Empty Saddles

EMPTY SADDLES

Michael Kennard

iUniverse, Inc.
New York Lincoln Shanghai

Empty Saddles

All Rights Reserved © 2003 by Michael Kennard

No part of this book may be reproduced or transmitted in any form or by any means, graphic, electronic, or mechanical, including photocopying, recording, taping, or by any information storage retrieval system, without the written permission of the publisher.

iUniverse, Inc.

For information address:
iUniverse, Inc.
2021 Pine Lake Road, Suite 100
Lincoln, NE 68512
www.iuniverse.com

ISBN: 0-595-27016-6

Printed in the United States of America

As a kid growing up in the early fifties I asked my dad if he knew any cowboy songs. He thought about it for a minute or so, then grabbing a pen and a scrap of paper, he wrote down the verses for me.

'Empty Saddles *in the Old Corral*'

I lost that piece of paper not long after he'd given it to me. Yet somehow those few words stuck in my memory. Empty Saddles, so mysterious and sad. The words excited my imagination. Now, I guess it's my turn to put pen to paper.

For my Dad

Acknowledgements

I'd like to thank the usual suspects, you know who you are. Alan, my son for helping me with the graphics and for his technical knowledge, computers and the like, without which Empty Saddles wouldn't have been written. My daughter Candice, for being well… Candice. Elaine, for all her help and support. Marion Emery for her painstakingly hard work in proof-reading this manuscript……….
…….And finally you the reader.

Chapter 1

Morgan Trelawney stared at his weather-beaten face in the mirror and despaired. He'd liked to have believed they were merely laugh lines, but years of squinting into the sun had taken its toll.

"Hell Laura, come next fall I'll be as old as Kennedy was when they up and killed him!"

"Ah, but you've still got your boyish charm," said Laura in a friendly but sarcastic manner.

Though not handsome by any means, Captain Morgan Trelawney's rugged features and pale blue eyes made him a hit with the ladies. A fact that Laura Trelawney had been struggling with most all her married life. Essentially decent and honest, Morgan had only one weakness he couldn't resist a pretty face. Not that Laura wasn't pretty. In fact you could say she had one of the prettiest faces in all of South Texas. She'd blamed the job for the break up of their marriage, but really it was his honesty that caused most of the ripples in their life. The nature of his work seemed to attract women. Morgan hadn't gone looking, it just seemed to find him. It might have been his neatness of dress, perhaps the star pinned on his chest, his charismatic charm and wicked smile, or the fact he was a member of a small select organisation known as the Texas Rangers. Whatever it was, it hadn't helped Laura none.

It was funny how a single sheet of paper had changed all that. Since the divorce, Laura and Morgan had found each other again. After years of fighting, making up and still more fighting, a calm had descended on their relationship. Gone was the tension and restraints of their life together; in its place an understanding and tolerance of each other's needs. The first time she slept with him after the divorce she realised not only that she still loved him but she actually liked the man. It had been the missing ingredient during those stormy years of marriage. In a strange way the break up had brought them closer together.

Laura was the first to admit it hadn't been all Morgan's fault. The little matter of her career had played more than a small part in the acrimonious split. With him now living in Laredo and her selling real estate in Austin, the odd weekend together seemed only natural.

"Morg, honey, I'll give you a call tonight," she said as she headed out the door.

"Yeah, I'd like that," he said affectionately.

Morgan had been working out of the field office in Austin for the past three years. He'd been happy there, but with a brand new divorce still ringing in his ears, the offer of promotion to acting captain came at just the right moment. It meant a move to Laredo. Given the choice he'd have opted for San Antonio, where he'd served in Company D for eight years and knew most everybody. But beggars can't be choosers, so they say, and of late there'd been talk of restructuring the organisation. More emphasis was being put on out stations like Laredo. Usually they operated with one or two sergeants, but with the increase in drug trafficking along the border, a higher profile was needed. He guessed how he handled the move would determine whether he kept the promotion.

If he shared a passion, it was women, horses and tradition, and not necessarily in that order. Women had been his downfall, as far as Laura was concerned, but much as he tried, he couldn't drag himself away from them. The mere presence of a beautiful woman almost invariably turned his head.

Now horses, that was another thing entirely. His love of horses could be traced back to his childhood. Most summers he'd help out on his uncle's ranch in the Hill Country around Bandera. For a time he even contemplated ranching for a living. During those long summer days Morgan became an expert rider and a pretty good judge of horseflesh. It was a passion he still pursed to the present day. When he moved to Laredo he made sure the house he rented had enough land supporting it, to graze his four horses.

Horses had been a way of life for the Trelawneys for generations. He'd found them indispensable when tracking a man across the rough tree-infested terrain of South Texas. Horses could go where not even a four-wheel drive could even contemplate. Both his father and grandfather served their time as law officers, and found the horse an invaluable animal. But it was his great grandfather Zachariah who had used the horse to its greatest potential, covering thousands of miles on horseback in his quest to bring justice to them that broke the law.

If the truth be known, that'd been the lynch pin as to why Morgan had accepted the posting to Laredo. Zachariah Trelawney was a man legends were built on, a hard man, a Texas Ranger of the highest standing. Around the turn of the century, the very mention of his name struck fear into the hearts of the country's worst bad men. He was a man who only saw things in black and white, a man who set standards and woe betide any man that crossed his line. Much had been written about his exploits and daring deeds, but his last few years were cloaked in mystery. In fact the last documented account of his life was the most mysterious of all. Zachariah along with two fellow Rangers crossed the Rio Grande into Mexico and just disappeared. What happened to them was anyone's guess, but the whole incident had been shrouded in legend ever since.

It had been late in the year of 1899, just a few short weeks to the turn of the century. There had been no news of Zachariah for almost a week, when Captain William Platt led a search party across the border into Mexico. For three long weary days the Ranger detachment followed the trail, until finally they came upon Zachariah's last camp. In a clearing nestled deep in the foothills of the Sierra Madre, Captain Platt and his troop stumbled upon their horses. They were tied to a couple of cottonwood trees, saddled, cinched and ready to go. Full canteens hung loosely from the saddle horns.

William Platt climbed down from his tall mare and ran his hand through the ashes of the fire. The embers were still warm. Setting up camp, Captain Platt and his band of Rangers waited until the following day. When no one showed up he organised and searched the surrounding area for a couple of days. He was without success. Zachariah and his fellow Rangers had vanished without a trace. A week later Captain Platt led the horses of the missing Rangers into the stockade at Laredo. The sight of those empty saddles spread like wildfire. His inexplicable end soon turned Captain Zachariah Trelawney into the stuff of legend.

Morgan's fascination with him had begun when he was just a child. His grandfather used to put him on his knee and tell him daring tales of great granddaddy Zachariah. From that moment on, Morgan set his heart on becoming a Ranger. The lure of law enforcement beckoned strongly in him. Following his father into the police force had seemed the obvious route for Morgan's chosen career. He'd already served his country in a military capacity for three years. A further seven up in Houston working for the police department gave him the civilian experience he needed. After that he joined the Texas Department of Public Safety as a Highway Patrol Trooper. Three years later he took the entrance examination and became a Texas Ranger.

Morgan Trelawney had twenty-two years experience as a peace officer. What he didn't know about police work wasn't worth spit. One of the many reasons why he'd got his posting to Laredo was his vast experience. It was expected to prove invaluable in his liaisons with the Department's Narcotics Service. Unfortunately it hadn't worked out quite the way he'd figured. He'd been there almost a year and he'd only assisted in a couple of drug busts. Most of his time was spent dealing with the usual misdeamours that a Ranger could be expected to handle along the border. His jurisdiction was vast, stretching from

Brownsville in the south, to Del Rio in the north. Though Laredo wasn't a walk in the park, the most excitement he'd seen had been a shooting at the local drug store.

Life in and around Laredo, as Morgan soon learnt, wasn't in the fast lane. Nor, as he learnt, was the traffic that Monday morning. It was like any other American city during rush hour. By the time he reached his office he was ready for the steaming hot cup of coffee that Jake Hamilton handed him.

"Thanks, that's just what I needed," said Morgan as he gave his 'in' trays a cursory glance and switched on his computer. Once he'd checked his Emails he was ready to relax and chew over the weekend with Sergeant Hamilton.

"Hell Jake, how was your weekend?"

"Much the same as most, Blythe had me clearing out the garage, you know the usual shit"

A lesser man would have resented a stranger taking command, but Jake wasn't in the least put out by Morgan's presence. He was four years older, a family man and looking towards retirement. Morgan found him a more likeable man than his appearance first suggested. With his close cropped sandy hair and bull neck, Jake Hamilton looked more like a Marine sergeant than a Texas Ranger. A likeable kind of guy withstanding, Jake wasn't the kind of man you crossed more than once. If Morgan ever had need for someone to watch his back then the man sitting opposite him drinking coffee was that man.

"Trooper" Orville Tyson, the youngest member of the team at thirty two, walked in with a bag of donuts, the bane of all policemen. He held the same rank as the Sergeant, but they called him Trooper on account he'd been a Highway Patrol Trooper for more years than Jake Hamilton could remember. But all that changed just over a year ago when Orville achieved his dream and passed the final exam and joined the illustrious ranks of Texas Rangers.

"Shit, it's been one hell of a morning!"

Neither Captain nor Sergeant looked up. Orville had been yelling the same line since Morgan first walked into the office eleven months earlier. Young, fresh faced and eager to learn. Orville was that new breed of Ranger, ambitious, clever and impatient. Notwithstanding that, he had a photographic memory and a Bachelor's degree, he was to all intents and purposes a career policeman.

"Throw me one of those there pastries, then grab yourself a coffee," cried Sergeant Hamilton. "When you're done drinking your coffee, I've got a job for you."

"Something major, I hope."

"Escorting a prisoner down to Zapata. You should be back by mid afternoon."

"Shit!"

A look of disappointment was etched across Orville's face. He'd been a Ranger for nearly eighteen months, and apart from the drug store shooting, which didn't amount to a hill of beans, most of his work had been dull and uninteresting. The smile reappeared almost as quickly as it had disappeared. There wasn't much that could keep the young Ranger down for long. He was cheerful to the extreme, and with good reason. His wife Tania was about the sassiest and sexiest young woman Morgan had ever clapped eyes on and so in love with her husband it hurt.

"You coming around tonight Morg. Tania's doing pot roast."

"Try and stop me," said Morgan. Tania Tyson was as damn fine cook as she was good looking. She was a real homemaker, with two kids below school age and a husband that loved her to bits. There wasn't much she craved in life. In Tania's eyes she had it all.

At first Morgan found it difficult to accept, after all he was straight out of a divorce. Looking at a woman as fine as Tania was really hard to take, especially since she was clearly in love with her husband. He remembered thinking after his first meal at the Tyson's that being Captain wasn't all it was cracked up to be, not when you compared it to 'Trooper' Orville Tyson's set up. But that was when he was in his cups.

Since then Laura had reappeared on the scene and her monthly visits soon put a smile back on Morgan's face.

Morgan and Orville's friendship came about when they were discussing the hundred and seventy odd years history of the Texas Rangers. Orville was especially interested in the story about Morgan's great grandfather.

"Reckon, with time and a little effort, you could sieve through the paperwork, ditch the untruths, embellish the facts and turn Zachariah's story into a damn fine book. Hell I'll even help with the research. Just think about it Morg, what a service you'd be doing future Trelawneys," said Orville, his enthusiasm becoming infectious.

"Future Trelawneys," the words struck a cord in Morgan's brain. Four generations of Trelawneys had taken up the badge. His son being the only one to break with tradition, electing to study business law at Tufts University in Boston. Morgan believed David blamed him for the divorce and had done it to spite him for all the years of his philandering, but Laura soon put him wise.

"It's nothing to do with your women," she spat bitterly, "it's about the years you spent away from him. It's the job. It's what you do. I know, I married into it. I went in with both eyes open, but when a father breaks his promise to his son as many times as you have, well there's bound to be a reaction. Our divorce was just an excuse."

Morgan reflected on Laura's words. It was true. How many times had he promised to be at his ball games, help with his homework, share an interest? He should have seen it coming, but he hadn't.

"When he's older he'll come round, you'll see," Laura added sympathetically.

Writing Zachariah's story wouldn't turn back the clock, but it might help David to understand why his father did what he did. Even Laura thought it would be the perfect gift to give her son when he graduated.

As it happened, Orville had connections up in Waco that you could shake a stick at, and soon had them faxing all the information they had on Zachariah Trelawney.

It was proving a monumental task. Sifting through sheets of old documents and following leads was going to take up most of Morgan's free time, but with Orville's enthusiasm he set about piecing together his great grandfather's life.

Zachariah was born in 1853, in Matagorda on the Gulf of Mexico. Not much was known about his early life, until he joined the Rangers around 1878. He was a popular figure and hung out with the likes of Jim Gillett and Dallas Stoudenmire, tough company for a man of such tender age. It was whilst rangering that he met and fell in love with Clara Boardman. She was the prettiest girl he'd ever seen. To say he was smitten was an understatement. They married in 1887 and at Clara's request he quit the Rangers. Their marriage produced two offspring, Morgan's grandfather Thadeus and a sister Roberta. For a time they lived in a small town not far from Fort Worth. Clara was a good and loyal wife, kind and caring, and a loving mother to her two children. Zachariah's life had taken on new meaning. He attended their local church, though not always as regularly as he should, mostly on account he'd take his son fishing. He was fast becoming a family man, and making a pretty good job of it too, until tragedy struck. Clara came down with Tuberculosis and died when the kids were very young. Zachariah was devastated, and it wasn't long before he turned to the bottle. Unable to bring his kids up in a proper family atmosphere, he took Thadeus and Roberta to live with a sister in Houston. About that same time he rejoined the Rangers.

Morgan scratched his head in amazement at the workmanlike way Orville had begun to structure Zachariah's life. In less than a week Orville Tyson had uncovered more information on Morgan's great grandfather than the Captain had thought possible. Then for a time, due to pressure of work and Morgan's introduction to the Narcotics Division, nothing much more was added to their file. Until…

It was an incredibly hot day, even at nine fifteen in the morning. Orville wearing that same old cheery expression strolled into the office as usual.

"Shit, it's been one hell of a morning!"

Morgan looked up and grinned. He'd been there a little over three months and found himself warming to the young sergeant. Orville looked across at Morgan, a distinct grin forming upon his face.

"Have I got something for you," he said shaking his head.

"What's on your mind? Spit it out," said Morgan in friendly frustration.

"Your great grand daddy made the papers, and then some. It's all there. Documented for all the world to see. Only thing that's left out is the eight months before he disappeared. If we work our way though the information in front of us we might just find a clue to his mysterious disappearance."

From the other side of the office, sandwiched between two fans both working overtime, a voice boomed out.

"Good work, now get yourself along to Travis High. They need a pep talk on road safety," shouted Hamilton.

"Shit Sarge, you're always spoiling me," Orville's sarcasm fell on deaf ears. Lecturing on road safety wasn't what he'd signed up for, but he accepted the assignment without anymore fuss. Not all police work was exciting, in fact most of it was purely routine. Even Morgan had lectured at the local high school on the dangers of firearms.

Morgan began looking at the microfiche pages of newsprint. The first thing he noted was the date of the newspaper. It was 1912, a full twelve years after Zachariah's disappearance. Carefully he began reading the first account of his great grandfather's life.

I remember the first time I caught sight of Zachariah Trelawney. It was a little after dusk and the streetlights had just been lit. It had been raining non-stop for two days, and there was no sign that it was about to let up. The broad expanse of Main Street was awash with the reflective glow from puddles that dotted his path. Sitting tall and erect he trotted his horse through the mud-laden street. I don't know why I singled him out, it was just something about the way he rode; like a man with a purpose. I remember as I stood looking up at him, how the rain cascaded off the brim of his hat and down the back of his slicker. His tanned features shone yellow from the gas lanterns that lined the sidewalk. I was only a kid at the time, but even I could tell from the look in his eyes he was a man hell bent on a killing. A man that couldn't be stopped. He turned his mount to the sidewalk outside the Alhambra. In awe I watched as the big man nimbly dismounted and tied his horse to the hitching rail. Slowly and purposefully he began to unbutton his rain slicker. In one smooth motion he swept the coat back, revealing a Colt 45 Peacemaker nestled in a fancy hand tooled holster. I gawked excitedly as he slid the rawhide thong from the hammer of the revolver. It was the first time I'd seen a man prepare for battle. In fascination I stared up at him as he stepped onto the sidewalk. His movements were slow and deliberate. Brushing some dirt from his pants he began fumbling in the top pocket of his vest. Coolly he withdrew a cheroot and lit up.

I was oblivious to the cacophony of sounds as he turned towards the open doorway of the saloon. His spurs jingled as he walked steadily into the smoke filled room. Rushing to the tobacco stained windows I peered inside. Through the grime I managed to see him step up to the bar and order a drink. The bartender reached down and produced a bottle and a shot-glass. Zachariah covered the room with the eyes of a hunter. Blowing dust from the glass he proceeded to pour three fingers of redeye, and in that moment his eyes centred on the man he'd come to kill.

Wide eyed with excitement I watched as he slowly drew the heavy Peacemaker. Stepping away from the bar he began to walk towards the farthest Faro table with the gun hanging loosely by his side. Within moments he was casting his dark shadow across the green baize table. Long Tom Carmichael slowly looked up into the imposing face of Zachariah Trelawney. The crowd scattered. The piano player stopped in mid tune. A dime dropped from the table. The room fell silent.

"You're a hard man to kill, Zachariah," said the seated man with resignation in his voice.

"Harder than you'll ever know!"

The hideaway gun leapt into the palm of Long Tom Carmichael's right hand, yet even as he felt the comforting feel of the ivory handle, he knew it was too late. Zachariah's Peacemaker was already levelled at his chest and spitting flame. Long Tom felt the searing pain as the 45 calibre slug smashed into his ribcage hurtling him backwards against the far wall. Mercifully, Trelawney's second shot entered his forehead, extinguishing Carmichael's lights forever.

Zachariah stole a cursory glance at the crumpled corpse and the crowd of white-faced onlookers. Turning his back, his spurs were the only sound in the silence of the bar-room, as I watched him slowly walk outside. The next I saw of him was minutes later as he turned onto Front Street and entered the adobe building that housed the sheriff's office.

Morgan was stunned and quite taken aback. The description was so vivid and real that characters just seemed to jump off the page.

"Shit, that was some hard son of a bitch," he exclaimed to Orville later that evening.

"Yeah well that's where all the hard work comes in. We need to find out what Long Tom Carmichael was into, and why Zachariah shot him down like a dog."

Their enthusiasm was quelled, as Tania cried out from the far flung reaches of the kitchen.

"Hey boys, it's time to put down your toys and wash up, chow's on."

Chapter 2

▼

Long Tom Carmichael ran the Faro table in Bob O'Reilly's No 7 saloon. He'd been in El Paso for eight months, coming there on the invitation of his friend, John Wesley Hardin. Long Tom arrived in the September of 1895 to find that John Wesley had expired in a shoot out in the Acme saloon the month previous. Not one to grieve, Long Tom soon established himself as an excellent card player and took over the running of the Faro table at O'Reilly's.

It didn't take long for the sporting crowd to learn that Long Tom wasn't a man who suffered fools gladly, promptly testifying to that fact when he was accused of cheating. The fool in question was a young man of twenty three, a miner fresh from the hills, having lost the past three months of his labours on liquor, women and gambling. Unfortunately at that moment, he chose to take the biggest gamble of his short life.

"I say you're cheating. No man has that kind of luck!"

"You're drunk son, apologise and go home!" Long Tom said it loud and deliberate for all to hear. His eyes had turned an icy grey. The boy hesitated, the challenge clearly ringing in his ears. Lose face, or play the cards he'd been dealt. His callused hand reached clumsily for the Smith and Wesson double action revolver. As his hand closed around the walnut handle, he realised his mistake. Long Tom pulled his Schofield 45 and held it out at arms length. It was but a whisker from the young miner's heart. The *blast from the gun in Long Tom's hand lifted the youngster off his feet. A ring of fire on the miner's shirt left no doubt that Long Tom Carmichael didn't take kindly to insults.*

There were those that claimed it was self defence, others that he could have given the boy a chance to back off, and the unspoken few that called it murder. In his defence, it was argued he could easily have killed the kid with the spring loaded derringer he kept up his sleeve for such dire emergencies. Needless to say, in a city that had released Old John Selman on bond for the killing of John Wesley Hardin, Long Tom only received a warning about discharging his revolver in a public place.

Zachariah Trelawney's entrance to El Paso was no less dramatic. He rode into town a full month before Hardin was slain. He looked weary and tired as he rode slowly towards the office of the town sheriff, behind him two pack mules, both laden with fly infested corpses.

Stepping down from his horse, Zachariah brushed the dust from his clothes with his hat. Replacing it carefully, he stepped onto the sidewalk and stared for a moment at the door to the office of sheriff. Taking off his worn out gloves he knocked loudly on the door, then entered.

"Howdy. I'm Lieutenant Zachariah Trelawney, Frontier Battalion, Texas Rangers. Outside I've the bodies of the Mendocino brothers. They're a tad ripe I'm afraid. I need verification of their identity, then they need planting pretty damn quick."

"Mendocino brothers, they didn't come quietly I bet," said Sheriff Mace Bigelow.

"Damn shot away my best horse. Me and Blue we rode all over the damn state for nigh on seven years," said Zachariah in a matter of fact way, as he stared out of the window at the town. "It's grown since I was here last."

"It sure has, El Paso is destined to become one of the culture capitals of the Western United States," said the sheriff proudly.

"You don't say," said Zachariah disdainfully. El Paso left a bad taste in his mouth. With his disinterest clearly showing, he made for the door. It

had been a long hard ride and he wasn't of a mind for conversation. Just as he was about to exit, he stopped and turned back towards the sheriff.

"Where's the best place to grab me a room and a bath."

"That'll be the Central Hotel, on the corner of First and El Paso street. Tell them Mace sent you, they'll give you a good rate."

"Thanks, I'll do that."

Stepping out into the sunlight, Zachariah ran his hand over the stubble on his chin. He needed a shave badly and his moustache was in need of a trim. He was surprised to see the hotel was located across the street from the Coliseum saloon. For a moment it took him back. It had been over ten years since he'd thought of the place. Looking across to the doorway of the Coliseum it only seemed like yesterday. 'If only I'd been in town on that fateful day, Dallas might still be alive.' It was almost thirteen years since Jim Manning had put a bullet into the brain of his friend Dallas Stoudenmire. Manning had stood trial but was acquitted because he had come to the aid of his unarmed brother Doc Felix Manning. Earlier Dallas and Doc Manning had been drinking together. An argument had ensued and shots had been fired. Both men had been wounded in the saloon and had grappled their way outside when Jim Manning fired that fatal shot. It was pointless to ponder the situation, Dallas was long gone.

Washed and shaved Zachariah felt like a new man. He'd been on the trail of the Mendocino brothers for all of three months. It was time to unwind, a good meal, a few drinks, a sociable game of cards, and then the luxury of a feather bed. No more sleeping under the stars, at least for the time being, thought Zachariah as he crossed the street outside his hotel.

Zachariah walked into the Globe restaurant. It was crowded but after ten minutes wait he was shown to a table. It was set neatly with clean cutlery and a red gingham table cloth. Glancing at the chalk board menu, he quietly ordered a steak dinner. While he waited for his meal he began remembering peaceful times around the dining table at home with his beloved Clara. He cursed himself silently, he knew he should have spent more time with her. Somehow he'd thought she was indestructible, that she'd always be there for him. It had been a devastating blow when she took sick and died within two weeks. It was a blow he'd still not fully recovered from, and possibly never would.

Before he'd met Clara he'd had the occasional drunken night of debauchery in the local bordellos. But from the moment he met her, his world changed. He never even looked at another woman. He'd found the perfect soul mate. She was sweet and innocent, and in his eyes far too good for the hard drinking but straight laced man that he'd become. During those few short years together she changed him, turning him into a warm and loving husband and father. In his own words, spoken at her graveside, he'd said she was too good for this world. He reckoned God must have thought the same and called her back to him.

Zachariah changed after her death. He began to drink heavily. He gambled rashly but he could never find it in his heart to go with another woman. Cheating on Clara's memory amounted to the worst kind of blasphemy he could imagine. Realising she wouldn't have wanted him to waste his life drinking and gambling, he decided to rejoin the Rangers. He'd served a spell with the Rangers during the late seventies and early eighties, working alongside such notables as Jim Gillett, John B Armstrong, and Zachariah's mentor and true friend Dallas Stoudenmire.

Dallas had taught Zachariah many things, the value of law being paramount. He was a man quick to act, relying on instinct and a willingness to take extreme measures at a moments notice. After the killing of his brother-in-law Doc Cummings, Dallas swore vengeance on the Mannings. The town council put pressure on Stoudenmire and the Manning brothers to keep the peace. Frustrated by the laws he'd stood by, Dallas turned to drink. Things took a decided down turn and the inevitable climax drew near.

Vowing not to walk in his mentor's footsteps Zachariah drank moderately and gambled only when the mood took him. His only concession to Dallas Stoudenmire's doctrine; no insults swallowed, no challenge left unanswered. It was the code he lived by and there was no deviation to that course, a fact that bad men on and around the Texas border began to learn and fear.

After his meal Zachariah strolled the two and a half blocks to the Acme saloon on San Antonio street. He looked an imposing figure in his long black frock coat as he pushed through the doors and entered the dimly lit saloon. Stepping up to the bar, he asked for a cool beer. So thirsty had the steak meal made him, that he downed the cool glass of beer in one lengthy swallow.

"Ah, that hit the spot. Same again barman."

"Coming right up," shouted the waist-coated bartender.

"Say friend, where can I find me a friendly game of poker?"

"In this saloon, the best game is the one in the far corner of the room. Stakes ain't high, but the company can be a little rough," warned the barman.

Zachariah looked to the far table. It seemed innocent enough.

"Obliged," he said.

Strolling over he greeted the table. "Hello gentlemen, is this a private party or can anyone join in?"

"If you're carrying hard cash, the seats yours."

Zachariah smiled and sat down. His companions seemed a harmless bunch, except for the dower-faced man with cruel dark eyes sitting across from him. Over the course of a few hands which he lost, and a couple that he won, he learned the names of the other players. He wasn't surprised when he learnt the identity of dark eyes. John Wesley Hardin was the deadliest killer that Texas had ever spawned. A man without fear, a man quick to anger, a man without compassion.

"You sir, now you've taken some of our money, your name?" Hardin's eyes never left those of Zachariah.

With a smile that held no warmth Zachariah spoke up. "Lieutenant Zachariah Trelawney, Fifth Company Texas Rangers, at your service." His eyes locked on Wes Hardin. The challenge clearly visible.

"How is that no good cur Armstrong? Dead I hope," said Hardin in a slightly drunken manner. The challenge was answered. Zachariah never for a second took his eyes off Hardin, quickly rose to his feet.

In a voice as cold as the grave, Zachariah gave his answer. "Sorry to disappoint you sir, John Armstrong is alive and well. As for your slight on his good name, a man that has had to endure Huntsville for the last sixteen years, it's only to be expected the lesser man would think ill."

The place went silent, apart from the scurrying of feet across the sawdust laden floor. People began edging slowly towards the doors. Hardin, his face not betraying a single nerve, sat looking up at the big Texan standing before him. Running his tongue slowly across his lips Wes Hardin forced a cruel smile. "I've heard of you Trelawney. They say you're a hard man, hard but fair. I like that in a man." Hardin's face softened slightly, his eyes never leaving the big man. "Sit down sir, and let me relieve you of the rest of your money!"

Zachariah ignored the gesture and without taking his eyes off the man, scooped up his winnings, tipped his hat and backed away from the table. In the centre of the room he turned and walked out the door. Within seconds the room was buzzing with noise once again.

Over the next few days, the talk was rife around El Paso. Some called it a Mexican stand off, similar to the one Hardin and Hickok had allegedly experienced more than two decades earlier. Others said Hardin had gone soft in his old age, that prison life had mellowed the Texas terror. Some even said Trelawney was lucky to be alive. Zachariah and Hardin both knew the truth. Two professional gunmen standing but yards from each other. It would have been a foolish man to risk his life in such circumstances.

They didn't see each other much after that, both preferring to move in different circles. Hardin staying in the Acme, while Zachariah found a card school in the Gem Saloon. When the news broke of old John Selman putting a bullet in the back of Hardin's head less than a month after their stand off, Zachariah hardly gave it a thought.

The killing of the young miner a few short weeks later, caused Zachariah even less concern. "If men continue to pull guns on each other, what the hell do you expect," was his only comment. It wasn't long after the Carmichael killing, that the Town Council sought a meeting with Zachariah.

They offered him two hundred dollars a month plus bed and board to take on the job of Assistant Town Marshall. Zachariah declined. "Thank you gentlemen for your trust, but I'm afraid it's not possible."

He'd been there nearly three months, getting the occasional orders through the telegraph wires. The nature of his job, and the vast distances he had to cover, allowed men of Zachariah Trelawney's ilk a freedom most men could only envy. After months of eating dust and sleeping under the stars, the company of his fellow man had beckoned. It had been his choice to hang around El Paso. While he was there he supplemented his meagre wages with a percentage of the house from the Gem saloon, where he soon became chief Faro dealer. A job he assured the proprietor that would be only temporary. Now after three months, he was getting itchy feet. Growing tired of El Paso, Zachariah made plans to visit with his sister and see his kids over in Houston. That was until he had a run in with Long Tom Carmichael.

"And that's as far as I've got," said Morgan over a beer in the Black Elk.

"Shit Morg, just when it was getting interesting," cried Jake, "so that's what's been keeping you and Orville busy the past couple of months."

"It sure as hell has," said Morgan. "Orville is like a dog worrying a bone. That guy just won't let up. Course having access to them files up in Waco sure helps. He's managed to dig up a tidy amount of information. My problem is putting it all down on paper."

"Well you be sure and finish it, you hear. I want to read it."

"Count on it."

"You having another?" said Jake as he caught the eye of the bartender.

"No, I'll take a rain check. I'm meeting Orville and Tania at Senor Lopez. Seems Tania's got a friend who's dying to meet me. Her words not mine," said Morgan raising his hands in mock surrender.

"Jesus Morg, I don't know how you do it. Now you've got women pimping for you." Jake laughed and shook his head in amazement. Morgan grinned and showed off a set of perfectly white teeth.

'Senor Lopez' was located two blocks from the international bridge. It claimed its enchiladas were the best this side of the border. Morgan reflected how many times he'd come across the same claim. "If I'd a dollar for each one," he mumbled to himself as he pulled into the parking lot behind the restaurant.

He hadn't met his date, but he suspected Tania would have set him up with a real doll. Her taste in everything was exquisite. Morgan grinned to himself, he knew Orville and Tania meant well, but at that very moment he wasn't interested in any serious relationships, and besides he had Laura's monthly visits to look forward to. Agreeing to meet his date was the easiest way out, offending his friends was the last thing he wanted. He'd known them a little over a year, but it felt as if he'd known them all his life. He enjoyed their company and their easy going ways. He loved their kids and above all the genuine warmth that radiated out from the both of them. Laredo wasn't the best place in the world, but with friends like the Tysons it ran a pretty close second.

Chapter 3

▼

Her name was Kathleen Delaney. She was thirty-three years of age, and what 'Senor Lopez,' lacked in the cuisine department, she certainly made up for, with her vibrant smile and flashing blue eyes. Even before Morgan could walk the short distance to their table, Kathleen was on her feet and introducing herself. Her mop of unruly blonde hair and those big blue eyes began working their charms almost immediately. To say he was knocked a little off balance was an understatement. She giggled at his awkwardness, then put him at ease a second or two later.

"I guess you were railroaded into this dinner date, the same as me," she said laughingly, indicating with her eyes towards the mischievous couple of matchmakers sitting expectantly at their table. His face broke into a grin, showing off a mouthful of pearly white teeth.

"I guess I was at that," he replied. "Buy you a beer."

"Sure, why not," she said, her eyes still dancing with laughter.

Morgan was surprised how quickly they fell into conversation. It didn't take but a few minutes for him to be mesmerised by her inbred Irish sense of humour and childlike qualities. Not long into their conversation he discovered that they shared a common ground. Though recently divorced, Kathleen made it quite clear from the start that she wasn't looking for a soul mate. Nor, she added quickly did she think he was either. He found her forthrightness and plain speaking a breath of fresh air.

The Tyson weekly barbecue, a couple of nights at the movies and a candlelit dinner for two followed during the next month. As predicted, it wasn't long before Tania started making broad hints about a serious relationship. Even Orville got in on the act.

"Shit, it's been one hell of a morning!"

As usual both Jake and Morgan kept their heads down. Not getting the reaction he'd hoped for, Orville grinned and directed his follow up remark to Morgan.

"The question is, was it one hell of a night!" Referring of course to the hot dinner date Kathleen and Morgan had shared the previous evening.

"Shit, Orville, if you wasn't so darn happily married I'd have thought you jealous," retorted Morgan in a playful manner.

"Hell, who wouldn't be, Kathleen is a peach."

Jake looked up for a moment, grinned then shook his head a couple of times before returning to his paperwork.

"Hey what's this?" cried Orville excitedly, forgetting his friend's romantic involvement, as he picked up a report from Jake's desk.

"Shit, it ain't nuthin, but as you're so damned interested you'd better check it out. Take a wide loop around the local farms and homesteads south of the barrio. Seems we've had us several reports of gunshots heard late yesterday afternoon. Damn illegals left it until this morning before they phoned it in. Why those wetbacks can't investigate it themselves is beyond me. Probably won't amount to a hill of beans. Just some fool kids shooting the crap outta a barn door. Just be visible. I want them damn chili-eaters seeing where their tax dollars ain't going."

"Gee thanks Sarge. Guess this is the break I've been waiting for," said Orville, barely hiding the sarcasm in his voice. He was beginning to regret his choice of location as a Ranger. He'd elected to work out of Laredo only because Tania's folks lived nearby. Both he and Tania were strong on family. Him especially, since he was brought up in an orphanage. Not having parents or grandparents, he thought it a good idea for his kids to grow up close to kinfolk. But in truth he'd rather have been working out of San Antonio. If he was going to obtain the promotions he wanted, then he needed the right kind of cases under his belt. Ones that you don't get in a sleepy border town like Laredo. 'Still maybe when the kids are a little older,' he thought as he pulled his hat on tightly and walked outside to his patrol car.

Morgan exchanged a wry grin with Jake as the office door slammed shut. "If I miss my guess, I'd say that boy's as sore as hell."

"I reckon," Jake replied dryly.

"Oh, almost forgot," said Morgan as he threw a manila envelope containing several pages of his manuscript, on Jake's desk. "This should keep you going for a few days."

"Obliged Morg, I'll give this a read during lunch break," said Jake as he pulled the loose pages from the envelope and began flicking through them....

Long Tom, still wallowing in the aftermath of gunning down the young miner, had himself an itching to see the man who had faced down his friend Wes Hardin. In his eyes the man either had plenty of spunk, or luck, or maybe a little of both. It didn't matter a damn to Long Tom. He intended finding out soon enough. Professional curiosity wasn't the only reason he decided to visit the Gem saloon that Sunday evening. Its location on one of the main routes into town made it a more profitable business venture, whereas O'Reilly's No 7 was down a side road and didn't get half as much clientele. He'd heard it said that Zachariah Trelawney was about to roll up his bedroll and visit pastures new. If that were true, then he intended giving him a shove in the right direction.

At his side when he walked through the double doors of the Gem saloon was a soiled dove who went by the name of Teresa Morales. She couldn't have been much more than seventeen, yet her eyes were that of the world weary. She operated out of a crib above O'Reilly's. To hear it told, Long

Tom won her in a poker game. At first Teresa had thought herself well off, trading the big hairy miner for the refined dandy. It was short lived, Carmichael soon turned out to be both cruel and sadistic, beating her whenever she brought him a poor nights takings. She didn't know what was worse, that or him sating his lust when she brought home the bacon.

Wearing her on his arm like a trophy, Long Tom stepped up to the bar. "Whiskey!"

"Coming up," said the bartender as he produced two shot glasses and a bottle.

"Leave the bottle," said Long Tom gruffly. El Paso was a growing town, and getting bigger by the minute, yet it didn't take people long to know who was who. Long Tom's reputation as a bad man had gone before him. He could see the fear in men's eyes when he addressed them. It was something he enjoyed probably more than sex. Power, to Carmichael, was a mighty impressive aphrodisiac.

Long Tom tossed down the first shot and refilled his glass. His eyes began searching the faces in the crowd. He knew he'd recognise Trelawney the moment he spotted him. Men that could kill without hesitation were a rare breed. Whether they were on the side of the law or those who had crossed the line, there was a certain something that set them apart from other men. No one could mistake the aura that surrounded them. Hickok and Hardin were prime examples of their breed. The same could be said for Zachariah Trelawney and Long Tom Carmichael.

Suddenly Long Tom's eyes centred on the man who'd faced down Hardin. Through a haze of cigar smoke, seated at the faro table, was Zachariah Trelawney. Wearing a white shirt and a dark cravat with a diamond stick pin, he looked every inch the house's man. Long Tom studied him as he deftly dealt the cards across the green baize table. His eyes appeared focused on the game, but Carmichael knew differently. Trelawney would have noticed him the moment he stepped through the double doors. He'd even have put a name to Long Tom's face. Such was the prowess of the man killer.

Carmichael tossed down the drink in his hand and, with Teresa on his left arm, walked casually toward Zachariah's table. A broad smile, devoid of warmth, spread across his face. "Good evening gentlemen, mind if a sit in for a few hands?" *The question was directed at Trelawney.*

"Feel free. I run an honest game and won't put up with cheats and liars. If you understand that, then you understand me!" *Zachariah's tone was abrupt and to the point. Long Tom noted the remark. He knew if push came to shove, there'd be no second chance.*

"Name's Carmichael, Long Tom Carmichael." *With a grin he studied the faces of the men seated at the faro table. It gave him a kick as he gauged the reaction to the mention of his name. His eyes lit up as he saw fear and edginess upon the faces of his fellow players, all except Zachariah Trelawney, whose eyes stared straight at him.*

"Yeah, I figured that's who you were," *said Zachariah, not giving out his own name or the names of his companions.*

Irritated by Zachariah's lack of reverence, Long Tom shouted, "Let's play cards!"

For the best part of two hours Zachariah studied Carmichael. What he saw, he didn't like. The man was ill mannered, aggressive and rude to the woman standing at his side. Twice during the course of the evening he warned Long Tom about his behaviour. As Zachariah dealt the cards, he braced himself for the trouble that was a coming. He didn't have long to wait. During a particularly bad run of luck, the pretty young whore advised Carmichael to quit. Without a single thought, he struck out at the woman, sending her sprawling across the dusty floor. Zachariah moving with the speed of a cat, pulled his Peacemaker and laid all seven and a half inches of barrel across Carmichael's head, splitting the scalp and dropping Long Tom to the floor like a stone.

"A man that beats on a woman ain't no man at all," *he said fiercely, his eyes ablaze. Zachariah looked at the woman and his face softened.* 'Hell she's no more than a kid,' *he thought as he saw the fear growing in her eyes.* "Forget him girl, he's past hitting on you." *Without realising it, Zachariah had placed himself as her protector. It was a responsibility he neither asked* for nor wanted. The simple fact was, Long Tom Carmichael would take it out on her when he regained consciousness. Even though they were moving closer to the new century, El Paso was still a bastion of vicious and ruthless men. It wasn't unheard of for whores to be beaten up so badly they either died or were crippled for life.

"I can't stay here, he'll kill me!"

Zachariah ignored her pleas and began relieving the unconscious man of his weapons. First the Schofield from his hip, then the two shot Derringer from an attachment located halfway up his sleeve. Once he was sure he'd retrieved all of Long Tom's arsenal, he unceremoniously grabbed both of his feet and dragged him outside.

Re-entering the saloon he looked across at the frightened young woman, "Right girl, where you originally from?"

"Nuevo Leon! But I'm not going back." The tall Ranger was surprised by the sudden outburst. His intention was to buy her a ticket and put her on the next stagecoach that was headed in that direction. From the look upon her face, the fear of her homelands was even greater than her fear of Carmichael. "I have family in San Antonio, Alicia my sister she'll take me in."

"Good." In the space of a moment the girl had made up his mind for him. "I'm heading for Houston in a few days, you're welcome to ride along. And don't you be worrying your head none about that scoundrel. Long Tom's a back shooter if I miss my guess. He's not the type to stand square on. It'll take him a couple of days of cursing and wailing before he plucks up enough courage to do something. By then we'll be long gone. In the meantime you can stay in my room, I'll sleep down the hall."

The girl began to smile, then hesitated. Zachariah smiled as if in reassurance. Where her smile had been, a contorted mask of fear appeared. He realised his mistake at the same time as he heard the lever of a Winchester jacking a round into the breech. Long Tom had recovered quicker than he'd thought possible and somehow had acquired a Winchester rifle. He stood framed in the doorway, dried blood, turning an ugly maroon, covering the left side of his head. Zachariah saw him for the briefest of moments before he felt the searing pain as two lead projectiles tore into his back. The sheer force from the blast sent him flying across two tables. Before he blacked out he heard the young Mexican girl scream out in terror. Screams that were punctuated by the sound of gunfire as Long Tom emptied the Winchester into the bar.

Zachariah woke up in his hotel room two days later. He'd lost a lot of blood, but by some miracle both bullets passed clean through his body, neither one of them hitting bone or a vital organ. Another half an inch to left or right would have proved fatal.

"The girl!"

"She's dead Zack. There weren't anything we could do. It all happened so fast. Carmichael just kept on firing until he ran out of shells." The bartender's face was still ashen as he relayed the story.

"Where is he?"

"He's gone. Once he left here he hightailed it back to the No 7, grabbed his gear and lit out."

"Where's he heading!"

"Don't worry your head about him. You're still too weak to move. Doc says you're lucky to be alive. You need at least a week's bed rest."

"The hell I do!"

Zachariah attempted to rise, opening the wound as he struggled to sit himself into an upright position. His head ached. He felt nauseous and the room became spongy. When he woke up next time it was morning and Long Tom Carmichael had more than a four day start on him.

Zachariah visited the grave of Teresa on the fifth day. There was no headstone, just a mound of freshly dug earth to show the world that once this poor pathetic creature had embraced life. It was a sad epitaph that her passing hardly caused a ripple amongst the townsfolk of El Paso. Standing alone, with the icy north wind whipping around the tails of his top coat, Zachariah Trelawney removed his hat and held it in front of him. The worn and tired Ranger bowed his head, then mumbled an almost silent prayer. When he was done he carefully replaced his dark wide brimmed hat upon his head. Swiftly mounting the tall mare, he cast an eye back to the *small mound. Then with a gentle jerk of the reins he negotiated his way out of the cemetery. At the gate he turned his horse east and headed towards San Antonio*

There was something wrong, Orville could sense it the moment he caught sight of the old Blevins place. Dogs! There were no dogs running back and forth barking his arrival. Switching off his engine he was surprised at how quiet the place had become. It wasn't a good silence. Orville couldn't put his finger on it, but there was something eerie about the place. Then he heard it. It was faint at first, barely a sound, but as he walked closer to the barn the noise increased. The low sound had become a gentle buzz. Then as he walked in the shadow of the barn, the noise became much louder. He spotted the dog first, its large canine teeth protruding from its open jaws. Its dead eyes staring into nothingness. The only movement was from the flies and maggots that infested the body. Then without warning, the stench reached out for him, clawing its way to the pit of his stomach and back again. The young Ranger began to retch. And then he saw the man, tied backwards across an old saw horse. It was something Orville could only imagine in his worst nightmares.

"Jesus H Christ!"

The man's dead eyes bulged with fear, his entrails such as they were, lay scattered across the dirt floor of the barn. His stomach had been slashed open from breastbone to groin. Apart from bruising around the face the rest of his body lay untouched. Whoever had done this had slashed him open and dumped his entrails on the ground. They'd left him to watch his own death as possums and rodents feasted on him whilst he was still alive.

Orville walked unsteadily to the car and phoned in. "Jake! Oh Jesus, you'd better get your ass down here now! I'm out at the old Blevins place just off south 40. They've butchered him."

"Orville, repeat it."

"I've got me a fucking homicide. I ain't seen nothing like it. It's bad man, it's real bad!"

"Morg and I'll be there in less than twenty minutes," snapped Hamilton.

"You'd better call in the sheriff's department, and a meat wagon!"

For a couple of minutes he sat in the patrol car, stunned and shocked by what he'd discovered. He'd wanted a real case, but this……. Pulling himself together he began searching the rest of the buildings. At the back of the house he found the woman. It was obvious from the disturbance of clothes and her positioning that she'd been raped and then shot twice in the chest.

"Oh God no!" His blood froze in his veins. He'd found what he'd most feared. There were two of them, a boy of about six and a girl of seven, both had been shot in the back of the head. Orville turned away. His body broke into a clammy sweat. Nausea kicked in and he began to retch again.

Allowing himself a minute he quickly wiped at his mouth with his sleeve. He tried not to look at the two broken bodies, but it was no use. "Why, why…." He kept mumbling to himself as his eyes filled with salty tears. "Jesus, why…" From his hip pocket he retrieved his notebook. He was still shaking as he wrote down the time of his arrival. "That's it, keep busy. I'm the first officer on the scene, there's plenty for me to do. God, where do I start?" He took a few deep breaths, gathered his thoughts and walked back to his patrol car. Leaning in the window he reached inside the glove box and brought out a 35mm camera. He stared at the grisly remains of the male victim. Steadying the camera he took several shots of the man from different angles. He noted that the man had been secured to the saw horse by wire and that one of his hands was almost severed from the wrist. He stared down at the corpse and wondered what motivated men to such cruelty.

Still shaken by the sheer butchery of the scene he walked unsteadily over to the body of the woman. Before photographing her, he looked over the scene. On the ground close to the body were shell casings from a .454. At a guess Orville figured they'd been fired from a Freedom Arms Casull. *It wasn't any wild guess, his pet subject whilst learning his profession was firearms.* What Orville Tyson didn't know about guns and ammunition wasn't worth printing. Noting down his observations he took a further group of photographs. Then steeling himself he walked over to the bodies of the two children. The sun glinted off a brass shell casing close to the body of the young boy. Orville hunched down and looked at the spent cartridge. It was a 10mm, probably fired from a Glock model 20, he thought. This told him the perpetrators weren't just random killers. He had a degree in psychology and although it wasn't an exact science, he reckoned the guy that carried the Casull suffered from an inferiority complex, hence his use of such a large calibre weapon. From his experience and the writings of certain psychologists, the man was probably of less than average height, a braggart and a coward, usually a loner but most dangerous when hunting in a pack. The Glock suggested a different kind of killer, cold and calculating. An even more deadlier fiend than his partner. It wasn't much to go on but he noted it down all the same.

Anger welled up inside. It was becoming almost too difficult to continue his work. But with the resolve of a Ranger he began taking pictures of the young bodies. For a split second the camera froze in Orville Tyson's hands as he saw his own children framed inside the viewfinder. It was enough to make him shake with fear, anger and frustration. He was still shaking when Morgan and Jake arrived.

Chapter 4

In less time than it took to whistle 'Dixie', the Blevins house and grounds were swarming with one agency or the other. The Sheriff's department believed they had full jurisdiction. The Border Patrol reckoned it had something to do with illegal immigrants, and the US Marshall's office wanted the case. When a small quantity of heroin was found, the DEA added their weight to the chaotic scene. Because of the newsworthiness of the case, every damn law enforcement agency in the state wanted a piece of the action.

Captain Morgan Trelawney not a man to take lightly, spoke up. "My man was first on the scene, this makes it our case. If you gentlemen want to co-operate that's fine by us. If you don't then butt out. There's a family butchered here, and all you can do is row amongst yourselves. I'm taking charge."

Twenty pairs of eyes turned in his direction. For a moment not a word was spoken, then…

"Now see here. There's drugs found at the scene of crime, that makes it our case," said a burly looking guy from the DEA. He was six one and looked like he still played pro football.

"You sir are very privileged. I normally only say things once. Due to the circumstances I'll accept that you didn't hear me first time," said Morgan, a nervous twitch appearing at the side of his left eye.

"I don't give a flying fuck what you said, we're taking the case," insisted the burly Drug Enforcement agent, his voice low and threatening.

Morgan grinned, then drew a line in the dirt with the tip of his boot. In a voice full of meaning he spoke once more to the DEA man.

"Cross that line, and I'll bust your balls."

Before he could do anything a restraining hand gripped the shoulder of the burly agent. "Leave it Lou, we'll seek further advice."

Morgan looked past the agent, and focused on his partner, a man of average height wearing a sharp looking suit. He had about him a military air, perhaps it was his close cropped hair and neatly trimmed moustache or the self assured way he addressed the Ranger. "Captain you'll be hearing from our commander within the hour."

Ignoring the threat, Morgan turned his back and began co-ordinating his men. The Sheriff, who for over an hour had believed the responsibility lay on his shoulders, breathed a sigh of relief. He'd worked with Morgan and Jake on a number of small cases and was only too pleased to leave the responsibility to the Texas Rangers. Sheriff Buzz Irvine a man that liked his job slow and easy, set his men to work cordoning off the area. Their hardest job at that moment was keeping the now forming herd of journalists from the crime scene.

"Fuck," said Morgan, uncharacteristically. "We've already lost two hours, and there is no telling what evidence those assholes have destroyed when they forced their way onto the scene."

"Fucking high fliers," spat Jake in disgust.

Morgan, not a man that angered easy looked across to his sergeant. "I'd like to know who tipped them off?" Like most men, seeing the bodies of the young children had really turned his stomach. He wanted to lash out. Jake couldn't miss the fire in Morgan's eyes, he reckoned that if that asshole from the DEA had crossed the line, well the chances were he'd be following the medical examiner back to hospital.

Leaving Jake to supervise, Morgan went in search of his friend Orville. He'd looked in an awful state when they first arrived. He'd seen death before, but nothing as bizarre as a multiple homicide, especially one that involved kids. He was still shaking when Morgan pulled up. His ashen features and the blank look in his eyes spoke volumes. It was obvious to Morgan that his young sergeant was in a state of shock. Tactfully he'd sent him for a walk down by the river. The sight of such carnage could send even the most hardened police officer over the edge. In Morgan's experience moving away from the scene of crime usually worked.

As he made his way down to the river's edge, he hoped the peace and serenity of the Rio Grande would have a calming effect on Orville's nerves. Minutes later he caught sight of his sergeant standing with his back to him, staring across the river into Mexico.

"How you feeling son? It's always rough the first time you come across such carnage."

"It's the kids Morg, who gave them murdering bastards the right to kill them. I've seen dead people before, many times, but not like this, not like this." He shook his head in disbelief.

"From the little the medical examiner could tell me, he reckons the kids were executed first, along with the dogs," said Morgan lamely. He didn't quite know what to say. The murder scene had affected him almost as much as it had Orville. "We found the bodies of three dogs scattered around the yard." Somehow he couldn't bring himself to talk about the murders. Even after his years of experience he still couldn't understand the minds of murderers. In his opinion the bastards that had done this had enjoyed their work.

Orville wiped his eyes and walked closer to the riverbank. "They raped that poor woman after they'd shot her two kids. Can you imagine it. What thoughts must have been going though her head as they raped her." Orville stared into the cloudless sky, "I want them Morg! I want them bastards in my sights. I'd kill em where they stand!" His eyes blazing with anger he added, "We've gotta get those sons of bitches!"

"We will Orv, you can bet on it!"

* * * *

Two weeks passed, and the memory of the slaughter at the Blevins homestead was still vivid in Morgan's head. Orville's angry outburst registered loud and clear. It mirrored his own emotions, but fortunately he had his great grandfather's manuscript to occupy his thoughts and evenings. Without that, he reckoned he'd have been feeling the strain almost as much as Orville.

Zachariah Trelawney rode for two weeks solid, sleeping in his saddle where need be, and catching a few hours shut eye each night when it became too dark to track. He was a hunter of men. Those that knew him said he was the best they'd ever seen. There weren't many men he'd hunted that would disagree.

Before he left El Paso he did some checking on Long Tom Carmichael. Zachariah's long experience had taught him that most men were creatures of habit. The man he was hunting was no different. He liked to work close to the Mexican border. He couldn't resist a game of cards, it was where he could brag about the men he'd killed. He was lightning fast with the sleeve device and had despatched two men using that method. Neither man would have had much of a chance. The killing in No 7 had been the most callous of them all. He already had the drop on the boy, there was no need for him to have killed the young miner. With the girl, this brought his killing tally to four people, although Carmichael would think it was five.

Just outside of Uvalde, Zachariah lost Carmichael's trail. He had a straight choice, either head for Del Rio and work his way systematically down the border towns, or head for San Antonio and break the news of the girl's untimely death to her relatives. The hunter in him opted for the border towns but his heart said telling her family came first. Tracking Carmichael could take months, 'To hell with it,' thought Zachariah. He'd been with the girl when she died, and somehow or other he felt duty bound to inform her next of kin. He stared longingly in the direction of Del Rio, then turning his horse, he headed for San Antonio. Long Tom Carmichael could wait a while longer.

Three days later, Zachariah arrived in San Antonio. He was of a mind to book into the Menger Hotel, but judging from the clientele he saw entering and exiting he thought better of it. It had become far grander than he'd last remembered. Giving it a miss, he took a room in a small inn over in the Mexican quarter. The more he thought about his lodging the more sure he was that he'd made the right decision. It stood to reason that his best chance of finding Teresa's family lay in the hands of the Mexican locals, not with the gentry that frequented the Menger Hotel. But before that, uppermost in his mind was sleep.

For days he'd dreamed of lying between cool white sheets. It was the one thing that kept him going during his arduous trek from El Paso. Zachariah was tired and plumb worn out. He hated to admit it, but age and the two wounds in his back had physically exhausted him. Finding Alicia Morales would have to wait until he'd had a good night's rest.

Zachariah woke to the incessant sound of a rooster crowing for all its worth. His first reaction was to look towards his revolver. He'd lain there, somewhere between consciousness and sleep, debating the fate of the noisy bird. The crowing was now grating on his nerves. In his mind the rooster took on monstrous proportions. Again he looked towards his weapon, then thought twice about it. If he wanted to ingratiate himself with the locals, then firing off his Peacemaker at the crack of dawn wasn't the way to go about things.

Sitting on the side of his bed he scratched at the stubble on his face and rubbed his eyes. Looking at his reflection in the worn and cracked mirror, he realised for the first time that he was growing old. He was forty-two years of age and looked well past that. It wasn't something that bothered him unduly but it was enough that morning to spur him into action. He took himself down the hallway and cleaned up.

Ten minutes later, in the privacy of his room, he surveyed the results. A more presentable reflection looked back at him. Only his eyes betrayed a hint of pain and sadness. The shooting in the Gem saloon had taken its toll, *weakening him both physically and mentally. His body ached from the long weeks of riding and from the fresh wounds. He'd been shot before, but that had been a long time ago, and with the elasticity of youth had mended very quickly. It was yet another sign that he should think about retiring from rangering.*

If Clara had been alive, he'd have forgotten about Carmichael and returned home. But Clara was gone, and he knew no other life than that of a peace officer. He reflected what life still had to offer him. Though not normally maudling, he found himself imagining his own passing. Somewhere out there was a trigger happy kid with an angry temper and a belly full of alcohol. It was a sad legacy for a man that had seen greater things. With the uncharacteristic stab at self pity pushed to the back of his mind, Zachariah dressed quickly and walked outside into the weak sunshine of a December morning.

After a hearty breakfast of spiced eggs and enchiladas, Zachariah began his quest to find Alicia Morales. It surprised him how easy it was to find her. In the brief moment of time that he'd known Teresa, she'd told him she came from the state of Nuevo Leon. From the expression on her face when she mentioned her homeland he'd expected she'd come from abject poverty. Somehow he'd imagined her sister eking out an existence in the poor quarter of San Antonio. Instead he found she lived in a large hacienda about thirty miles outside of town.

It was early in the day and Zachariah wasn't the type of man to let grass grow under his feet. With a full canteen and a day's provision of food he set out at a gentle lope towards the Morales ranch, which happened to be twenty seven miles south of town. The day's journey was both arduous and long. More than once Zachariah contemplated his pending old age.

Zachariah could see the ranch in the distance. It couldn't have been more than a mile ahead. He also spotted two outriders keeping abreast of him. Ignoring their presence he rode steadfastly towards the looming hacienda. Within half a mile the two riders began to converge. As they drew closer he could see they were both Mexican. The Mexican to his left was about his own age, while the rider to his right was probably in his mid twenties. Neither man looked friendly, especially since they rode with their reins in one hand and a Winchester, held pointing in his direction, in the other. The younger man motioned Zachariah to stop. Easing himself in the saddle the mare moved into a walk then halted.

"Gringo, what is your business at the Morales ranch?"

Zachariah didn't like his tone. In his book bad manners was just a step higher than hitting a woman. Choosing to ignore the man's bad manners, mainly because of the Winchesters now pointing directly at him, Zachariah looked him straight in the eye.

"My business is with Senora Morales. It's personal and I'd be obliged if you gentlemen would let me pass."

"Senor Xavier Morales has given us orders not to let anyone pass without finding out who and why," said the tall young Mexican.

"My name is Lieutenant Zachariah Trelawney, Texas Ranger." His hand was now resting on the walnut butt of his Peacemaker. "I repeat, my business is with Senora Morales and her alone."

The young Mexican, for a second taken aback by the abruptness of the reply, looked across to his companion for reassurance. With a nod the older man accepted they'd reached an impasse. Spurring his horse forward he rode ahead while the younger Mexican and Zachariah trotted in behind him.

In the courtyard Zachariah saw the older Mexican talking to a man in a white shirt. Moment's later, white shirt disappeared back inside the house. Kicking his horse into a trot, the Mexican rode back to the tall Ranger.

"Un momento, we wait for Senora Morales."

"Gracias," said Zachariah politely. All the time his eyes watching the younger man who still trained the Winchester on him. And then he saw her. She was a vision of such loveliness that he locked that moment in his heart forever.

Alicia bounced out of the house and walked across the dusty courtyard and looked up at Zachariah. "Buenos Dias Senor. My name is Alicia Morales. How can I help you?"

Her beautiful brown eyes and dark flowing hair stunned Zachariah. She looked tiny from his vantage point upon the tall mare, yet she was probably close to five six, slim and willowy with an air of vulnerability. It was the warmth in her face that threw him. He'd known her but seconds, yet it was as though he'd known her all his life. To his embarrassment he felt his skin tingle and begin to colour. To cover his blushes he said gruffly, "For a start you can tell that vaquero to point that damn thing in another direction."

She smiled, pleased by the impression she'd made upon him, "Rafael, the gun. Remove it!" Then turning back to him she smiled again. "I'm sorry he's only acting on orders from my husband. He's so protective."

'So would anyone be if they were married to such a beauty,' thought Zachariah. He felt himself blushing again at his uncharacteristic thoughts. "A wise man," said the Ranger.

"Thank you sir," said Alicia as she felt herself being drawn to the rugged man on the tall horse.

"May I get down, it's been a hard ride and my bones ain't getting any younger."

"I'm sorry. You must excuse my manners. Please come inside," she said apologetically.

Climbing down from his saddle he felt his wounds pull. It made him grimace with pain. He should have listened to the doctor's advice, he thought with the benefit of hindsight. Handing the reins to a servant, he stretched his long legs and brushed the dust from his clothes before entering the hacienda.

"Ma'am, I've news of your sister Teresa! I'm afraid it's not good." Zachariah saw the anxious look spread across Alicia's face. He wished it had been different, if only he could have protected her from his news. "I'm sorry, Teresa's dead. She was killed in a gunfight in the Gem saloon in El Paso a month ago." He watched as the colour drained from Alicia's face. He wanted to reach out and hold her, comfort her, tell her everything would be all right. Strange thoughts for a man that hadn't held a woman in his arms for years.

Recovering herself she invited Zachariah to sit. Then she insisted he tell her the full story. In vivid detail he told her everything he knew about Teresa's life up to the moment she was cut down in a hail of bullets by Long Tom Carmichael.

"I only knew her for minutes, but she seemed a nice kind gentle person that had taken the wrong path in life. She died too young. I intend tracking down the man that killed her and I shall bring him to justice."

She winced at his rough talk, then slowly her warm smile reappeared.

"It's getting dark, you can't possibly ride out tonight. I'll get someone to make up a bed for you in the spare room."

He started to protest, but found himself accepting her offer far more readily than he'd have expected.

"My husband will be home soon. He'll want to meet you. Dinner is at six. Cristina will show you to your room."

Before he could say anything, Alicia walked swiftly out of the room. At the door she paused and looked back and beamed the sweetest smile he'd ever seen. Zachariah's heart beat a little stronger than it had of late.

Chapter 5

Tania was worried about Orville. Since the horrific discovery of the slain family, he'd become obsessed. He neither joked with his comrades nor played with his kids. Most of his free time had been taken up with compiling facts and other data concerning the killings. As Tania put it, single-minded to the extreme.

"It's not healthy Morg," said Tania. She'd called into the office when she knew Orville would be out. "I understand solving the case would help his prospects, but he's taking too much of a personal interest. When he's at home he should put it to the back of his mind. But he won't. He says he has to keep trying. He says there's something not quite right, that things just don't add up."

"It's his first big case Tania. Believe me, seeing those bodies was horrific. Even Jake winced at the sight of them." The very mention of the killings brought it right back to him. "It's not unusual for police officers to be affected after witnessing such carnage," he added.

"Yeah but it's been three weeks since the killings," said Tania.

"There's some I've known that would go on a week long drunk, others that channel their anger and frustration into sports, and others that disassociate themselves all together. Everyone reacts differently. He'll come out of it soon."

"I wish you'd have a word with him. Tell him to ease off," pleaded Tania.

"I'll do just that, but I don't think it'll do much good. That husband of yours is one stubborn mother."

"Thanks Morg."

"I'll tell you what, get Orville to bring you and the kids out to my place this week-end. You can take the kids riding. Then when I get a chance I'll have a quiet word with him."

"That's real nice of you, but I suspect he won't come."

"Tell him, that's an order," joked Morgan, except it was an order. Since the Blevin's massacre as it had become known, Morgan had been called away to Brownsville to give evidence in a trial. It was only routine procedure but it had taken him away from Laredo for more than a week. Since he'd arrived back in town he'd been unable to speak with Orville.

"I will," said Tania.

Once again Morgan reflected how his friend Orville Tyson was one lucky son of a gun. With a young wife like Tania to back him, the young Ranger couldn't fail to make good. Solving the Blevins killings would assure his promotion.

There was only one problem. True to his word the DEA man had got back to him. By early evening almost the entire case had been turned over to them. Someone in Austin had pulled a few strings and the Rangers had been sidelined. Morgan had really gone into one. He argued and cajoled until he was blue in the face. The only concession he managed was for Orville to be allowed to work the case in conjunction with the Drugs Enforcement Agency. Anything he turned up was to be handed over immediately to agents Jordan and Thurston.

According to the DEA the murders were part of a wider set up. A drugs cartel operating out of Guadalajara had been sending massive supplies of heroin via illegal immigrants in a blanket cover of the Mexican border stretching all the way from Tijuana to Matamoros. Morgan didn't buy it. Why hadn't the Department of Public Safety's narcotics division known of the deal? He'd been in law enforcement for most of his adult life, he knew that shit happens, but this was more than a pile of crap. Yet he wasn't going to let being hampered by the DEA shake him. All it did was make investigating the murders more difficult but not impossible.

In Orville he'd found a more than willing recruit. He wouldn't let it drop, and if the truth be known, Morgan actively encouraged his enthusiasm. Orville had taken an instant dislike to the burly DEA man, and solving the case before them would give him the greatest of pleasures.

From Morgan's own experience he knew this was no ordinary murder. One thing the DEA had got right, drugs were at the heart of it. From the scant evidence they'd found, he believed it wasn't a random killing. Revenge was possibly the motive, a warning to others more likely, but something told Morgan it was more than that. What little facts they had, suggested the carnage had taken place over a period of several hours. Whoever carried out the massacre took great delight in the suffering of others.

Orville's dogged police work had uncovered several new facts. The guns used for the killing had both been fitted with silencers. There would have been no report of gunfire. Either an illegal immigrant stumbled on the bodies and called in, which wasn't likely, or someone connected with the killings made the call. That would explain why so many agencies appeared on the scene at the same time. Morgan figured it was a deliberate ruse to destroy what evidence was left at the old Blevins homestead.

Whoever they were, they hadn't bargained for the thoroughness of 'Trooper' Orville Tyson. Another more startling fact had emerged, more by accident than design. When Morgan appeared on the scene he could see how distressed Orville had become and he'd ordered him to take a walk. As Orville's watery eyes stared across the river, he noticed the tracks of several horses entering the shallow waters. Bringing it to Morgan's attention they were able to deduce five horses had entered the American side of the border and five horses had exited. Morgan, in light of being relieved of the case, elected to keep that information strictly between himself and his fellow Rangers.

A couple of days later they received a forensic report on the bodies. It confirmed what they already knew. Four men had raped the woman over several hours, while her man lay strapped to the bench dying. Forensics had come up with traces of semen in every orifice of her body. She'd been brutalised and tortured far worse than the gutted man. Contrary to their original theory, Orville now believed the woman was the main reason for the murders. It was something else he kept from the DEA. Whoever ordered the killings wanted the woman to suffer.

Their green cards showed them to be Alberto and Felise Hernandez. Extensive enquires showed both green cards were forgeries. Their national security numbers were none existent and the kids weren't registered in any schools. From the little information Orville had managed to extract from the local residents, the family had arrived three months before the killings and had squatted in the old Blevins homestead. Keeping themselves to themselves they eked out a meagre living from the soil. And then from a quirk of fate they were brutally murdered. It didn't wash in Morgan Trelawney's eyes. The woman was the key, he was certain of it.

* * * *

Morgan was surprised and pleased when Kathleen showed up with the Tysons. They hadn't seen much of each other since the Blevins murders. She'd been busy in LA, then when she got back, he took off for Brownsville. His pleasure was twofold. Kathleen Delaney was a sight for sore eyes. The fact that she rode meant she and Tania could take the kids riding for an hour or so, leaving Orville and Morgan to chew the fat.

So intent at shortening the stirrups for Mary Beth and Jimmy's mounts, Morgan failed to see the look of disappointment in Kathleen's eyes. A fact noted by Orville, for reference later that evening.

"We'll see you gang in an hour or so," said Morgan. He waved impatiently as the girls mounted up and walked their horses towards the east pasture. He could see a glint in Orville's eyes, from past experience he knew his friend had something really important to say.

"For Christ sake spit it out," Morgan said, under his breath as Kathleen gave an exaggerated wave and loped off after Tania and the kids.

"You ain't hardly gonna believe what I've found out."

Morgan was pleased to see Orville in high spirits, but found his knack of stringing things out mighty infuriating.

"I've been gone a damn week, and all you can do is grin."

"Mr and Mrs John Doe, well we know for certain they ain't the family Hernandez. Their real names are Antonio and Juanita De la Fuente. He's originally from Monterrey, comes from a long line of De la Fuentes. Seems he got cut out of the will when he took up with our Juanita. By all accounts her family ain't what you'd call respectable. Anyway Antonio's so much in love with the girl he gave up everything and moved in with her family." Orville grinned, he couldn't wait to see the look on Morgan's face.

"Come on, get to the point," said the Ranger captain.

"The point is my friend," Orville paused for effect, "Juanita De la Fuente's maiden name is Morales!"

"What!"

"Morales, as in Alicia Morales,"

"It's a coincidence, Morales is a common enough name," said Morgan.

A look of self satifaction spread across Orville's face. "I had me a friend in Monterrey, check back on the records. Seems our Juanita's from an old Mexican family that live on a vast ranch that reaches up into the foothills of the Sierra Madre, not far from the town of Apodaca." Orville licked at his parched lips and asked for a beer. Morgan reached into the cool box and threw him an ice cold Budweiser. "Thanks," said Orville as he snapped the cap off the bottle with his penknife and took a mouthful. "That tastes so good."

"Go on," said Morgan, who was now all ears.

"Oh yeah, the story. It's funny, the old hacienda had lain derelict and home to rattlesnakes and scorpions for close on a century. Then about fifteen years ago a silver haired guy of about fifty five shows up. Seems he's a Senor Salvador Morales from Guadalajara. He's got deeds and documentary proof that he's the rightful owner of the old place and promptly moves in. Within months he's had the old place remodelled and restored to it's former glory. He ain't alone, he's brought a full entourage of servants and some very shady characters including two sons Diego and Ignacio, both in their twenties. Now there's also an illegitimate daughter called Juanita, who was treated no better than a servant. According to my source, her birth and subsequent establishment in the household caused more than a little resentment. Old man Salvador was a very powerful man in a certain part of Guadalajara. He'd seen Juanita's mother when he passed though her village. So captivated by her beauty was he that he decided to have her for himself. Returning to her village a week later he abducted her." Orville took a swig of beer. "He took her on her wedding day."

"What! Didn't the Federales do anything?"

"You're forgetting, this is Mexico we're talking about. Obviously someone got paid to look the other way."

"What about her husband?"

"There was talk Salvador cut the husband's throat but that's hearsay. He kept her until she became pregnant, then the bastard threw her out onto the streets. With nowhere to go she would have starved. Without a choice she turned to the oldest profession known to man. When the baby was born she begged him to take her in, for the sake of the infant. Finally Senor Salvador Morales relented and allowed her back into the servants quarters. Within a year she died giving birth to a still born son."

"Jesus! That mother fucker!" Morgan had become stonefaced as Orville relayed the story. "What happened to the baby girl?"

"An elderly servant took the child and brought her up as her own. Salvador's only acknowledgement that he was the father of the child was to insist she bore the Morales name. It was more to spite his two ungrateful sons than any show of affection, in his eyes she was his property."

"I'd like to meet the son of a bitch," interrupted Morgan.

Orville, ignoring Morgan's outburst, continued with his narration. "As the years passed Juanita grew into a beautiful young woman and Salvador's heart began to soften towards her. At the age of eleven he finally acknowledged she was his daughter by installing her into the main building of the old hacienda. This was more a calculated act than a charitable one," added Orville with a note of caution. "For years Salvador had ruled his sons with a rod of iron, neither giving nor receiving love from them. He was cruel and ruthless, and his sons Diego and Ignacio would have killed him in his sleep if it wasn't for his bodyguard and faithful friend Clemente Ramos. Although still mentally strong, Salvador could feel the onset of old age. Long years of living in the city, a poor childhood and many years of ill treating his body were finally taking their toll. Unbeknown to his sons Salvador was suffering from Tuberculosis. The move to the mountains was supposed to do him some good. Now old and frail before his time, he craved the love and affection that he had always denied himself." Orville took another swig from the bottle and motioned for another one. Taking the cap off, Morgan handed it to him.

"At first Juanita was afraid of the man that for years had denied her birthright. But as the weeks stretched into months and finally years, a strange bond formed between them. Although still fearful in his presence, a great yearning to be loved overtook her. This love, though misguided, seemed to have a strange effect on Salvador, turning the hard and cruel man into a softer and gentler person. So much so that his sons Diego and Ignacio took it as a sign of weakness." Orville shooed an irritating fly from his nose, stood up and stretched his legs. Having a young family made him ever protective towards them. Relaying this sorry tale didn't bode well with him. He hated injustice.

"On the eve of her fourteenth birthday Juanita lost her innocence. Ignacio, the far kinder of her two brothers had been showing more than a passing interest. What Juanita hadn't realised until that fateful day was, she'd become a woman. Her innocence and naiveté had allowed Ignacio to lure her to an out building at the far end of the hacienda. Within minutes he'd torn her clothes from her back and was forcing himself inside her. She tried to scream but Ignacio's powerful hands muffled her cries, while his heavy body kept her pinned to the hard ground. He was about to climax when he was flung back with such tremendous force." Morgan took a swig and wiped his mouth with the back of his hand. "The colossus that was Clemente Ramos, towered above him," continued Orville. "For a second Ignacio thought he was about to die. Though forty five, Ramos had the strength of ten men, and in temper twice that. Grabbing the younger man by the throat he began squeezing the life out of him. Ignacio though strong and powerful was powerless to stop the behemoth that held him in a death grip."

"No please stop!" screamed Juanita. "Please stop, you're killing him!"

"The sound of her voice alerted Clemente and he loosened his grip on Ignacio's throat. Turning towards her, his eyes softened and he reached out. Juanita began to sob uncontrollably, while Clemente held her gently in his arms until the sobbing subsided. Bewildered and traumatised by what Ignacio had done she begged Clemente not to tell Salvador."

"Don't worry little one, your secret is safe with me."

"From that day until the day she married Antonio De la Fuente, he was never far from her side. Something in little Juanita had brought out a spark of compassion in Clemente Ramos. He became her friend and protector. A fact not lost on Antonio when he first came calling.

Yet over the months of their courtship, Antonio began to like the gentle giant that never seemed far from Juanita's side." Orville swiped at the pesky fly with a fly swat, then reflected on what might have been if Antonio's family hadn't been so pompous and arrogant. "The De la Fuentes are a proud and noble family that didn't take kindly to their youngest son marrying into the rich and decadent Morales family. Antonio blinded by Juanita's beauty, renounced his family and moved in. It wasn't long before he realised something was terribly wrong. But by then it was too late. Juanita was heavy with child and Antonio's family had cut him off without a penny. Not a man to shy away from hard work he took a job as a vaquero on a nearby ranch. The pay was poor but it was enough for them to live on. By then they had a baby son and another child on the way. Life was a struggle but for a time they were truly happy. Then Salvador died and Clemente Ramos disappeared mysteriously. Within a week of Salvador's death, Juanita and Antonio together with their two children disappeared. That was five years ago. Nothing was heard of them until now."

"You know this for certain, those people at the Blevins place are definitely Juanita and Antonio De la Fuente?"

"I'm certain," said Orville, the strain clearly visible on his face.

They sat for a while, both lost in their own thoughts. Orville had told an extremely sad story, made more poignant by the manner of their deaths. It was clear to Morgan that his friend was taking their deaths to heart. It was time to change the subject. Getting up from his chair Morgan opened another couple of beers.

"Come inside, forget about work, well at least for the rest of the day." Orville grinned half-heartedly then followed Morgan into the house.

Handing Orville a sheath of papers Morgan added, "I want you to tell me what you think about the latest development of my story."

As his sergeant mulled over the papers, Morgan turned towards the window, his mind racing over whether there was a connection between Juanita and Alicia Morales

Chapter 6

▼

Zachariah Trelawney set out for Laredo early the next morning. His head whirling from too much wine and the face of Alicia still vivid in his thoughts. He'd been surprised when he was introduced to Alicia's husband at dinner that evening. Xavier Morales must have been Alicia's senior by at least thirty years. At fifty-six Xavier was still in fine shape. His magnificent frame and sinewy body were that of a far younger man. Only his hair gave way to age. Even that, though now almost completely white, contrasted and complimented his tanned and well structured face. But it was his gleaming smile, half-hidden beneath a well trimmed moustache, that was his most striking feature. It didn't take Zachariah long to understand how a woman of Alicia's tender age could fall for such a man. He cringed with embarrassment at the thoughts that had been running around inside his head. Even allowing for the ten years that he had on Xavier Morales, his dour, stuffy and Victorian attitude were as nothing compared to the charm and wit of this most charismatic of personalities. Silently he cursed himself for being such a damn fool.

Yet as the Morales ranch disappeared from view, Zachariah became troubled. Things had happened to him, strange wonderful feelings. His brain had become addled by Alicia's beauty. It was ridiculous, he knew that, but for a time he'd imagined she'd shown more than a passing interest. And was it his imagination, when towards the end of the evening, Ali-

cia seemed slightly uncomfortable in her husband's presence? These were indeed strange thoughts for a man that only days before had contemplated his own demise. Concentrating his efforts on the mission at hand Zachariah rode hard and fast for the town of Laredo.

A week later he rode into the sleepy border town. Outside the Grand Hotel he handed the reins of his horse to a small boy who, for a dollar, took his horse to the livery stables and cared for it. A service of the very Grand Hotel Laredo, leaving Zachariah to check in at reception. Grand it was by name and grand it truly was, purporting to have the only hot and cold running water bathhouse in town. Zachariah had to see it to believe it. Back in El Paso he'd seen one of those horseless carriages and wondered what the world was coming too. Now he'd seen, more than that he'd even bathed in a hot tub that had running water on tap. For the briefest of moments he allowed his imagination to run wild at what the new century had in store, but then invariably his thoughts returned to Alicia.

After he'd washed and brushed up, he walked across the street to the Oriental and ordered a cool beer. The long and dusty trail soon took care of the contents of the glass. Over a second beer Zachariah enquired of the bartender whether Long Tom Carmichael had been seen in Laredo.

"Can't say as I recall, but if he's low life you'd more likely find out more if you try Dog Town."

"Thanks," said Zachariah. "Now if you'll be so kind as to point me in the right direction, I'd be obliged."

"Sure can, turn left out of here. Ten blocks straight. You can't miss it, damn shanty town is crawling with dogs. Two legged as well as four," said the bartender adding a note of caution.

"Obliged," repeated Zachariah as he swilled the remains of his beer and strolled purposefully toward the double doors of the saloon.

* * * *

Dog Town lived up to its name. A few mangy curs patrolled the many bars and flop houses that made up the entire town. Situated the closest to

Mexico, it attracted the worst kind of badmen from both sides of the border. Gambling, whoring and drinking were the order of the day. In comparison Laredo, though in itself a sleepy border town, was from another world. Not for the first time Zachariah contemplated his fate. Only this time it was different, it scared him somewhat. Without realising it, Alicia Morales had gotten under his skin and he couldn't shake her loose. The farther he'd come from San Antonio the more sure he was that he wanted to see her again. Ridiculous as it sounded, he kept telling himself he needed to go back and enquire if she was happy. He tried pushing the nonsense to the farthest reaches of his brain but it was no use. In the end he had to face up to the truth, he wanted her like he'd wanted no other, not even Clara. Yet until he'd found and taken care of Long Tom Carmichael there was no way he could go back.

He knew he was in trouble the moment he walked into the Jade Palace. Five pairs of cruel eyes looked up at him as he walked towards the bar. He wasn't wearing a badge, but his sheer presence and demeanour suggested he couldn't be anything else but the law.

"Turn around and walk back the way you came, law dog!"

Zachariah felt the hairs on the back of his neck stand on end. It wasn't an order, it was a challenge. In a flash Zachariah surveyed the room and thought what a fool he'd become. Thinking about that little Mexican girl had got him killed. Each of the five men looked ready and able to kill at a moments notice. If he was lucky to clear leather before the first bullet found it's mark, the best he could possibly hope for was to drop one man, maybe two if he moved fast enough. By then his body would be looking like a sieve.

Desperate to gain time Zachariah looked straight at the man that'd spoken.

"You die first!"

It was a gamble, unsettling a man was the best way of destroying his aim. Zachariah had already picked his targets. The man to the right of the voice and then the large gentleman at the far left. There was but one chance, if he downed the two that in his opinion looked the most dangerous, the others might get discouraged and high tail it. He doubted it the moment he thought it.

"Kind of unfriendly odds, Mind if I deal myself a hand!"

Voice and his four friends turned and looked straight into the twin barrels of a Greener loaded with double O buckshot. The guy holding the shotgun didn't look much, he couldn't have been more than five six, but his pale blue eyes told a different story. Zachariah risked a glance, then looked back at the voice ready for the last go round.

"Pull those pistols boys, and tonight you'll dine with the devil!"

Blue eyes finger tightened on the trigger.

"Easy man, we were only foolin!" The voice began to blubber.

"Yeah man, it was only Henry's idea of a joke," added the big man at his far right.

"Okay Harley, tell your brother and the others to make light with the hog legs and we'll call it quits."

Harley slowly eased his Remington from its leather scabbard and placed it gently on the green baize table. Looking across to his brother he ordered him, "Do it damn you, before you get us all killed." Henry's eyes stared with rage as he reluctantly followed his brother's advice. The three others quickly followed Harley's lead. All the time the shotgun never left the belly of Henry Tanner.

"You boys just done the smartest thing you'll ever do in your lives," said the sandy haired guy that shouldered the Greener.

"You ain't heard the last of this Tom Tenpenny!" Henry Tanner was starting to feel brave now he'd thrown in the towel.

"I'm here when you want me Henry," said Tenpenny as he motioned the five toward the door with the barrel of the twelve gauge.

"You're time's coming," mumbled Henry Tanner. Then as he backed towards the saloon doors he looked defiantly towards Zachariah Trelawney. "Next time law dog! Next time!"

Tom Tenpenny waited awhile before releasing the hammers of his shotgun, then he walked into the main body of the saloon.

"Thanks partner, I'm obliged," said Zachariah.

Up close Tom didn't look as young as he'd first appeared. Zachariah guessed he was in his early thirties, thirty five at most. His ruddy complexion and unkempt walrus moustache made his face seem far more serious than it needed to look.

"A guy like you can't be too careful. Jesus man, you got Ranger written all over. I seen you one time back in 87. Amarillo that's where it was. You were standing face on in the middle of the street. Man, that was the finest shot I seen in my entire life. You just stood there as Johnny Behind the Deuce blasted away. You levelled your pistol, cool as all get out, and shot that son of a bitch all the way to kingdom come."

"That was a long time ago. What's buried's, buried."

Zachariah had taken men's lives in the name of law and order. In his book most had deserved the fate he'd bestowed on them, yet although he shed no remorse at the men he'd killed, he took no pleasure from it.

"Name's Tom Tenpenny, some time lawman, most times law breaker. At the moment I'm between vocations."

"Zachariah Trelawney, Lieutenant, Texas Ranger. Guess I owe you a beer."

"Guess you do at that!"

Zachariah kept his eyes peeled on the entrance to the saloon. "You'll excuse me if I seem a mite preoccupied," said the Ranger, "Only I'd rather not underestimate man's foolishness."

Tom Tenpenny noted the Ranger's remark, and tried putting him at his ease. "Henry's a back shooter, so's Harley for that matter, but bringing the fight to us, hell that ain't their style. Give it three or four weeks, a dark lonely street, enough liquor in them to promote courage, well then I'd say you've got a problem. By then I'll be long gone. If you've a mind you'll have left this town too."

"I'm here only as long as it takes. I'm looking for a gambler feller. Dark greased back hair. Carry's a Smith and Wesson Schofield in a cross belly rig. Runs a mean game of poker. Goes by the name of Long Tom Carmichael. You heard tell of him?"

"Yeah, now that you mention it, there was a feller here a couple of weeks ago. I didn't get his name but he wore his gun, butt forward and it was a Schofield. I only noticed it because the Schofield's a rare gun in these parts. Most people favour a Colt or Remington. Well that's how I see it. He was bragging too. Seems he took down a peace officer a while back. Guess he didn't make too good a job of it."

"This galoot say where he was heading?"

He didn't tell me, but I'll ask around. Where you staying?"

"Over to the Grand, but you can catch me in the Oriental if you've a mind," Zachariah kept glancing towards the door. Memories of Long Tom Carmichael opening up with the Winchester, still fresh in his mind. He'd walked with death most all his adult life, it wasn't something he feared, until now.

"I'll give it my best shot," said Tom. Zachariah, still nervy about an ambush thanked the sandy haired man once again, and bid him goodnight. Then cautiously he walked out into the darkness.

On the way back to the hotel Zachariah cursed himself for the damn fool that he'd become. Alicia Morales was almost twenty years younger than he, he'd known her for but a few hours, he'd met her husband and had enjoyed their hospitality. What kind of a man lets his heart run free, so free he'd almost gotten himself killed into the bargain. If it hadn't been for Tom Tenpenny's timely intervention he'd have been propped up in the undertakers parlour posing for photographs.

Fate had brought Tenpenny into his life, just as surely as it had brought him together with Alicia. It had to be fate, what other reason could there be for him having her on his mind. He'd only known her one single evening but the more he thought about it, the more certain he became that something was amiss. One thing was clear in his mind, once he'd finished his business with Carmichael he was heading back to San Antonio.

* * * *

Tom Tenpenny found him around mid-day, languishing over a rare steak in the restaurant of the Grand Hotel. Zachariah looked up as Tom reached the edge of the table. "He's heading back north. Seems he was overheard telling a pretty young whore that he was going to try his luck in Carrizo Springs. Seems he'd a friend at the Alhambra saloon there, that needed a good faro dealer."

Zachariah contained his excitement at the news and cut his steak into inch square chunks and began forking them into his mouth. "Good steak, here try a piece," he said extending a piece at the end of his fork. "Tom, I can't thank you enough, not just for this news but for last night. You probably saved my life. If ever I can repay you, you only have to ask."

"When you heading out?"

"In about an hour," said Zachariah.

"Mind if I tag along a ways. I've got me a hankering for those pretty little gals up in San Antonio. And besides the air around Laredo ain't what it once was," he said referring to the Tanner boys.

"I'd enjoy the company, but when I ride into Carrizo Springs I ride alone. This thing between me and Carmichael, it's personal." Zachariah left Tom Tenpenny in no doubt.

"I'll ride with you as far as Artesia Wells, if that's okay."

"Get your gear," said Zachariah as he put another cube of meat into his mouth.

* * * *

They made camp around seven that evening, under a couple of scrubby oaks. While Tom gathered wood and began putting together a fire, Zachariah went in search of game. He returned a while later having shot a large hare. Between them they skinned it and cooked it over an improvised spit.

It turned out to be tough, and made Tom wish he'd ordered himself one of those steaks that Zachariah had consumed with such relish.

Tough meat and bad coffee apart, Tom began telling his life history. His grandparents had come over from Ireland just after the Potato famine and tried homesteading. It wasn't long before they found themselves up against a foe as deadly as the foppish English. Two skirmishes against the Comanche was enough for Michael Tenpenny. He wasn't a man to ride his luck too far. 'Twice I kept my hair, I wasn't risking it a third time,' he could often be heard saying at his blacksmiths stall in Fort Worth. Shoeing horses became his trade until he died. Later his son, Tom's dad fought outlaws as well as Comanches when he drove cattle up the Chisholm Trail. "I guess between them they fought most of the battles there was to be fought. That's why I tried me luck along this here border. Hell Zack this whole damn country's getting too civilised."

Zachariah warmed his hands in the glow from their fire. He remembered a time when all he thought about was high adventure. Righting wrongs, having the respect of your peers and the thrill of living on the edge. Well he'd certainly seen a thing or two in his colourful career. Some of it good, most of it bad. Not the least, the degeneration into drunkenness as life takes one ugly turn after another. Dallas Stoudenmire his closest friend had been a prime example. Until a little over two weeks ago Zachariah had believed his life would follow the same path, that was until he'd met Alicia Morales. He was fooling himself thinking that one little smile could mean so much, yet that smile had made him come alive.

It was on their second night together, that Zachariah realised Tom wasn't just a happy go lucky Irishman. Tom had broken open a bottle of whiskey and was sharing it with Zachariah. After the second drink the tall Ranger refused another.

"One of us at least needs to be in control of his faculties," *said Zachariah. He'd stayed alive as long as he had, because of his vigilance. One mistake now could rob him of ever seeing Alicia again.*

"Hell Zack, you do what you must. Me, I'm past caring!"

For two days he hadn't let up with his wise cracks and tall stories. On the first night he'd drunk himself to sleep. Zachariah hadn't thought anything of it, being Irish, he supposed it was in his blood. Tom's comment had intrigued the older man.

"Past caring, now what's that supposed to mean?"

Tom's face twisted in anguish. A wounded look appeared in his eyes. Quickly he pulled on the bottle. He let out a gasp as the whiskey found its mark. "Ahhh, that's better. I love that warm glow you get when you've had just enough of the blessed stuff."

Zachariah grinned in way of acknowledgement. It was the way of the frontier to take people on face value. Zachariah knew better than to pry. Most men who had worked both sides of the law had some kind of past. He expected Tom Tenpenny was no exception.

"I was married once, pretty young thing she was too. Had myself a dry goods store up near Fort Worth." Tom's eyes stared up at the night sky, lost in his own world. "We'd stayed open late that night on account a bunch of cowboys from one of the local ranches was picking up last minute supplies for a drive up north. I'd stayed open as a favour for the foreman of the Bar 6, a friend of mine." Tom took another pull on the bottle, wiped the back of his hand across his mouth and slowly shook his head. "I was out back shoeing one of our horses. My Sally was out front minding the store. To this day I don't rightly know what happened, only that I heard a shot and a tinkling of glass. I rushed inside and found Sally lying in a pool of blood." Tom's eyes filled with tears, his voice began to break up.

"Tom, there's no need to go on. It's none of my Goddamn business," said Zachariah.

"No Zack, I want to tell you. I want you to know the kind of man you're riding with." He offered Zachariah the bottle. The tall Ranger took a swig and handed it back to him. "She was gone Zack, one minute she was full of life, the next she's lying there dead." Tom threw a log on the fire and watched as the burning embers flew up into the night sky. "They said it was an accident, a young kid green as all hell, excited about his first cattle drive. It weren't his fault, the damn drovers had got him liquored up, a

sort of baptism so the sheriff informed me. The kid was just showing off. Trying to prove what a marksman he was, shooting at the old wooden cigar Indian we had sitting on the sidewalk next to the front door." Tom stopped for a moment, his mind far away. *"If only I hadn't stayed open, my Sally would have been alive today."* Tom wiped at his eyes. *"The sheriff locked the kid up for the night, so I'm told. I was so distraught with grief at losing Sally that I didn't care. Some well meaning friends handed me a bottle, I drank to steady my nerves, then I drank to obliterate the memory of what happened, then I passed out. When I woke up I learned the owner of the Bar 6 had posted bail and the kid was on his way up the Chisholm Trail with a herd of ten thousand cattle. My grief turned to anger. Where was the justice? I rushed into the street, my anger turning to frustration. Then I saw him. I didn't know it was him at first, just a kid on an old mangy horse. He rode up to the store and dismounted. He looked sick and shaken as he walked towards me. He was unarmed and frightened. It was then that I realised who he was. He took off his hat and nervously stuttered, 'Mr Tenpenny, it was an accident. I didn't mean to do it. I'm so sorr....' I'll remember that look of shock and disbelief, for the rest of my days. I shot him dead in the middle of the street. He was just a kid, sick with remorse at what he'd done. He couldn't face the drive, he had to come back. He wanted to beg for my forgiveness. What did I do? I didn't give him a chance, I shot him down like a dog. He was just a kid."*

Zachariah reached over for the bottle and took another swig before handing it back to Tenpenny.

"You see who you're riding with Zachariah? Me, Tom Tenpenny, Murderer of children. Turns out he lied about his age, he was only fifteen. Without thinking I went back into the store room and grabbed up some supplies and hightailed it before the sheriff knew what had happened. That was fifteen years ago, yet I still see them every night. Sally's smiling face and the boy, I don't even know his name. I see his tortured expression, then it changes into one of bewilderment and shock as he feels the bullet that ended his short life. I thought losing Sally was the worst thing that could happen, but it pales when I think how I took away the life of that child."

Tom stood up and walked away from the fire and stared out into the darkness. Ten minutes later he returned to the fire, his composure returned. "I don't tell that tale to many folks. I ain't known you but a gnat's life, but I respect you Zachariah. You stand for everything that's right in this world. I just thought you ought to know what company you're keeping." For a moment the air was thick with silence. "Another drink perhaps," said Tom as he held the fast emptying whiskey bottle up. Zachariah smiled and beckoned Tom to sit down before he fell down.

Chapter 7

▼

"Yeah but I still don't see the connection between Juanita and Alicia," said Morgan.

"You will, I can feel it in my water," replied Orville.

"So it's just a hunch."

"I didn't say that. There are certain things I'm working on that suggest there is a connection. I want to keep it to myself until I'm sure they'll pan out," said Orville by way of explanation.

The sound of hooves pounding the earth caused Morgan to stare off into the distance. There was no mistaking Kathleen's mop of unruly yellow hair as she weaved back and forth whilst she closed the four bar gate behind her.

Orville couldn't help but notice the attention she was getting from his captain. He couldn't contain himself a moment longer, "She's a pretty fine horsewoman. Damned if she wouldn't make some cowboy happy!" His grin almost split his face in two.

Morgan chose to ignore the inference his friend was making."Well I guess we better get that barbecue lit. I reckon those kids of yours will be mighty hungry when they get back."

Mary Beth and little Jimmy proudly trotted their horses into the yard, with Tania and Kathleen a step or two behind them.

"Take a picture Pa," cried Mary Beth. "Take a picture of me and Jimmy."

Orville laughed and quickly left the barbecuing chores to Morgan while he ran to the car for his camera. Reaching into the glove box he realised excitedly that the camera contained film of the murder scene. With the onslaught of several agencies descending on the homestead, and the subsequent handing over of the case to the DEA, he'd forgotten about the film in his camera. The sheriff's department had brought in their official police photographer, who'd taken all the relevant photos.

Orville walked back towards his kids, thinking that perhaps his film contained a vital clue that had been missed. After all, his negatives would have been of the scene before half a dozen law enforcement agencies had trampled over the area. Deciding to keep the knowledge of the film to himself, at least until he'd had it developed, he began taking pictures.

"Let's have another shot for the family album," cried Orville as he snapped away at his kids on their horses.

By late afternoon the day's excitement had left the grownups in a spin. Morgan had forgotten how tiring kids could be. Mary Beth was still pleading with her father for a pony, but the day's activities had exhausted little Jimmy, he'd fallen asleep in his mother's arms. Tania thanked Morgan for his hospitality, and with the help of her husband managed to bundle the kids into the car without waking little Jimmy.

Kathleen made no move to get up and surprised everyone by inviting herself to stay for a night cap. A fact that registered very high on the Tyson's Richter scale. The look between Tania and Orville said it all. Morgan knew that it would be all round the station house before lunchtime.

Kathleen Delaney watched as Orville's tail lights disappeared from view. "They're a great couple, aren't they," said Kathleen.

"They certainly are," replied Morgan automatically. His mind on the rest of the evening, if the truth be known he hadn't given Orville and Tania a second thought. He'd been as surprised as they were when Kathleen said she was staying. 'I guess this looks like the end of a beautiful friendship,' he thought as she advanced towards him. The look in her eyes was enough to tell him that side of their relationship was about over.

*   *   *   *

Unable to wait until morning, the undeveloped film still paramount in his head, Orville dropped Tania and the kids off and went in search of a one hour photo lab. If the film contained nothing then, then so what. But if there was anything on the film that had been overlooked then he was in with a fighting chance of solving the case. Two blocks from his house he found the local K-mart still open. Showing his credentials to the manager, Orville was introduced to the lab technician. Within minutes he was being given a crash course in the art of one hour processing. Knowing the film would turn even the most hardened law officers' stomachs, there was no way he was going to give the lab technician nightmares if he could at all help it. Orville soon learned the workings of the machine and after a dummy run was all set to print. He sat down and set the enlarger. In less than half an hour he had thirty six 8X10 glossy photos including half a dozen of Mary Beth and little Jimmy. He shuddered at the thought of his kids on the same film as the Blevins killings.

Thanking the assistant Orville pulled out his wallet and handed over a twenty dollar bill. Not waiting for change he exited the building and drove home.

In his study later that night when Tania had gone to bed, he began scrutinising each and every photograph. The photos of Antonio De la Fuente were stark and horrific, unreal and macabre. For hours he checked every single print with the aid of a magnifying glass. If it hadn't have been such a brutal killing he'd have chuckled to himself, as he realised he was turning into a latter day Sherlock Holmes. So thorough was Orville that he listed every item that he viewed. Even though he knew the photos wouldn't reveal a single clue he wouldn't let it go until he'd identified each and every item on his list against the official police evidence book. Only then would he believe his photos held nothing of interest. There was only one problem, the evidence book which wasn't a book at all, but a computer program, was held in the local office of the DEA.

From the start Orville had met strong opposition from Lou Thurston the heavy set DEA man and his partner Frank Jordan, the chief operatives working the drugs side of the Blevins homicides. Thurston was especially obnoxious, blocking Orville's access when he first asked to see the murder files.

"You'll see them when we're good and ready," said Thurston. His halitosis repelled Orville for a couple of seconds.

"I'll see them now!" shouted Orville. At the same time he jammed his index finger into Thurston's chest, "As first officer at the scene it's my right!"

"Your right my ass!" Thurston pushed forward, Orville fell back into a fighting stance. Boxing was yet another of his attributes. The only thing dumb about Orville was his damn name.

"Leave it Lou. The boy's got jurisdiction," said Jordan as he pulled Thurston away.

"One day boy!"

"Anytime, you tub of guts!" Orville was mad as all hell and wanted to set the ball rolling. Thurston made a lunge in his direction, but Frank Jordan stepped in between. Orville didn't know what was bugging the DEA man. He could only assume that Thurston knew he didn't have a cat in hell's chance of solving the case.

As the weeks flew by Orville was sure someone had looked over his notes. It wouldn't have been the first time that a detective had tried to steal someone else's thunder. He'd thought to tell Morgan about it and their non co-operation but knowing the hassle it had caused at the start of the investigation he decided to keep it to himself. Besides the way Thurston had been riding him of late, Orville fancied a showdown.

Arriving at the DEA office Monday morning, Orville found his luck was in, both Lou Thurston and Frank Jordan were down the street having breakfast when he arrived to look at the evidence book.

"Still trying to solve the crime of the century Tyson," said the desk sergeant Lewis Mahon, when he handed over the password to the computer.

"Just running a few facts is all," said Orville cautiously.

Glancing at the clock, Orville typed in the password, then the words evidence book. He waited a moment while the machine did its calculations. Typing in Blevins brought up every shred of evidence that had been found at the scene of the crime and listed them in alphabetical order. Looking at his watch Orville ran through his list against the computers. He crossed off every one on his list except for one item. The Ranger had it listed as **see through wrapper**, just a plain see through wrapper. It probably wasn't listed because it had blown away between the time he'd photographed it and when the DEA stuck their nose into the case.

Lou Thurston walked into the office. "What the fuck you doing here. I didn't see your horse tied up outside. Ranger station's three blocks down, through the time warp and a century away." He began to laugh at his own witticism. Orville thought this was kind of dumb, seeing as the Texas Rangers were privy to the most up to date equipment money could buy. Orville screwed up his list and, without drawing attention dropped it in the waste basket and quickly closed the files he'd been looking at.

"Yeah, I was just leaving," said Orville. He wanted to bust the asshole's balls, but decided to wait until he'd cracked the case wide open.

* * * *

It was Kathleen's suggestion and after the night he'd had, how could he refuse her? Besides, her inquisitive brain and her youth might help him solve the mystery of his great granddaddy's disappearance. During the evening he'd shown her the latest draft of his manuscript. Instead of giving it a cursory glance, she'd devoured it with great interest, so much so that she'd suggested a visit to the Morales home in the foothills of the Sierra Madre.

"It's not like you're taking a day off. While you're investigating Zachariah's disappearance you're doing background work for Orville's case," said Kathleen, with a wicked glint in her eye.

"Okay you win, I'll leave a message on his voice mail, tell him I'll be back late afternoon."

"Yeah do that," said Kathleen as she sipped her wine and began to re-read the latest draft.

At a fork in the road, just outside the small town of Artesia Wells, they halted their horses For most of the morning both men had ridden in silence. Now at the parting of ways Zachariah turned his horse towards Tom Tenpenny.

"Tom, what you did was wrong, you don't need me to tell you that. But it was an understandable mistake. One that you've regretted every day of your life since. You can't bring Sally or the boy back." Zachariah pulled at the reins as his horse grew restless. "What you can do, is live your life. If that boy had lived, think what his life would have been, living with the guilt of taking a young woman's life. You above all others know the hell he'd have to live with." Then Zachariah put his hand to the brim of his hat, "Live your life."

"Thanks Zack, I'll try to do just that. You take care, you hear," then Tom Tenpenny spurred his horse forward and headed along the trail to San Antonio.

Dark clouds greeted Zachariah as he pushed on westward. Within a mile he had to stop and put on his rain slicker. It started slowly, one raindrop then another, until pretty soon it began to pour. After enduring eight miles of driving rain the temperature dropped a few degrees and a new hazard forced Zachariah to seek shelter. Hailstones the size of robins' eggs had caused his horse to spook and the road ahead had become like a small river. For miles he'd weaved in and out of oak groves but now he was out in the open. Shelter came in the form of a lone oak. It wasn't much but it allowed him a respite from the main storm. That night Zachariah slept fitfully propped up in a sitting position against the tree the reins of his horse wrapped tightly round his right hand. When he did sleep, he dreamed of Alicia.

He awoke to a grey sky. It was still raining but it had eased. Mounting up, he headed towards Carrizo Springs. By dusk he could see the gaslights of the town below him. Finding a wall of rock that allowed a little shelter from the rain, Zachariah dismounted and checked the Peacemaker at his side. He knew he'd only get one chance, and he couldn't afford a misfire.

Zachariah walked his horse down to the outskirts of town and halted just before the broad expanse of Main. The street was alive with dancing colour, caused by the gaslights reflective glow. He knew from what the bartender at the Oriental had told him, that the Alhambra saloon was halfway up Main Street on the left hand side. Zachariah's heart raced. He knew there was the possibility that within a few minutes either he or Long Tom Carmichael would be lying dead. He had the element of surprise. More than that, as far as Carmichael was concerned Zachariah was already dead. Yet the Ranger didn't let that fool him for a second. Underestimating the foe had cost many a man his life. If Long Tom was in the saloon, he'd only get the one chance.

For a brief moment Alicia invaded his thoughts. He lingered for a while contemplating his fate, then steeling himself for battle he spurred his horse forward. He sat tall and erect as he trotted through the mud-laden street. The rain began to beat down heavily as he reached the middle of Main Street. He passed the hardware store, the assayer's office, the bank and the barber shop. On the right he noticed a small ladies' dress shop, and a restaurant. The beginnings of the hotel and gaming houses took over from everyday life. The tinkling of a piano filtered out from the Texas Lady. A group of early-evening revellers looked up as he rode past. On the sidewalk, near the Alhambra, he spotted a small boy playing with a wooden gun. When Zachariah turned in at the hitching rail, the boy stopped what he was doing and stood watching. The big man stole a glance in his direction as he dismounted.

Unbuttoning his slicker he swept the coat back, revealing the gunmetal blue of the Peacemaker that nestled snugly in its hand tooled holster. He slipped the rawhide thong from the hammer of the pearl-handled revolver and stepped onto the sidewalk. Absentmindedly he brushed at a splattering of mud on his pants and then fumbled in the top pocket of his vest. Bringing out a small cigar, he lit up. He had to stop his hands from shaking. Most other times he hadn't the luxury of time to react. Instinct took control and he'd walked away from the scene unscathed. This, however, was different. This time it was personal.

A drummer, in a dark bowler hat of the time, pushed open the door to the saloon, took one look at Zachariah and sidled off to the right very hastily. From the open doorway a cacophony of sounds burst forth. The tall man in the rain slicker walked steadily into the smoke filled room and stepped up to the bar. Holding up three fingers he shouted his order over the noise of the saloon. Zachariah blew dust from the shot glass and poured himself a generous measure, all the time his eyes searching the faces of the crowd.

Tossing the drink down, the Ranger's eyes centred on the far card table. Long Tom Carmichael, with his back to the wall, was sitting dealing faro. Zachariah couldn't be sure if the gambler had seen him. He prayed he hadn't. Slowly he drew his Peacemaker from its scabbard and held it by his side at arm's length. Through the noise of the piano and the incessant chatter of people, the sound of the single action revolver being cocked went unnoticed.

Zachariah pushed his way through the crowd and soon stood over the green baize table. Long Tom remained composed as he looked into the eyes of a man he thought he'd killed.

"You're a hard man to kill, Zachariah." said Carmichael, knowing his only chance was to react immediately.

"Harder than you'll ever know," came the reply as the muzzle of the Ranger's Peacemaker levelled on his chest. Even as the hideaway gun leapt into Long Tom's hand, the barrel of the Peacemaker was spitting flame. Carmichael's body was propelled backwards into the far wall. Wide eyed with shock, the second bullet found its mark and closed Long Tom Carmichael's eyes forever.

Chapter 8

Apodaca was a sleepy little town that owed more to another time, than to the bustling metropolis of Monterrey a few miles farther south. Kathleen and Morgan had arrived a little before lunch time. As a courtesy Morgan called into the local police station. He wanted it known why he was there, and that his people in Laredo also knew where he was. It was a simple precaution. It wasn't unknown for people to dissappear whilst visiting out of the way places. More than that, he didn't want to run foul of the Mexican police. As it was, once he'd shown his credentials and outlined Zachariah's story, he was shown all the courtesy of a visiting dignitary. With a promise to send the police chief a signed copy of his book when it was published, Morgan and Kathleen drove away with not only directions to the Morales ranch but chapter and verse about their activities.

"I'm not sure we should be going there," said Morgan.

"Why, because I'm a woman?"

"In a word, Yeah! We already know Ignacio raped his half-sister."

"We don't know that for sure, all you've got is hearsay," said Kathleen defiantly.

"Right if we must go, we stick to my story about researching Zachariah's life. We don't breathe a word about the killings at the Blevins place. Understand?"

"Yes boss, anything you say boss," replied Kathleen, half-serious, half-joking.

Half an hour later they pulled up at the outskirts of the vast and sprawling ranch. Even from a distance the hacienda looked spectacular with its cream stucco walls and red tiled roofs. Spanish in style, with more than a hint of eastern influence; notably the two Moorish towers which appeared to touch the snow capped mountains that sparkled in the background.

As the hacienda grew ever closer, Morgan began to have second thoughts. Approaching the wrought iron gates he realised it was too late to back out. Already the electric operated entrance had swung open and two hulks in matching white shirts armed with Browning Auto-5 12 gauge shotguns beckoned them through. It was obvious to the Ranger that they were expected.

Without giving the two guards a second look, Morgan drove through the entrance and followed a long paved driveway until he came to a magnificent circular courtyard. In the centre of which stood an equally impressive fountain complete with trumpeting cherubs. Pressing gently on the break, Morgan came to a halt outside the entrance way to the hacienda.

He cast a professional eye over the courtyard and surrounding buildings. In each of the Moorish towers he'd noticed heavily-armed guards, and across the courtyard he spied three more. The place was like a fortress, which is what he would have expected from a drug overlord. And then Morgan saw him, a tall and imposing Mexican, standing against a backdrop of two highly polished hand carved oak doors. His dark smouldering eyes looked first at Kathleen then focused on Morgan.

"Buenos Dias. Welcome to Hacienda Morales. Allow me to introduce myself, my name is Diego Morales. You are the captain of Texas Rangers, Morgan Trelawney. And this young woman, this vision of loveliness, must be Miss Kathleen Delaney," said Morales with an unmistakable twinkle in his eye.

Morgan grinned, but he could feel the hairs on the back of his neck stand on end. In front of him was a very dangerous man. He'd half expected the police chief to be on the phone the moment they'd left Apodaca. After all, it was the Mexican way. What he hadn't bargained for was the outright way Morales had made his presence felt. His almost casual manner, his knowing leer. It was all part of his show of defiance, his utter contempt for the forces of law and order.

"Buenos Dias Senor Morales," said Morgan as he held his hand outstretched. Diego took the hand and shook it firmly. The Ranger watched as the Mexican took Kathleen's hand and kissed it gently. The twinkle was becoming more than just a leer, only Kathleen hadn't seen it. Not for the first time, Morgan wished the nine millimetre was at his side, instead of in the glove box.

"You must be hot. Come inside and I'll send for some cool lemonade." Then with a flourish of his hand he bid them enter.

A servant came in and placed a large tray with a pitcher of lemonade and several glasses on the great oak table.

"Refreshments!" gestured Diego Morales.

Morgan cursed himself for putting Kathleen's life in danger. He'd been a fool to allow her to come. Yet could he have stopped her? Kathleen was her own person. Nothing he'd have said or done could have dissuaded her. Quickly he stole a glance in her direction. She seemed relaxed and at home with her surroundings. She was oblivious to the danger they were in.

"Captain Blanco informed me you were coming and of the purpose of your visit," said Diego. Morgan didn't react. He knew that anything he said in the next five minutes could determine whether they lived or died. Diego Morales was playing with them. He wanted the Ranger to inadvertently know that every minute he breathed in Hacienda Morales could be his last.

"Right, I'll come straight to the point. For the past six months I've been researching my great grandfather's life, and so far as I can tell, he met up with a woman called Alicia Morales. This would have been the late 1890's in San Antonio. I have my manuscript in the car, if you're interested."

"Senor, allow me to stop you there," said Diego as he poured a glass of lemonade and handed it to Kathleen. "Firstly, Morales isn't an uncommon name." The Mexican looked directly at Morgan, paused for a brief moment then asked the question, "What makes you think your Alicia Morales is related?"

Morgan grinned. The Mexican was clever, very clever indeed. Without actually coming out with it, he'd gone for the jugular, the real reason why Morgan was there. If he lied who knows what would happen? If he came clean would the outcome be the same?

"You're obviously aware of the killing a month ago of your sister and her entire family," Morgan waited for a reaction before adding, "Of which you have our deepest sympathy."

"Yeah I heard, but save your sympathy," said Diego, the twinkle having gone from his eyes.

Aware of the look of surprise on Morgan's face he smiled and then added, "Allow me to explain, she was my half sister and that part's debatable. She tried taking my father for all she could get. God rest his soul." He crossed himself, then continued, "She left when she saw there was no provision for her in his will. That was about five years ago. I haven't seen her from that day to this. I'm not surprised she met her death so violently. She mixed with a bad lot."

Kathleen looked acutely embarrassed and a little shocked by his outburst.

"I'm sorry Senorita if my words offend you, but I have to say what is in my heart."

Morgan knew everything hinged on his next few words. "No I'm sorry, I didn't realise how you felt. You see I'm working on this book, when suddenly up pops Juanita Morales, coincidence or what? Not long after we arrive they find a cache of drugs and that's it we're off the case and the DEA take over. Me, anything for an easy life, but I'm left wondering if they were related. And that my friend is about it."

"Well then, that is that Senor. I'm afraid your journey has been in vain. I have no knowledge of any such relation. As I said before, Morales is not uncommon."

"Thank you for your time and hospitality," said Morgan, maybe a mite too quickly.

"And your home is most beautiful," added Kathleen, now fully composed, "Would it be presumptuous of me to ask for a tour of the house and grounds now that we are here?"

Morgan couldn't believe his ears.

"But of course," said Diego, slightly taken aback himself. "Unfortunately it will have to be a brief visit as I have guests to attend to later this afternoon."

For more than half an hour Diego played the congenial host, showing them both the interior of the hacienda and the magnificent courtyard.

"The roof, it's not original if I miss my guess," said Morgan, trying his damnest to appear relaxed.

"That is correct Senor. When my father inherited the old place it was but a ruin. The main body of the hacienda, in fact the area where we took our lemonade, was all completely renovated. Many years ago there was a fire that swept through that part of the building."

From his body movements Morgan could see that Diego was getting slightly edgy. It was time for them to leave whilst they still could, "Senor Morales, it has been a pleasure. Thank you for your time." Morgan handed him a business card, "I know you said there was no relation, but if anything comes up regarding Alicia Morales I'd appreciate you getting in touch," he added.

Diego took the card and walked outside with them. At the side of their car he kissed Kathleen's hand again, "Senorita, it has been a pleasure." Turning towards Morgan he added, "Vaya Con Dios," but his eyes told a different story.

As they passed through the entrance and found the main highway Morgan turned to Kathleen, his relief turning to anger, "Don't ever do that again, we're lucky to be leaving there in one piece."

"What! I don't know what you're talking about," said a surprised and indignant Kathleen. "I found Diego a very handsome and charming man, and honest too. He didn't have to tell us how he really felt about Juanita, but he did!"

"Of course he'd say that!"

"Well I don't agree, in fact I might take him up on his invitation."

"You can't be serious!"

"What is it with you? Morgan Trelawney. You're jealous!"

"Jealous my ass! Pushing your luck might be your way of getting kicks but it sure as hell ain't mine."

It was a sour note to end their day and Kathleen not surprisingly slumped down in her seat and fell into silence.

Morgan brooded on the things he hadn't told her; the reasons why he was so edgy. A little bribe back in Apodaca had thrown new light on Orville's investigation. He'd learned the brothers were into drugs, pornography, and child prostitution, not to mention the little matter of a number of mysterious disappearances.

* * * *

Back home in his study, Orville scanned the photo of Juanita's broken body onto a compact disc. Then with the aid of his computer he zoomed in on the wrapper. Enhancing it to life size, he could make out the letters Ma on one side of the cellophane and…xell on the other. Together they formed the word Maxell. Orville shuddered at his first thoughts. He already knew the perpetrators of this hideous crime had enjoyed their work, but this was too horrific even by the Blevins case to be real. It couldn't be true, but what other explanation could there be for the cellophane wrapping from a video tape?

He'd heard of Snuff movies in the past, but always thought that was beyond belief. He was a family man. The thought of anyone actually filming the slaughter of human beings seemed unreal. Yet as a police officer he knew there were plenty of sick people who'd pay to see such atrocities. Everyone knew of the hoax movie that played to packed audiences in Times Square back in the seventies. But that's what it was, just a clever hoax. Orville thought over his assumption. If it was true, then these people had to be stopped at all costs. Technically anyone who saw such a movie, was an accessory after the fact. More importantly it made anyone sick enough to pay to see such horror, a contributor to murder. Shaken by his discovery Orville switched off his computer and filed away his paperwork. He'd unearthed a terrible secret, one that left him nauseous and dizzy. Stepping outside he made a conscious decision. In the absence of Morgan or Jake, he'd decided to phone through his finding to headquarters in Waco, but first there was something he had to collect from the office.

He stood by the side of his car and took a few deep breaths. He'd stumbled onto something so horrific he was beginning to feel out of his depth. The case was becoming too big, he needed to talk to someone and fast.

"Shit, it's been one hell of a morning," he shouted in frustration. Jake was off with the flu and Morgan had left a message on the voice mail to say he'd be in the office late afternoon. 'Jesus Christ, we try all ways to get Kathleen and him together, when they finally do it's the wrong time.' Jumping into his car he turned the air conditioner on full blast. Within half a minute the heat inside the car had gone. The interior had turned cold. Adjusting the temperature to normal he drove out onto the highway. Then his pager went off. Orville checked the screen. **Blevins Homestead 4.30 pm. Juanita and Alicia, I've found connection, Morg.** 'At last,' thought Orville as he checked his watch and did a U turn on one of Laredo's busiest streets.

* * * *

Kathleen's sulks lasted until near sundown. "Sorry, I guess I was wrong back there, but I was funning that's all," she pouted in a school-girlish sort of way that was designed to melt the coldest of hearts. With the sun's fading light bathing the inside of Morgan's car with a soft orange glow, Morgan grinned. Encouraged by his warm smile Kathleen snuggled up to him. "Am I forgiven?" Glancing at her puppy dog eyes, he realised that at thirty-three she was still a little girl, lost in a big bad world. Something happened to Morgan at that moment, he couldn't put his finger on it, but he realised there was no way he could stay mad at her for a minute longer.

"Nothing to forgive darlin. It's just that Diego Morales as charming as he seems, is capable of anything." The relief of getting Kathleen away from the Morales hacienda swept over him. Kathleen snuggled even closer, resting her head in his lap. On the brow of a hill he pulled off the road and brought the car to a gentle halt. It was his favourite time of day. The sun had painted the heavens a spectacular shade of red. They watched in awed silence as the golden sun dropped from the horizon.

"It's so beautiful here," said Kathleen.

Morgan smiled and held her very close. Together they gazed out at the desert as it took on a softer more gentler glow. Not for him the mountain peaks and valleys of emerald green. He preferred the desert. In his eyes it held an even greater beauty. It could be harsh and unfriendly, offering unrelenting heat during the day and freezing temperatures once night had fallen. But there was more to the desert than most folks imagined. Morgan had lived most of his life in desert regions. He knew the names of every flower and brush, every animal that hunted and every reptile that slithered or crawled across its barren landscape.

Kathleen listened as Morgan reminisced about his childhood, then she pulled him towards her and kissed him gently on the lips. He looked into her deep baby-blue eyes, her sweet angelic face and soft lips, and returned her kiss with another, more passionate and stronger. Kathleen responded, devouring him in a sea of unbridled passion. Their kisses becoming more urgent, more savage, more uncontrollable.

It was nine thirty when they swung by the office. Almost all the lights in the building were on. The place was a hive of activity. Morgan looked across to Kathleen. "No prizes for guessing who's working late," he joked.

Stepping out of the car, the first person that Morgan saw was Jake, and he looked like shit.

"What's up?"

"Oh Jesus Morg it's bad, real bad."

Kathleen clung tightly to his arm, as Morgan looked past Jake to the crowd of strangers milling around the office. "What's bad? Where's Orville?" The atmosphere was electric, the tension on their faces spoke volumes. Morgan knew instinctively that something serious had gone down.

"That's it Morg, Orville's dead!"

"Orville!"

Jake waited a moment to let the news sink in, "He was found at the Blevins place. He'd been shot twice in the chest."

"He can't be dead, I was with him only yesterday." His mind conjured up pictures of their last afternoon together. The look of nervous tension on Orville's face as Mary Beth and Jimmy mounted the horses for the first time, the relief when they returned unscathed. The love he openly displayed when playing with his kids. The seductive looks he swapped with his wife Tania. The thought that some asshole had destroyed all that filled Morgan with rage.

"Have you any idea who did it?" Morgan's mind was racing, "What the fucking hell was he doing out at the Blevins homestead?"

"He nailed the son of a bitch before he died," said Jake, with a troubled look on his face. "It was Lou Thurston, that asshole from the DEA."

"What!"

"Yeah, I know it's bizarre, but from the start of the Blevin's case Thurston's been railroading Orville. Seems he was hell bent on glory and Orville was in his way," added Jake, not too convincingly.

"Hell Jake, that don't wash. There must be more than that involved."

"Yeah, that's what I thought, but the case has been taken out of our hands."

"The hell it has!" Morgan pushed his way into his office. "Okay which of you guys is in charge?"

"For the time being I am," said Sheriff Buzz Irvine apologetically. "It seems that our masters are sending in a special force to investigate what happened. In the meantime I've been given full jurisdiction. From now on the Rangers and the DEA are officially off the case." He wiped sweat from his brow then added, "That includes the Blevins case."

"No way, no fucking way!" Morgan shook his head. In less than a moment his world had been turned on its ass. His eyes brimmed with tears, as he thought of Tania and the kids. He looked at Kathleen and realised she'd had the same thoughts. His arm reached for her and brought her in real close.

"Has anyone informed Tania?"

Jake looked down at the floor, "Sorry, I thought it would be best coming from you. Honest I'd have told her if we'd known sooner. You were his best friend, he looked up to you," then the big man began to choke up.

"Easy Jake, I understand. It's my duty anyway."

Jake grimaced then turned away. At that precise moment Morgan felt a hand grip hard on his shoulder.

"I hope you're satisfied. That murdering bastard killed one of the finest policemen I've had the privilege to work with!"

The Ranger swung around in anger and stared into the hostile face of Frank Jordan. Morgan's own face quickly turned purple with rage. His vocabulary was reduced to that of the gutter. At last Morgan had someone to pound on."I'll fucking kill you!"

Jake moved quickly, intercepting the expected exchange of blows.

"Cool it, you ain't going to solve anything going for each others' throats," he shouted.

"That's the very reason your two agencies have been taken off the case," added Sheriff Buzz Irvine.

Frank Jordan shrugged off the restraining hand of Jake, "Anytime Trelawney, name the place." Jake's powerful arms pushed the agent towards the door, then turned quickly to restrain Morgan. Agent Jordan gave out a hateful stare, then walked out of the room.

"Come on Morg, we'd best break the news to Tania," said Kathleen as she laid a gentle hand on his arm.

* * * *

Sleep was impossible for him. It was three fifteen and his brain wasn't about to shut down. He kept reliving the moment when Tania opened the door. She didn't know what had happened but she knew from Morgan's face that it was something bad. The colour drained from her cheeks. At first she couldn't take in the news. He had to repeat it, but even then it took time to sink in. He thanked God Kathleen was there to help. Without her comfort and support he didn't know how he'd have coped. He remembered thinking, the kids were upstairs asleep, oblivious that their world had been turned on its head. He wished that he was asleep too, that when he awoke he'd find it was only a bad dream.

Chapter 9

▼

It was gone midnight when Morgan left them alone. He hadn't wanted to leave, but then he didn't want to stay either. Having Kathleen with him had been a godsend, and when she said she'd spend the night with her friend he decided to drive home.

He'd tried sleeping but the events of the day kept running around inside his head: If only I hadn't taken off into Mexico, if only I'd made Orville drop the case, if only I'd been there for him. If only…the inevitable if onlys. Sleep was impossible. Switching the light on he gazed across the room at the pages of unread manuscript that Orville was supposed to read. What were they now? Empty words that would remain unread. At the time they'd seemed important, but that was because Orville had been the driving force behind the manuscript. Now they were destined to gather dust in the corner of his office. 'What would he have wanted?' thought Morgan as he perused the pages of his novel. The answer was obvious, "Finish it!"

Killing had never sat well on Zachariah's shoulders, the death of Long Tom Carmichael doubly so. Had he killed in anger, defence, or in protection of someone, he could have understood, but killing to avenge was something completely different. What troubled him most was the thought that perhaps revenge wasn't the main reason. He had to ask himself if he was driven by an even greater force, the lure of a woman's skirts.

That Long Tom deserved to die, he had no doubt. But did he have the right to proclaim himself both judge and executioner? He was struggling with these thoughts when he rode into the town of Big Wells. Big it wasn't, just a tiny hamlet with no more that a handful of shops and stores, a cantina and a small blacksmith's forge. He'd barely left the saddle when an excited voice called his name.

"Trelawney, it's that time."

Zachariah recognised the voice instantly. Turning round he stared into the grinning and excitable face of Henry Tanner, together with his brother Harley. Both men had guns drawn, though they weren't actually pointing in Zachariah's direction.

"Time for what Henry," said Zachariah as he calculated his chances.

"Time to kiss your ass goodbye, lawdog…"

Zachariah took three fast strides into the middle of the street, at the same time he began to draw his heavy Peacemaker. Henry shot first, missing by a mile. Harley the steadier of the two, took careful aim and caught Zachariah with a bullet in the fleshy part of the thigh, spinning him around like a top. Henry's second shot tore a great chunk out of the hitching rail. In his excitement he ran up to the lawman for a shot at point blank range. It was the stupidest mistake of his whole stupid life. Zachariah knocked Tanner's gun arm away and pulled him onto the barrel of the waiting revolver. The shot tore through his stomach and exited his back, tearing out half a lung and leaving a great mass of torn tissue in its wake. Using Henry as a shield the Ranger then levelled his pistol at Harley. Tanner's second shot tore into his dead brother's shoulder, tearing him away from the grip of the lawman. Zachariah steadied himself for the killer shot. With his arm at full stretch he cocked the hammer and took careful aim. Harley's third shot flew harmlessly past his left ear. The Ranger fired, hitting Tanner just below the ribcage, stopping him in his tracks. As the echoes of gunfire died down, Zachariah realised he'd been hit. His instinct for survival was never greater than on the field of battle. There was no way of *knowing whether the other three had followed along with the Tanners. Taking no chances the big Ranger staggered across the street to his horse. He wanted to put as many miles between himself and Big Wells as was possible. A small crowd began forming on the sidewalk. They appeared frightened and bemused by what they'd just witnessed. Without stopping to give an explanation, the Ranger using all his strength pulled himself into the saddle. Turning his horse he rode off without taking a second look at the dead body of Henry Tanner and the mortally wounded Harley.*

An hour out of Big Wells and Zachariah was forced to stop and rest. Weak from the loss of blood he slowly slid off his horse and collapsed on the ground. Undoing his pants he began to examine the wound. With relief he saw that the bullet hadn't hit bone or a vital organ, but it was still there lodged just beneath the skin. He knew if he didn't manage to extract the bullet the chances were he'd die of blood poisoning. With no time for cleanliness the Ranger drew his Buck knife and cut at the protruding flesh. It split open like a ripe plum, revealing a slight protrusion of lead. Sweating with the exertion, he clenched his leather belt between his teeth and probed at the bullet with the point of his knife. He screamed silently as he began to inch the lead bullet from his thigh. Through excruciating pain he watched as the bullet finally dropped silently into the dirt. He'd already lost a great deal of blood and now the wound was open he was in danger of losing even more. With his left hand he pressed firmly on the wound, while with his free hand he grabbed at sticks until he had a small pile of kindling. With a match and some pages which he'd torn from his old bible he made a small fire. From a lifetime of experience on the frontier, Zachariah knew his only chance of stopping the bleeding was to cauterise the wound. Leaving the blade of his Buck knife in the fire he prepared himself for what was to come. He knew when he laid the red hot blade on his flesh the chances were he'd pass out. To protect himself from dying from the cold he dragged his greatcoat over his shoulders. As he took his hand away from the open wound he could see it was still bleeding freely. There was no time to think, he grabbed the handle of the knife and pressed the red hot blade across the open wound. All he remembered was a searing pain, the smell of burning flesh, then nothingness.

It was dark when the cold brought him back to consciousness. His eyes opened and he looked directly at the night sky. In that precise moment Zachariah thought he was in heaven. Then with consciousness came the pain and the cold. He knew if he was to survive he had to combat the freezing temperatures. With a great effort he somehow managed to pull his coat back across his shoulders. He looked up at the stars and judged it to be around midnight. Too weak to move, he knew if he made it through the night, the chances of him living would increase tenfold. With that thought in mind he drifted into a fitful sleep.

He was awoken by the false dawn, its translucent light lending the land an aura of mystery. Zachariah wasn't in a fit state to appreciate the mood. His head ached and his mouth and tongue cried out for water. Luckily he had water. It was in his canteen, which was wrapped around the saddle horn.

"My horse!"

He panicked. The horse must have wandered off in the night. At that moment, caught between an all powerful thirst and sheer panic he heard a faint whinny. Looking up he caught sight of the mare, she was chewing on a tuft of grass not more than thirty feet away. His relief was such that he almost smiled. Mustering up enough spittle he pursed his lips and managed a faint whistle. The mare looked over, then dropped its head and continued chewing the cud. Zachariah whistled again, the horse looked up and edged closer.

"Here girl, easy now," coaxed the Ranger.

As the horse drew near, Zachariah reached for the reins that trailed on the grassy floor. Grasping them he gently pulled the horse closer, then favouring his good leg he eased himself into a kneeling position. With his left arm he was able to get himself in to a crouch. With luck and God's will he was ready to make a grab for the saddle horn. He knew he would only get one chance.

"Easy girl, easy does it, easy."

Zachariah grabbed for the saddle horn, but the sudden movement spooked the horse, causing the Ranger to cry out in pain. His grip held and he managed to hoist himself up to full height.

"Easy, easy," whispered the Ranger as the horse shifted nervously. Beads of sweat ran down his face. He looked to his pants for the tell tale sign of fresh bleeding. His luck was holding. Supporting his weight on his good leg, Zachariah unhooked the canteen from the pommel and took a drink. The ice cold water tasted like nectar as it trickled down his parched throat.

By the time the sun had cast its spider like rays across the land, Zachariah had managed to pull himself into the saddle. Judging his direction from the sun's position he pointed the mare north. With luck he hoped to be in Frio Town by nightfall. If he got there, his chance of seeing the lovely Alicia again would have doubled from the night previous.

Frio Town wasn't much bigger than Big Wells, but what it lacked in comfort it made up for by having a veterinary who doubled as the town doctor. Pruitt Slocum patched the Ranger up, dressed his wound and administered to his other needs. Slocum was a stubborn man, possibly his stubbornness was even greater than that of the Ranger.

"When I fix a man up, he stays fixed. That's why you're gonna do as I tell you and stay in that damn bed." To weak to argue, Zachariah did as he was bid, but by his second day he was getting restless. The lure of San Antonio and Alicia were becoming too much.

Morgan sadly stacked the pages of manuscript and settled himself down for what was left of the night. His last thoughts before he slept were of the two Rangers, Zachariah the hard nosed son of a gun and 'Trooper' Orville Tyson his modern day counterpart. From what he knew about his great grandfather, he reckoned him to have been a hard but fair man. The year he'd spent getting to know Orville, he knew his friend hadn't killed Lou Thurston without a good reason. Just before sleep overtook him, he looked up towards the ceiling, "No matter what it takes, I'll find out what really happened. And when I do, someone's gonna pay!"

Chapter 10

Morgan knew the moment he saw the body of Lou Thurston that Orville hadn't killed him. Rangers, like most other law enforcement agencies, are taught to snap off two shots to the body. Thurston was killed with a single head shot. There was no doubt that the shot had been fired from Orville's nine millimetre, but in Morgan's opinion, after Orville had been killed. Not only that but the head shot was of pin point accuracy, not the kind that had been fired in the heat of a gunfight. For the time being Morgan kept that knowledge to himself, that and the package that arrived in his mail box the day after the shootings.

The package contained a single compact disk. The cryptic note attached, left Morgan in no doubt it was from Orville. Loading the disk into the computer, he gave it a cursory viewing. His young sergeant had been far busier than he'd possibly imagined. He'd compiled an almost complete dossier on the Blevins killings. From the little Morgan read, the file seemed to suggest there had been a cover up at the highest level. In the Ranger's opinion Orville's death confirmed it. His dogged police work had gotten him killed. The case smacked of conspiracy, and sooner or later someone would come looking in Morgan's direction. The disk was dynamite. It could get whoever held it killed. With no time to study the disk, he was left with no other choice.

There was only one person smart enough to piece together Orville's dossier. He didn't want to involve her, but she was the only one he could really trust. The envelope he re-addressed and sent with a brief letter of explanation to Laura in Austin.

The 'Dead Mustang' was a bar frequented by truckers and the occasional biker. It was on a straight stretch of highway a little north of Laredo. Since the freeway had been built, the road had fallen into disrepair and apart from the clientele of the bar, it wasn't used much. Jake drove down the lonely stretch of highway, and couldn't help but wonder why Morgan had asked him to this out of the way bar on a late Sunday afternoon. Pulling into the parking lot he spotted Morgan with a pair of binoculars trained on the road he'd just come down.

Jake parked his Ford Explorer and walked over to his captain. "Jesus Morg, what's with the cloak and dagger stuff?"

Morgan lowered his binoculars and smiled at his sergeant's bemused expression. He'd chosen the Dead Mustang for its out of the way location and its positioning. From the parking lot you could see for miles in all directions. If Jake's Explorer had been followed, Morgan would have been able to spot it with his field glasses.

"Come inside, let me buy you a beer," said Morgan.

Inside, the bar was decorated with radiator grills, hub caps and Harley memorabilia, not to mention the many neon Miller High Life signs. Grabbing a table away from the bar, they sat down and Morgan ordered a couple of beers.

"Okay Jake, what I'm about to tell you, could get you killed. On the other hand if I don't, you might just get killed anyway," said Morgan as he handed him a foaming Budweiser.

"Hell, everyone's gotta die sometime," replied Jake. There wasn't much that spooked Jake Hamilton. He'd done his tour of duty in Vietnam, and he'd seen his share of hell. More importantly, he'd come out the other side.

Morgan paused for a moment. Apart from Laura and Kathleen, his sergeant was the only person he could trust. "What do you know about snuff movies?"

The question threw Jake Hamilton. "What!"

"What do you know about snuff movies?" Repeated Morgan. "What I mean is, have we got any case histories, any known pornographers, any fucking known perverts who would watch this kind of filth?"

"Hell Morg, I ain't got a clue. As I recall, there was a case about twenty years ago. I think it was Death Valley. Anyway it turned out to be a hoax. Other than that, I ain't heard of such a thing. Don't get me wrong, I ain't saying it don't happen, all I'm saying is, as a police officer, I ain't heard of it happening."

"They killed Orville, so you won't hear of it! Some sick bastard filmed the massacre at the Blevins homestead, Orville found out and they killed him for it."

Even under the neon glow Jake's ruddy complexion turned a shade darker. "Those no good sons of bitches. If I could get my hands on them, I'd kill em myself."

Morgan ignored Jake's outburst, but lodged it in the back of his mind. "If I miss my guess, I'd say the persons that ordered the Blevins killings got scared we'd find out, and used their influence to have the investigation sidelined. I say persons because I think I know who did it." Morgan took a swig from his bottle and ran a cursory eye over the bar. "The day Orville was killed, Kathleen and I drove down to Apodaca in Mexico. I wanted to find out for myself whether there was a connection between Alicia Morales and Juanita De la Fuente. I found out purely by chance that Juanita's half brothers are big time drug dealers. I can't prove it, but I think the brothers Diego and Ignacio ordered their sister's execution."

"But why?"

"I don't know…revenge? Hatred. Maybe they knew too much. All I know is Diego Morales gave off an incredible aura of pure evil. If we'd said or done one thing wrong, I doubt if I'd be talking to you now. I tell you Jake, his arrogance was only matched by his Latin charm."

"Where's the connection to snuff movies?"

"Orville found a wrapping from a video tape. It's not conclusive proof, but it would have warranted an investigation. Besides it fits in with what I found out about Diego and Ignacio Morales. Not only are they into drugs, they're involved in child prostitution, and pornography. Hell that's one step away from snuff movies."

"Yeah, but in all due respect, you ain't got diddly squat."

"Maybe I ain't, but between us we can change that. You in?"

"If it'll help catch Orville's killer, you bet. But how are we going to do that? We're off the case?"

Morgan threw Jake a knowing look, "First we've Orville's funeral to attend. Tania's going to need all the support we can give her. Afterwards we make a noise about kick starting the investigation. It's what they'd expect. Then, when the uproar dies down, we settle back into our usual routine."

"You said they?"

"Yeah, I did. I've a strong suspicion Orville was lured to his death by one of our own, and I don't mean Thurston. Someone high up is running scared, someone that's had dealing with the Morales brothers in the past. We find out why the De la Fuentes were killed, we find Orville's killers."

"Just point me in their direction," said Jake.

"Good man. Talking of good men, Orville's replacement arrives the day after tomorrow. His name's Tony Valdez." Morgan then added, in a way that suggested far more than he'd said, "He's our kind of people. I worked with him up in San Antonio a few years back."

With the sky painting a golden tapestry, Morgan drove out of the parking lot of the Dead Mustang. Driving along that lonely stretch of highway, he couldn't help comparing Tony Valdez with Orville. He undoubtedly was the right man for the job, a worthy successor to Orville Tyson. But he couldn't replace the man. No one could. Morgan owed his young sergeant a big debt, bigger than he'd first realised. His friendship and family had meant so much to Morgan after the divorce. Orville's introduction into his family had saved him, not only from loneliness, but from himself. The young sergeant had an uncanny way of understanding what was missing from life. So much so, he'd actively encouraged Morgan in starting the manuscript. He'd suggested making friends with his ex wife and together with Tania, he'd introduced him to Kathleen. Those first few months would have been hard if it hadn't been for their warm affection and understanding. He owed it to Tania to find Orville's killers. More than that he owed it Orville to finish the job he'd started.

* * * *

Pruitt Slocum had fixed Zachariah's wounds up real good, so much so, that after the second day of enforced bed rest the Ranger began complaining about burning daylight. Slocum did his best to dissuade the big man from travelling, but his words failed to register. In respect for what the veterinary had done Zachariah told him of his quest to avenge the death of young Teresa. When he told Slocum of his meeting with Alicia Morales he was surprised by the man's attitude.

"Abandon your mission, you've done what is honourable, now turn away before it is too late."

Zachariah tried questioning him some more, all he received in reply was. "Xavier Morales is not a man to take lightly!" All Pruitt Slocum's advice did was to reinforce Zachariah's belief that all was not well between Xavier and Alicia. Ignoring the good doctor's advice the Ranger saddled up and left within the hour.

As the skies darkened above him, and the rain began to fall, he hurriedly donned his rain slicker. Before he could button it fully, the rain had drenched him to the skin. Zachariah shivered and began to wish he'd stayed in that warm comfortable bed in Frio Town. Ahead of him lay a vast expanse of trees. With luck he thought, they should help shelter him from most of the inclement weather. Hardening his resolve, the Ranger kicked his horse towards San Antonio.

Tired and weary Zachariah rode into the town two days later. It had been a difficult journey. The rain had continued to fall all that first night. Pushing his way through the trees had been hard going, but worse was to come. By morning, when the rain finally stopped, he realised he'd drifted off his route and added another five miles to his journey. He couldn't have given a tinker's damn. His limbs ached and he was burning up with fever. Climbing down from the mare, he began gathering up a huge pile of dead wood. Within fifteen minutes he had himself a roaring fire and snuggled close to it. As he lay there with the chills and fever, sleep eventually overtook him. When he awoke, he found every conceivable bone in his body ached but the fever had gone. Thanking God for his good fortune, he grabbed a hurried breakfast of beef jerky and washed it down with a generous swallow from his canteen and pointed his horse north.

Now lying in the comparative comfort of his room above the saloon he thought about what he would say to Alicia when he saw her. The killing of Long Tom Carmichael, the shoot-out with the Tanner brothers, the incessant rain, the cold, the fever, they were problems he was equipped for. But problems of the heart, that was something Zachariah Trelawney knew very little about. What if he was wrong? What if Alicia, was happy with her husband? What if he'd read more into her gaze than was there? Now that the time was drawing near Zachariah began to doubt himself. He'd been resigned to a lonely life, with only a grisly death to look forward to, and then he'd met Alicia. In the space of an evening she'd captured his heart, reawakening feelings he'd believed were dead and buried along with his beloved Clara. Alicia had shown him a way back, but was he fooling himself? Did he have the courage to find out? That's what frightened him. What if all there was, in the end, was a lonely existence.

It was too late in the day to do anything about it. Already he could hear the faint tinkling of the saloon piano far below him. Pretty soon he'd hear the shouts and cries, the yells and laughter of other poor wretches. He reminded himself that he wasn't alone, that the frontier was crawling with people like himself. Tom Tenpenny, a man he'd only just met, was a prime example. A man desperate to flee his past, a man destined for the same fate as himself. But why should that be, thought Zachariah. Despite what Tom had done, he was a good man. A man not unlike himself.

"Company, that's what I need," said Zachariah as he looked into the cracked and worn mirror. He was forty-three years of age. His hard sun-tanned features, laid testimony to the fact. His recent gunshot wounds, weeks of sleeping rough, a bad diet and the constant need to be forever alert had aged him beyond his years. Only his eyes gave away the young man straining to get out. Unfolding his razor he began to scrape away three days worth of stubble. When he was finished he put on his old but still functional grey shirt, his cravat, his brocade vest and his black frock coat. He swept his hair back with his hand and placed his black hat upon his head. He wasn't one to admire himself in the mirror, vanity was something reserved for the young. Again he had self doubts, Alicia was twenty six, maybe twenty seven, how could he possibly think she'd be interested in him. With a sigh of resignation he pulled himself away and headed out the door.

From the balcony at the top of the stairs, Zachariah studied the Friday night crowd. This was his world, a place of excitement and danger. These were his people, the drinkers, the gamblers, and the ladies of the night. They were the same in every town he'd been in. Every one of them, searching for their own private dreams. Some found it in a bottle, others in the pleasures of the flesh, and some never found them at all.

San Antonio was a big town, and for some, a lonely town. Zachariah though by nature a solitary man, at times felt the need for company, an urge to talk, to clear his head. He could while away a few hours with any number of saloon girls, but it wasn't his style. He needed the company of his own kind. Someone who would understand his needs. Someone like Tom Tenpenny.

* * * *

Tenpenny had arrived in San Antonio a week and a half earlier. For fifteen long years he'd been drifting aimlessly. A man tortured by his past, searching for release from his pain and suffering. He'd gone the way of many a man in the same situation. Drinking, gambling and whoring. It was his only way to obliterate the past. Yet deep down the guilt at what he'd done wouldn't let him forget. Tom Tenpenny was neither a man who sought trouble nor a man to step aside when the chips were down. Without wanting it, he'd become a dangerous man on the fast shrinking frontier. Death walked in his wake. Not counting the boy, he'd killed three men, two of them in the line of duty, whilst the third in a drunken brawl. To those who knew of him, he was becoming known as the undertaker's friend.

Negotiating a percentage of the house, he'd taken over the job of Monte dealer in the Military Plaza saloon. It was a game with Spanish origin, and popular with the Mexican clientele. Tom was a natural with the cards, yet he was a fair man and ran a straight game. In the short time he'd frequented the Military Plaza, he'd managed to ruffle a few feathers. Most people liked him, but in his chosen profession there was always one or two bad eggs in the basket.

He'd been dealing Monte for almost a week when Barclay McCulloh and Josh Randolph sat in on a game. Because of his slight stature and unassuming ways they'd misjudged the little Monte dealer and thought him a push over. On the orders of Jasper Kendrickson, a well known proprietor of two large gambling establishments, they instructed Tom in the way business was handled in San Antonio.

"It's like this see. Each week we collect fifty percent of your cut. We don't ask for it for nothing, we make sure no trouble comes your way. Call it an insurance," said McCulloh as he grinned at the smaller man.

"McCulloh! You wouldn't happen to be Clay McCulloh of Amarillo."

"The very same," said McCulloh, pleased that his fame had spread this far south.

Tom grinned back, "Thank you gentlemen for your kind offer, but I'm afraid I can't accept." His eyes turned to blue diamonds as he watched the pair.

"You misunderstand," said Josh Randolph, "we ain't asking, we're telling!" His right hand slammed down hard on the green baize table sending chips and playing cards crashing to the floor.

No one saw him move, but quick as a flash Tom Tenpenny pulled a slim bladed knife from nowhere and stabbed it through Randolph's right hand, pinning it to the table. With his other hand he'd drawn his short barrelled nickel plated pistol and held it an inch from McCulloh's nose. "No gentlemen, you don't understand." Then in a level voice, devoid of emotion he uttered the words. "I don't take shit from any man, especially back shooters." His eyes fixed on McCulloh. Unceremoniously he yanked the blade out of Randolph's hand. Josh swirled with pain and lunged at the little Monte dealer. He stopped in his tracks as Tom shifted the nickel plated pistol to the middle of his forehead. Clay McCulloh, the thinker of the two pulled his comrade away.

"You're dead Tenpenny! Next time I see you, you're dead," screamed Randolph as he and Clay McCulloh made a hasty exit.

That had been four days ago and nothing had happened since, although the tension in and around the Plaza was still electric. The altercation had done nothing but good for the Military Plaza saloon. The San Antonio grapevine was soon buzzing with the tale of the short Monte dealer that had backed down two of Kendrickson's men.

Everyone knew Jasper Kendrickson wouldn't take it lying down. He had a stake in most of the gambling establishments on both sides of the San Antonio river. When he heard what happened, it irked him some, but no more than that. He knew one man standing alone, wasn't going to cause him to much of a problem, despite his quickness. Josh Randolph was a brute of a man yet when it came to a thinking game he just wasn't equipped. Clay McCulloh on the other hand, was a thinking man. He'd have judged the situation and wouldn't make the same mistake twice. More importantly McCulloh didn't take kindly to being made a fool of, he'd want retribution and would be more than ready when his boss gave him the order. Kendrickson sat back and thought about his next move.

Tom had taken to working without his jacket on, revealing a brace of nickel plated Colts sitting snugly in matching shoulder holsters. No one saw fit to inform the little Monte dealer of the city ordinance forbidding the carrying of firearms within the city limits. Most people believed the infringement would only be temporary. Death wasn't something that Tom feared, but it didn't mean to say he intended going to Hell without a fight.

He watched them as they slowly mingled with the Friday night revellers, first one, then another. 'Back shooters, I reckon,' thought Tenpenny. A lesser man would have taken it to them there and then, but Tom knew how these things worked. Kendrickson wouldn't make his play until he had all his men in position. Even then he would want to make a show of it, allowing would be revolutionaries a showy warning. Unperturbed Tenpenny continued dealing the cards.

A little after eleven fifteen, Jasper Kendrickson walked into the Military Plaza saloon flanked by Clay McCulloh and Lucky Charlie. Josh Randolph brought up the rear. A nervous hush settled over the crowd. While some stayed perfectly still others rushed for the exit. Tom soon found himself surrounded by empty chairs.

"Now that ain't nice, you've frightened away my guests," he said, glancing briefly to the shotgun in the corner.

"My name's Jasper Kendrickson, and I ain't a nice man. But I am a reasonable one. Agree my terms and that's the end of the matter. After all we're both businessmen."

Tom weighed up his situation. Kendrickson was no slouch, and Tom could see it in his eyes. Clay McCulloh, he'd heard tell, had killed himself a number of men and Lucky Charlie looked like he'd seen action a time or two. As for the three others, Randolph was slow, and he guessed if he let the scattergun off in their direction, they'd do exactly that. The trick was to get Kendrickson before the others opened up.

"That's my point, I can't do that," Tom's eyes turned to stone.

"Then we have no choice," said Kendrickson his tone sounding low and menacing.

"There's always a choice Jasper," came a cold voice from the edge of the bar, "You can choose to live, or you can choose to die."

All eyes turned in the direction of the bar at the tall man in the black hat and dark frock coat which had seen better days. More importantly they gazed at the long barrelled Peacemaker hanging from his right hand, the hammer already cocked.

"Zachariah Trelawney, what in blue blazes you doing in this neck of the woods?" There was no warmth in Jasper Kendrickson's words.

"I'm here to help my friend deal Monte," said the tall Ranger, not taking his eyes of Kendrickson for a second.

"I wish you'd said you were with Mr Tenpenny before now. It would have saved me some embarrassment." Kendrickson looked uncomfortable. He tipped his hat and ordered his men out. Framed in the doorway of the saloon Clay McCulloh lingered for a moment longer. Barely able to control his temper he sneered across at Tom and pointed his loaded finger in a symbolic gesture. "Next time." Then he too, was gone into the night.

Tom looked across at his new friend and smiled. "Guess that makes us about even!"

"I guess it does at that," said Zachariah. "Buy you a beer?"

Chapter 11

Tania stood proud as a bugler played 'The Last Post.' Clutched in her hands, the neatly folded flag of the sovereign state of Texas. Her heart was breaking, yet she held herself with dignity. Just as she knew Orville would have wanted. Behind the grieving widow, standing with the children, were Tania's parents. Little Jimmy stared around in bewilderment. Mary Beth, barely old enough to understand, cried as the metal casket was lowered into the ground. Morgan looked across helplessly at the broken family and wept.

It had been a moving ceremony. Even the most hardened of law officers could be seen wiping their eyes. Orville had been liked by all who'd come into contact with him. There wasn't anyone who he'd truly known in his short life, who hadn't been touched by his warm affectionate character.

'All except the bastards that killed him,' thought Morgan darkly. He could feel the bitterness rising in his chest as an uncontrollable rage deep within him threatened to spoil the sombreness of the occasion.

Morgan and Jake watched as Tania, helped by her ageing parents bundled the children into the limousine and drove slowly away from the cemetery. She'd asked them back to the house, but the Rangers politely and respectfully declined.

"I'm in need of a drink," said Jake.

"Me too," replied Morgan.

As the sun died, they entered 'The Lone Star.' It was late afternoon, and the place was empty apart from a couple of old bar flies. If it had been a little later the bar would have been crowded and their ceremonial dress would have raised a few eyebrows.

"Hell Jake, here's to Orville! A finer Ranger never lived."

"I'll drink to that," said Jake, though he wasn't of a mind to enjoy it.

One drink became two, then several. It wasn't long before the two Rangers had notched up a fair sized bar tab. Their tensions eased as the alcohol kept a coming.

"One minute you've got everything…the next, it's all gone," said Morgan.

"Yeah, life's funny, Vietnam was like that. We were under heavy fire, Charlie had us pinned down real good. I'd bought the farm for sure, when out of nowhere these choppers appeared. A month later Blythe's standing there on the tarmac with a banner welcoming me home. After that I just stopped trying to figure it out."

"To Orville" said Morgan for the umpteenth time as he raised his glass and sank his fourth tequila. A screech from the amplifiers of the local band busily setting up for the evening sounded across the bar-room. Jake glanced at his watch.

"Shit Morg, we better get outta here." He'd already spied a few unsavoury characters entering the bar. In the wrong kind of neighbourhood, dressed as they were, it wouldn't take long before there was more trouble than they could handle. To hang around any longer would be verging on suicide. A few faces had begun to stare in their direction.

Morgan was about to get up and go when he looked straight into the face of a dark haired girl. The redness of her lips widened into a smile. Her eyes invited him to play. Perhaps if Kathleen had been there he'd have followed Jake's advice, but she wasn't. She'd been called away unexpectedly by her uncle up in Austin. Unfortunately it was just when Morgan needed her most.

"One dance Jake, then we go."

Before Jake could move, Morgan was off his bar stool and heading towards the brown eyed girl.

"Ma'am, let's dance!"

She grinned, showing off a set of pure white teeth, slid seductively off her bar stool and sauntered onto the dance floor. Up close she wasn't as pretty as she'd looked, but she turned out to be one hell of a dancer. Pretty soon they'd attracted a number of the Lone Star's clientele, including the two hundred and thirty pound hulk that claimed brown eyes as his girl friend. Jake spotted him the moment Morgan walked in her direction, but it was too late. The uniform was enough to cause a fight. Add that to the misdemeanour Morgan was committing on the dance floor and it only added up to one thing, trouble as large as the T in Texas.

"Oh shit!" Jake could only watch as Morgan played out the scenario. Too late, he realised what his captain was up to, as he escorted the girl back to her boy friend. Before he could leave his stool it was all over. There was an exchange of words, an arm grabbed the girl roughly and then the big feller lunged forward. Morgan neatly side-stepped and tapped him one just below the left ear sending him flying into a table and knocking a bunch of chairs six ways to Sunday. Tapped was probably the wrong word. The rage that had been festering in Morgan's head had channelled itself into his right fist. The big feller sat on the floor dazed. Quick as a flash Jake left two twenty dollar bills on the counter and raced over to Morgan.

"What's got into you man!"

Without waiting for an answer Jake hurried Morgan outside and into the street.

"We gotta get outta here, and fast!" Jake looked towards the door of the Lone Star. Already the big feller, and three of his friends, were charging through it.

"Hey asshole, we ain't finished," he cried as he lashed out at Jake. The blow caught Hamilton off guard, hitting him high up on the cheek bone, sending him hurtling into a bunch of garbage cans. Recovering himself quickly the ex-Marine bunched his fists and launched himself at the big guy, landing a hay maker to the bridge of the man's nose. A stocky Mexican in faded Levis and sleeveless white tee shirt, slammed a powerful left at Morgan's head. The Ranger parred the blow and followed through with a short punch to the man's solar plexus. A Hispanic man with a blue bandana tied around his head, lunged at Morgan. Jake hit him with the lid from an overturned garbage can, stopping the man in mid flow.

"Ahhh," cried Morgan as another guy slammed him from behind with a piece of timber, knocking him to the ground. Jake stopped him from dealing another blow with a vicious kick to the man's crotch. Morgan scrambled to his feet and drove his head into the muscular chest of the guy wearing the white tee shirt. Seconds later the familiar blip and siren of a Laredo patrol car tore into the action. The four men broke from the affray and scattered in all directions, leaving Jake and Morgan battered and exhausted. The cop, on seeing the tangled mess of uniforms, relaxed and asked if he could be of any assistance.

"Thanks, you already have been," said Morgan. Sitting propped up against an old pick-up he grinned across at Jake, "Now ain't that better?"

Jake grinned back, "I guess it is," then he shook his head. "Though next time warn me before you start something." Then he began to laugh. Somehow the fight, short as it was, had helped to free the demons in Jake's head. His laughter became infectious and pretty soon they resembled a couple of hyenas. As they staggered towards the car Morgan's mood became more thoughtful. The benefit of the adrenaline rush was beginning to wear off, his euphoria clouding over.

"Let's get closer to home, and have us a real drink."

"I'm up for that," added Jake.

* * * *

Jake Hamilton lifted his bruised and battered face and looked into the dark eyes of a good looking Hispanic man. The star pinned on the breast pocket of his shirt left Jake in no doubt. Tony Valdez was reporting for duty.

"Jesus man, what happened to you?"

Jake didn't respond. Just at that moment the door opened and in walked Morgan. His eyes were sparkling despite the cut above the left eye, which was now turning a bluish-red. Tony's face broke into a broad grin, "Don't tell me, you're just good friends, right!

It wasn't love at first sight. Jake hated wise guys, especially when nursing a medium sized hangover.

Morgan extended a hand, "Good to see you Tony."

"Good to see you too, Morg" said Valdez, his mood changing ever so slightly as he added, "I'm here because I owe you."

Morgan smiled, showing off a mouthful of white teeth, albeit two were loose from last night's brawl. Choosing to ignore the last remark, Morgan did the introductions. "This old reprobate, he's my sergeant. Jake meet Tony Valdez!"

"Nice to meet you Jake."

"Likewise," said Jake though not too convincingly.

After Jake and Morgan had explained their bruises, and exchanged a few more pleasantries Tony excused himself. He'd only just arrived and needed to find himself somewhere to stay. As he closed the door behind him, Jake cast a worried glance at Morgan.

"Believe me, he's a pistol," said Morgan. "I know what you're thinking, but you couldn't be more wrong."

"He's too sure of himself for my liking."

"Valdez is like a chameleon. He can be what he wants to be, given any situation. Don't let first impressions fool yah." Morgan could see Jake wasn't convinced. "Okay, I'll give you a run down on Valdez. His father was Mexican. His mother, God rest her soul was one hundred per cent Texan. Believe me, being half white and half Mex ain't a picnic. Even though San Antonio has a large proportion of Hispanics there's still prejudice."

"So, it's something he had to deal with," interruped Jake.

"From a kid he always wanted to be a Ranger, he wanted to be looked up to and admired. He succeeded better than any man I know. He worked for a time for the border patrol, catching and sending back illegal immigrants. The abuse he received from them and from his own kind was unbearable. From his colleagues it was even worse, the snide remarks, the practical jokes, the verbal abuse. Needless to say Tony got into more fights than he could handle. But his biggest battle was when his father killed his mother!"

"What!" exclaimed Jake.

"I met him when he first joined the Rangers. From the moment he was assigned to my company I could tell he had a chip on his shoulder the size of the San Jacinto monument."

Morgan filled his cup to the top with coffee, his mind far away remembering. "I only ever knew his ma as Hannah, but from the little time I spent in her company I could tell she'd been a real hell-cat in her time. Sassy and full of beans, I can imagine she'd have had people talking every which way when she upped and married Filipo Valdez."

Morgan sipped his coffee and squatted his butt on the side of a desk. "Filipo wasn't a bad man. He'd always provided for his family, brought them up real good too. Along with Tony there was another son and three daughters. Bringing up five kids in a mixed race family might have had its draw backs, but you sure as hell wouldn't know it. Hannah and Filipo had forged a marriage anyone of us would have been proud of. But then shit happens. Filipo was in his mid fifties when he got laid off from the oil refinery. You might just as well have cut off his hands, Tony's dad was a proud man, and not being able to support his family came as a heavy blow. He tried getting other jobs, but because of his age he found it nigh on impossible. For weeks he endeavoured to find work, but all he was offered was menial, in the kitchens of restaurants he'd once frequented. It wasn't that they were destitute, on the contrary, Hannah had a good job with a law firm in San Antonio. It was Filipo's pride. He hated the thought of not providing for his family. He became demoralised and started drinking. Hannah begged him to stop. She told him he'd done his share of work when the kids were young. She reminded him that never in their lives had the Valdez kids gone hungry. He'd provided them all with a good education and had nothing to prove. She told him it was her turn to bring in the gravy. He wouldn't listen. He didn't consider himself a man if he had to accept charity. That's when Hannah really lost it. She flew into a blinding rage, telling him if he didn't stop drinking then she would sure as hell leave him. Whether it was her raised voice or the threat of leaving that made him see sense, I don't know. Anyway for a month or so Filipo played the perfect house husband, cleaning, cooking and getting the groceries from their local store."

The telephone rang in Jake's office, "Shit! Hold it one second while I answer the goddamned phone."

Morgan finished his coffee and grabbed a refill. He didn't like talking behind Tony's back but it was important for Jake to know the kind of a man he'd be working alongside. The Ranger captain had a gut feeling who'd done the killings at the Blevins homestead, especially since his visit to the Hacienda Morales. Proving it was going to be a difficult, and extradition between Mexico and the States had always been tricky. Orville's death had changed things. Now it was personal. That's why he'd brought in Tony Valdez. His sergeant had a right to know the calibre of the man who was riding shotgun.

"Sorry about that," said Jake, at the same time he grabbed himself a refill.

"Right, where was I. Groceries, that's it. Filipo did a great job for a time. When he was done, he'd hop in the car and travel into town to pick Hannah up from work. It was a good arrangement, until…. No one knows why he started drinking again, only that on the day it happened he'd been on the sauce pretty heavily. Whether she noticed the drink on his breath as she climbed in the car, I guess we'll never know. Anyway it wasn't until they were on the freeway that it happened. Hannah wasn't the type to take matters lightly. She must have realised he was drunk and tore into him. She'd have demanded he stopped the car at once, and knowing Filipo, he'd have put his foot down hard on the gas. What happened next is anyone's guess. She probably grabbed for the ignition. Anyway the car swerved out of control, hitting an old pick-up, then side swiping an Oldsmobile, and that was that. The car must have spun over at least three times before finishing up in an irrigation ditch. Filipo staggered out unhurt, but poor Hannah, well she was beyond help."

"Jesus!" Exclaimed Jake.

"It gets worse, much worse," drawled Morgan. "Filipo was charged with manslaughter and sent to prison for three years. Tony took his mother's death real hard, but instead of wallowing in self pity he threw himself into his job as a Ranger. During that time he equipped himself real well, earning one commendation after another. He'd finally earned the respect of his peers, and believe me, that meant a lot to him."

"I can understand that," said Jake sympathetically.

"Life finally took an upward turn when he started dating a pretty young thing. I can't recall her name right now. Anyway, he was really smitten and it wasn't long before they started looking for a place to live. He moved out of the family home and they moved into an apartment overlooking the Frost bank. And then Filipo was released from prison. Of course he took it to heart,. The dumb fuck hadn't learnt anything whilst he was away. Tony tried reassurring him it was only a coincidence that the lease had become available at that time. Filipo didn't believe his son and they had a tremendous row and Tony walked out. Secretly though, I think he was glad to get out of the old man's hair, you see, he'd never been able to forgive him for Hannah's death.

What happened a week or two later, I can recall as clear as day. We were out on routine patrol, when the call came in. Tony was just getting a couple of chilli dogs from the stand on the corner of Commerce and Main when they radioed through. "We're to go to the Acme refinery on West Fifty Third and Travis," I said. 'Hey that's were my old man use to work,' says Tony. He can see it in my eyes, there something I ain't telling him. 'What the fuck's going on,' he snaps at me. I tell him it's his old man. First reports are a little sketchy, but it looks like he took that old hunting rifle of his and shot dead his old boss. I told him that wasn't the half of it. He's holding several hostages and claims he'll kill one every hour unless his demands are met. 'Shit Morg, what fucking demands!' screams Tony. 'He wants your forgiveness. Claims you ain't spoke a single word to him since he's been let out.' I press the metal to the floor and speed off in the general direction of the refinery. Anyway the upshot of it is, we arrive and find the place in a siege situation. Fearing for his father's life he strips his gun off and walks into the wide open yard and proceeds to walk up to the refinery building. He's within ten yards of the door when some asshole with a bullhorn bellows that if the hostages ain't released within five minutes they're coming in. Tony shouts back, 'Give me time!' I could sense the panic in his voice. 'Hey pa, let's talk about it.' I see that big old hunting rifle and it's trained right at Tony's chest. It seemed like an eternity but it couldn't have been more than five minutes before Tony had convinced his old man to give up the hostages. The door opened and one after another the hostages started to leave the building. All the time Tony's standing perfectly still, the rifle pointing right at him. 'Jesus pa, give it up,' says Tony. 'I can't,' he cries. 'Do it for me pa, do it for me and ma.' I can tell you, my heart was in my mouth, and then suddenly Filipo lowered the rifle and shows himself at the door. Even from where I was standing I can see tears in the old man's eyes. 'I'm sorry son, please forgive me...' It sounded like a dull thud, but there was no mistaking the shocked look on Filipo's face as the bullet tore into his chest. 'No!'

Screamed Tony as he raced to his father's side. But it was too late, the old man died in his son's arms."

"Oh Lord," exclaimed Jake.

"For six months I did all I could for the boy. His relationship with the girl folded and for a time I thought he would up and quit the Rangers. Then one day we're confronted with a bank robbery that had gone horribly wrong, two bank employees dead and three taken hostage. I'm putting on my flak jacket and thinking about the similarities to the oil refinery situation, when Tony cool as ice steps into a vicious firefight against three heavily armed bank robbers. He killed two and seriously wounded the third. His courageous, though foolhardy action undoubtedly saved the lives of one young bank clerk, the head cashier and a security guard. He was awarded our highest decoration."

Jake looked across at his captain, "Are you telling me the boy has a death wish?"

"Nope, well maybe. After that he volunteered to work under cover in Mexico. Dangerous wasn't the word I'd use, but he came through it. What I'm trying to say is, Tony Valdez gets the job done. And where we're heading you need to be a mite crazy."

Morgan had been a Texas Ranger for more years than he could remember. He knew how things worked, he knew that sometimes the good guys didn't win. That's why he'd brought in Tony Valdez. There had been stories, unconfirmed stories that Valdez could be a ruthless mother fucker, and for what Morgan had in mind Tony was the man for the job. One way or another justice was going to be served.

Chapter 12

▼

Zachariah opened his eyes, then quickly closed them. Lying perfectly still he willed the pending headache away. It was a forlorn effort, he'd known that from the moment he'd woken. There were the old tell tale signs, the nausea, the hammering inside his head. It had been years since he'd really tied one on, but some feelings you just don't ever forget. In an effort to forestall the inevitable hangover he began recalling all he could of the previous night's altercation.

He'd known Tom for less than a month, a month in which both men had saved each other from certain death. He'd watched Tom's eyes as he openly embraced death. It held no fear, it was as if he welcomed its coming. He'd seen that look before, on the faces of men like Dallas Stoudenmire, John Wesley Hardin and Long Tom Carmichael. He'd worn that look himself. He'd been one of them, a man without hope, without a future, a man who few people would mourn. What was there to fear? But now, what right did he have to hope, to feel, to love? Was he a fool? Was he stupid enough to believe that Alicia Morales might want him? All he knew for sure was she'd made him vulnerable. He wanted to live, to feel, to touch. More than anything he wanted to taste those sweet lips of Alicia's.

Seeing Tom again so soon pleased him. "You're in town only days and you get Kendrickson gunning for you. How did you manage that?"

"My personal charm, I guess."

"Good to see you Tom," said Zachariah, the warmth of his greeting not lost on his new friend.

Tom flicked his hat in way of acknowledgement. "I take it you found Carmichael," he said, and poured them both a generous measure of tequila.

"Yep," said Zachariah. "I come across the Tanner boys in Big Wells too," he added without going into details.

"You don't say!"

Zachariah looked at him thoughtfully, "How long you planning on staying in San Antonio?"

"I ain't really thought about it. I'm earning a living, and San Antonio does have more than it's share of pretty women," said Tom.

"Only, I figure San Antonio is a mite more civilised than you give it credit for," said Zachariah. "While I'm around Kendrickson won't touch you, but I can't be sure about the guys that hang with him."

"Hell Zack, I ain't of a mind to worry about the likes of McCulloh."

"You're missing the point. You might need protection from the authorities. This part of the country has taken to law and order in a big way. Now if I was to make you an acting Texas Ranger, the law would find it hard to go against that if it did come down to a fight."

"How would I earn my pay?"

"Just be there when I need you," said Zachariah. He hadn't thought about it until Tom mentioned it, but having him around made going back to the Morales ranch just that little bit less hazardous. He hadn't forgotten Pruitt Slocum's words of warning.

Late in the evening, over too many beers and a bottle of Mescal, Zachariah brought up the subject of Alicia Morales. "I tell you Tom, she's so pretty it makes my heart bleed. Those dark eyes of hers, they're mischievous, they're suggestive and at the same time they're sweet and kind and gentle. I tell you Tom, I ain't looked at another woman since my Clara died, but this one, well she's different."

"They're all different when you're smitten. Seems to me you got it bad. I guess the only way to find out is to dangle your hook in them murky waters and see just what's biting," said Tom advisedly.

* * * *

Zachariah poured a pitcher of cold water into a bowl and sluiced his face. Staring right back at him was an old man with bloodshot eyes, "Oh Jesus," he said as his headache kicked in again.

An hour later, after forcing down breakfast, he walked across to the livery stable. Though not feeling a hundred per cent, he couldn't put off the inevitable a moment longer. Before he left town he stopped by the telegraph office and sent a telegram to Austin, confirming Tom Tenpenny's position in the Rangers. Then he stopped by the Military Plaza and gave Tom a circular badge with a single star in the centre of it. Emblazoned on the badge were the words Texas Ranger. "Gee, I sure hope this protects me," mimicked Tom.

"More than you'll know," said Zachariah as he turned his reins and spurred his horse into a fast trot out of town.

It was around three in the afternoon when Zachariah spotted the two men riding on his flanks about three hundred yards distance. On his last visit he hadn't questioned why there were such precautions at the Morales ranch. If the opportunity arose he was going to ask. As the hacienda loomed closer and the outriders drew nearer, he recognised the younger man as Rafael. He was a good lookin son of a bitch, thought Zachariah, apart from his dark merciless eyes. The familiar Winchester was still pointing towards the Ranger's mid section. Zachariah ignored their presence, and spurred his horse faster. The Hacienda grew to an imposing stature as the Texas lawman rode through the entrance. Nearing the house he slowed to a fast trot, then as he entered the courtyard he brought the horse to a walk. His heart began pounding as he looked for Alicia. His anticipation of their meeting was quashed as Xavier came out.

"Buenos Dias Senor Trelawney," greeted the old Mexican.

"Buenos Dias yourself, Senor Morales," said Zachariah, his disappointment clearly showing. A slight movement behind Xavier, caused the

Ranger's heart to almost leap out of his chest, as Alicia walked up beside her husband.

"Buenos Dias Zachariah," she said, her eyes dancing like two mischievous imps. "You must be tired from your ride, please come inside." Then turning towards the young vaquero, she indicated the lawman's mare. "Rafael, take care of Senor Zachariah's horse."

Did he detect a slight flinch from Xavier when Alicia said his name. He couldn't be sure. Climbing down from his horse, he saw the smile now fixed firmly across Xavier's face. "I judge from your presense, you bring us news that is both disturbing and welcome. Unfortunately we are mere mortals and the need for vengeance is within us all." Zachariah felt his hackles rise, had he just been warned off, or was Xavier just being courteous.

In the huge dining room Alicia turned, her hands clenched together in front. Zachariah could see she was nervous. "Senor, I take from your arrival. you bring me news of my sister's killer." The Ranger stared into her dark brown eyes and saw fear in them. Fear of what? Xavier? Was he keeping her prisoner? Were Rafael and the other outrider there to watch for intruders or were they her guards? Zachariah's head buzzed with questions.

"The man Long Tom Carmichael, the killer of your sister is dead. I caught up with him in Carrizo Springs. The man offered me no choice," Zachariah cringed at his own pomposity.

Alicia feigned shock then reached out for the Ranger's hand. Her tiny fingers grasped it gently as she raised it to her lips. She kissed his hand softly and her eyes took on a look of gratitude. "I abhor violence but unfortunately it is as my husband says, a fact of life. My thanks to you for bringing Teresa's killer to justice."

Had she squeezed his hand tighter as she raised it to her lips? Zachariah's head was in a spin as he fought against his emotions. Alicia was far more beautiful than he'd first believed. To him, she was an exquisite work of art. More than that, her dark smouldering beauty came from within. How else could he explain the love he so earnestly felt for her?

Don Xavier Morales broke the spell, "Senor Trelawney, it would honour me if you would dine with Alicia and myself. There are things I'd like to discuss with you."

Zachariah looked towards Alicia, her eyes telling him to stay. "I would be delighted, except I feel I am intruding upon your hospitality." Did he detect a look of disappointment in Alicia's eyes?

"Nonsense, my friend. You have brought to justice my sister-in-law's killer, and besides, what I have to discuss with you could be of mutual benefit," said Morales as he placed a hand on Zachariah's shoulder and led him to the table.

"Then I've no choice, I accept your gracious offer!"

"Maria, make up the spare room for Senor Zachariah," shouted Alicia rather hastily.

The evening went well, Don Xavier Morales was a genial host, and Alicia the perfect hostess. On the surface they seemed devoted. A marriage of convenience perhaps, but other than that, they seemed happy enough. Zachariah feared that his misgivings about their marriage had been unfounded. Throughout the evening he couldn't help looking for signs than Alicia was unhappy. To his dismay she seemed much brighter than the first time he'd seen her. But then she would, he thought. After all, I had just given her news of Teresa's death.

Despite himself he warmed to the old man. Xavier was far more knowledgeable than the lawman. His range of topics and subjects so vast, that a month of evenings such as this, wouldn't have been enough to quell the Ranger's interest. Or was it the dark and beautiful Alicia, who delicately sipped from a wine glass opposite him, that held his attention?

Towards the end of the evening Don Xavier offered Zachariah a job as range detective. The ranch was huge and could take a man several days to ride the fence line. As with all large spreads, the problem of rustlers was reaching epic proportions. Even with his crew of trusted vaqueros he hadn't been able to scare off those that preyed on his herd. It was impossible to stop the rustling, but with a known Ranger doubling as range detective, there was the chance that his presence might frighten off the rustlers.

Don Xavier swilled the brandy round in his glass, then looked Zachariah straight in the eye, "From what I've heard about you, you're not a man to give up easily. These rustlers will continue to raid my herds unless they're brought swiftly to justice. I'd pay you a generous monthly retainer, you'd be free to roam as you will. The only time I'll call on you is if and when I get rustled. That's when you'll earn your money. I'll expect you to track these men down and bring them to justice."

The job was more than he could have hoped for. It would bring him into contact with Alicia on a regular basis. But what good would that do him if she really loved Xavier? The Ranger thought the matter over carefully. "Don Xavier, it is a most generous offer, one that I find very tempting. Can I sleep on it?"

"I'll await your answer first thing in the morning. Now if you'll excuse me, I'll bid you goodnight."

Zachariah arose from the table, but too late, Don Xavier had turned swiftly and was already halfway up the stairs. As he watched the elderly gentleman climb the stairs, he sensed Alicia's eyes on him. The swiftness of Xavier's exit had unsettled him. To be alone with Alicia had been his most constant thought since he'd first met her. Now sitting across from her, he found he had nothing to say.

Alicia came to the rescue, "Forgive my husband his abruptness. He's been up since five this morning." She looked fondly towards the top of the stairs, "He's such a sweet man, a kind and gentle man," she added.

"Alicia are you happy?" Zachariah couldn't believe the words had come from his lips. The colour rushed to his cheeks. "Please forgive me, I can't think what possessed me to say that."

Though startled by the suddenness of the question, Alicia smiled and after a moment's hesitation said, "There is nothing to forgive. I admire your honesty and forthright question. I have to admit it's not the first time that question has been asked of me. My answer... why shouldn't I be?"

Embarrassed beyond reason Zachariah began to fidget in his chair.

"I'm sorry, I did not mean to cause you discomfort," she said with a mischievous glint in her eyes. "You ask because there is such a difference in our

age. That is true. Xavier is thirty years older than me. Do I love him?" She paused, preparing herself for his reaction. "Yes, I love him. If it hadn't been for Xavier, who knows? Maybe I would have ended up in a filthy saloon and met my death, like…like Teresa. We came from a poor village on the outskirts of Monterrey. It was the festival of our Lady of the Nativity. I was standing in the village square when suddenly I saw this dashing looking man staring at me. I snubbed my nose at him and turned my face away. Yet my eyes were drawn to him. He flashed a smile, then began to laugh. Fascinated by him, I didn't realise he'd moved forward until it was too late. Moments later he was standing at my side. It was then that I heard him speak for the first time. His tone was soft and gentle, lulling me, calming me. I was still a virgin, but I knew what men were capable of, yet somehow I could sense Don Xavier Morales wasn't like other men. Within a week I was madly in love, a month later I married him. Throughout the years he has been good to me. I still love him, though now more as a brother. We are happy together and I wouldn't do anything to hurt him."

"I thought…"

"I know what you thought, I could see it in your eyes," said Alicia. "You're a man of both physical and mental strength, a man capable of great things, yet I could sense a great sadness." Alicia rose from the table and walked towards the open balcony. "Please join me."

Zachariah followed her outside. It was a balmy night and the dark velvety sky cloaked the forecourt in darkness. Looking up she pointed to the North Star. "That's you, you're like the North Star. Whenever I look up, it's always there, so dependable, so bright, and yet so alone. From now on when I gaze into the heavens and watch as it twinkles and shines I shall be remembering you. You fought for my sister's honour. You stood alone at her graveside, you hunted down and brought justice to her killer. But most of all I shall remember a man of great sadness."

Zachariah's heart swelled with love. He wanted to reach out and touch her…to kiss her sweet inviting lips, but he couldn't. She belonged to another. A man whom Zachariah had been prepared to hate, to kill even. But now standing beneath the starry skies he could feel only love and admi-

ration for a wondrous woman. A woman of dignity, a woman of extreme class, a woman who would never be his. Yet somehow being around her made him feel ten feet tall. In that instant he knew what his answer to Don Xavier's question would be.

Chapter 13

Morgan kept up a continuous barrage of Emails to headquarters in Waco, demanding to be allowed to investigate the death of one of their own. The response was almost always the same, "**Due to the delicacy of the situation, both the office of Texas Ranger and the Drug Enforcement Agency are excluded from the investigation. Please be assured, no stone will be left unturned until the matter is satisfactorily resolved.**"

"Bullshit!" Morgan screwed up the latest Email and threw it into the waste paper basket.

Tony Valdez looked up at Morgan's outburst, then returned his gaze to the funnies spread out across his desk. "How much longer are we gonna keep up this charade."

"Not much longer," replied Morgan. He'd sensed Tony's restlessness a few days after he'd arrived. Valdez wasn't the most patient of men. "It's only been three weeks since Orville's funeral, give it another week."

"At the outside," said Tony, his inpatience showing. "I've been in this godforsaken town almost three weeks and I ain't had me a single piece of pussy. If things carry on like this I guess it'll shrivel up and die."

Valdez's comments struck a cord. The tension in the office was reaching fever pitch. Tony had made it quite clear from the off that he wanted to get the show on the road. Mundane police work had never sat well with him. His constant bitching was getting on Jake's nerves and it was beginning to show. Morgan's sergeant had, not so much in words, more in deeds, let Tony know he didn't like him. A night out at one of Laredo's hot spots might be the tonic they all needed. All three of them needed to let off some steam. Casting an eye across to Jake he outlined his plan. "Ain't it about time we took a break and had a night out together. Tony's bitching so hard I thought we'd fix him up with the best piece of ass this town has to offer. Let her break his balls!"

It had been a while since Morgan had tied one on. He hadn't wanted to since his involvement with Kathleen, but that had somehow petered out. That was the funny thing. Kathleen had hit it off with him from the start. True, they'd not been what Tania would have called an item, but then things had changed. Suddenly from nowhere they had the hots for each other, hotter than Morgan would have thought possible. In fact he was crazy about her and he thought she felt the same. Then, as abruptly as the affair had started, it fizzled out. Morgan thought it was reaction to Orville's death, but after the funeral he called her. All he got was the answering machine. After trying unsuccessfully for a week, he began to get the distinct feeling she was probably there listening. He didn't want to give up, but if she wasn't responding what could he do? He could ask Laura her advice, but maybe that was being a little insensitive. He remembered how he felt when she told him she was dating a realtor. It hurt, in fact it hurt like hell, knowing the woman that had given birth to your kids was seeing another man. But this was the nineties, surely honest and open relationships were the norm. Before he went out that Friday evening he placed a call to Laura in Austin.

✶ ✶ ✶ ✶

It was Friday night and the whole of downtown Laredo was buzzing. Morgan and his two sergeants were sitting in a booth at 'Los Lobos,' downing a few beers and casting their eyes over the local talent. At least Morgan and Tony were. Jake was a confirmed family man and although he took the occasional look he never touched.

"Well I reckon it's about time I took that little vacation into Old Mexico," said Tony as Jake handed him a beer.

"Hold your horses a while longer. You'll find Laredo's a real nice town," joked Morgan.

"That's as maybe, but up until now I ain't seen anything to keep me here," he said while looking at a pert ass in a pair of designer jeans.

"Well do it! I'm fed up with your constant whinging and whining. A good man lays dead, and what do they send us in replacement? You!"

Tony looked up and sneered.

"I don't care what Morgan has to say, from what I've seen you ain't worth shit," Jake continued. He'd stood it as long as he could. "I'm sorry Morg, I'm outta here!"

Jake grabbed his coat and made for the door. Morgan started to go after him, but Tony laid a hand on his shoulder. "Easy Capitan, I think this is one argument me and old Jake ought to settle alone."

Morgan slumped back in his chair and took a swig from his bottle, "Don't get yourself beat up too bad, I need both of you!"

Tony raced after Jake and caught him up in the parking lot. "Jake, hold on now. I'm sorry if I don't come across the way you want, but that's me. Take it or leave it. I ain't your all American boy. I'm Tony Valdez, half-breed. I've spent most of my godamn life proving I'm as good as you. It ain't been easy, but now I'm happy with who I am. If I choose to whinge and whine, that's up to me. If you've got a grouse then let's get to it."

A split second later Tony landed a punch that split Jake's lip. "You son of a bitch," cried a startled Jake, who immediately retaliated and caught Tony one in the stomach, doubling up the smaller man. Hamilton took a step backwards, and waited. Tony recovered quicker than the bigger man expected and caught him with a right hook to the left eye. The sergeant saw red and smashed his fist hard into Valdez's face, then sizing up his opposition he drove his other fist into Tony's solar plexus. For a time he knocked the wind out of the smaller man.

"Had enough?" shouted Jake Hamilton.

"Nope," gasped the Mexican-American, as he lowered his head and drove it straight into the large gut of the big sergeant, knocking him into a pile of garbage cans. They scrabbled about in the dirt, kicking and gouging at each other like a couple of tigers. Jake managed to get to his feet and, with lightning fast reactions, he grabbed Tony in a neck lock.

"Okay little guy, you've proved your point. Now can we talk awhile."

Tony, knowing that the bigger man's strength could keep him there until hell froze over, managed to spurt out, "Sure, that's what I've been trying to say all along," Jake immediately released his grip. "Hey man, you hit real hard for an old guy."

"Fuck you. Now if you've got something to say, say it."

"Okay asshole. Do you think I'm here by choice? Believe me, there are a thousand and one places I'd rather be right now. I'm here because Morgan called in a debt. You see, I owe him, I owe him big time. That can mean only one thing, he intends doing something that ain't exactly legal. In fact what he's got in mind could get us all killed. Now me, I couldn't give a flying fuck, but you, you've probably got a nice wife and a couple of kids. Both at college, and doing well, I bet. You don't need the trouble Morgan's liable to buy yer! You mean well Jake, but you ain't a killer." Tony's eyes turned cold and mean. "You see I am!"

A prickling sensation began creeping up Jake's spine. There was no question in his mind the Mexican-American was speaking the truth.

He'd always known Morgan wouldn't let the death of Orville rest, but until that moment he hadn't known to what lengths he was prepared to go: now he knew.

"Orville was my buddy too. I want them bastards as much as Morgan. Whatever it takes, I'm in!" Then to ease the tension between them, he grinned, "Even if it means putting up with your whinging and whining."

"Good, I'm glad we cleared that up," said Tony, "Now you can step back in this here bar and buy me a beer."

An hour later Jake left to go home to his wife. He mused on the fact Tony Valdez had him pegged. He'd given him chapter and verse on his family, and the only thing he'd left out was the names of his kids. Earlier over a few more drinks Morgan had left him in no doubt; if the law didn't take care of Orville's killers then they would. On the drive home it troubled him some, but then he remembered the folded flag that was given to Orville's widow. Jake knew whatever else he was, he was a true son of Texas, and eversince San Jacinto, Texans have aways had their own sense of justice.

Tony Valdez had no such misgivings. He was there for a specific purpose. Not as Morgan thought, to repay an old debt. Nor to avenge the death of a fellow Ranger, though that fact alone did stick in his craw. But for now he was content to let Morgan think it was to repay the debt.

He'd lived with that night for eight years. It wasn't something he'd been proud of, and though the memory was fading, it still haunted him.

Things had changed for him after the foiled bank robbery. His fellow officers began to treat him with respect. His heroic rescue of the bank officials was now written into the annals of Texas Ranger lore. For a time he was compared to Manuel T (Lone Wolf) Gonzaullas the famous 1940's Ranger. One small incident, foolhardy or otherwise, had restored his self esteem and confidence. Tony Valdez was now a celebrity, and for a time he was flavour of the month. It was about then whilst riding high in the popularity stakes, that he met a young Hispanic girl called Lucita. She was married to a guy who worked the night shift at a local factory. To Tony it was the perfect arrangement.

A secret arrangement that lasted for all of three months. Until a hot and torrid Friday night at the back end of June, when his luck finally ran out. He'd finished a late shift and as usual had parked his car three blocks down from where Lucita lived. Exhausted by their furious lovemaking, Tony took a cat nap. It was around one thirty when shots were heard coming from Lucita's apartment. By the time the police arrived, Texas Ranger Tony Valdez had matters in hand. His version of the story was as follows. He was driving past the apartments at approximately one thirty when he heard shots fired. Investigating the scene he found the woman Lucita Alvarez dead in bed, two shots to the head at point blank range. Lying fully clothed at the side of the bed was the body of her husband Roberto, in his hand the recently fired revolver that had ended Lucita's life. Two slugs not more than an inch apart had hit him in the chest, killing him instantly. In Texas Ranger Valdez's expert opinion, the woman had been in bed with a lover when her husband happened on the scene. The lover must have been in the bathroom taking a leak when the husband crept into the house. Hearing the shots he must have opened fire with his weapon, killing the husband. It was a theory that the investigating detectives concurred on. Which isn't surprising since that's exactly what did happen. All Tony could do was hope the detectives working the case didn't ask to see his weapon. He was in luck, they didn't; Morgan did. He'd had his suspicions that Tony was seeing someone he shouldn't, and on an occasion had seen his car parked just down the street from the dead woman's apartment. Couple that with the two shots from a nine millimetre only an inch apart, Tony's exceptional marksmanship with a handgun was legendary and it left Morgan no choice but to challenge his officer.

"Honest Morg, I swear to God, it happened just the way I said it happened. If I could have saved Lucita, I would have dropped the son of a bitch and taken the consequences. He killed her Morg, at point blank range, almost tore her fucking head off. He was a no good son of a bitch, he beat her regularly. That mother beat the living shit out of her on at least three occasions that I know of, I told her to leave him before it was too late."

"It doesn't change the facts. I'm gonna have to take you in," said Morgan.

"What good's it going to do, giving me up? If I'd been on duty I'd have done the same."

"But you weren't on duty!" Morgan was close to reading Tony his Miranda. Of Tony's version of accounts he had no doubt. He knew that, but for the grace of God, went a great many men, and that would have included himself.

"In a court of law, I might go to prison. Then again I might not. But my career as a law officer would be over. Morg, all I ask is a chance!"

Morgan thought long and hard. The law was the law, but Tony Valdez had fought against insurmountable odds to get where he was. Bad luck and bad judgement had brought him to an impasse. Tony wasn't a favourite of Morgan's, yet to turn him in seemed unfair, so unjust.

"If anyone finds out, you're on your own."

"You won't regret it," said Valdez, the relief clearly visible, "Anything you need, anytime. I'm yours." Morgan might not have regretted it, but Tony Valdez had. He'd spent the past eight years waiting for the call. He mused on the fact that Morgan had chosen his timing to perfection. In the past eight years Tony, because of his Spanish looks, had worked undercover in conjunction with other agencies in the war against drugs. He'd spent a great deal of time working the border around Del Rio. On more than one occasion he'd had to use his special skills in a life and death situation. Now after Morgan had highlighted what they might have to do, he realised his rash promise could get him killed. It could also make him very rich.

Laredo lived up to Morgan's claim. By the end of the night Tony Valdez had been laid, in more ways than one. Jake had laid him on the parking lot, the tequila had him on the dance floor and a pretty blonde had laid him in the back of his car. Which is where Morgan found him at seven thirty the following morning.

During breakfast Morgan mused over the previous night's incidents. He'd spent the last few hours in the motel bed of a twenty-nine year old divorcee. She'd given him great head, it was her speciality. It had been fun, but it left him cold. He felt empty inside. Only two women had ever made him feel complete, one was Laura, the other Kathleen. The emptiness of last night only highlighted his loneliness. It made him more determined than ever to get it together with Kathleen.

*   *   *   *

Up in Austin, Laura woke from a fitful sleep. Morgan's call had troubled her. She'd known about Kathleen. She'd known about all his women. She'd thought Kathleen was no more than a friend, well a bit more than a friend, but nothing serious. Now it turns out she'd been much more than that. She had to be some lady to turn Morgan Trelawney's head so easily thought Laura, with a touch of envy. But above all what troubled her most was the disk he'd sent to her. She'd spent an awful long time unravelling Orville's notes. What she found out, she couldn't hardly believe. She knew Morgan wasn't going to like it one bit.

Chapter 14

Tom Tenpenny stood framed in the doorway of the Military Plaza Saloon. He was relaxed and had been feeling in good spirits since the arrival of his friend. Even the slight altercation with Josh Randolph earlier that evening couldn't suppress his well being. Randolph and another of Kendrickson's hired help, a man called Newt Padbury, had been seen drinking in several saloons and boasting about what they were going to do to the little Monte dealer when his protector had left town. When they walked into the smoky atmosphere of the Military Plaza the tension mounted. Propping themselves up at the bar they stared defiantly across at Tenpenny. Tom, unperturbed by the appearance of Randolph, continued to deal cards, despite the growing edginess of his card playing customers. It was plain to everyone in the saloon that Josh Randolph, his damaged hand now bandaged, was spoiling for a fight. Yet as big as he was, he knew Tenpenny would cut him down before he'd cleared leather. The Monte dealer's Colts were conspicuously on open display. The courage he gained from the bottle dissolved when Tom Tenpenny spoke to him.

"Randolph, would you mind doing what you've come here to do, you're upsetting these nice gentlemen!" The colour drained from the bigger man's face as Tom Tenpenny stood up.

"We're here for a drink, we ain't tangling with Johnny Law!" Randolph motioned to the star pinned on the little Monte dealer's vest.

"Cut the crap Randolph, pull that hog leg or get out!"

For a split second it looked as if the big man was going to make his play, but the timely intervention of Newt Padbury saved his life. Under his breath Padbury said, "Leave it, there's always another way. Let's get outta here."

Within minutes the place was buzzing with music and noise. The back slapping began in earnest, something that Tom Tenpenny found false and inappropriate. The nature of his job and his lifestyle didn't usually allow for such luxuries. Though normally of friendly disposition, he could count few men his true friends. They were acquaintances, men that patted you on the back during the good times, yet so easily changed sides when the chips were down. Zachariah was more than that. He was a true friend and without hesitation had dealt himself a hand. Despite Tom's scepticism and good humoured remarks concerning the wearing of the star, he was secretly pleased that the tall lawman had seen fit to appoint him as a Ranger.

In the doorway Tom fingered the badge that he wore proudly on his vest. Lighting a smoke, he stretched his legs and began to breathe in the night air. Looking up the street he could see the lights of the big hotels and restaurants, the bright lights of gambling halls and similar establishments to the Military Plaza. San Antonio was growing, its embrace of the next century becoming more apparent each waking day. 'Civilisation, that's what they call it,' mused the little Monte dealer.

A fusillade of small arms fire peppered the entrance to the Military Plaza, hitting Tom and sending him hurtling backwards into the saloon.

"They've done for Tenpenny!" came the cry from the revellers of the Military Plaza.

"Get a doctor, get Doc Adams, and get him fast," shouted the bartender. One of the saloon girls became hysterical and had to be silenced with a slap from the Military Plaza's resident madam. People began crowding around the body of Tom Tenpenny, eager to take a look at one of the last great shootists of the era. Others just stared in morbid fascination, already forming the stories they would tell their grand kids, 'They were there when the 'Undertakers Friend' dealt his last hand of Monte.'

Bob Schaffer the barman of the Military Plaza cleared the crowd back and bent down to examine the body. After feeling for a pulse he slowly stood up.

"We're sure as hell gonna need an undertaker now. Tom's alive! Tenpenny ain't dead!" *Miraculously Tom had been hit only once, a flesh wound to the side of his left temple. Dazed and bewildered, he allowed Bob to help him into a chair, while Loretta, a young prostitute who worked both the Military Plaza and Frenchie's Palace, bathed his temple. Her perfume and gentle touch were enough to tame the fiery Monte dealer as he allowed her to wrap an improvised bandage around his head.*

As Tom's senses returned, he looked up at the girl and smiled. He'd seen her before, she worked the saloon. What was her name? Lorna? Lorraine? Loretta? Yeah that's it, Loretta. Pretty girl, I wonder why I hadn't paid her more attention?'

"Thank you ma'am, you're most kind," *he heard himself say.*

"It was nothing," *she said, blushing into the bargain.*

"We need to get Tom out of the saloon just in case those back shooters return," *cried Bob urgently.*

"He can stay in my room! I'll keep watch," *volunteered Loretta"*

Too nauseous and weak to protest, Tom allowed Bob and Loretta to help him up the stairs. She rushed ahead and opened the door to her room. Once inside she drew the top blanket back, while Bob eased him onto her cot. "You'll be safe here, you rest now," *he heard her say faintly, as he drifted into sleep.*

When he awoke, he thought he'd been on a real bender. His head ached like nothing he could describe. His tongue was parched and most disconcerting of all, he didn't recognise the room he'd just spent the night in. Then he saw her. She was fast asleep in a chair by the door with one of his pearl handled Colts hanging loosely in her small delicate hand. Then it started to come back to him. The last thing he remembered was taking a stroll outside: A hail of bullets, a scream, a crowd looking down on him, then Bob Schaffer announcing he was alive. And the girl! Tired from the mental exhaustion, Tom let his head fall back onto the pillows and dozed.

The smell of coffee and bacon invaded his nostrils and brought him out of his slumber. Loretta was standing over him with a steaming hot mug and a full breakfast, "Hell, I'll get shot more often if this is the kind of treatment I'd receive."

Loretta blushed, "Hush now. Eat your breakfast. The sheriff's downstairs and wants a word when you're good and ready." *Tom sat up and took a swig of coffee. He was ravenous and soon demolished breakfast.*

When he'd finished he found there was a bowl of hot water, soap and a towel all laid out for him. "Thanks Loretta, you're spoiling me. I ain't used to such luxuries."

She smiled back at him, "I seen you dealing Monte. You take a drink, you're polite, which is a rarity, but you don't go with the girls. Why's that?"

"Jesus Loretta! You have a way of coming straight to the point." *Now he could feel the colour rising to his cheeks.* "I guess I ain't met one that's taken my fancy…until now." *Tom flushed with embarrassment. 'It must be the reaction to being creased by that bullet,' he thought.*

"Oh," *she said, but it was enough.* "I'll leave you to it." *She slid out the door leaving him more confused than when he'd first woken.*

* * * *

Confusion wasn't just restricted to Loretta's bedroom, since leaving the Morales ranch, Zachariah's thoughts had been troubling him. He'd agreed to act as range detective, more so because it allowed him an excuse to see the lovely Alicia, than the bounty Xavier had placed on every rustler he captured. Yet why had he done so when Alicia had left him in no doubt that she loved her husband? Was it his imagination that something wasn't quite right, or was it the figment of an old man's fantasies? Whatever it was, he still had the distinct feeling she was more than a little attracted to him.

The sun was going down as he entered the city limits. Spurring his horse forward he headed for the telegraph office. Quickly Zachariah jotted down his report requesting time off to act as range detective at the Morales ranch. He left word that he could be contacted at the Military Plaza saloon, then with that chore under his belt, he mounted up and headed towards the Plaza.

It was just turning dark and the street lights were being lit when he reined in at the Military Plaza. He'd just dismounted and tied his horse to the hitching rail when he happened to glance through the double doors of the saloon. Just inside he noticed a mean looking man sitting down. Cradled in his lap was a double barrelled shotgun. Stepping through the entrance he couldn't help but see the splintered wood and the bullet holes in the door frame. His hand automatically rested on the butt of his revolver. Peering up the stairs he spied another man, also heavily armed. Bob the bartender was also wearing a gun. Zachariah's eyes darted towards the far corner of the room. With relief he saw Tom Tenpenny busily playing solitaire. As he drew closer he noticed the purple blue wound above Tom's left ear.

"What in blazes happened to you?"

"Josh Randolph, Newton Padbury and I can't be sure, but I think McCulloh. They bushwhacked me last night."

"You get any of them?" enquired Zachariah.

"Nope! But I aim to rectify that omission pretty damn soon. From now on the Military Plaza is off limits to Kendrickson and his men. If anyone of them sets foot in this establishment, they'd best come heeled. One wrong move and I'll kill any of them on sight."

"If that's what it takes, but just remember, you are the law. A rope or a bullet, it don't make no difference, dead's dead. This town ain't got much use for the likes of Kenrickson, or us for that matter," warned Zachariah.

"Yeah, so Sheriff Clem Taylor informed me. All the same, if any of those sons of bitches draws down on me, they'd better make sure I'm dead next time." Tom poured himself a measure of redeye and grinned, "How was your day? How was the lovely Alicia?"

Zachariah sat down, ordered a beer, waited for it, took a swig and settled in the chair opposite Tom Tenpenny. Just the very mention of her name was enough to transform the gruff Ranger, "Hot damn, she's prettier than the first time I saw her. What's more, she appears happy. I guess I was wrong. I was probably reading more into it than there was. Her husband even offered me a job."

"You didn't take it! Tell me you didn't take it."

"Subject to headquarters approval."

"Holy shit! Since you've been gone, I did a little checking on Senor Xavier Morales. He ain't dirty, well not so's you'd notice, but he's got a string of hand picked vaqueros working for him that make all but a few of Kendrickson's men look small potatoes. My advice to you my friend…Stay away!"

Zachariah swallowed a mouthful of beer, wiped his arm across his moustache and said, "I can't do that."

"Oh shit!"

✸   ✸   ✸   ✸

A week later Zachariah received a telegram from Texas Rangers headquarters in Waco. His request to work as range detective was denied, but as his duties in the San Antonio area included the apprehension of rustlers, he could take in the Morales ranch and surrounding areas as part of his jurisdiction. Due to Anglo-Spanish tension in the San Antonio area, his command was to be increased by one. Corporal Ethan Book would be joining his section within the month. Overall command was now in the capable hands of Captain William Platt, a Ranger of the highest integrity. He was operating out of Austin. In essence Zachariah was now second in command of the south Texas contingent. Funds for quarters were imminent, in the meantime a letter of credit was being brought by Corporal Book.

"Which don't mean shit," said Zachariah after reading the telegram. Another man was needed, of that fact he couldn't deny. He'd never met Ethan Book but from what he'd heard, the man could be hell on wheels. Tension was riding high at the Military Plaza and across the plaza at Frenchie's Palace, the headquarters of Kendrickson. With luck the presence of a third Ranger might cause Kendrickson to pull back from the brink.

Though Zachariah doubted it. Tom's challenge to his authority wasn't something he would forget in a hurry.

Tom Tenpenny was a friend, but he was becoming a problem, he was shouting his mouth off about what he'd do if McCulloh showed his face. Much as Zachariah liked Tom, he was creating more tension than was necessary. The shooting that nearly cost Tom his life was festering in his brain. Zachariah had seen it before, the killing of Dallas Stoudenmire's brother-in-law Doc Cummings had started the rot that finally got the tall Ranger killed. It was coming and there wasn't a damn thing Zachariah could do except wait. Ethan Book might tip the balance, and with the news that a detachment of Rangers was within a day or two's ride, there was still the possibility of avoiding bloodshed. Zachariah hoped desperately that Book would arrive before Tom talked himself into entering Frenchie's.

But the die was cast, Loretta Marcus had entered the scene. It had taken Tom Tenpenny less than a week to fall hopelessly in love. She was twenty nine years of age, though surprisingly she didn't look it, considering the cattle towns and mining camps she'd frequented over the past ten years. She was pretty too. Years of abuse had done nothing to mar her beauty. It didn't matter to the little Monte dealer that she'd slept with numerous men, all he cared about was the future. In Loretta he'd found that special person, someone to eradicate his past. Everything would have been all right, except prior to seeing Tom, she'd been Clay McCulloh's girl. Loretta told him about McCulloh after they'd made love on the second night he slept in her room.

"It ain't something I'm proud of, but it ain't nothing to be ashamed of either," shouted Loretta, when Tom reproached her for it. "You know the kind of woman I was, you knew before you made love to me. I thought you were different Tom, but you're like all the rest. Now get out!"

Tom left, descended the stairs, grabbed a bottle and sat down. Zachariah found him some two hours later, drunker than a skunk and twice as mean. If McCulloh had shown his face in the bar, Tom Tenpenny would have shot it off.

"Tom, from what you've told me, the girl has true feeling for you. And by the look of you I reckon them feelings are mutual."

"Yeah, but that low life McCulloh! How could she?" slurred Tenpenny.

"The same ways as she did with you. It's her profession for Christ's sake," said Zachariah, growing tired of the smaller man's ramblings. "Sober up. If she don't mean anything to you, forget her, if she does, then you better get down on your bended knees and beg her forgiveness."

He'd woken with a spliting headache and Zachariah's advice still ringing in his ears. It was a little after six thirty when Tom knocked on her door. In his hands a bunch of wild flowers he'd picked from a nearby garden. Tired, red-rimmed eyes stared around the door at the posy held self-consciously in Tom's hands. Her mouth faltered, her eyes sparkled, as she flung the door wide open. The posy was knocked from his hands as Loretta rushed into his arms. The door made a hearty slamming sound as Tom kicked it shut behind him, leaving only the discarded posy, to bear testimony of their love.

Inevitably the news of Tom and Loretta's relationship reached the ears of Clay McCulloh. "She's a cheap whore, but she deserves better than that runt of a card player."

The words inevitably spread like wild fire, a powder keg had been lit. The showdown grew every closer. "If he steps into the street I'll shoot him down like the dog he is," said Tenpenny, on hearing of McCulloh's outburst.

"Not this side of the fourth of July you don't," said Zachariah. "You and I have a job to do out to the Morales ranch. I need to explain why I can't take the job."

"You don't need me for that," said Tom defiantly.

"No that's right I don't, but I can't leave you here on your own."

"I've lived this long without your help," shouted Tom angrily.

"Tom, you're my friend, you know the reason I'm going, but if you got yourself killed in my absence, I'd feel responsible. And besides, I need someone to watch my back. Sure I'm going because of duty, but we both know the real reason I'm going." The thought of her conjured up visions. He so *desperately wanted to see Alicia, to smell her perfume, to wallow in her beauty.* "Two days! That's all I ask."

Tom smiled, "Two days."

Chapter 15

Crossing the International Bridge the lights of Ciudad Acuna appeared welcoming and friendly, Tony Valdez knew different. Here he'd spent many a hallucinogenic weekend. Blurred by the effects of too much cocaine, washed down with an abundant supply of Mescal, not knowing nor caring if his cover had been blown. His life became one big gamble. Death from infection, the pox, or the burning sensation of a switchblade as it sliced through his windpipe? This was the everyday life that Sergeant Tony Valdez had volunteered for in the misguided belief that he could make the difference.

And now he was back in that living nightmare that most decent people called Hell. Not for Tony the luxury that he was there to do something worthwhile; maybe save some poor unfortunate wretch from destroying his life. Nor was he, as Morgan believed, there to seek out and execute the men responsible for killing Orville Tyson. He wasn't revisiting the jaws of Hell for revenge. He was there for the far baser emotion of greed. Cash…hard cash! Five hundred thousand dollars worth.

During Tony's time as an undercover agent he'd amassed a small fortune from illegal transactions. It was part of his cover, but it hadn't taken him long to realise a man could get seriously rich along the way. Together with a partner, a small time drug dealer called Tito Vargas, they'd stashed half a million dollars inside an Addidas sports duffel and then placed it in a waterproof bag and hidden it in an old sewer. It was the perfect hiding place, just a stone's throw from the back entrance of 'Madero's', the favourite hangout of the Montoya cartel. Suspicious and paranoid that Tony was going to double-cross him, Vargas accidentally stumbled on the fact his partner was a narcotics agent. Tito, greedy to get his hands on all the money, made the biggest mistake of his life. He should have informed on his partner before going to the sewer. It was a fatal error. Tony was waiting for him.

In a dark alley, not far from 'Madero's' night club, Tito Vargas begged for his life. Whether Tony would have spared him remained unanswered. His boss and overlord of the Montoya cartel, Esteban Montoya, happened to drive up. His bodyguard, the fearsome Francisco Ramirez, was driving him.

Esteban lowered the electric window on the passenger side. "What's up man?"

Without hesitating Tony's Beretta Model 92 9mm Parabellum spoke, silencing Vargas forever. "Get outta here! We're about to be raided," shouted Tony over the sound of the gunshot.

Francisco without question gunned the stretched Cadillac and disappeared down a labyrinth of side streets. That was the last time Tony Valdez had seen Esteban Montoya.

During the ensuing hours a joint Mexican-American initiative swooped on several locations and arrested many key players from Montoya's drugs cartel. In Tony's panic at being discovered, he'd unwittingly helped Esteban to escape justice. Before he could retrieve his money and disappear across the border, he was picked up and arrested.

Thrown into a Mexican prison, he remained silent while he waited foolishly for his government to free him. It was months before the American authorities moved in that direction. In their words, it was for his own protection that they left him there. 'Bullshit,' thought Tony. Every stinking cockroach infested minute he spent in that prison was etched into his brain. The inedible food, the inadequate sanitation, the threat of gang rape, the constant fear of being discovered, all that and much more turned Tony Valdez into what he was now. Morgan Trelawney had called in an old debt, and given Tony his chance to work close to, and across, the border. From the nature of his conversation with Trelawney he knew it was both dangerous and illegal, but it provided him with the cover he needed. Three years he'd waited. Now he was back to claim the drug money that was waiting in the old sewer. That money was his by right. He'd earned every cent and he'd kill anyone who tried to take it from him.

Tony parked his Blazer in the back streets of Ciudad Acuna and walked two cobble stone blocks until he saw the red and blue neon of 'Madero's.' His heart beat faster. His palms began to sweat, and his body started to shake. His first instincts were to go for the cash. Instead he found himself staring at the entrance to the night club. He knew once inside 'Madero's' he would be at the mercy of Esteban Montoya.

He'd seen at first hand the cruelty of his ex-boss, witnessing the murder of a man who'd, had the courage to grass to the authorities. He'd watched helplessly while three of Montoya's henchmen held the man down. Esteban's cruelty knew no bounds as he explained in gruesome detail what he was about to do. Tony remembered only too well the smell of fear as the man's bowels gave way. Montoya, unperturbed by the stench, ran the razor-sharp knife across the man's throat in a slow, exaggerated movement. The look of pleasure on his face as the blood pumped from the severed jugular, turned Tony's stomach. Howls of laughter came from Esteban's men, as the defenceless victim thrashed about, gasping desperately for air. It took Tony all of his will power to stop from emptying a clip into the cruel laughing face of Esteban Montoya.

Entering 'Madero's' would be the gamble of his life. Tony's only hope lay in the fact he'd been the one to tip Montoya about the police raid. His rash act had ensured the freedom of his boss. The execution of Tito Vargas should have been enough to convince the drugs overlord of his loyalties. Yet Tony knew Esteban Montoya wasn't a man to take lightly. He was cruel, ruthless and cunning. The drug dealer might have him taken out back and killed, or he might welcome him back with open arms. Either way Tony was putting his life on the line. Montoya was his passport to the drugs scene in north-east Mexico, and he knew only too well that he needed an in if he was going to infiltrate the Morales family further east. Taking a deep breath he wiped his palms, checked the clip of his nine millimetre Beretta, crossed himself and walked inside.

It could have been yesterday, nothing had changed. Perhaps the lighting had been updated, the music a little wilder, the women a trifle younger. The hookers that frequented the bar had changed faces, but the dialogue was no different. The sweet smell of marihuana, the buzz of danger, the noise of the disco all embraced him like a long lost son as he mingled seductively in the smoky atmosphere of Madero's. Tony looked at his reflection in the grubby age-old mirror at the back of the bar and grinned to himself. He was back and running on pure adrenaline. He needed a fix. He grabbed a bar stool and ordered.

"Tequila, Dos Equis," he said, holding up two fingers.

Almost immediately a slim young woman sidled up to him. "You want some action," she purred and her thin hand rubbed his crotch, feeling for his hardness. Her breath smelt of fresh come, while her scent, a cheap overpowering imitation, barely concealed her body odour. Tony neither pulled away nor re-acted any differently than he had three years before, except that between his legs there was hardly a quiver. Not surprisingly as his eyes had just locked on to Esteban Montoya.

"Not at the moment babe, but stick around, I might be interested later," under his breath he mouthed the words, "if I'm alive." He tossed the tequila down, wiped the neck of his beer and looked again at the drug dealer. Near panic, Tony fought for control, as he weighed up the situation. It was useless to run, he was committed. Esteban was sitting towards the back of the club on the second level. From his vantage point he could see all beneath him. Rising slowly from his stool Tony smiled across and began walking towards the stairs that led up to Montoya's table. Climbing the stairs slowly, he could see his old boss had put on a few extra pounds. His jet black hair, once so neatly styled, now unkempt and greying. Time hadn't been kind to Esteban Montoya, yet his swarthy features and cruel piercing eyes could still strike fear into the hearts of younger men. Around the table sat Francisco, Esteban's personal bodyguard, a man of limited personality, yet quick to act in defence of his master and Rico and Ruben Torres, two of the most ruthless killers Tony had ever seen. To their right, Emilio Ortiz, the number two in the organisation, fat and slimy, a man ready to sell his own mother without a second thought. Glancing back over his shoulder to the exit, he recognised Alfredo and Jesus. From the looks of their ill fitting suits, he reckoned they both carried enough firepower to drop an elephant. As he saw it, he had two choices, he could draw his piece and try to take out the whole table or he could brazen it out. He chose the latter.

"Nice to see you Tony, when did you get out?" Esteban pushed a large piece of tortilla into his mouth and waited for the reply, his eyes giving nothing away.

"Just over a year ago," said Tony, remembering the grey prison pallor that had taken six weeks to disappear. "Good behaviour," he added with a smile.

"Why did it take so long for you to rejoin us?" An air of suspicion creeping into Montoya's tone. A flake of tortilla dropped from his long and untidy moustache. 'He's still a pig,' thought Tony. Three years hadn't helped him with his table manners.

"Mother fucker of a parole officer, had me looking up my own ass!" The Mexican nodded his understanding. A supply of coke magically appeared on the table. Tony looked at it hungrily, "Shit man, for a damn year I ain't bin near the stuff." He watched as Montoya wiped his mouth with a napkin, "Hell man, I'm in need of rehabilitating," he continued nervously.

That last line tipped the balance as Montoya's reservations seemed to disappear. "Pull up a chair Tony boy, we got some re-educating to do." Esteban smiled, "If it wasn't for this man, I would be rotting in some stinking prison." 'And that part was correct,' thought Tony. His killing of Tito Vargas had forced the hand of the agencies into moving quicker than they'd originally planned. "Fore warned, is fore armed," Montoya added. Tony flinched as the drug dealer produced a switch blade and began working the small pile of powder into four neat white lines. Esteban pointed the familiar looking knife in Tony's direction and smiled. "Join me."

Tony snorted two lines and waited for the rush. Ever present of the danger he was in, his mood began to change. He felt euphoric. He felt on top of the world. His Chameleon like qualities swung into action, as a strange cocktail of drink and drugs began to relax him. A sixth sense, an ability to think straight, had always been his secret weapon. His instinct for survival was never greater than when he was on the edge.

Esteban, a man of more than average intelligence continued to probe, seeking that one fatal flaw in his story that would cost Tony his life.

"Why are you here?"

"I'm passing through."

"Where are you going?"

"Tampico."

"Why Tampico?"

"Why not," came the glib reply. "I've a cousin lives right on the beach."

"Plenty pussy!"

"Plenty everything man. One thing prison taught me, freedom is the ultimate. The rest sucks. I'd rather die than be chained to someplace I don't want to be." Inadvertently it was Tony's way of telling Montoya he was only visiting. "Come see me. Tampico's a nice town."

Tony watched as the suspicion in Esteban's cruel eyes disappeared. Cocaine and booze and a pretty young hooker, caused Esteban Montoya to tire over his questioning. Leaning back in his chair Tony felt great, he'd forgotten how good it felt as the booze and drugs worked their magical spell. Coupled with the relief he felt at not having had his throat cut, he became wildly excited and horny as hell.

"You want a woman," laughed Emilio Ortiz, pointing to the noticeable bulge in Tony's trousers. Rico and Ruben both stole a glance, while Francisco remained impassive to their laughter.

"Serafina, she wants you. She's been staring at you all night," said Esteban, pointing to the hooker who'd accosted him three hours earlier. Unable to protest Tony smiled as Emilio Ortiz beckoned the woman over. "My gift. Serafina is most gifted in the art of making love." Tony tugged at the bottle of Mescal, the smell of her still fresh in his mind. He wanted to tell Ortiz to fuck her himself, but thought better of it. Serafina slid onto his lap and nuzzled her face close to his. The smell of too much booze on her breath was an improvement.

He awoke to find himself staring up the ass of the woman called Serafina. Too drunk to perform, they'd both fallen asleep in the sixty nine position.

"Oh Jesus!" he cried as he unceremoniously pushed her off.

"Fuck you!" she cried as the violent action forced her awake.

"Get outta here!" he yelled, still trying to discover whether he'd actually made it with her. In the end he gave up. It wasn't worth the effort and if he did remember, would it haunt him for the rest of his life?

* * * *

With Tony supposedly working out of Del Rio, Morgan assigned Jake the everyday running of the Laredo office, which left him free to investigate Orville's apparent shoot out with Thurston. There were a few anomalies he had to clear up. One of them was Frank Jordan.

From what he'd seen, Jordan and Thurston had always worked as a pair. Where was Frank Jordan when the shooting took place? It was a question that needed an answer.

Morgan burst into Jordan's office, slamming the door behind him. Frank Jordan looked up from his desk.

"Can I help you?" The voice was calm, devoid of any emotion.

"You can start by telling me where you were when the shooting occurred?"

"I might ask you the same question," replied Jordan.

Morgan thought about it for a moment. Under normal circumstances he'd have been in the office, and Orville would have just called in. But he wasn't. He'd been spending a pleasurable day with Kathleen. 'Perhaps that's why she's not been in touch. If we hadn't been down in Mexico, maybe Orville would still be alive.' The thought troubled him. He'd been quick to assume Jordan was always with Thurston. The same could be said for himself and Orville.

"If you must know, I was in a meeting with my bureau chief and a couple of Senators. Are you satisfied now!" Jordan rose from his seat and stepped around his desk. "Listen Trelawney, Lou Thurston was a good cop, a little ragged around the edges, I'll grant you. I dare say Tyson was an all round guy too. I'm in the dark as much as you, perhaps we're looking far too deeply. Maybe, just maybe, what we've seen is what really happened."

Minutes later Morgan was gunning his sedan down Main and feeling a damn fool. He didn't buy Jordan's explanation of events, but he couldn't fault the man on his opinion. 'Perhaps I'm too close to the investigation,' he thought, doubting the wisdom that had seen him pushing his way into Frank Jordan's office. The clues were there, he was sure of it. Why else would someone break into his house and access his computer? He'd never have known, except for a single strand of blonde hair lying across the keyboard. Kathleen hadn't been there in weeks, so there was no way it could be hers, which meant it belonged to an intruder. There was only one thing left to do; he needed to look closely at the evidence Orville had amassed on the disk that he'd mailed him. Not for the first time he was pleased he'd had the good sense to send the disk to Laura. Now was the time to take a closer look. It was as good a reason as any to visit Austin.

When he phoned and told her he was coming up, Laura had said, "That's funny, I was thinking of paying you a visit." He'd panicked, and insisted it would be better if he came to her. "Fine, no big deal," replied Laura a little surprised by his sudden urge to visit. Realisation came to her in a flash, the moment she put the receiver down. There was more than one reason why he was coming to Austin. Kathleen Delaney had given up the lease on her apartment in Laredo and rented a condo not far from the Capitol building in Austin.

Chapter 16

"Your timing is excellent," said Xavier, looking up at the two riders. "They killed Paco and run off thirty of my herd," he continued. "Rafael will round up seven of our best men. They are to go with you."

"Hold your horses compadre. I've come here personally as a courtesy to explain why I can't take the job." Zachariah looked past Xavier, hoping for a glimpse of Alicia.

"Why is that senor?" Xavier's face changed to one of disappointment.

"Here, best you read it," said Zachariah as he offered the telegram. Xavier read and re-read the few lines on the piece of paper.

"From what this says, Hacienda Morales comes under your jurisdiction."

"That's correct. Guess you get me for nothing," said Zachariah. "Though I must stress, I'm here to administer the law, the law of the great state of Texas," he added as a codicil. The tall Ranger stretched in his saddle and surveyed the courtyard. A hint of disappointment clearly visible on his rugged face.

"You wonder about my Alicia?"

"Just wondering that's all," said Zachariah uncomfortably. He fought desperately to bring his embarrassment under control, while appearing unconcerned by her absence. "This is Tom Tenpenny, one of my men."

Buenos tardes, Senor Tenpenny." He nodded briefly at Tom then returned his gaze towards Zachariah. *"Alicia has gone to visit relatives in Mexico, she'll be sorry she missed you."*

"And I her," he answered.

Don Xavier flinched.

Quickly changing the subject, the Ranger asked which direction the rustlers were heading.

"Southwest, towards Uvalde. They'll have crossed the Hondo, but you should catch up with them before the Frio," said Xavier.

"How many are we up against?"

"Five, maybe six," chipped in Rafael, now mounted and impatient to ride.

"Good, in that case they'll be easy to follow. Take your men and head for Frio Town. Once there, if you haven't caught up with the rustlers, follow the river north. Tom and I'll head due west towards Uvalde, if we ain't picked up their trail we'll follow the river south until we meet up. With luck we should catch these desperados within a couple of days."

"Don Xavier," cried Rafael in frustration.

"A good plan," said Xavier reassuringly, "Simple, but a good plan." Rafael's anger was barely contained as he pulled viciously on the reins of his horse and turned towards his patron.

"Adios," cried Xavier, his eyes glowing red hot at his nephew's insolent attitude. Rafael's horse reared as he dug his rowels into the animal's flanks. Seconds later he was heading out of the courtyard at full gallop.

"Man's in an all fired hurry to get himself killed," commented Tom.

"Ah! The vitality of youth, my friend," replied Xavier, his composure now fully returned. "Gentlemen, pardon my manners. You have travelled far, and must be hungry." Xavier Morales clapped his hands and two servants appeared as if they'd been waiting behind the door. "Juan, see to their supplies. Manuela, food on the table."

"Thank you Senor Morales," said Zachariah climbing down from his mare, "We're obliged."

"Yeah thanks," Tom added. "but I'd a soon we were hightailing it after them varmints before nightfall."

"We will," replied Zachariah absentmindedly. Struggling with his disapointment at not seeing Alicia he addressed his next question to Xavier, "Alicia, she's gone where in Mexico?"

"Not far from Monterrey, near Apodaca. We have a large hacienda, many cattle and many relatives. Alicia is visiting her mother," he added in way of an explanation.

"How long has she been gone? That journey can be mighty rugged and dangerous," said Zachariah.

"Fear not, my friend. Alicia is in good hands. No harm shall come to her. But thank you for your concern, it is appreciated."

* * * *

At best it was an hour before sundown when Zachariah and Tom Tenpenny rode out through the gates of the Morales ranch. "Hell Zack, I thought we'd only be gone a couple of days. I reckon we'll be gone the best part of a week."

"More than that if I miss my guess," mumbled Zachariah.

"Damn you! You knew all along we'd be lucky to be back in San Antonio before the week's out."

"Two I reckon," said Zachariah. "You and McCulloh have been spoiling for a fight. One, maybe both of you'll end up dead. Two weeks ought to cool both of your heels some."

"Well let's get to it before that head honcho of Morales gets his hands on them."

"Relax. Remember we travelled this way not that long ago. Did you see many watering holes between here and Frio Town? These boys bin rustling Xavier's cattle for quite some time. My guess is, they got a buyer closer to Ulvade than Frio Town."

"Hell Zachariah, you're smarter than you look."

They continued into the night, walking their horses at an easy pace. The creak of leather, the dull metallic clunk of bridle and bit, and the soft padding of hooves on the grassy plains, were the only sounds to be heard. Above them a vast blanket of stars shone down, lighting their path. As soon as night descended Zachariah had set his direction by the north star. Glancing up, he remembered another night and imagined Alicia by his side, her perfume lingering in the cool night air. The thought of her left him sad and unsettled. She was another man's wife, he had no right to covet. Yet he couldn't help himself as he realised he was hopelessly in love. Looking again at the star she'd named for him, he wondered whether she felt the same.

At first light they discovered Zachariah's hunch had been right. At the Hondo they found tracks of six riders and some thirty-five head of cattle. On closer inspection they found the cows had been watered as they crossed a shallow part of the river. On the far bank Tom came across the remnants of a small fire. Running his hand through the ashes he was able to deduce the rustlers weren't more than a day ahead.

"We should catch sight of them by late afternoon," said Tom.

"I reckon," agreed Zachariah.

It was nearing dusk when they heard the mooing of cattle. Zachariah pulled his field glasses from his saddlebag and, from the cover of a few junipers and tall brush, he scanned a small valley. The cattle had been bedded down for the night and Zachariah could just about see the figures of five of the men. He reckoned the sixth was riding night herd.

"We hit them at first light," said Zachariah.

In the ghostly haze of the false dawn Zachariah and Tom saddled up. Solemnly, without a word spoken between them, both men checked their guns. Tom was carrying his nickel-plated Colts and a Greener shotgun, while Zachariah was favouring his single action Peacemaker and his Winchester. Neither man liked killing but they were the law and they would not shirk their duty.

Getting close to the rustlers camp was going to be risky. A spooked horse could mean the difference between living and dying. Tom, using an old

Comanche horse thieving trick, tied rags around their horses hooves to muffle their approach.

They got within a hundred yards of the sleeping rustlers when Zachariah halted his horse. Both men quietly dismounted and let the reins of their horses hang in the dust. Zachariah silently directed Tom to his left, while he approached from the right flank. They advanced quietly to within ten yards of the sleeping forms. 'With luck the men will come quietly,' thought Zachariah, as the sound of the twin hammers of Tom's shotgun registered loud and clear.

"We're Texas Rangers, don't anybody move!" Zachariah's words were punctuated by the lever action of his Winchester as he jacked a round into the breech. "No one has to die!" Four tired heads slowly and cautiously emerged from beneath their bed rolls.

"There must be some mistake. We bought these cattle," said a bearded man in a faded yellow shirt. "I've a bill of sale to prove it." Slowly he rose to his feet and studied the two Rangers. "Easy with those irons, I'll get it."

Zachariah motioned with his rifle for the man to move. Tom, holding his shotgun firmly in the crook of his shoulder, glanced across to Zachariah. "Didn't you say there were five in the camp." A slight movement out of the corner of Zachariah's left eye caused him to spin around and fire. The tall Ranger saw the gun, that only a fraction of a second earlier had been levelled at his head, spin harmlessly into the air. The man's eyes grew wide with shock as the 44-40 projectile tore into his stomach, knocking him backwards in the dirt. Lightning reactions and the instinct to survive had saved his life. Jacking another round into the Winchester, Zachariah turned as yellow shirt began firing wildly with a double action Colt Lightning, which had appeared from out of the man's saddle bag. Tom spun his Greener in the man's direction and gave him both barrels. Yellow shirt was blown across the camp and landed in the dying embers of his own campfire. In the heat of battle Tom dropped his shotgun and pulled one of his pistols. A man, dressed only in red underwear threw his hands in the air. The sudden movement cost him his life as Tom pumped two shells into him.

"Don't shoot! Don't shoot!" The two remaining rustlers threw their hands skyward.

"Enough Tom! Hold your fire," shouted Zachariah. The two men cowered in their bedrolls.

"Easy boys, move nice and easy, shuck your hardware and stand over by that rock," said Tom gesturing with the nickel-plated pistol to the rock's general direction. Zachariah, seeing Tom had himself and the prisoners under control, raced into the open. The night rider had begun to race back towards the camp. Seeing the tall Ranger raising his Winchester to his shoulder took all the fight out of the man. Reining his horse to a halt, a cloud of dust masked him from view as he changed direction and raced away from the scene. Zachariah levelled his Winchester on the fleeing rider and began to squeeze gently on the trigger. Five years before he wouldn't have questioned it, but were a few cows worth a man's life? Zachariah lowered his rifle.

Returning to the camp Zachariah saw the men Tom was covering weren't much more than boys. "Shit," not for the first time he began to question his vocation. The three men they'd killed looked to have been in their late twenties, maybe early thirties. "How old are you boys?"

"I'm nearly eighteen sir, Johnny here, he's a tad younger," said the boy from under a mop of unruly blonde hair.

Tom looked in horror at what he'd nearly done, and the past flooded back. Holstering his gun he turned and walked away from the scene of carnage. Zachariah gave him a knowing look.

"Right boys, you got yourselves a busy morning. First thing is you're gonna tie your friends across the saddles of their horses, then you're gonna help us take these cattle north. Do as I say, no harm will come to you. You have my word. We're Texas Rangers out of San Antonio. My name's Zachariah Trelawney and that guy there is Mr Tom Tenpenny. Give us an easy time of it, I'll speak up for you back in San Antonio. Make it hard, I'll kill you."

"Yes sir," said Franklin, as he nervously ran his hands through his unruly blonde hair.

Leaving the kids to pack the bodies of their friends onto the horses, Zachariah walked over to Tom. The sandy haired Ranger was staring emptily across the open plain, his eyes red and watery. "Jesus Zack, if you hadn't called. Those kids they ain't much older than that boy I killed."

"I know. But the important thing is you didn't." There wasn't much more that Zachariah could say. It was up to Tom to work it out for himself. The taller man patted his friend on the shoulder. "Stay here awhile. I'll rustle up breakfast."

* * * *

Two days later they'd crossed the Hondo. Tom's spirits had returned, more thanks to the two boys than anything else. Young Franklin had taken to the two Rangers and quickly fell into conversation with them. He told an all too familiar story of how they'd gotten themselves into the trouble. Bored with life on the farm, the boys had set out to seek their fortune. In a small border town they'd fell in with a bad crowd, guys that talked hard and threw their money about. Eager to prove their manhood the boys agreed to go along with them on a rustling expedition. They'd spoken of taking a cow here, a calf there. To the boys, it hadn't seemed much more than a prank. Off one of the big ranches in South Texas the odd heifer wouldn't be missed. The risks would be minimal. Then the older guys began to get greedy. Zachariah and Tom had been down the same road themselves a time or two when they'd been young and learned from their experiences. Both Rangers thought the boys had been given a valuable lesson in life. Seeing their friends cut down in a gunfight had probably taught the boys far more than the few years they'd spend in Huntsville.

Johnny was a bit quiet, more concerned about his pending prison sentence than anything else. Three or four times Tom had caught him crying. The sandy haired Ranger tried telling him that once Zachariah had spoken up, the most he'd get would be five years. "Who knows Johnny, you might, because of your age, get out in two." It lifted the boy some, which kind of made Tom feel a whole lot better.

Franklin, the more talkative of the two, had accepted his fate and was only too willing to fill in the gaps in the rustling operation. Logan Kincaid, the fellow in the yellow shirt, was the gang leader. It was him that had killed Paco. The vaquero rode up just as they'd cut the cows from the main herd. The Mexican understanding immediately what was going on, had tried making a break for it, but Kincaid pulled his rifle from his saddle boot and gunned the man down. Dan Weems was the fellow in the red underwear. Tom had seen a flyer on him back in Laredo. He was a mean son of a bitch. Knowing that, made the knowledge that he'd killed an unarmed man that much more bearable. The man who Zachariah had killed was John Quinn, the meanest of the bunch. A man that killed without hesitation. He always packed two bedrolls and always slept apart from the rest. Zachariah's instinct for survival had almost certainly saved his life.

"The night rider, who was that?" It was almost as important for Zachariah to know the name of the man whose life he'd spared, as it was to know the names of the men he'd killed.

"That was Martin, my younger brother. He was so frightened when Logan killed that Mexican. He'll most likely keep riding. I reckon without me he'll head for home, at least I hope so."

Zachariah remembered the kid's back, in the sights of his Winchester, and thanked God he'd stayed his hand.

About an hour out from the Morales ranch, Tom spied a cloud of dust coming from the rear.

"Shit," said Zachariah, "I was hoping we'd outrun them. If I miss my guess, I'd say that's young Rafael, and about now I'd reckon he's hopping mad."

Tom halted his horse, looked again at the cloud of dust, then carefully checked both of his pistols. "Trouble?"

"Could be. That vaquero's itching for a fight." Zachariah pulled his long barrelled Peacemaker from its holster and checked his loads. "Guess we pushed these cattle far enough. Best we leave them for Rafael and his vaqueros. That should hold them up a while. Give us enough time to call

on Senor Xavier Morales, and be on our way to San Antonio before nightfall."

"Mr Trelawney, with all respect, is that wise?

Zachariah looked across to Franklin, whose blonde unruly hair hung across his eyes, masking the fear that registered behind them. "Son, you're in my charge, no harm's gonna come to you two boys. Senor Morales is an understanding man."

They rode up to the ranch with Rafael and two others less than a quarter of a mile behind them. As they walked their horses into the courtyard Xavier Morales walked out to greet them.

"My congratulations, somehow or other I knew you would get to them first. Rafael is good, but he is young. He still has much to learn." The smile was relaxed and charming. "You didn't kill them all, that is good. You must be tired and hungry. Step down from your horse and allow me to pamper your every need. Tonight we have a great fiesta in your honour. Yours too, Mr Tenpenny," he added. "Then for our grand finale we hang those two murderers from the gates of the Morales ranch!"

Chapter 17

Tony Valdez had a problem, and that problem was Emilio Ortiz. When Serafina left, she didn't leave quietly. She made enough noise to wake the dead, which was how Emilio Ortiz was feeling that morning as Serafina ranted and raved past his bedroom. Ortiz threw on his clothes and banged loudly on Tony's door.

"Hey man, don't you know better than to cross a whore first thing in the morning. Damn bitches raise fucking hell. Now grab your clothes, lets go eat."

Somehow in Tony's drugged state, he'd partnered up with Ortiz and Serfina. The thought of it made him feel ten times worse. The three of them staggering along a corridor of flaking walls and threadbare carpets stinking with cats' piss sprang to mind. That and Serafina giving Ortiz head, just before he passed out.

He was stuck with Emilio Ortiz. He knew the little man wouldn't let him out of his sight. Somehow or other he'd allowed himself to become caught up in Morgan's plans. It would have been so easy to have taken the flashlight from the glovebox of the Blazer and enter the sewer, but instead he walked into Madero's. 'Was he going soft? Perhaps there was some decency still left inside, or was it that the killing of a fellow Ranger rankled. Hell he didn't know Orville Tyson, yet he knew Morgan. He knew him well enough to know he wouldn't put his life on the line unless he believed that what he was doing was right. It wasn't the way Tony wanted to play it. He should have grabbed the money and hightailed it across the border. Instead he'd re-entered the nightmarish world of drugs and prostitution.

Tony watched as Ortiz stuffed his face with hash browns, three eggs, a sausage patty and six sides of bacon, all smothered in a hot chilli sauce. The man was a pig at the table, the bar and in the bedroom. Tony had never liked the man. He had no redeeming features, but he was Montoya's second in command and as such would be useful in making contact with the drugs' operation in Monterrey.

One night in the presence of evil had turned Tony's stomach. He wanted to cut and run. Looking across at Emilio Ortiz, he realised that the war against drugs was already lost. Cut down ten Montoyas and another hundred would willingly take their place. At best, all they could hope for was to stem the tide. The money was his escape. Yet the thought of animals like Ortiz and Montoya growing fat from the human misery they had perpetuated sickened him. The money had waited three years, it could wait another few weeks.

Ortiz looked up from his breakfast, "Tampico, it's a nice town. When you think of going?"

"Oh, in a day or so. I figure to take a leisurely drive down, stopping off a time or too. Sample the merchandise as I go. Make a few scores along the way. Why, you interested in tagging along?"

Ortiz looked up and smiled. "That isn't as bad an idea as you might think. I've contacts that could be of use to you."

"Hah, Esteban wouldn't allow it." Tony knew his ploy would incite Ortiz into going.

"Fuck Esteban! I'm my own man. If I say I'm going, then there's nothing else to be said," screamed Ortiz.

"Easy man! Easy." Tony smiled inwardly. He'd been in Mexico less that twenty four hours. He'd been high, he'd been laid and now over breakfast he'd been guaranteed the safe passage and credentials he needed to infiltrate the Morales family. Steering Ortiz towards Apodaca would be child's play.

True to his word Emilio told Montoya he was joining Tony on his journey south. As predicted Esteban hadn't liked it, he hated change. Paranoia from too much Peyote abuse had changed the drugs' lord from a very dangerous man to an extremely unstable dangerous man. The arrival of Tony Valdez he'd viewed with suspicion. Though why he did, he didn't rightly know. And now his second in command was taking off without a by your leave, it was becoming too much. He was sure Ortiz was plotting against him. What other explanation could there be?

As an outsider Tony could see more clearly than those who surrounded Esteban Montoya. When the drugs' lord called Valdez to one side, Tony's diagnosis was confirmed. His old boss's chilling words still ringing in his ears. When they left early the next morning, no one was more relieved than Tony Valdez.

*   *   *   *

Jake Hamilton looked across the breakfast table at Blythe, his wife of nearly twenty years. They'd been childhood sweethearts, destined to marry, but Vietnam had interrupted their courtship. When Jake returned home, he was different. No longer the boy she'd loved and stayed faithful to, but a man who had seen the horrors of war and was still paying the price. Like the girl she once was, Blythe fought hard and tough to save her man's sanity. He was nineteen when the army took him away. He was nearing thirty when she finally got him to the altar. Not once in that whole time had he looked at another woman. His family was his pride and joy, but he was risking it all, and for what? For a man he'd barely known for but a few short months. Morgan hadn't exactly told him what they were going to do, only that it was dangerous and probably illegal. Jake weighed up the situation and realised the reason he'd agreed to risk all wasn't because of a piece of folded cloth, but because the very thought of going into action had sent a double dose of adrenaline coursing through his veins.

Left to mind the store while Morgan chased up to Austin, Jake began an investigation of his own. He'd known Lou Thurston since their days together in Vietnam. Though not friends, Jake knew him well enough to know he wasn't into murder. He was undoubtedly a bully, yet a good cop all the same. The chances were, both Orville and Thurston had been lured to their deaths. Whatever way he looked at it, the finger kept pointing back to Frank Jordan. Okay, so Morgan had thought the same and had drawn a blank. Having the boss of the agency and a couple of senators as an alibi might get him off the hook, but Jake Hamilton didn't buy it. Years of experience hadn't gone amiss. Jake was like a terrier with a bone. The more he chewed at it, the sweeter it became. If Jake probed deep enough he was sure he'd find marrow.

Too busy to check out Frank Jordan's alibi, Morgan had left Jake a note. **"If you get a chance, check out Jordan's meeting."** It wasn't much to go on, and Jake was sure the alibi would hold up, but he checked into it all the same. The only meeting the Bureau chief and the senators had on that Sunday was at an informal cocktail party. The bone had begun to crack. Jake managed to get a peep at the party guest list. Frank Jordan's name was on the list, along with his Bureau chief and a number of senators. Running his finger down the page his heart skipped a beat, and the marrow oozed out.

*　　*　　*　　*

Laura looked worried when she answered the door to her ex husband. "Hello Morgan," she said in an overly polite manner. Morgan smiled and stepped inside. Instantly he knew something was wrong. He'd lived with the woman for more years than he could remember. He knew every mood, every frown, every facial tic. Laura's body language was screaming at him.

"What's wrong?"

"Nothing's wrong," she replied too quickly.

"Laura, it's me you're talking to. We've known each other too many years for me not to know when something's bothering you."

Laura looked down at the floor, the walls, the door, but she wouldn't look him in the eye. "Can I get you a drink?"

"I'll take a beer." He watched her as she turned and walked into the kitchen. She opened the refrigerator door and reached inside. "Laura," he said as he placed both hands on her shoulders, "What's wrong, you know you're gonna tell me sooner or later."

Handing him an ice cold bottle, she said, "Here, take it. Let's sit down." Morgan twisted off the cap and took a swig from the long-necked brown bottle. Laura fiddled with her bottle but never raised it to her lips. "I've been going over the evidence you sent me." She was shaking and she'd turned the colour of parchment. 'I think I know why Orville was killed. More than that, I think I know who's responsible for his death."

Morgan sat forward in the chair, his attention fixed firmly on his ex wife. Laura was the smartest woman he'd ever known. If she said she knew why and who, the chances were she was right. "Go on," he said and took another swig from the bottle.

Chapter 18

▼

"These men are my prisoners and as such are under my protection as a Texas Ranger!" The words were loud and threatening, but the sound of twenty rifles being cocked was deafening.

Unflustered by the refusal, Don Xavier said, "If my men had caught up with them, they would all have been swinging from ropes. For centuries men of property have administered the justice of the rope."

"That is true Senor Morales, but these men were caught by us and are entitled to our protection." To emphasise his words, Zachariah rested his hand on the butt of his revolver.

"Give it up Senor Trelawney, you must realise you are out-gunned," the words cold and mocking. Rafael sat only yards behind the Rangers, his revolver cocked and pointing towards Zachariah's back.

"They're only boys," shouted Tom. *"For pity sake, they're kids."*

"Paco wasn't much more than a kid," said Xavier.

"If you take these boys, I'll come back for you. You'll be committing murder. You'll swing at the end of a rope, I'd see to it personally."

"What makes you think you'll get the chance," countered Rafael.

Tom swung his horse in Rafael's direction. "You die first," said the sandy haired Ranger.

The Ranger's defiant stand caused Xavier to to pull back from the brink. "Enough! I am a reasonable man. You agree, I could kill you. Go before I change my mind!" He waved his hand in a gesture of dismissal.

Rafael stole an angry glance at his patron, then moved his horse out of the way of the Rangers and their prisoners.

Zachariah acutely aware of the dangerous situation they were in, quickly turned his horse and kicked it into a trot. Tom glared angrily at Rafael, then he too turned his horse. Zachariah summoned the boys to follow. As he rode past Johnny he could see the boy was still shaking, "Easy son, we're heading for home."

'Crack! Crack!'

Both boys fell from their horses. Zachariah spun his horse around and raced back to Xavier. The Mexican stood there, his revolver still outstretched and smoking.

"You murdering bastard! Why?"

"Don't preach to me of killing. You, the killer of men. You the man who lives by the gun. Tell me, did you kill that man Carmichael in the name of justice, or did you kill him because of a woman? Don't you think I don't know. It's written all over your face. You want a woman that you can't have…my woman! Get out before I change my mind and have you both killed!"

Zachariah glanced back at Tom. The little Ranger was white faced with shock and anger. He shook his head. "They're both dead!"

Zachariah's eyes glared with hate. "Next time we meet, one of us will die!" Spinning his horse around he rode away, neither looking back, nor worrying about the bullet that might follow. Tom stared down at the two still figures of the boys, his nightmare continuing, then he too kicked his horse into a gallop.

For a mile neither man spoke as they rode side by side away from Hacienda Morales. Tom broke the silence, "Zack, what do you make of that?" He pointed back towards the gates of the ranch.

"Jesus Fucking Christ! They've hung them boys from the gates, and set them on fire!"

"Holy Mother!" Tom halted his horse and crossed himself. "Zachariah, those boys, they were dead?"

Zachariah looked off into the distance at the two burning effigies and shook his head, "I hope so." Then he turned away and kicked his horse into a lope and headed for town.

※　　※　　※　　※

"If only we'd skirted past the ranch, those boys might still be alive," said Tom solemnly. Across the camp fire, Zachariah stared into the burning embers. Ignoring Tom's remarks he reflected on the horrific events of a few hours earlier. His world such as it was, had been turned ugly by a single act of barbarism. He knew Xavier hadn't killed those boys for rustling his cattle. He'd destroyed them because of Zachariah's love for his wife. "In the open, I reckon we could have scared them off. Any how, it would have been better than this. What fight did we put up? We turned and ran. We should have stood our ground," grumbled Tom.

"It was my fault. He knew how I felt about Alicia. Those boys died because of me."

"Don't torture yourself. I'm as much to blame as you," said Tom sympathetically.

"How many guns do you reckon Xavier has working for him?"

"Thirty, maybe forty. More than we can handle my friend."

"First thing I'm gonna do when we get back to San Antonio is to send a wire to Austin. Soon as I can get Captain Platt and his troop of Rangers here, the better."

"Didn't we just agree that Morales must have between thirty or forty guns. As I recall, a troop is six men. Counting the captain that's nine including ourselves,"

"Ten. You forgot Ethan Book," corrected Zachariah.

"Oh yeah, ten. That should make all the difference," said Tom as he grabbed his bedroll and settled down for the night.

Zachariah nursed his coffee cup and continued to stare into the fire. Did Alicia know to what lengths her husband was prepared to go? Thank God she was away from the ranch. Would she believe him when he turned up with Captain Platt? Would she turn against her husband? Would she turn against him? He awoke just before dawn, his questions still unanswered.

Red white and blue ribbons still hung limply from the false fronts of Main, even though the celebrations had been over for almost a week. "Looks like we missed one hell of a party," said Tom as they rode past several of San Antonio's finest hotels. Zachariah chose to ignore Tom's efforts at lightening the mood and continued to stare directly ahead. At the Military Plaza, Tom veered his horse from the main drag and walked it to the saloon's hitching post. "Catch you later Zack."

"Yeah, see you in an hour," said Zachariah without turning his head. His mind composing the telegram he was sending to Austin. He'd earned the enmity of Xavier Morales and the battle lines had been drawn. The moment Morales pulled his pistol and gunned down those boys, Zachariah knew there could be no going back. Alicia was lost to him.

Tom Tenpenny peered cautiously into the Military Plaza Saloon, the splintered wood of the door frame a knowing reminder of what might be waiting for him. Even though he wore the badge of a Texas Ranger, Tom knew there were men who'd readily kill him if the chance arose. The saloon was empty apart from three late afternoon drinkers who looked too far gone to even notice his entrance. Bob Schaffer looked up from cleaning bar, a nervous smile slid across his face. "Tom, Tom Tenpenny when did you get back?"

"Just a minute ago," said Tom as he brushed the surplus dust from his top coat. "Where is everybody?" Schaffer lowered his head and continued to polish the brass rail at the end of the bar. "Hey Bob! I asked you a question," shouted Tom.

"Oh Jesus! You got to understand, there weren't anything we could do," stuttered Schaffer.

"You're talking in riddles, you couldn't do what."

"We couldn't save her, she died in my arms," said the barman.

"Who died?" It was a stupid question, from the look on Bob Schaffer's face, Tom knew it couldn't be anyone else. "Who died, damn you? Who died?"

"Loretta. It was an accident, a number of boys from Frenchie's Palace got a mite too liquored up and began shooting their guns off. Loretta was upstairs minding her own business when the shooting started. Curious to what was going on, she looked out the window and took a stray bullet high in the chest."

"Who did it?

Bob Schaffer knew enough to know you didn't pussy foot with Tenpenny. "Kendrickson's son, Nathan."

"He's a dead man," screamed Tenpenny. A sickness welled up inside of him, he couldn't believe it was happening to him over again. "Where is he?"

"He's over to the jail," volunteered Schaffer.

"Well he's about to go free," said Tom, as he pulled one of his nickel plated pistols from it's holster and began to check his loads.

"No he ain't!" The voice belonged to a man sitting in the shady part of the room. A half-finished meal sat on the table in front of him.

Tom stared at the voice, as the man unfurled himself and stepped away from the table. He was tall, probably as tall as Zachariah, but thin and wiry. Tenpenny judged him to be about thirty five, but the long blonde hair and the goatee made him look older. He wore a Remington 44 calibre revolver across his left hip, butt forward. On the table lay an old Sharps buffalo gun, and judging by the shine it looked well cared for. More importantly it was cocked.

Tom had seen death many times, and he knew at that moment he was staring it in the face. "Who says?" said Tom. his hand closing on his pistol.

"I do. Kendrickson is in my custody." There was a twinkle in the man's eyes. Tom had seen that look before, and only a few men carried it. Those that did, killed faster than a snake's tongue. "From the cut of you, I'd say you were a fellow Ranger. My name's Ethan Book. I'm sorry about your lady, but the whole affair was as Bob says, just a freak accident."

"*Freak accident my ass! The man's gonna pay.*"

"*Not while he's my prisoner.*"

"*Tom, listen to the man,*" shouted Bob Schaffer, "*He walked into Frenchie's Palace and took Nathan in front of McCulloh, Randolph and half a dozen more of Kendrickson's men.*"

"*I understand how you feel, but let the law deal with it,*" said Book, his demeanour softening.

Tom thought of the young boy he'd gunned down in the street so many years ago. If only he'd stopped to think, that kid would be alive today. What good would it do? Loretta was gone. Much as he hated to admit it, Ethan Book was right. For once he should let the law deal with it. "*Okay, I'll leave it to the courts, but if the kid walks, he's mine.*"

"*I have no problem with that,*" said Ethan Book.

Tom turned back to Bob Schaffer, "*Where is she?*"

"*She's buried in the little cemetery behind the Alamo.*"

"*Obliged,*" said Tom. *He walked out of the saloon his head bowed. Bob followed him to the door and watched him mount up and head east towards the old mission.*

An hour later Zachariah strolled into the Military Plaza saloon. At the telegraph office he'd learnt the news of Loretta's death and the subsequent arrest of her killer. He'd heard of Ethan Book, a man much like himself. A man of principles. A man who had ridden with the law most all his life. It didn't take Zachariah more than a few moments before he recognised the tall long haired stranger. Holding out an outstretched hand he said, "*Howdy, I'm Lieutenant Zachariah Trelawney, fifth company Texas Rangers, you must be Ethan Book.*"

"*Nice to meet you, I've already met Tenpenny.*"

Zachariah looked across to Bob Schaffer. A look was all he needed.

"*Tom take it hard?*"

"*You could say that, almost threw down on me,*" said Book.

"*I'm sure glad he didn't. Chances are both of you'd end up dead. When's the trial?*"

"Circuit judge set the arraignment for the twenty seventh of this month."

Zachariah said nothing, then after a few moments of deliberation he spoke to Ethan Book, "Kendrickson knows that if his son is acquitted Tom will kill him. Between now and the trial he's going to try provoking Tom. My guess would be Clay McCulloh, with Randolph and Pudbury as his back up."

"That's how I figured it," said Book as he extended his hand in friendship.

Zachariah grasped the man's hand, and gave a semblance of a smile, "Welcome to San Antonio. If I miss my guess, I'd say, you just bought yourself into a little war."

✳   ✳   ✳   ✳

Tom Tenpenny stood over the small mound of earth, his head bowed and his eyes brimming with tears. Bending down he placed a small bouquet of flowers, not dissimilar to the posy he'd brought to her room less than three short weeks ago, upon the foot of the tiny grave. In the short span of time that he'd known her, she'd become his salvation. Where once there had been the chance of a new life, there was only bitterness and anger. He knew Kendrickson would be sending someone for him, he couldn't afford not too. The boy would walk, and Tom would surely kill him. Tom Tenpenny was entering the arena he felt most at home in. He was going to war and no one, not even Ethan Book or Zachariah Trelawney, were going to stop him.

Chapter 19

▼

A look of disbelief formed on Morgan's face. He'd sat there patiently listening as Laura poured out her theory. He'd even stopped himself from interrupting when she said Senator Delaney was involved, but her suggestion that Kathleen was somehow implicated, that was too much to take.

"Kathleen Delaney! That's ridiculous!"

"Face it Morgan. Who lured you away on the day that Orville was killed?"

"Now I know you've flipped! Kathleen! You don't even know her. If you did, you'd know how foolish that sounds." He started to laugh. This was a joke. Laura was tugging at his tree. Yeah that's it. It's a joke. But the look in Laura's eyes told him it wasn't so.

"Morg, I'm so sorry," said Laura as she tried reaching out for him.

What was she playing at? Why was she saying such dreadful things? His anger welled up inside. "Get away, get away from me," he said and pulled away from her embrace.

"Morg, listen to me," she pleaded. "I didn't want to be the one to tell you. Believe me, this is one of the most painful things I've ever had to do."

Angrily he shouted at her, "You're jealous! Why else would you say such things? She's younger than you, and you don't like the attention

I've been giving her. You're trying to turn me against her. Well it won't work."

Laura's face twisted in anguish at the vicious words. She'd been expecting it, but the look and tone were more than she could stand. Even during the divorce Morgan hadn't spoken with such venon. In desperation she tried one last time to make him understand, "Morgan it's true, believe me. I wish to God it wasn't. I love you, I wouldn't hurt you for the world."

"You say you love me, but how can you?" His face became contorted with rage.

"I do, I do. That's why I had to tell you," she pleaded.

Ignoring her plea, he hardened his resolve, "I shouldn't have come. You've got Kathleen all wrong. I've gotta get outta here!" Brushing Laura aside he took three giant steps and wrenched the front door open. For a second he hesitated. She had to be wrong. Then he slammed the door behind him.

Despairingly Laura slumped into her chair. It was useless to chase after him. The tears streamed from her eyes, and she began to sob uncontrollably. Now came the self doubt. She'd given him the facts as she perceived them. 'Could she be wrong?' Burying her head in her hands, she jumped as the phone rang.

Grabbing a tissue she blew her nose and wiped at the tears, "Hello," she said barely disguising the tremor in her voice.

"Hi. Laura have you seen Morgan? I need to speak to him right away."

She'd only met Jake Hamilton twice but she recognised his voice immediately. "Jake, no, I mean yes. He left in an almighty hurry."

"Shit. Excuse me, I kinda forgot my manners. When you expecting him back? Only I got something mighty important to tell him."

"I can't say Jake. We had us a fight." The more she thought about what she'd told Morgan the more she was beginning to doubt herself.

For a moment there was nothing then a gurgling sound like someone clearing their throat. Then Jake spoke. "The name Delaney didn't crop up by any chance?"

Laura jumped from her chair, her heart pounding out of control. Perhaps she'd been right after all, "Jesus Jake! What do you know?"

The excited tone of her voice told Jake Hamilton all he needed to know. From what Morgan had said about Laura, he knew she was one smart cookie. "Listen Laura, if Morgan gets in touch, tell him to stay put. I'm coming up. I reckon I should be with you in a little under four hours."

"Hurry!"

Laura placed the receiver back on its cradle and poured herself a large drink. She looked towards the open bedroom door and thought about the full packet of Camels resting in the bottom drawer of her bedside table. "Shit!" Six months of abstinence flew out the window.

Morgan's head was spinning, he couldn't believe Laura could be so vindictive, yet what if it was true. 'It couldn't be true, Kathleen wasn't that type. What type was she for Christ sake! Kathleen involved in murder, it just didn't make sense. His first reaction as he flung open the door to his car was to race around to Kathleen's condo and have it out with her. As the door closed he realised he needed to sit down and think it through rationally. He was confused, his whole world was being torn down around him. If Laura was lying and he confronted Kathleen, he'd surely lose her. If she was telling the truth, then there must be a reason, there had to be a reason. He needed time to think, to rationalise.

Morgan drove to Kathleen's building and parked his car on a red zone opposite the Capitol building. He climbed out and began walking until he found the nearest bar. Once inside he slid into a booth in the far corner and ordered a Shiner Bock and a whiskey chaser.

Normally he'd have believed every word Laura had told him, but Kathleen, that was asking too much. Laura had seemed ill at ease, troubled in fact, but he'd sat there coaxing her to lay it on the line. She'd looked him straight in the eye and said, "Okay, here goes. Orville's enthusiasm got him killed. He'd made it quite clear from the start that he wasn't backing down." Morgan nodded his agreement. "As you're aware he'd found evidence that suggested the murders at the Blevins homestead had been filmed, well I'd like to leave that aside, Orville didn't know that until about a day before he was killed." Laura paused, then looking her ex husband in the eyes she continued. "Answer me this, why did so many law enforcement agencies descend on the crime scene so quickly?"

"Way we figured it out, someone phoned them all, probably the killers. Everyone was falling over themselves. It was chaos," said Morgan.

"Exactly. With nothing much to go on, Orville turned his attention to why there were so many agencies involved, especially the DEA. We have our own Narcotics division in the Department of Public Safety, why was the DEA even involved? What's more, why were they handed over the jurisdiction of the case?" Laura saw that she had Morgan's undivided attention.

"Go on," he said.

"I've been through that file with a fine tooth comb. Orville was a stickler for detail. He somehow managed to get records of all phone calls concerning the tip off. The Rangers were called first, then the Border Patrol and finally the Sheriff's department. There were no calls to the Drugs Enforcement Agency!" She paused and studied his reaction.

"Jesus, I never thought to check that out." Morgan knew Orville's eye for detail was second to none, but until that moment he never realised just how sharp that eye was.

"With nothing else to go on, Orville began checking up on Lou Thurston and Frank Jordan. Both men have exemplary records and separately they had received commendations for bravery. Of the two, Frank Jordan was the thinker. He was of a higher than average IQ for the department, ambitious, cunning and ruthless. Add all that to his many contacts with influential business men and several politicians, including Senator Joe Delaney and there's your man."

Morgan's jaw dropped open, but he said nothing.

"Okay, so it's only circumstantial, but it's just possible that because your Kathleen was a friend of Tania's, that Orville showed more than a passing interest in Delaney's affairs." Laura tried judging the reaction on Morgan's face, she wasn't sure she should have begun something that she had no control over stopping. "Two days before he was killed, Orville received a list of Frank Jordan's phone calls, his home line, his mobile and his work number. Around the time the agencies received news of the Blevins killings Jordan took a call at his home address. It was from the same public phone booth." Laura took a sip from her beer.

"So what's that got to do with Kathleen's uncle?"

Laura had hit a nerve, she knew by the tremor in Morgan's voice. "Immediately after receiving the call he phoned Delaney's office."

"Yeah so what does that prove?" There was now irritation in Morgan's speech, he'd known Laura too long not to know she was building up to something.

"Jordan placed another call to that office an hour and a half later. One can assume it was after your confrontation with Thurston and Jordan. Anyway Delaney placed a call to the headquarters of the Texas Department of Public Safety explaining that a big DEA operation was about to be compromised. To this date no operation concerning the DEA has been recorded concerning the Blevins' slaying."

"There's no evidence to suggest that Delaney was involved. Sure it could put both Thurston and Jordan in the frame, but it could have been anybody in Delaney's office."

"You're right Morg, but prior to the discovery of the bodies at the Blevins homestead, Frank Jordan received a long distance call in the early hours. It was from a public phone booth in the little Mexican town of Apodaca."

Morgan's face turned white, he didn't like where this was leading. "I see where you're coming from, but there still isn't any proof he's involved."

Laura twisted uncomfortably in her chair. She knew what she was about to say would hurt like hell. "Remember that weekend when Kathleen was away at a convention in LA."

"Yeah," he said cautiously.

"Well it's true she went to the convention. What you don't know is that she was called back to Austin by her uncle. After that you didn't see much of her until that weekend just before Orville was killed." She looked for his agreement. He nodded. Taking a deep breath Laura went for it. "How much of the investigation did you tell her? More importantly who suggested taking the day off when Orville was killed?"

After that the rest became foggy. He'd said some terrible things. Hurtful things, words that couldn't be taken back. In the cold light of day, he was beginning to believe that Laura might somehow be telling it as it was. The more he mulled over what she'd said, the more it made sense. Ordering another round of drinks he began reflecting on what a fool he'd been. He and Kathleen had been friends, but then suddenly she'd come on to him. He remembered how surprised he'd been, but he never questioned her motives. Their lovemaking that night had seemed a little stilted, but he'd put that down to nerves. When she'd suggested taking the day off he'd gone willingly. Was he such a fool? Had Kathleen known she was clearing the way for Orville's execution? The logical side of his brain came to the rescue. She couldn't have known, he recalled their lovemaking in the desert south of Laredo. There had been no inhibitions that time, she'd given herself to him. It was fantastic, it was beautiful, no it was out of this world. There was no suggestion she was faking it. They'd made love in the truest sense of the word. He was as confused as when he'd first stepped into the bar. Throwing the fiery liquor down his throat Morgan rose unsteadily to his feet and walked out.

Fifteen minutes later he was peering up at the pink stucco building that housed Kathleen's condo. His heart began to pound as he climbed the steps to her doorway. Morgan checked the number of her condo and rang the bell.

"Morgan!" she exclaimed.

"Kathleen, we need to talk."

"You'd better come in."

She was more beautiful than he remembered, but her hang dog expression told him she knew why he'd come. "I thought we had something," he began. "I worked slow so as not to rush you. Then when we finally get together you move away. I tried telling myself it was only temporary, that you'd come back, but I was only fooling myself." All the time he was wishing she'd stop him and declare her undying love, but he already knew that was a forlorn hope.

"Why have you come?"

"I think you know why. Did you really feel for me, or was it just orders from your uncle?" His heart sank as she didn't flinch at his question.

"I didn't know, I still don't know the truth. Uncle Joe said the Texas Rangers were compromising a drugs investigation and as I was friendly with you, would I help. I refused at first, but he persuaded me that it would be in your interest."

"What did he mean, in my interest?" The anger was welling up inside him.

"A drugs' bust was supposed to be going down on the Monday that Orville was killed. My uncle said it would be better if you were out of town, because if things went wrong, you were liable to be blamed. I did it to protect you, I didn't know anyone would get killed!"

"So it was all an act," he asked aggressively.

"No! I've got feelings for you, I didn't know how much I cared until Mexico. I thought I was going to lose you. Until that moment I didn't realise just how much I cared. Sitting in the car after we'd made love, I knew what I felt was real. I loved you, I still love you." Tiny droplets of tears began forming around her eyes.

"When we got back to Laredo, why didn't you tell me about your uncle?" The anger was clearly showing.

"I was frightened, I thought you'd never forgive me. Believe me, I didn't know Orville would be killed. I still don't know why."

Morgan continued unabated. "After Orville's funeral you packed your bags and moved back here, why?"

"My uncle said Orville was involved and that possibly you were implicated. I didn't know what to believe. I had to believe Uncle Joe, I've known him all my life. Yet my heart said you were innocent. I didn't know what to do. I had to get away." The tears began to flow.

He didn't know what to believe, his mind was in turmoil. He wanted to reach out to her, to tell her everything was all right, but things weren't all right. They'd never be all right. She'd been duped just as surely as she'd fooled him. Her Uncle had used her in the worst possible way. Her stupidity and naiveté had cost a man his life, robbing a wife of her husband and depriving their children of a father. Even though his heart cried out for her, she was lost to him forever.

He raced down the steps and turned the corner. In his heart he wanted her to call him back, but his stubborn streak would only have spurred him further away from her.

"Tequila," he demanded the moment he walked into the dimly lit bar. Slumping into the booth Morgan began to get drunk.

Jake found him there three hours later. Paying Morgan's tab he hoisted the big man up and half dragged, half carried him to his waiting Explorer. Hamilton turned on the ignition and gunned the sedan to the nearest motel. "Guess you need to sleep it off. I reckon Senator Joe Delaney can wait until morning."

Chapter 20

"What do you know about Cuba?" The frustration and anger in his voice caused Ethan Book to look up from his midday meal.

"It's an island a couple of hundred miles off the mainland. Why?"

Shaking with rage, Zachariah pushed the crumpled telegram into Book's hands. "Read it! Then tell me what's so damn important that we're to leave murderers go free."

Ethan uncrumpled the paper and read the telegram. **"Under no circumstances arrest Xavier Morales stop. Sympathetic to Cuban insurrection. American interest must repeat must not be compromised. Repeat do not arrest Xavier Morales stop."** It was signed simply, **Captain William Platt.**

"I know Captain Platt, if he says we don't arrest anybody, you better believe he means it. He's a good man, but a hell of a stickler for the rules." Book pushed his half eaten dinner into the centre of the table. "Face it Zack, the whole Plaza's a powder keg, we got ourselves enough to handle."

"Damn politics, damn them to hell!" Zachariah grasped at the telegram and screwed it into a ball before throwing it into the nearest spittoon. "Where's Tom?"

"Last I seen of him he was sleeping off a drunk. Which is just the way I like him. When that man's conscious he's as mean as a snake. Trial or no trial, trouble's a coming!"

"Yeah, I reckon you're right. I should have killed Kendrickson years ago. If you hadn't gone after Nathan, old Jasper would have found another way of getting at me."

"What! There's bad blood between you and Kendrickson?"

"You could say, I killed his brother up to Amarillo a few years back. Jasper had his chance then, but he didn't take it. He came on the prod, liquored up and crazy as a tree'd coon. Said how he was gonna cut my heart out and cook it over an open fire. My hand closing on the butt of my gun and I said, "Get to cutting!" I caught him off balance. He was drunk and mean as hell, but he sobered pretty quick when he seen I was about to have at it. Jasper backed off. He ain't no coward though, just a man that likes to play the percentages."

"And you ain't seen him since then?

"Yeah, a time or two, but we mostly kept outta each other's way. I reckon it would have carried on that way if Tom and I hadn't braced him. In the reddy glow of the saloon lights, I saw the hatred in his eyes. That son of a bitch aims to kill me." Zachariah paused then added, "Or me him."

"He's got quite a bunch, I seen another new face only yesterday," said Ethan.

"Yeah I heard another two rode in this morning. Whatever the outcome of the trial, Kendrickson intends having at it. Right now I'm feeling as mean as all hell. I reckon it's time I took the fight to them sons of bitches."

"Hell no Zack! You cain't let that damn telegram make you do something stupid."

"It ain't the telegram," shouted Zachariah, which was a damn lie.

His frustration at not being able to ride to the Morales Ranch and arrest Xavier Morales was eating him up, but his real concern was at not seeing Alicia. She'd been figuring more and more in his dreams of late. All was not well with the Morales family. He'd sensed it the first time he'd set eyes on Alicia. If he could have arrived in force, maybe just maybe he'd be able to free her from the tyrant her husband had become. His hands had been tied by a stinking telegram, and his anger was rising to the surface.

"*Them boys over too Frenchie's Palace is wearing guns in contradiction of the City Ordinance. I aim to see what those boys are made of.*"

"Let's get to it," shouted Tom Tenpenny.

Zachariah looked up at his friend standing at the top of the stairs, checking his guns. His anger was such that he was prepared to fight an army, but it was his fight and he didn't want anyone else getting involved. "Not so fast Tom. If I take you with me, there's no way I can avoid bloodshed."

"From what I've heard, Kendrickson wants your blood. You tell me how you're gonna avoid it," roared the sandy haired Ranger as he descended the stairs rather unsteadily. "Someone's gotta watch your back!"

Zachariah's obsession with Alicia had drawn other people into his fight, he didn't know how to cut loose. Angrily he shouted at his new found friend. "No Tom, look at yourself. You've got the shakes far worst than a rattler. You're liable to get yourself killed the moment you cross the Plaza."

"That ain't fair Zachariah! And you knows it."

That maybe so Tom, but you ain't invited this time."

Tom cast a hurt look towards his tall friend, "Let me go Zachariah."

Ashamed at the way he'd spoken to his friend Zachariah tried reasoning. "It's six days until the trial. I'm gonna need you in one piece. Get a square meal, sober up. If I miss my guess, I'd say this here fighting's only just beginning."

Tom was confused, his only friend had spurned his offer of help. As he looked at himself in the ornate mirror behind the bar, he knew the reason why. His pallor was grey. His hands shook and he was bathed in sweat. *Zachariah's right. Look at what I've become. I'm not fit to call him my friend.*' At that moment Tom didn't care whether he lived or died.

"I'll go!" Ethan Book stood up and motioned Bob Schaffer for the scatter gun he kept behind the bar. Tom glared at the long haired Ranger, but stifled his tongue. He didn't much like Ethan Book, but his tall Ranger friend needed someone he could rely on and Book was stone cold sober. If he was as deadly with his Remington as he liked to make out, then Zachariah was in *good hands.* Casting an eye across the room at the tall rangy blonde lawman, Tom said weakly, *"You take care of him, mind."*

Whether Ethan heard him or not he gave out no reaction.

It was a fight of his own making. One that he'd been prepared to tackle alone, but fate had taken a hand, Zachariah had no choice but to nod his thanks. *"You ready!"* he heard himself say.

"I reckon," came Ethan's reply.

Both men stepped outside and stood on the sidewalk for a moment, acclimatising their eyes to the brightness of the late afternoon sun.

"How do you want to play this Zachariah?" said Ethan.

"As it comes."

Striding purposefully across the Plaza they stepped onto the sidewalk outside Frenchie's. Somehow luck had played a hand and they'd not been noticed. Zachariah slid his Colt 45 from its holster and cocked it in one smooth motion. Ethan drew back the twin hammers of the Greener, and nodded his readiness.

As one they entered Frenchie's Palace in a rush. Zachariah discharged a round into the wooden floor of the saloon. The noisy interior of the room came to a deathly quiet, all eyes turned towards the open doorway and the heavily armed Rangers. *"Gentlemen, your full attention!"* The calmness of his voice left no one in any doubt that he wasn't to be trifled with. *"You gentlemen are in contravention of the City Ordinance concerning the wearing of firearms within the City limits. Take them off and put them on the table in front of you."*

For a moment there was silence, then.... *"The Hell I will!"* Josh Randolph pushed his way forward. His gunbelt clearly noticeable around his large frame.

"Keep a coming and Hell's where I'll send yah!" The tone was unmistakable as Ethan levelled his shotgun at Josh Randolph's belly. The bigger man stopped in his tracks. Unsure what to do, he looked towards McCulloh for support. Clay McCulloh wasn't adverse to trouble, but he knew when the deck was stacked against him. Without hesitating he unbuckled his belt and placed the rig on the nearest green baize table.

"You!" Zachariah pointed his Peacemaker at two young men in their early twenties. "Schuck them weapons now!"

The look in his eyes was enough for them to obey his command. Only Josh Randolph had not made a move to give up his weapon. Without warning Zachariah spun round and in one blinding motion brought the seven and a half inches of cold steel gun barrel pounding down on the big man's head. The man dropped heavily to the floor.

Zachariah's blood was up. Every man in the room knew death was a split second away. "Jesus Trelawney, there was no need," protested Clay McCulloh. Ethan turned his Greener in McCulloh's direction, causing the man to throw his hands in the air. "Easy with that scattergun." The words were polite enough, but his eyes remained hostile.

"Tell your boss no one has to die. It can end here now!" Zachariah spoke the words directly towards McCulloh. Then holstering his revolver, he pulled the unconscious Randolph into the street and cuffed him to the hitching rail. Stepping back inside he gathered up the men's weapons. "You can collect these from the sheriff's office when you leave town." A feeling of relief wafted over the tall Ranger. He'd acted in haste and got away with it. Inside he could feel the shakes beginning. He above all knew how lucky they'd been. If the bar had been filled with Kendrickson's men, there was no telling what the outcome might have been. Cautiously both men backed out of the saloon.

When they returned to the Military Plaza saloon they found Tom Tenpenny packing his saddlebags. His badge was lying discarded on the centre of the Monte table. Zachariah gave him a quizzical look.

"You got yourself a back up. Guess I ain't needed anymore," he said by way of an explanation.

"Tom, you know damn well you're needed. It's just…"

"Just what? I'm a liability, I'm a drunk. If I stay, you know there'll be blood split. Book's with you, I ain't needed anymore. Loretta's gone. There ain't much more this town has to offer. That's why I'm getting out of this civilised town while I still can."

It was of the tall lawman's making. He'd forced a showdown and got away with it, at the cost of losing his friend. He knew Tom well enough to know his pride was hurt and there could be no reasoning with him. Regret mingled with relief. Under normal circumstances Zachariah would have tried telling Tom the truth. Yet the more he thought about the situation the more he had to admit that with Tom out of the way, there was a pretty good chance they could avoid a shooting. Zachariah accepted the little man's explanation with a heavy heart. "I'm sorry to see you go Tom. Where you heading?"

"I got some folks up towards Fort Worth. Thought I might visit awhile."

"Why not wait until morning? It's starting to get dark," said the tall Ranger, reluctant to say goodbye.

"Nope, best I go now."

"Take care, you hear," then Zachariah shook his friend's hand. "It's been a privilege."

"Likewise."

Tom turned away and strolled out of the saloon into the night's darkness. Standing on the sidewalk he gazed across the plaza which was bathed in an orange glow from the gaslights that lit up the square. All looked peaceful and right with the world. Tom felt a sudden sadness at his leaving and would have stayed if Zachariah had given him one word of encouragement. With a sigh of resignation he threw his saddlebag across the rear of his horse. Grabbing the saddle horn he was about to mount up when he felt the hair on the back of his neck rise. Turning quickly he stared into the face of Clay McCulloh.

"Law dog, when you fixing to release Randolph?" McCulloh jerked his thumb in the general direction of Frenchie's Palace at the moaning body of Josh Randolph still chained to the hitching rail.

One glance told Tom that McCulloh was unarmed, "It ain't none of my business anymore," he said, before turning his back and putting one foot into the stirrup, He added, "Far as I see it, he can stay there forever."

"Why you son of a bitch!"

In that moment Tom realised McCulloh was reaching beneath his jacket for a hideaway gun. Tom pushed himself free from his horse and grabbed at McCulloh's gun hand, desperately trying to force the gun from the bigger man's grasp. They grappled into the middle of the street both fighting desperately to win possession of the short barrelled Colt. McCulloh landed a punch with his left hand and sent Tom sprawling into the dirt. Staggering backwards McCulloh discharged his pistol, missing Tom by a fraction. Unperturbed by his poor aim, he began cocking the hammer for a second shot. The little man was on his knees and rising. Grabbing for his pistol he got off a shot. By luck the bullet tore off McCulloh's thumb just as he cocked his weapon. With the instinct to survive he grabbed at the pistol with his left hand, but it was too late. Tom had risen to his feet and was firing at almost point blank range. His second bullet tore into Clay McCulloh's shoulder, his third and fourth were less than an inch apart tearing the life from Tom's would be assailant.

Zachariah and Ethan rushed out of the saloon, guns drawn and ready. "What the hell's going on!"

At the same time as Zachariah arrived on the sidewalk Jasper Kendrickson and six others ran across from Frenchie's.

"You'll pay for this Tenpenny. My man was on an errand of mercy."

"That's far enough Kendrickson!" Zachariah's Peacemaker was levelled at his head. "Unless you want to have at it!"

Kendrickson stared into the muzzle of the Rangers' long-barrelled 45 and froze. To Zachariah's left was Bob Schaffer, in his hands a twelve gauge shotgun. On the wooden sidewalk half hidden in the darkness Kendrickson detected the unmistakable octagonal barrel of a Sharps 'Creedmour.' He figured that was Book. He'd heard tell how Ethan Book had taken down a bank robber at two hundred and fifty yards. The man was dead before he back-flipped off his galloping horse. Across the Plaza he couldn't have been more than twenty feet away. Jasper wasn't a man prepared to commit suicide. Backing up he threw his hands high in the air.

"Zachariah, this is nothing less than murder. Your man killed McCulloh in cold blood. I intend to see that justice is done." Then looking

down at the small Monte dealer he shouted, "Tom Tenpenny you're gonna hang for this!"

Zachariah bellowed at the small crowd that had begun forming. "Back off, back off I say!"

"Tom, get your ass inside now," shouted Ethan Book.

Tenpenny, still dazed and shaken scurried into the saloon. Bob Schaffer followed him in. Kendrickson and his crowd began milling around outside Frenchie's. It was obvious to Zachariah that Kendrickson was trying to stir up the crowd. Zachariah began walking across the plaza, while Ethan Book adjusted the sights on his Creedmour. At the centre of the plaza the lawman spoke to the crowd of onlookers. "What happened here will be investigated to the fullest extent of the law. Tom Tenpenny will be questioned and if necessary be prosecuted in accordance with that law. Now go home, all of you!" A few murmurs of angry dissent, then a withering look from the tall Ranger and the crowd began to disperse.

"It ain't over Trelawney. Your boy walks, so does mine!"

"We'll let the law decide." Zachariah holstered his gun and turned his back on Jasper Kendrickson. For a split second the owner of Frenchie's Palace was tempted to draw his pistol and let the Ranger have it, then he remembered the octagonal barrel of Ethan Book's Creedmour.

Kendrickson watched as Zachariah reached the entrance to the saloon. Ethan Book emerged from the shadows and then both men re-entered the Military Plaza Saloon. He continued to stare for minutes after they'd locked and bolted the doors. Taking out a fine Cuban cigar from the breast pocket of his brocaded vest, he proceeded to light it. He was a gambler and always played the percentages, which was why he was still alive while many of his contemporaries were in lonely graves scattered throughout the West. Trelawney had been dealing the cards and had won the last few hands, but that game was over. McCulloh was dead, killed by a quirk of fate. Well McCulloh wasn't the only gun hand in Jasper Kendrickson deck. Now it was his turn to be the dealer and the name of the game was death. He puffed on his cigar and a grin began to form.

Chapter 21

As Morgan lay there contemplating the strange ceiling, the events of yesterday slowly began filtering back. For one brief moment he thought he'd dreamed it. His euphoria was short lived as he turned his head and saw the sleeping form of Jake Hamilton. He'd expected the sudden movement of his head would bring on the inevitable hangover. From the amount he'd consumed he knew it was lurking somewhere in the depths of his skull, waiting for the most inappropriate time to begin.

Lying there, he gathered his thoughts. He'd been bullish and mean. He'd treated Laura shamefully. Instead of thrashing it out with her, he'd chosen to attack her verbally. He'd called her for everything. She was a good woman, yet he'd treated her no better than a whore off the streets. She was a liar, she was jealous, she was old. Cruel words, uttered in anger. He could see it now, in the cold light of day. He could see it now. Laura had a forgiving nature, but this time he'd gone too far. He'd asked for her help, and then he'd thrown it in her face.

Why, if he didn't believe Laura did he verbally attack Kathleen? Somehow after all he'd said, he knew his ex-wife was telling the truth. He'd hoped Kathleen would have denied it, but she didn't. Even when she broke down and cried, he kept the hard exterior. He'd torn into

Kathleen and ripped her heart out, as surely as the truth had broken his own.

Sitting up he was surprised his headache hadn't arrived. Pushing his luck he ventured into the bathroom and took a shower. As the water cascaded over his head and shoulders he began planning his next move.

Jake stirred, the sound of the shower bringing him out of a restless sleep. The events of the day before came quickly to mind. They'd stumbled on a nest of rattlesnakes, and no matter which way one turned someone got bit. He wished, oh how he wished, he hadn't sent Orville on that fateful call that led to the Blevins homestead. He wished he could turn back the clock. He wanted to quit, that's how much the case turned his stomach. It had been a dirty business from the start, its deadly tentacles affecting everyone that came in contact with it. He wondered just how many lives would be ruined before the dust finally settled on the case. Jake was no less a Ranger than Morgan and he'd sworn to see the job through no matter what the consequences. But not for the first time, he though of his wife and kids.

"We gotta talk," said Morgan as he walked out of the bathroom, towel-drying his hair.

"Over breakfast," said Jake as he walked into the steamy bathroom.

Neither man spoke much, each deep in their own private thoughts. Dressing quickly, they made there way downstairs to the motel restaurant. Seated in a quiet booth they waited until the waitress had taken their order before speaking.

"Thanks for last night," said Morgan.

"Forget it," said Jake abruptly. "Laura's a good woman, she didn't deserve what she got. She told me everything, and it fits nicely with what I've discovered. You should have listened to her instead of flying into one."

"Look Jake I know you mean well, but don't you think I know that."

"Yeah I guess you do at that." Jake smiled as the waitress filled their cups with coffee, "Thanks."

"Kathleen told me all she knew, and before you say anything, I believe her," said Morgan. He took a sip of his coffee and wiped his moustache with the back of his hand.

"This has gone big time, what with the Senator and all. If I'm to continue working on this case, I mean to know what you're all planning."

"Yeah I guess you do at that. First thing I'm gonna make Joe Delaney spill his guts. I don't rightly know why he's involved, but with a little persuasion I think we'll be able to loosen his tongue."

"Right, I'm with you as far at it goes. Once we know where it's heading I'll let you know if I'm still with you." Morgan reflected how, in the time he'd known Jake, he'd never seen him as serious. "Right now I think you'd better give Laura a ring." Two loaded plates interrupted their conversation as the waitress smiled and set their breakfasts in front of them.

Half an hour later both men drove in silence the seven blocks to the Capitol building. Within minutes they were climbing the concrete steps to the entrance. Going through several security checkpoints, they arrived at Senator Delaney's front office. A formidable secretary tried quizzing them on their visit. After minutes of interrogation, she reluctantly phoned through to find out whether the Senator was busy. To her extreme chagrin and surprise, she learned the Senator was expecting them.

Senator Joe Delaney came from around his desk, his hand extended in greeting. A politician's smile spread across his face.

"Gentlemen, I'm a very busy man, but not too busy to see two members of our illustrious Ranger service. How can I help?" Even when both men rebuffed his handshake, he remained cool. Ignoring the snub he walked back round his desk and sat down. "Take a seat," he continued, gesturing with an open hand to the comfortable leather button studded chairs in front of his desk.

Ignoring the invitation Morgan stared the man squarely in the eyes. "I think you know why we've come."

"You must be Morgan Trelawney. Kathleen has told be so much about you. All good I hasten to add."

"Cut the crap! I want answers and I want them now!" Morgan slammed his hand down hard on the mahogany desk. The senator's face turned a deathly white and his Adam's apple bobbed up and down.

"Okay," he said, holding his hands palm forward in way of submission. "I'll tell you all I know. You stepped into a delicate operation and nearly blew six months of surveillance. Because of my timely intervention I was able to save your career. Kathleen phoned me last night in tears. She told me how you didn't believe her, how you practically accused her of being an accessory to murder." The senator's face was turning the colour of beetroot, his anger plain to see. "Why she'd bother with the likes of you is beyond me. She's a great girl and has a bright future ahead of her. She helped me because she thought she was helping you. If you're smart you'll head back to Kathleen's apartment and beg her forgiveness."

Morgan was taken aback by the senator's manner. He'd half-expected him to crumble and spill all. Instead he'd hit back, skilfully turning the tables. 'Perhaps I've got it all wrong, maybe there really is a drugs deal that I haven't heard about.'

Encouraged by the attitude of the senator, Morgan began to believe there was still hope for him and Kathleen. Lost in his private thoughts he hardly heard Joe Delaney utter the words, "I'm sorry a Ranger got himself killed. That was most unfortunate."

Jake hadn't. Incensed by the last remark, he reached across the desk and pulled the senator out of his chair. "What the……"

Jake brought his clenched right hand into contact with the senator's stomach, causing him to double up with pain. Surprised by his sergeant's act of violence, Morgan rushed to intervene. "Sorry Morg, this asshole had it coming. What he ain't telling you is Frank Jordan and him were in Vietnam together. It was something Thurston told me just before we were air lifted out of Vietnam. Seems he'd got a friend who had himself a number of photographs. Said how they were gonna make his fortune. I didn't pay much attention to it back then, every soldier in that Goddamn war had horror stories to tell, me included." For a moment Jake seemed to go into himself, then quickly he pushed Delaney back into his chair. "Yeah you know what I'm driving at, don't you asshole!"

Joe Delaney's face remained impassive. If there was one thing he'd learnt it was to admit nothing. "I haven't the faintest idea what you're talking about. Get out before I call security."

"Tanh Linh!"

The senator's face crumbled and the colour drained from his face.

"Oh Jesus No!"

Morgan threw his sergeant a quizzical look.

"You remember Mylai, Pinkville, Lieutenant Calley. Well Tanh Linh was a much smaller affair, so small it hardly got more than a mention in the newspapers back home. Thirteen women and small children herded into the centre of their village and systematically raped and then executed on the orders of Captain Joseph Delaney. After the story broke on the Mylai massacre, it became almost a witch hunt on the part of the radicals to punish every known atrocity. Our senator here, well he was well connected with the folks in Washington and the little matter of rape and murder were brushed neatly under the carpet. All would have been well if it hadn't been for Captain Delaney's sergeant who turned out to be none other than Frank Jordan."

"Enough! You don't need to go on. You must remember it was a time of war. None of us were ourselves. It was madness!"

Jake stared hard at the senator, searching his face for remorse. There was none, only blind panic that his secret past had finally caught up with him. "What was it, blackmail?"

The senator looked up, "I hadn't seen or heard from Sergeant Jordan for almost thirty years, until a little under three months ago. He called this office and asked me a small favour. Something about a small matter of jurisdiction. I told him there was nothing I could do.

"Remember Tanh Linh," he said. Memories that I thought I'd erased, flashed before my eyes. I said it was in the past, it happened a long time ago. I even said I'd sue the pants off him. He just laughed at me and asked how many photographs I'd like as a souvenir of our phone call. "What photos?" Then I remembered Sergeant Jordan was a habitual photographer who'd captured some of the most moving scenes of that war. My future was at stake, I had no choice." He looked up at the unsympathetic faces of the two Rangers, imploring them silently.

"Go on. When did you involve Kathleen?" Morgan's tone was mean and menacing.

Nervously the senator continued, "I thought that would be the end of it, but I was wrong. Jordan paid me a visit a few days later, said how a certain Texas Ranger captain and one of his sergeants were still poking their noses where they didn't belong. I said I didn't know how I could be of use. He smiled and said, "You've a pretty niece lives down to Laredo, seems she's been seeing this Ranger captain for a while. That's how." I refused, then as if he'd already figured my move, he threw a photograph onto my desk. It wasn't pretty. After that I had little choice. Believe me, I didn't know anyone was going to get killed."

"So what you're telling me is Kathleen knew nothing about Frank Jordan."

"Believe me," said the senator. "She's given me Hell since that Ranger was killed."

"One last thing senator," said Jake, the disdain clearly apparent in his voice. "If you so much as call Jordan, I'll be back, and next time I won't be so polite."

✶   ✶   ✶   ✶

Morgan stared at the doorbell of Kathleen's condo. After dropping Jake off at the motel he'd driven straight there. On the way over he thought about what he was going to say, now as he hesitated over whether to ring the doorbell or not, the words wouldn't come to him.

The decision was taken away as Kathleen opened the door. Her eyes under that mop of unruly blonde hair looked red and swollen, but it didn't diminish her beauty. It just seemed to radiate from her gentle smile. "I saw you from my window," she said sweetly, "come in."

Nervously Morgan walked into her living room and sat where she indicated. He wanted her. He wanted to reach out and hold her in his arms and say everything was all right, but somehow the magic of their relationship had become tainted. There were questions that needed answering. Questions he was afraid he already knew the answers too.

"Tell me, did you ever really fall in love with me?"

"Oh Morgan, I think you already know the answer. Yes of course I did."

"Why didn't you tell me the truth when we found out Orville was dead?"

"I couldn't. I was confused. I didn't know how you'd react, I was frightened."

"You left without reason. I kept calling you and you never answered."

"Morgan, you have to believe me. I was attracted to you the moment we met in 'Senor Lopez'. We were two of a kind. Neither of us were ready for a serious relationship, though I think I could have been persuaded. When Uncle Joe said you were prejudicing a drugs operation I agreed to help, to stop you getting into trouble. I didn't expect to fall in love with you but I did. When we found out about Orville, I was in a state of confusion. I had to clear my head. Yes I ran. I ran as fast and as far from you as possible. You see I felt responsible. I thought you'd never forgive me."

"I'm sorry too. Sorry that I thought you were involved."

"My Uncle's a good man. If he did something wrong it wasn't of his doing."

Morgan didn't have the heart to tell her about Tanh Linh. She would know soon enough. "Perhaps, after this is all over, we can become friends," he said.

"I'd like that."

At the door to her apartment he turned and lowered his head towards hers. Gently he kissed her salty lips and stroked the mop of unruly hair. Sadly, he broke from their embrace and walked down the steps to the concrete sidewalk. Looking up he smiled, then with a heavy heart turned away.

He'd only just left the city limits when his thoughts turned to Laura. He'd tried ringing her after breakfast and had got no answer. He tried ringing her office and was told she hadn't reported in yet. Stopping at a pay phone Morgan dialled her number, there was no answer. He called her work and was told she'd phoned in and was taking a few days vacation. "Where," he'd asked.

"She didn't say," came the reply. Before he climbed back inside his vehicle he stared at the city lights of Austin. Somewhere in that city of half a million people were two women whom he'd loved and lost. 'Perhaps this was the way it was meant to be, no ties, no commitments, no one to mourn if I don't come back.'

His first thoughts when he woke the following morning were of Kathleen. If somehow he could solve the murder of Orville without involving the senator, then there might be a chance he and Kathleen could get back together. It was a slim chance, but one worth considering. What did he care, that the senator was a war criminal? It had been thirty years. What point would there be raking up so many painful memories. If he could get to Jordan and find those photographs, then none of the Senator's past need come out.

With a spring in his step Morgan climbed inside his sedan and drove off down the highway. For a time he drove parallel to the Rio Grande. Then as the International Bridge came into sight, with its cargo of humanity crossing back and forth he pulled into the curbside and radioed though to the office. "Hi Jake, how's it going?" His tone was jubilant and full of optimism.

"Morgan, I've been trying to reach you. He deserved it the son of a bitch, but it still came as quite a shock."

"What came as quite a shock?" Alarm bells rang inside Morgan's head. The optimism of earlier was slowly evaporating.

"The senator. They found him this morning. He'd stayed late, locked the double doors to his office and hanged himself from a ceiling beam."

"Oh Jesus!" Morgan's optimism hit rock bottom. His chance at making a go of it with Kathleen had been severed, as surely as the rope had strangled the last breath from the senator's body. His second thought was how Frank Jordan was home free. The only evidence to link him to Orville's death had been the Senator. Morgan forced a smile, the inevitability of it had been there since he'd started researching his great grandfather's life. Their lives had taken on strange parallels. From the moment Orville had pointed out the tracks on the bank of the Rio Grande, to the coincidence of Alicia and Juanita, he'd known his destiny would lead him into Mexico. He looked over at the foreboding 'Welcome to Mexico' sign and knew somewhere in the foothills of the Sierra Madre he would find the answer to so many questions, even the mystery of death itself.

Chapter 22

A back street bar in the worst part of Monterrey was where Tony found what he'd been searching for all his life. An angel, an angel of such loveliness that she took his breath away. No older than nineteen, slim with dark hair that reached almost to the small of her back. Sexy, seductive, and very sensual, dangerous with more than a hint of wickedness. She was every man's dream and every woman's nightmare. Her name was Lupe Chavez. She'd been a whore from the age of thirteen. She was unusual in as much as she hadn't been driven into prostitution. She'd openly embraced it from the moment she realised her own sexuality. Older than her years, she soon learnt what men wanted. More importantly, she learned how to hold something back. By the time she was fifteen Lupe only went with the richest of men. At seventeen, one man had died for her affections. Why she operated out of the back streets instead of the posh hotels in the centre of town was anyone's guess. If anything the danger added to the thrill of bedding Lupe Chavez. Her name was enough for the rich and the well connected to seek her out. To those who knew her she had indeed earned her nickname as 'the Dark Angel of Monterrey.'

Tony had observed her up close. She was everything he wanted in a woman. Mesmerised, he concentrated on a small bead of sweat as it trickled between her pert breasts and channelled itself between her cleavage. Driven by lust Tony insisted Ortiz gave him an introduction. "Jesus, Emilio that is one hell of a foxy lady! I've got to have her!"

Ortiz laughed, "She'd eat you alive, my friend!"

"That's what I'm counting on!"

Ortiz grinned, grabbed his companion affectionately around the neck and pushed his way through the crowd towards Lupe Chavez.

"Hello Lupe, it's been a long time," said Emilio Ortiz.

"Not long enough! I thought you were dead."

"No! I'm very much alive. Sorry to disappoint." In the steamy nightclub the air around them became icy cool. "I'd like to introduce you to a friend of mine."

"Forget it. Any friend of yours can't be worth shit!" Lupe spun around and slinked away.

Tony motioned the waiter, "Champagne, French!" Emilio laughed and turned his back. Unperturbed by the brush off Tony walked over to her at the end of the bar.

"Fuck off!"

"That's not the way to treat the man that you're gonna marry," he said and smiled just as the waiter brought the French Champagne. "Leave it," said Tony as he motioned for the bottle and glasses to be left at the end of the bar. Handing the Waiter a hundred dollar bill he added, "Keep it."

Lupe smiled and said, "I thought I told you to fuc......"

"Shush," said Tony as he placed two fingers against her mouth. "Firstly, there's no way I'd call that piece of shit, a friend. Secondly I meant what I just said."

"What!"

"I mean to marry you," he said again. His Latino smile revealed a row of perfect white teeth. "Now I've got you're attention, Champagne?"

Lupe's smile was that of a true professional. "If I'm to marry you, it would help if I knew your name, and what you are doing in such company."

"Tony Valdez. Ortiz is a business associate."

"The drugs business," she added.

"Whatever."

For half an hour he turned on the charm. His wit and repartee soon had her eating out of his hand. He'd always had a magic touch with the ladies. Lupe was no exception. She was like a favourite glove. Her charismatic seductiveness and his charm only increased their interest in each other. Lupe was enjoying herself more than she had for quite some time. That was, until she happened to glance in Emilio Ortiz's direction. He smiled with a knowing leer, it was enough to make her heave. Quickly she turned her face away.

"He's bad news Tony. I meant what I said to him. I wish the scum were dead."

Tony laughed. 'If only she'd known of his last conversation with Esteban Montoya. The drug lord of Ciudad Acuna was high on Peyote when he gave Emilio and Tony his blessing on their departure. As a parting instruction he'd whispered in Tony's ear, "When you come back, make sure that pig doesn't!"

"I'm intrigued. what has Ortiz done to you that's so bad?"

"He raped me!"

"When? Why?"

"It was two years ago. It was at a party in Apodaca."

Tony pricked up his ears, "Apodaca!"

"You know it?"

"No, but I've heard of it." The conversation was beginning to affect the evening, but Tony knew he had to know more. Go on."

"There were several of us girls, enough to go around. It was a swinging party at a large Hacienda in the desert. Everyone was having a good time, until that filthy pig Ortiz said he wanted me. I laughed. At the time I was seeing the guy whose party we were attending. I knew I was safe from that fat creature's clutches. Diego was stoned and laughed, "I give her to you," he said. Like I was a piece of meat. I couldn't believe my ears. I told them both to screw themselves. Diego and Ortiz both laughed. I grabbed for my jacket and made to leave. Before I could reach the door Diego had pinned me to the floor and that beast was astride me. He fucked me in front of everyone. He only took a few minutes, but his face is forever etched in my mind. You see Tony, I ain't an innocent, I don't even know the meaning of the word. I like fucking. But I fuck on my terms. I've fucked more men than you'd ever be able to count. I've been fucked so many ways you wouldn't believe me if I told you." The recollection had soured the evening. Lupe looked Tony square in the eyes and said defiantly, "Well, do you still want to marry me?"

"Yep, marry you and kill that animal into the bargain."

The anger and hatred in her face vanished immediately, as she broke into laughter. That had been two days ago, and Tony was in love. Lupe knew more tricks than he'd thought possible. On their first morning together he awoke to find her straddled across his face, and for one unforgettable moment he thought he'd died and gone to pussy heaven.

Laying in each others arms she said, "You still want to marry me?"

"More than ever," he said.

"I'd fuck your best friend, I'd fuck your brother. I'd even fuck your old man."

"I doubt that. He's dead."

"Sorry." She smiled again and said wickedly, "I'd never be able to remain faithful."

"I don't care."

"When you gonna kill Emilio?"

"Soon. How come you don't feel bad towards this Diego feller?" It was his first chance to bring up the name of the man he'd been sent to kill. If it was him.

"Mucho bad hombre. Him and his brother make Emilio Ortiz look like a boy scout." For the first time he sensed her fear. Gone was the wickedly decadent fun-loving persona, in her place a vulnerable, frightened woman. "You don't speak ill of Diego and Ignacio Morales," she said under her breath.

"Why not?"

"Best you don't ask. I'm bad, worse than you'll ever know, but the Morales brothers are in a league of their own. They were born from Hell's womb." Lupe crossed herself and huddled up into a small ball.

*   *   *   *

Ortiz left him alone for almost two days before he knocked on Lupe's door. "Get your ass down stairs, I got two guys that you'll want to meet."

Lupe shot Tony a look of fear. "Be careful, it's them. I feel it." Reaching behind her neck she undid the clasp of her gold necklace and before handing it to him she kissed the gold crucifix. "For luck, Vaya con Dios."

Checking the nine millimetre, he quickly tucked it in his pants at the small of his back. "Just in case," he said reassuringly. At the door he turned and blew her a kiss. She was the wildest woman he'd ever met. By her own denouncement she was far wickeder than he could imagine. She had no conscience. She had no shame, but looking back, all Tony could see was a frightened young girl.

Chapter 23

San Antonio courthouse was straining with crowds of people. Most there not for the trial (both men were expected to be acquitted) but for the ongoing feud that had reached boiling point. When the verdicts came in, the court room exploded with noise.

As predicted Nathan Kendrickson was acquitted on the charge of unlawful killing and fined two hundred dollars for a breach of the peace. The outcome was never in any doubt. Loretta's social standing and Kendrickson's money had both played their part. Zachariah had wisely kept Tom from attending, suggesting he kept himself as far away from the courthouse as was possible. Understandably Tenpenny was seething with anger but with his own arraignment following so closely after Nathan's court appearance he chose wisely to spend the morning visiting Loretta's grave.

Jasper Kendrickson was ecstatic. He'd never doubted the outcome. With the trial over his biggest fear was for his son's life. He'd hired two ex-lawmen, Billy Owens and J W Barnes, both tough and capable men. Billy Owens, it was alleged, faced down Long Haired Jim Courtwright and Luke Short on the same night. Whether that was true or not didn't concern Kendrickson. The gunning down of two soldiers outside the White Elephant was enough to ensure his reputation. J W Barnes, a more deadlier man you couldn't wish to meet, heralded from Miles City, where he hired out as a stock detective. He'd come highly recommended. At least five rustlers had lost their lives to the bark of his Winchester carbine. Some say he was lucky to get out of Montana territory alive. These men didn't come cheap, and Jasper had more important things for them to do, apart from entrusting them with spiriting Nathan away from the courthouse. Jasper and several others stayed in their seats, eagerly awaiting their chance on the witness stand.

Zachariah and Ethan Book, both heavily armed, brought Tom to the city courthouse fifteen minutes after Nathan's acquittal. Tension between both factions left the Sheriff with a monumental task of arranging security. Everyone, except law officers, were searched for concealed weapons. The tension in the courthouse was electric.

Tom Tenpenny was found not guilty on the grounds of self-defence. Jasper protested, Bob Schaffer cheered, the crowd went wild. After the roar and hullabaloo had died down, the judge ordered Zachariah and Jasper Kendrickson to sign a peace agreement. 'Little good that did Stoudenmire when the city councillors ordered him and the Mannings to sign such an agreement,' thought Zachariah. Though no words of warmth passed between the two factions it looked as if peace was finally being restored in the part of town known as the Military Plaza.

For days nothing major happened in and around the plaza. Kendrickson kept his men under control, while Tom Tenpenny went back to his Monte table. The killing of Clay McCulloh and the ensuing trial had sobered Tom dramatically. So much so he'd agreed not to cause trouble, a fact that relieved Zachariah immensely.

Just as things had settled back to normal the inevitable happened. Trouble looked imminent when Newt Padbury and Josh Randolph entered the Military Plaza saloon five days after the trials. Bob Schaffer reached behind the bar for his shotgun.

"Easy man! We ain't packing," said Padbury as he pulled back his coat to reveal he wasn't armed. "Just want us a friendly game is all."

Bob looked across at Tom, who nodded that it was okay. Nevertheless the vigilant barman kept the scatter gun within easy reach. Tom kept his cool and made light of the situation, a fact that caused Randolph's temper to flare. "Any time you've a mind," said Tom with the practised cool of a man killer. Newt Padbury somehow managed to calm the big feller down and order was restored. Bob gave Tom a worried frown, which the little gambler shrugged off. Tense as the night had been, there was no trouble, though Tom thought long and deep about how easily Padbury had been able to restrain Randolph.

It wasn't long after that, perhaps a couple of days before Jasper Kendrickson paid the Military Plaza a visit. He walked in unannounced and walked over to the table where Zachariah was dealing Faro. "Mind if I play a few hands. Professional curiosity, you understand," he said and grinned at the tall lawman.

"Your money is as good as any," replied Zachariah.

"I'm glad to hear it," said Jasper.

He stayed about an hour, joked with the crowd and made a show of friendliness. Zachariah smiled in turn, but no warmth emanated from his eyes. It was unlike Kendrickson to leave things be, but to all intent and purposes that's exactly what he was doing.

Over the next two weeks, the tension that had existed between both camps eased considerably. Ethan moved from the Military Plaza saloon into a boarding house not more that six blocks away. He'd told Zachariah he preferred it that way.

"I ain't saying I don't like Tom, just that I don't make a habit of sleeping in a house that is packed with high explosives."

"I understand," said Zachariah with a wry grin, "But when trouble's a brewing I'm glad Tom Tenpenny's a friend rather than an enemy."

"You reckon Kendrickson will try something?"

"I feel it in my bones. He's playing the waiting game. Soon as we relax, he'll hit us." The easing of tensions only seemed to increase Zachariah's anxiety.

"If you want me to hang around for a few days?" said Ethan.

"Nope, you best head out and check on the rustling over to the McAllister spread."

Ethan tipped his hat, "See you late Saturday night."

"I'll be here," said Zachariah, then he called after the slim Ranger. "If you've a mind, ask around, see if Alicia Morales is back from Mexico." Zachariah had tried sounding casual, but his tone was anything but. Ethan threw him a knowing look, then disappeared through the bat-wing doors of the saloon.

Long hours of waiting for the inevitable had told on Zachariah. With time to kill he'd begun to drink more, and his thoughts inevitably turned to Alicia. She could never be his, she was a married woman. It didn't matter that her husband was a murdering scoundrel. What counted in the eyes of her church were the vows she'd taken. He was a fool to waste time thinking about her. Drink wouldn't solve his dilemma, all it would do was get him killed. In his heart he wanted it over with. He wanted Kendrickson out of the way.

If he was still alive after that then he had himself a notion to ride out to the Morales ranch and check if Alicia was all right. If she was happy then he had a mind to let it be. He'd say his farewells and then leave Texas. He knew he'd never forget her, that she'd live forever in his heart, but her happiness came first. Putting distance between himself and Xavier Morales was the safest thing for all concerned. He'd seen the look in her husband's eyes. The old Mexican had wanted to kill him, just as surely as he'd taken the lives of those young boys.

'But why?' thought Zachariah as he looked at the world from the bottom of his glass. The answer hit him like a thunderbolt. So blind had he been, he'd thought it kindness, but the old Mexican had known. Deep in Xavier's heart he knew he was losing her. His jealousy raged like a fiery furnace, the flames fanned by passion, scorching everyone that stood to close. It was burning out of control. The sudden thought caused Zachariah to exclaim out loud, "Those boys weren't killed for rustling. They were killed as a warning to me. A warning to stay away!"

The drink had a numbing effect, yet it distorted his thoughts. One day he'd be up, the next he was down. He'd sensed there was something between them, yet his stoic Victorian upbringing had forced it to the back of his mind. Why would she look at a man like him? The realisation that she cared for him seemed to lift his spirits. He couldn't explain it, but every day that passed seemed to draw him closer to her.

It was Friday night and Zachariah was in a jubilant mood. He'd made up his mind. He wasn't going to wait any longer. He was going out to the Morales ranch the day after Ethan Book returned. With Ethan and Tom to mind the store, he reckoned to be gone no longer than two days. If things worked against him and he came home alone, then Kendrickson could have at it, Zachariah was ready to fight.

"Hey Bob, join me in a game of stud."

Bob Schaffer whipped off his apron and strolled over to the green baize table. "I don't mind if I do," he said and pulled up a chair. A sickening thud caught Bob high in the chest. He didn't hear the crack of the rifle, only the tinkling of broken glass cascading to the floor. In his death throes his hand gripped tightly on the back of the chair and he crashed heavily to the ground. Zachariah threw himself flat, drawing his gun as he landed. One glance was enough for him to see Bob Schaffer was dead. His eyes already misting over as they stared emptily at the ornate chandelier that hung from the centre of the ceiling.

"Zack you okay?" shouted Tom from his vantage point close to the door.

"Yeah, they killed Bob! Can you see anything? That shot came from the direction of Frenchie's, if I miss my guess."

"I'd say," agreed the little Monte dealer. "That was one helluva shot. From that distance there's only two men who could have done it, and one of them is out looking for rustlers. Guess that means it's the work of that no good back-shooter J W Barnes."

"I reckon," agreed Zachariah.

Tom saw the peril of their situation. Illuminated by the chandeliers, they were sitting targets. "Douse the lights!" Tenpenny shouted across to a scared and bloodied Fanny Shelton, the resident madam. She'd been within touching distance of Bob when he was killed. Crawling as fast as she could, Fanny made her way to the back of the bar and found the tap. Quickly she turned off the gas, and the saloon was plummeted into darkness.

Eager to avenge his friend, Tom shouted across to Zachariah, "I say we rush the sons of bitches!"

"No Tom! That's what Kendrickson wants." Zachariah's first reaction was to do as Tom had suggested. He wanted it over, but his instinct for survival kicked in. "We wait, the sheriff and his committee should be along in a while. We sit tight until he arrives."

"Shit!" The anger and frustration in Tom's voice was mirrored by the tall lawman on the other side of the room. Sitting tight wasn't Zachariah's style, but sometimes the waiting game paid off. It was only a single shot but the news would soon reach the other side of town, that the Military Plaza saloon was under siege.

It seemed an eternity before Sheriff Thadeus Youngerman and his ten strong committee, all heavily armed, descended on the plaza. "Secure the area," they heard Youngerman shout. Running footsteps crashed on the sidewalks as the committee fanned out around the plaza. Once the sheriff was satisfied everywhere was secured, he walked into the darkness of the Military Plaza saloon.

"What happened here?"

"Bob Schaffer's dead. Killed by Kendrickson's men," shouted Tom angrily.

"Hold your horses. You caint go making accusations," said Thadeus Youngerman.

"The hell I caint!"

"This is my town! You do what the fuck I tell you!" countered the sheriff. "Zack, best you come with me. Tom you stay put! You hear!" Tom swore at the sheriff.

"Easy Tom," said Zachariah, doing his best to calm the fiery Ranger.

Not wanting to get into a quarrel, Thadeus turned on his heels and walked rapidly towards Frenchie's, "Hello the saloon, this is Sheriff Thadeus Youngerman, so hold those shooting irons." Zachariah walked at his side, both men mounting the sidewalk together. Inside the saloon they found Kendrickson, Nathan, Padbury, and Billy Owens sitting around a card table.

"Can I help you gentlemen?" Jasper Kendrickson said mockingly. Without warning Zachariah wrenched him from his chair and threw him across the room. Jasper was on his feet in seconds and coming at Zachariah with an eight inch Bowie knife.

"Keep a coming," said Zachariah as he cocked the hammer of his Peacemaker. Kendrickson was mad as all hell, and within spitting distance of doing just that.

"Easy, dammit! There's been enough violence for one night," screamed Sheriff Youngerman.

Jasper halted in his tracks and put the blade back in its sheath. "I think I could have taken you," he said.

"Thinking ain't doing," replied Zachariah.

At that moment one of the committee members came running into the saloon excitedly, "Sheriff, we just found a spent cartridge in the alley between the saloon and the dry goods store!"

Without taking his eyes off Kendrickson, the tall Ranger uncocked his revolver and holstered it. "Let me see that damn cartridge," he said. Grabbing it from the man's grasp he sniffed at it. "Guess this is it, its recently been fired." It was a 44.40 calibre, the same calibre as J W Barnes used in his Winchester carbine. "Where's J W Barnes?"

"He's over to the Bon Ton on Fremont," said Billy Owens. His eyes coldly calculating the cut of the lawman, like an undertaker measuring his client. "J W owns a Winchester sure, but so does half the population of San Antonio."

Zachariah gave him a harsh look, then turning to Sheriff Youngerman he said, "J W Barnes is a suspect in the killing of Bob Schaffer, I intend bringing him in for questioning."

The sheriff knew better than to ask whether that would be alive or dead. Turning before the sheriff could object, Zachariah stalked out of the saloon. Outside he gathered his thoughts quickly. The Bon Ton was four blocks west of the Plaza. If he moved swiftly, with luck, he could catch the man unawares.

Five minutes later, Zachariah stood breathlessly outside the Bon Ton. Catching his breath he pushed open the doors to the saloon. A sudden thought caught him, 'How many similar such doors had he passed through in his career not knowing whether he would live or die?' Through the crowded smoky atmosphere he advanced. As the crowds parted he spied the man he was looking for, sitting at a table with his back to the adobe wall. He knew it was him by the cut of his hat, and the beady eyes that were staring straight at him. Most Texans wore wide brimmed hats to keep the sun from their faces. Cowboys from the northern plains wore hats with a narrow brim and were more prone to wear it with a Montana peak. (the crown had all four sides pushed in to form a single peak). Zachariah moved closer to J W Barnes. The Winchester carbine lay propped against the back wall. It was too easy. Something was wrong. At that moment Zachariah realised he'd been suckered. The Montana gunman grinned and stood up. A Remington 44 calibre pistol lay within easy reach on the table in front of him. The tall lawman knew then that he should have retired one door ago. The trap had been sprung and he was about to enter purgatory. Determined to take the Montanan with him he brought his gun up and aimed at his adversary. "You're under arrest!"

J W Barnes was a mite slower, but that didn't matter in the full plan of things. Josh Randolph and Lucky Charlie, both standing a few yards behind the lawman, were about to turn the Ranger into a sieve.

"Boom!"

Josh Randolph's face just managed to register a look of surprise as a .44/90 slug from Ethan Book's Creedmour tore the life out of him. J W Barnes tried desperately to thumb the hammer back as the flash of flame from Zachariah's Peacemaker spat death.

Lucky Charlie unnerved by the sudden appearance of Ethan Book, threw his gun to the ground and raced out of the saloon. It was Friday the thirteenth of September and Lucky Charlie's luck had finally run out. Ethan barged his way through the double doors and took a stance in the middle of the street. Taking careful aim, he waited a few seconds before squeezing the trigger. The bullet made a swacking sound as it entered the back of Lucky Charlie. The momentum of the bullet propelled him several yards before he finally fell to ground.

Zachariah looked at the crumpled body of J W Barnes and thought of what might have been. He glanced up as Ethan Book walked through the door of the Bon Ton. "If I miss my guess I'd say you was a day early."

"I'd say you'd better get yourself over to the Menger Hotel. There's a certain senorita just checked in."

Zachariah looked at his saviour and couldn't believe what he was saying. "You mean..?"

"Well, who else would I mean?"

Chapter 24

He'd phoned Kathleen immediately he heard the news. The hostility in her voice was unmistakable. She blamed him for her uncle's death.

"What did you say to him? What did he do that was so bad? You killed him as surely as if you'd placed the rope around his neck!"

She didn't know why he did it. Confused, tortured by grief and frustration she hit out at the man she considered responsible. She wanted answers, all she knew was that it was connected to Morgan's visit.

He wanted to tell her it was far more complex, that his visit was just the final straw, that thirty years of guilt had finally caught up with the senator. The temptation to tell her the full gory details was almost too much, but somehow he managed to bite his tongue. What good would it do if she learned the bitter truth? Would it bring Kathleen and him closer together? 'Would it hell,' he thought angrily.

"I'm sorry. I'm so sorry."

"Sorry don't cut it. Goodbye Morg," and then his phone went dead.

Frustrated and numbed by the turn of events, Morgan stared at the receiver for a few seconds before placing another call to his ex-wife's office. She still hadn't checked in.

"Damn! Damn! Damn!" he shouted and thumped the dashboard. Controlling his anger, he looked again across the river at the 'Welcome to Mexico' sign.

Everything pointed to Hacienda Morales. From the moment he and Kathleen had stepped inside the house he'd sensed a feeling of pure evil. That the Morales brothers were Jordan's paymasters he had no doubt. That they'd murdered their own sister and butchered her family he wasn't one hundred percent sure. To kill in such a way was without precedence. What reasons lay behind so evil an act he couldn't begin to imagine.

With the death of the senator, Morgan's case against Frank Jordan had crumbled. Without Joe Delaney's testimony there was nothing to link the DEA man with the murders of Orville Tyson and Lou Thurston. They were back where they started. The only thing in Morgan's favour was the small fact, that Frank Jordan didn't have the faintest idea the Rangers were on to him.

He'd known almost from the day that Orville had been murdered what he would have to do. He'd hoped there was another way, but with the senator's untimely death that avenue was closed to him. He drove down to the river's edge and sat there staring at the muddy waters. After what seemed like a moment, but was in fact half an hour, he patched a call through to Jake and arranged a meeting at 'the Dead Mustang'.

Jake Hamilton drove with the window of the Explorer open. The air conditioner had packed up. Another sure sign he should trade it in for the new Ford Expedition Blythe had been nagging at him to get. As he turned off the freeway and began motoring down the old highway Jake spotted a flash of light, probably from Morgan's binoculars, he thought absentmindedly. The neon sign of the 'Dead Mustang' was barely visible in the afternoon sunlight as Jake turned into the parking lot.

"Seen you a mile off. Those glasses are a surefire give away," said Jake motioning towards the binoculars in Morgan's right hand.

"I guess they are, but they told me aplenty. The fact you ain't been followed proves one thing. Frank Jordan thinks he's home and dry, which tells me Tony's cover ain't been blown. With the senator dead, things can work in our favour. Let's go eat."

In the booth at the far end of the bar, they ordered a couple of cheeseburgers and a bottle of Budweiser a piece. Morgan waited until the waitress had taken their order before speaking.

"So far we got three names, Diego Morales and his brother Ignacio, what proof we've got against them ain't worth spit. At this moment we've got the senator's word that Frank Jordan blackmailed him into taking the case off us. We got documented proof that the senator was contacted by Jordan and that he in turn had been contacted by person or persons unknown from a call box in Apodaca."

"The evidence is too vague, we'd never get a conviction," said Jake as he removed his hat and wiped the sweat from his forehead. "Even if we did, those chilli eaters are so well connected we'd never get an extradition warrant." Jake looked across the table at his captain. "Jesus H Christ! You ain't thinking what I think you're a thinking."

Morgan's face remained passive, but his eyes told a different story. "We take em out!"

"You cain't be serious!"

"More serious than I've been about anything in my entire life," Morgan's tone was low and menacing.

"You've known all along. You've known we wouldn't get enough evidence to convict. That's why you brought in Valdez."

"Jake, you're a good man, and I'll understand if you ain't with me."

"Oh Jeez Morg, it ain't that! I agree those sons of bitches need killing, but it's going against everything we stand for."

"I got no other choice."

"Hell Morgan, everyone's got a choice. Okay, so Kathleen's history, but what about Laura? I know she still loves you!"

Morgan snapped back angrily, "Leave the Goddamn women outta it!"

"If you had Laura to go home to, you'd think twice about risking all," countered Jake.

"That's maybe so, but I cain't let those butchers roam free. Hell it'd stick in my craw."

"How can you be sure they're guilty?"

"Good question. That's why Tony's risking his life at this very moment. I won't move until I'm absolutely sure we've got the right men."

"Morg, it's Blythe and the kids. I cain't risk it. I'll help as far as it goes, but when you cross that line, you're on your own."

"That's all I can ask Jake."

* * * *

"Hey Tony, when are you gonna ditch the slut?" shouted Emilio Ortiz across the restaurant floor.

"Emilio, that's no way to talk about the woman that's going to become my wife," he retorted playfully.

"I hate the fucking pig! Why do we have to dine with him?" moaned Lupe in a half whisper.

"Because he's important to my plans and besides don't you want to be there when I bust a cap on him?" said Tony in the matter of fact manner he'd so recently adopted.

"Oh Tony, you say the sweetest things," for a moment she smiled then just as quickly it disappeared. "Just make sure I'm sitting as far away from him as possible."

Ortiz was proving himself invaluable. His contacts were both interesting and useful. The Morales brothers had been a revelation. When he descended the stairs of Lupe's apartment, he'd expected to meet two oversized grease balls, with hair tied back in pony tails. Instead he'd found them both muscular and well-groomed men, expensive suits and Italian shoes. Mexico's answer to Goodfellas, thought Tony, tongue in cheek. Diego, older by two years was both handsome and charming, a real ladies' man, though his smile lacked warmth. Ignacio, an inch shorter, wore his hair long but made no attempt to tie it up. He smiled sparingly through his thin cruel lips, giving the impression of a man who had little compassion for others. His high cheekbones and pockmarked face were the only concessions to a childhood of poverty, but this hardly detract from his playboy looks now. But it was their arrogance towards all kinds of authority that struck Tony the most. More than that, both men thought they were invincible, invulnerable to harm, almost Godlike in their belief of total power.

Intrigued by Emilio Ortiz's tale of Tony's silence, the Morales brothers were interested in meeting him. Valdez told them of his plans to rest awhile in Tampico before eventually going back to Ciudad Acuna. How he was hoping to make a few scores along the way and how grateful he'd be, given a helping hand.

"There's money to be earned here," said Ignacio, "if you've the stomach for it."

Tony neither flinched nor made any reaction, other than to ask how much.

Ignacio laughed, "Amigo, you're either one cool dude or one crazy bastard."

"Take your pick!"

Even Diego laughed, "Hey brother, I think this mother fucker is shitting you."

Ignacio's face turned into an ugly snarl, "Is that true? Are you shitting me?" A stiletto appeared as if by magic, in his hand.

Tony raised his hands. There was a seriousness to his voice, "Hey man, do I look stupid?"

Ignacio looked puzzled, unsure what to say next. A nervous tic played at the side of his mouth. He looked to his brother for support. Diego grinned reassuringly. Ignacio's eyes lit up and without warning, he threw his right arm around Tony's shoulders, "Hey, I like you man. Mucho grande cohonies."

Tony's laughter was hesitant at first. Then realising he'd passed inspection, he began to laugh more heartily. He'd walked into the lair of Esteban Montoya, with his heart in his mouth, not knowing whether he'd live or die. He'd known the enemy. He'd lived side by side with them for months on end. Yet the constant danger of them turning on him had never been far from his mind. But these two brothers were different somehow. More unpredictable, more dangerous than any one he'd ever known. Tony couldn't quite put his finger on it, until he remembered what Morgan had said about entering Hacienda Morales. Evil, that was it. An aura of evil surrounded both men like nothing else. Tony could feel his heart pounding. He was beginning to sweat. He hoped the smell of Calvin Klein helped to mask his fear. Ignacio played with the point of the stiletto, then absent-mindedly closed the blade and put it away.

Years of working undercover had perfected Tony's chameleon-like qualities. His instinct for survival was never sharper than when bleeding in a pool of sharks and at that precise moment, if they'd asked him to blow away the city's chief of police he wouldn't have hesitated.

Five days had passed since his first meeting with the Morales brothers and thankfully he'd not had any dealings since, until now. Ortiz had phoned and demanded he meets with him in the restaurant.

"Diego has a proposition for you," said Ortiz through a mouthful of refried beans. "He's invited you and…" the hesitation was intentional, "your lovely fiancee to Hacienda Morales. He's throwing a party and expects you there."

Lupe threw Tony a look of apprehension and tugged at his arm. "I ain't going!"

"Don't worry slut, I'm already spoken for," said Ortiz with a knowing leer.

"Hey, watch your mouth! She's with me, you tub of guts!" Tony kicked himself for his outburst, and tried sounding like he didn't care, but his tone was unmistakable. What's more Emilio Ortiz had picked up on it.

It was approaching dusk as they drove through the gates of wrought iron. Tony stared in fascinated horror, as their limousine edged closer to Hacienda Morales. The amber rays from the dying sun danced across the red tiles and splayed out like a demonic angel's wings. The Moorish towers, blackened silhouettes against the blood red sky, lent themselves an aura of pending evil.

He'd counted two guards at the gates, another three patrolling the courtyard and at least two manning the towers. 'Jesus, Morgan must be the world's biggest optimist. At a guess I'd say this outfit had another couple of men riding fence, twenty-four hours a day. Some wage bill.'

The party was in full swing when they arrived. Ortiz excitedly pushed his way forward and promptly disappeared into an array of bodies. Lupe stuck close to Tony as they mingled with the thronging crowd. Here and there she smiled, rebuffed sexual advances, exchanged innuendos, grabbed at the crotch of a stranger, gave the come on to all and sundry, but not once did she let go of his arm. This was her world, an ocean of decadent writhing flesh. But in a week she'd changed. No longer hell bent on self destruction, but a woman who had finally found what she'd been searching for all her young life. The realisation frightened her. Everywhere people were shooting up, sniffing cocaine, performing acts of gross indecency. An orgy straight from the court of Caligula. It was stepping back in time to the days of the Roman Empire. Suddenly Lupe Chavez understood. In the midst of this decadence she'd finally found a man worthy of her. She hoped, as she moved through the writhing mass, that fate hadn't conspired against her.

For an hour they mingled and chatted, with the police chief, several local politicians, a fading matinee idol, an up and coming tennis player, in fact a who's who of Monterrey. Then Ortiz re-appeared.

"You're wanted upstairs," he said. Tony grabbed Lupe's hand and turned towards the stairs. "Just you!" The pleasure in Emilio's voice was undisguised.

Lupe exchanged a fearful look with Tony. "Don't leave me!" Tony's eyes glared at Ortiz, the words unspoken.

"No need to worry I'm coming with you," hissed Ortiz

"Don't worry baby, I'll be back as soon as I can."

Tony and Ortiz ascended the stairs two at a time. At the top Tony glanced back at Lupe who'd been monopolised by the police chief and his wife. At that moment he realised how beautiful she was, and how much she'd transformed his life. More and more he began to think about his stash hidden in the sewers, not far from Madero's. When his mission was over he was heading back to Ciudad Acuna. With the money he could disappear, start a new life, perhaps even a family. And in his thoughts Lupe Chavez figured prominently.

They walked along the corridor until they came to a double door. Ortiz smiled and turned the knob. A tall albino Mexican with a glass of scotch in his hand looked across then ignoring the intruders continued to share a joke with a man in a white shirt. They were by the side of a well-stocked bar, while a short guy, American if Tony wasn't mistaken, sat at a small table cleaning a massive looking revolver, so big it looked as it didn't belong to him. Lounging on an easy chair watching a porno movie was Diego Morales. His brother Ignacio was helping himself to a drink from behind the bar in the far corner of the room. Acknowledging the visitors, Ignacio asked what they wanted to drink. Ignoring their requests he grabbed a couple of glasses and filled them with ice then poured over a generous helping of pure malt. The scotch fizzed and crackled in the glass as Ignacio handed them the drinks.

Diego freeze framed the television and stood up. From his jacket pocket he produced an envelope. "There's fifty thousand dollars, it's yours," he said and slapped it into Tony's palm.

"Who do I have to kill?" It was the standard one liner, but the moment Tony said it, he wished he hadn't.

Diego reached into his jacket again and brought out another envelope. "His name is Rodrigo De la Fuente! Everything that you need to know is contained in that envelope."

Ignacio looked across and smiled, "You may well ask why we've paid you in advance." Then in a voice so devoid of emotion he added coldly, "As far as we're concerned the job is already done." The implication wasn't lost on Tony Valdez.

Masking his nervousness Tony asked as casually as was possible,"When's it got to happen?" He needed to know how much time he had.

"It's all in the envelope," said Diego. "Go back down, enjoy the party." Dismissing Tony he sat down and pressed the remote control. The blonde with the extra large tits awoke from her freeze frame position and continued sucking the huge cock. "Wait a minute," cried Diego, "I'd like to share something with you, it's my favourite bit." Diego looked at the small crowd, at the tall albino in the sharp suit in particular and laughed, "Did I say bit, what I meant to say was bits!" The crowd roared at their boss's attempt at humour.

Tony's eyes involuntarily sought out the flickering of the television screen. In a macabre surreal slowing down of time he forced himself to watch. As the story reached its climax he was left wondering if the woman filling up the screen knew what was about to happen, he hoped to God she didn't. Forced by an unreal fascination his eyes stared in horror as the screen turned red in an orgy of violence, "Ohhh......." Tony's legs almost buckled, the bile retched forward. Stealing himself he swallowed back the vomit in his throat, and turned deathly white.

"I think we understand each other," said Diego.

Chapter 25

Zachariah stopped at the front entrance to the Menger Hotel and brushed the dust off his suit. He'd just killed a man, normally his revulsion at the deed would have had him reaching for a bottle, but the knowledge that Alicia was in town had pushed the death of J W Barnes to the back of his mind. He'd dreamed of this moment so many times in the past months, yet now the time was upon him, he began to have doubts. Nervously he walked into the grand lobby of the hotel.

Making sure his badge was prominently displayed, he adopted an air of authority and walked over to the reception desk. The desk clerk looked up as the Ranger towered over him. "Yes sir, can I help you."

"Senorita Morales, what room?"

"Eh, let me see now," he said rather timidly. "Ah here it is, room 207. If you look to your right, there's a flight of stairs. She's on the second floor."

"Obliged," said Zachariah turning on his heels and advancing to the stairway.

"Sir, the young lady, she's not in any trouble?"

Zachariah looked uncomfortably at the hotel clerk, ignored the question, then turned back to the stairs and began to climb. At the top he walked along a beautifully decorated corridor. 'Things have changed considerably since I last visited,' he mused as he admired the lime green and gold wall-

paper that adorned the walls. Nervously he counted down the golden numbers on each of the doors, until he reached Alicia's room.

An hour before he'd faced certain death in a grimy saloon, but the fear and apprehension was as nothing compared to how he felt at that moment. Only the dark green door stood between him and destiny. Hesitantly he removed his hat and nervously ran his fingers through his dark greying hair. Self-consciously he smoothed at his moustache, only to discover he hadn't shaved for the past two days. He was about to flee as his nervousness turned to blind panic, but it was too late. Sensing someone was about to knock, Alicia opened the door.

"Zachariah, you weren't thinking of leaving?" Her eyes took on a mischievous glint as she realised she'd caught him in mid flight.

"Alicia!" He stared in awe. She was far more beautiful than he'd first remembered. Dressed only in a night gown, her hair still damp from washing, she looked a vision of loveliness.

"Well, who else would you expect." She stifled a grin as the great brute of a man began to blush.

"I mean…oh hell I don't know what I mean. One of my men said you were in town." It was all coming out wrong. 'It's a mistake, what the hell am I doing here,' his mind raced for answers.

"Zachariah, come here!"

Even though her forthrightness shocked him, he instinctively took her in his arms and pulled her to him. "Alicia," he cried, not knowing, nor caring, where their embrace would take them. She tilted her face up towards his, her eyes, dark limpid pools of unfathomable depth, probing his very soul. He was lost in a garden of such beauty that the harshness of his life seemed so very far away. He had an irresistible urge to kiss her sensual lips, but he'd forgotten how. Instead he gazed lovingly into her delicately sculpted face. For one unstoppable moment he thought the outcome at the Bon Ton was a mistake and he was being greeted at the doors of heaven by one of God's dark angels.

Alicia's mouth trembled as she waited for the expected kiss. "I tried, I tried forgetting you. That's one of the reasons why I went home, that and the business my husband has gotten into." Pausing for a second, her eyes misted over.

"Alicia, are you all right?" Her sudden change, frightened Zachariah.

Shrugging off the melancholy mood, her eyes took on renewed life, "Sorry, please forgive me, ever since Don Xavier got involved with the Cuban insurrection he's become a changed man."

Zachariah hardly heard her, so caught up in her embrace, the sweetness of her breath, the intoxication of her perfume. So many years of denying himself the comfort of a woman, had caused him to lose all sense of reality. He'd dreamed of this moment, never really believing it could happen. Yet now it had, he was frightened to let go, afraid the spell would be broken forever. He so desperately wanted to kiss her. Sensing his need Alicia reached up on tip toes and found his mouth. The gentle brushing of lips sent a charge of electricity running through Zachariah's veins. Pulling her closer to him, his lips fused with hers. His whole body came alive, adrenaline flew out of control, he wanted the kiss to last forever. When finally Alicia was able to break away she stared up at him, her breath ragged with desire, her eyes dark and smouldering. Pulling him down, her mouth sought his, coaxing, teasing until his kisses became stronger and more passionate. Stepping backwards into the room, Alicia managed to get a toe to the door.

The moon cast its glow across the room. As the shaft of blue-grey light shone into his eyes, he awoke and sat up in bed. Was it a dream? So vivid, yet surreal. Could God be so cruel? The answer lay at his side, snuggled up beside him like an innocent child. His heart beat a little faster as he recalled the events of the night. How clumsy he'd been at first. Her understanding of how years of celibacy made the act of making love just that little bit harder. Yet patiently she'd coaxed him, with tender words of affection, until he became comfortable with their nakedness and intimacy. And finally the sheer joy of coupling, the ecstasy of it all. He'd never known the art of making love could be so beautiful.

Climbing naked out of bed, he walked towards the open window. It was a beautiful night, with the moonlight casting an eerie glow over the limestone walls of the Alamo. Not for the first time, he thought about those brave men who had given their lives so fearlessly in the fight for freedom. Everyone knew of the Alamo and its gallant defenders, but as the new century loomed, Zachariah wondered whether it would still seem so glorious a hundred years hence.

Zachariah looked up at the North Star and wept. He was happy, happier than he'd been his whole life. Yet his life was in constant turmoil. Making love to Alicia had been the most moving and memorable moment of his life. She was everything he could ever want in a woman, but had she come too late? Earlier that evening he'd stared death in the face, and laughed at its impetuosity. He was embroiled in a fight to the finish, and the game was only half done. If he survived the coming weeks and months, would they be able to start life anew? After the excitement of their affair, would Alicia so young and full of life, still feel the same? He didn't know what was worse, wanting her for so long, or the thought that now he'd got her, would he be able to keep her?

Before he'd time to delve too deeply into his melancholic world, Alicia slipped up behind him and embraced his waist. "Zack darling, why look so sad?"

"I'm not sad, I've never been happier."

"Well come back to bed and show me just how happy you are," she teased.

The looks they received as they came down for breakfast, caused Alicia to break into fits of laughter. Zachariah loosened his collar, the embarrassment was almost unbearable, until he looked at the bright young face that stared across the table at him. 'To hell with Victorian values, most of those stuffy men with their disapproving wives would give a fortune to be sitting where I'm sitting.'

Over breakfast Alicia filled in the gaps of her life. She told him how she'd truly loved Xavier, despite the difference in age. Was it love? Well Alicia liked to think so. Young and innocent, Xavier had swept her off her feet. He'd been her mentor, a man she could look up to, a man to love and respect. He'd taught her everything. He'd been a wonderfully kind and *gentle lover, teaching her things she'd never dreamed possible. Teasingly Alicia said she'd been a willing pupil. Zachariah told her to skip over that part of her life. She smiled and laughed off his pomposity. He looked sombre and sad until she stuck out her tongue. He broke into a smile, then laughed. Such was her spell over him. He asked her to continue. She gave him an impish grin then told him that until Xavier happened along, she'd never ridden a horse. The closest she'd come to a horse was an old tired donkey that fetched and carried for her village. Xavier was a fine horseman and soon taught her to ride. "He was good to me in so many ways. He taught me to read and write. He taught me history and Latin, he was everything to me. And then it was over. He'd taught me too much to soon. If I'd had children, maybe things would have been different." She paused and took a drink of water. "Don't get me wrong, I still loved him, but it was turning into a different kind of love. I loved him as a brother. I tried not to show my feelings, but Xavier is a man of the world. It didn't take him long to understand what had happened." Alicia looked around the breakfast room, they were the last people there. "Oh I've talked too much, we'd better go."*

"No it's fine, go on, I'm fascinated," said Zachariah.

Alicia looked hesitant, "It's just that everything turned ugly after that. I don't mean he beat me or anything like that. But men only had to look at me and he'd go into a jealous rage. He changed. It was gradual, but as the years moved on, it became more frequent. He even accused me of having an affair with Rafael, just because he took me riding every Sunday before church. I told Xavier he was being ridiculous, that I only had eyes for one man. I was always able to talk him around. After each outburst we'd make love and things would go on much as they had before. Until that awful night a few weeks before you rode up to the ranch for the first time. A young man a vaquero from the old country happened by. We were always excited about news from home and listened avidly as he regaled us with stories of people and places we all knew. And then one morning he was gone, no explanation no goodbyes, he just simply vanished. I found out a week later, he'd made a terrible mistake. He happened to ask whether Don Xavier's daughter was spoken for. After I had retired for the night Xavier had him taken to the barn and stripped. Then my kindly husband took a whip to him. By the time Xavier had vented his feelings the poor man's back was just a gaping mass of torn flesh. I think my husband would have killed him if it hadn't been for one of the servants who bathed the young vaquero's wounds and sent him on his way. When I learnt the truth I threatened to move out. It was more than Xavier could bear. He began to cry and begged me to stay. He begged for my forgiveness. He promised never to do anything like it again. You must understand this man had given me everything. He'd made me what I am. In the end I couldn't leave him. That was a week before you came."

"I see, it all fits," said Zachariah, understanding only too well her husband's torment.

"In Xavier's eyes you were no threat. You were stuffy, stand-offish, Victorian both in manner and attitude, you were no threat to him. But my husband was wrong. The moment I first laid eyes on you, I knew you were the one." Her eyes glowed warm and she reached across the table and brushed playfully at the three days growth of beard. *"I knew you'd return. It was on your second visit that he began to suspect I had feelings for you. Right after that my husband sent me back to the old country on the pretext I was visiting relatives. I was, but his reasons were twofold. He wanted me out of the way when you next came to visit. I think he had plans to have you killed. As luck had it, you came with a friend and there had been an incident with rustlers. I think he saw a way of using you to capture the cow thieves and have you killed into the bargain. When I got back and found out what he'd done to those two young rustlers I knew I had to leave him. By then I knew he'd never let me go, so I waited my chance. I took it, when he personally took a shipment down to Old Mexico."*

"Shipment? What shipment?"

"Your government have been supplying the Cuban revolutionaries with weapons. The American government, though sympathetic to their cause, couldn't be seen to be supporting the insurrection against Spain. So they employed men like Xavier to be their go-between. As a citizen of Mexico he

could come and go as he pleased without causing any suspicion. Once a month we've been sending consignments of weapons to the coast, to a place called Laguna Madre where a blockade runner takes the guns and ships them to Cuba. It's very political, there are some members of your government who advocate a war against Spain, but others who will go to any lengths to avoid it. According to Xavier they won't be able to stay out of the conflict for much longer."

"So that's why he has immunity against arrest," said Zachariah more to himself than Alicia. "When are you expecting Xavier to return?"

"In about a month."

"Good, at least we've time," he said thoughtfully.

"Time for what?" she countered mischievously.

"Time to get to know each other," he said with a wink.

* * * *

When later that morning he rode into the Military Plaza, he found the place crawling with soldiers. Tying his horse to the hitching rail he stepped onto the sidewalk, only to be confronted by two soldiers blocking his path. Pulling his jacket back he revealed his badge. "That don't mean shit to me Reb!"

"Sonny, the war's been over for thirty years. If you've a mind to use that rifle get to it before I shove it up your ass!"

The young soldier realising he'd caught a grizzly on his home ground, swiftly moved aside. The older soldier with him, grinned, took out some chewing tobacco and said, "Don't mind him, he's still wet behind the ears."

Zachariah grinned, and stepped around the two soldiers. No one was going to spoil the mood for him that morning.

"What's with the soldiers?" he said as he walked into the saloon.

Tom Tenpenny looked up from the card table. "Where the hell you bin!"

"You don't need to ask," said Ethan from across the other side of the room.

"Jesus, Zack. You up and kill a man, then you're off sparking with a woman. Well don't that beat all," said Tom as the roasting began.

"Yeah enough about me, what's with the soldiers?"

"Sheriff Youngerman called them in to keep the peace. The whole goddamn area's under martial law," said Ethan, then he added, *"Tom, she's a looker, a real lady, cain't see what she sees in the old feller."*

"When am I gonna meet her, Zack?"

"Soon enough."

"Jesus, that long drink a water rides back into town, kills two men and even steals a glimpse at Zachariah's lady. While me, his oldest friend, caint seem to get any of the action," said Tom, to no one in particular

"You'll get it soon enough, Kendrickson won't take what we did to him lying down."

"What, we got to kill em all before it's over? McCulloh's dead, Josh Randolph and Lucky Charlie won't be gracing this establishment anymore, and that shooter from Montana, what was his name, J W Barnes, he cashed his chips in this morning."

"I reckon," said Zachariah. With Alicia on the scene, things had changed. He wanted to take off, to dispense with his old life. He wanted to get as far away as possible. He'd thought about it over breakfast, imaging what it would be like to take off. They could put all their belongings into a couple of cases and take the next train out of the state. With luck they could be in San Francisco before next weekend. It was an impossible dream.

He was involved in a blood feud, a fight to the death, against an adversary so twisted with hate, that there could only be one outcome. Under those circumstances there was no way he could leave his two friends to face it alone. Hopefully with the Military Plaza under martial law, there would be a respite from the killing. Never in his life had time seemed so precious. He prayed peace would last long enough for him to get to know Alicia.

Chapter 26

He sat staring at the computer, his mind struggling with the document he had before him. A colleague from San Antonio, knowing that Morgan was researching his great grandfather's life, had come across what until recently had been classified information. It put a new slant on the legend of Zachariah Trelawney.

It had come at a very opportune moment. Until he heard from Tony Valdez there was nothing he could do except phone Laura at every opportunity. He'd tried her home, he'd tried the office, yet each time he was either told she was still on vacation or he received an unavailable tone. The thought that she was deliberately avoiding him did more than cross his mind. In all their years of marriage he'd never spoken to her so cruelly. He was beside himself with guilt, and wanted to make amends if it was at all possible. He so desperately wanted to speak to her, to make things right between them. He'd asked for her help, no, more than that, he'd actively sought her opinion. When she'd given it, he'd thrown it in her face. All Laura was guilty of was trying to help him. And Morgan in his pig headed way, had driven a wedge through their relationship. Even their divorce had been conducted in a far more civilised manner. It was only now, now that he'd truly lost her, did he realise her true worth. Trying not to dwell on it, he began shuffling through the paperwork on his great grandfather.

The information in front of him was a revelation, a discovery that Orville would have found downright intriguing. It was a welcome distraction from his own troubled thoughts. Enthusiastically he began putting together an as yet unknown part of his great grandfather's life.

* * * *

Jake sat down to dinner with Blythe and thanked God he hadn't agreed to go with Morgan into Mexico. It wasn't that he didn't share his friend's views, sure he wanted the perpetrators brought to justice but there was something far more important to him. The wonderful woman that was sitting opposite him had swung the balance. Vietnam had deprived them of each other for almost ten years. It had even played a part in nearly destroying him altogether, until Blythe took a hand. Life over the last few years had taken on a far sweeter edge. He owed it to her and the kids to be there for them. He'd been more fortunate with his children than many of his friends. They were both straight A students, they'd steered clear of drugs and in his opinion were destined for greater things. Yet why after he'd taken stock of his life was there a gnawing at his soul. He'd done his bit for his country, hell he was still doing it. Patrolling the mean streets of Laredo was anything but a picnic. Blythe smiled across the table at him, and he quickly dispelled any niggling thoughts or doubts.

* * * *

Tony stared in disgust at the money on the table. 'Three days, that's what the bastard has given me. Three fucking days or else my ass is in a sling. Fuck! If this Rodirigo De la Fuente was a dealer, I'd willingly take the guy out. But he ain't, he's a mother-fucking rich kid, who's looking for answers to his brother's death. Hell who could blame him, gutted like a chicken. If someone did that to my brother, I'd cut his liver out. Three fucking days!'

Tony was scared, more scared than he'd been all his life. He'd seen what Diego Morales and his brother were capable of. The video tape of that poor girl had been strictly for his benefit. He'd winced, then as casually as he could, he pocketed the cash and got the hell out of the room. Lupe had smiled up at him as he descended the stairs, 'Christ, she's high already.' he thought angrily.

"We're leaving, now!"

He grabbed her by the arm and began pushing his way though the melee of stoned bodies. Lupe grinned at him stupidly, but she neither protested nor resisted. The show of force in the upstairs room was meant to scare the shit out of him. It had worked, and Tony saw no reason to linger. The aura of evil that he'd felt when they first arrived was never stronger than in the presence of Diego and Ignacio. When he thought about the big inhumane looking albino he began to shake, not just with fear, but with an anger that he found difficult to control.

As he drove through the gates of the hacienda he reached into the glove box and took out a small flask. Putting the silver vessel to his lips, he began to drink greedily. It was only when the lights of Hacienda Morales disappeared in his rear view mirror, that Tony stopped shaking.

Unnerved by his experience at the hacienda, he checked that he hadn't been followed then swung by the nearest Holiday Inn. Spending another night in Lupe's seedy room was more than his nerves would take. In the room he double locked the door and checked his nine millimetre. Grabbing a drink from the mini bar he threw the two envelopes on the table.

"What's that?" Lupe clawed at the large sealed envelope and revealed a bundle of fifty dollar bills. "Who you gotta fucking kill?"

Tony indicated the second envelope. Lupe tore it open and her face changed.

"Mother of God! This is bad, this is so fucking bad."

"Whatdya mean?"

"If you kill him, your life won't be worth a plugged nickel."

"If I don't, I'm as good as dead."

Calmly he spread the contents of the envelope across the bed, and with the little information Lupe could tell him about the family, he was able to piece together the reasons why the Morales brothers wanted Rodirigo De la Fuente dead.

The De la Fuente family were one of the most influential families in Monterrey. The father was a wealthy industrialist, very powerful with strong political connections. His wife Dolores, a member of the local chamber of commerce, and a woman of very high social standing, had mourned the death of her youngest son. But it was the shame of his marriage to the Morales woman that had caused her the most grief. When he entered into marriage with her, in Dolores De la Fuente's eyes, he was already dead. As for the children, she wouldn't let herself believe they were blessed with De la Fuente blood. The nature of their deaths, though terrible in the extreme, was inevitable. What good would crying out for vengeance do, it couldn't bring him back. It was better to draw a veil over the whole affair.

Rodirigo had seen it differently. He loved his younger brother, and someone was going to pay for his death. A brief hurried phone call from his brother, only weeks before his death had pointed Rodirigo in the right direction. It didn't take him long to find out who was responsible for the deaths of his brother and family. With his money and connections he began putting the wheels in motion to prove it. Inevitably it wasn't long before the Morales brothers got to hear about it. Normally they would have dealt with him themselves, a public execution, in full view of the blind eyes of Monterrey. Deaths in public places were becoming the Mexican way. But Rodirigo was his father's favourite son. He was high profile and anyone that killed him couldn't expect to live long. Diego and Ignacio needed a patsy. Emilio Ortiz, their friend from Ciudad Acuna, had generously supplied them with one. Tony knew only too well that once he'd carried out the contract killing his life wouldn't be worth a plugged nickel. The Morales brothers would have him killed and present the De la Fuente family with a fait accompli. He had three days.

It was around three in the morning when Morgan picked up the phone.

"Morg, it's one hundred percent, they're behind it. I can't say for certain who pulled the trigger but there's an albino Mexican that works for them called Geronimo Menendez. I'm almost certain he did the butchery. There's a short American guy works for them called Aldo Chudzik. He fits Orville's profile of one of the shooters. More than that, he carries a Capsull .454. Treats it like it's a better friend to him than his dick. Then there's Emilio Ortiz. He ain't involved in the killings, but just in case I ain't around, he should be on the list."

"Why, what's up? Have they made you? If they have, get the fuck out now!" The alarm in Morgan's voice trembled down the phone line.

"Nah, I'm okay. I've got three days."

"Three days?"

"Yeah. Then my life ain't worth two bits! I gotta go."

It was minutes after the line went dead that Morgan placed the phone back on it's hook. Any thought of sleep was banished from his mind. He had the names, or at least the names of the chief players. It had to be enough, now time was of the utmost importance. Tony had said three days and he wasn't a man that scared easily.

In the hours before dawn he went over his plan. Plan, that was a joke. Who the fuck did he think he was? The Lone fucking Ranger, blazing away with two six guns from atop a white horse. Taking on the Morales outfit would need more than silver bullets. Yet as he went over his cock-eyed strategy he realised one thing was right in the overall scheme of things. The Morales brothers contempt for law and what it stood for was never more apparent than at Hacienda Morales. There, they were at their most vulnerable.

✱   ✱   ✱   ✱

"Tony, they're gonna fucking kill you!"

"I know baby, but it's the only way I can stay alive," he said.

With the realisation of the situation sinking in, Lupe became both protective towards him and extremely aroused.

"I can't help it baby, danger does that to me. My adrenaline goes sky high and I can't help myself." She'd slipped to her knees between his legs. Her head inches from his crotch. She looked up at him with her seductive dark eyes and smiled wickedly at him. Her delicate fingers stroked at the hardness in his jeans, then slowly, ever so slowly, she tugged at his zipper. Tony's mind slipped out of gear as she forced her tiny hand inside his fly. He gasped as her cool fingers gently prized his penis from his jeans. He stifled a cry of ecstasy as her seductive red mouth closed over the end. Expertly she worked on him, bringing him close to the edge. Then at the last moment pulling back from the brink, only to tempt and tease until he was ready. Struggling to control and forestall his excitement, he pushed her backwards on the floor and lifted her dress. He tore at her panties until he'd exposed her magnificent thatch of mahogany. Then rising to his knees, he undid his belt and top stud of his jeans. Within moments he was inside her, pumping, heaving, thrashing around like a crazy man. Desperate to prevent his inevitable climax, he withdrew and buried his face into her dark wondrous pubic forest.

Tony awoke around ten, his body sore from their marathon night of passion. He stared at the ceiling and began reliving the most lustful night of his life. 'Lustful,' he thought, 'no, that does it an injustice.' They'd been like wild animals, depraved, savage, devouring every ounce of pleasure from their bodies, until Tony could stand it no longer. He erupted inside her like Mount Vesuvius spurting his fires of passion. And afterwards, he found something beyond his wildest emotions. A warm and tender feeling of love, a need to comfort, to protect, a feeling worth dying for. And as he gazed into her eyes he saw they'd softened and that she too was feeling the same emotions.

He'd come to Mexico to kill, to destroy, to reek havoc on the vile empire of the Morales brothers. He'd come for the three quarters of a million dollars hidden in the sewers underneath Madero's. Nothing had changed, yet everything had changed. He hadn't banked on finding love, yet there was no other word for it. He was in love, and it frightened the hell out of him. He wanted to run, flee with Lupe over the border. Start a new life, build a home, have kids. It was a dream, fifty thousand dollars, his cache of drugs money and Lupe. It was so simple, but then the dream would become the nightmare. Diego would never give up. There would be nowhere to hide. He'd unleash his dogs and the giant albino's shadow would one day fall upon his door.

His only salvation lay in Morgan's plan. His only hope of spending his life with Lupe was to kill the Morales brothers. Kill them, then with Lupe at his side, drive to Ciudad Acuna, recover his money and disappear. It was a good plan. It was a shit plan. It was his only plan.

Getting up, he showered, then dressed quickly. "Lupe, wake up! We have to go." She stared at him through sleep-laden eyes, but she was just as beautiful. 'The fucking plan has to work,' he thought as he smiled down at the most beautiful specimen of womanhood he'd seen in his entire life.

When she'd showered and dressed, he asked her if she was prepared for a new life. She looked up at him with love in her heart and softly mouthed the word yes. It was enough, it was more than enough. He took her in his arms and looked longingly at her sweet kissable lips.

"I love you," he said softly.

"And I you," she replied as their lips touched and their hearts became as one. After they'd caught their breath Tony sat her down on the bed and began to outline his plans. He didn't tell her anything of Morgan's involvement, only that fifty thousand and three days grace was their only chance. He said he had things that needed doing and would have to leave her for a couple of days. She wasn't to ask questions. She just had to go to her apartment and pretend that everything was normal. He looked at her seriously and told her she had to trust him. Her face grew pale and her eyes took on a haunted look. She was afraid he was running out on her. Her lip trembled, her heart skipped a beat. He was going. He was leaving her for good. Lupe looked at him hesitantly, unsure, frightened, like the kid she really was, and then her eyes locked on his and she saw how much he loved her.

He took her tiny face in his cupped hands and smiled at her. "There's things I have to do, I can't explain it now, but if you think I'd be crazy enough to leave you, well you've gotta be out of your head. I love you, I could never stop loving you, you're everything to me. Reaching down he placed his lips upon hers, and in the sweetest moment of their short time together, he kissed her.

* * * *

Morgan stared at the clock on the wall. 'We're due for another paint job,' he mused as he studied the flaking walls that surrounded it. Beige was a functional colour but nicotine and the process of time had turned the walls a dirty ivory. 'To hell with departmental cutbacks. After Mexico I'm gonna make sure this damn office gets a fresh lick of paint.' "After Mexico?" He questioned his own optimism. 'What the fuck's keeping Jake,' he mumbled under his breath. It was ten o'clock and Jake hadn't shown. He was normally in the office by nine at the latest. If he could reach him on the radio or the mobile it would have been something, but he'd tried them and got no response. It was beginning to irritate him some. He was already on edge since Tony's call, now with Jake God knows where, it was putting the whole operation in jeopardy.

He sat watching the clock as the minutes ticked by. Marion, his secretary come gopher, brought him a cup of coffee and placed it on his desk. He neither looked up, smiled or acknowledged her presence. She might just as well have been invisible. She muttered something under her breath and gave him an off handed look as she closed the door behind her. Morgan tilted back in his chair and put his feet on top of the desk, absentmindedly sipping his coffee. It was all going off. After months of investigations he was finally going into Mexico. From the start he'd had a gut feeling, but when they killed Orville he knew it was inevitable. He didn't blame Jake for not coming with him. In fact, given different circumstances, maybe he might have cried off the whole idea.

Where the fuck's Jake?' It was bad enough smuggling himself into Mexico, without having to worry about his Sergeant. His nerves were at breaking point. The course of action he'd instigated could get a fellow Ranger killed. Tony had sounded scared. Fuck, he was scared too! He stared again at the clock. It was eleven fifteen, and there was still no sign of Jake. Looking at the nicotine-ingrained walls, he laughed nervously. Chances were, he wouldn't get back from Mexico alive. The chances of a new paint job were just as slim.

Jake burst through the door, his eyes bulging murderously from their sockets. It didn't take a rocket scientist to see that something bad had happened. Morgan dragged his feet from the desk, "What's up?" he cried.

"Whenever you're planning on going into Mexico, I'm in," he said bitterly. His face had become a dark mask of unbridled hate. The veins in his bullish neck stood out like branches of an oak. Morgan had never seen him quite so worked up. And from the dishevelled look of his clothes it was obvious he'd been up all night.

"Jake, for fuck's sake tell me what's up?" Somehow or other he managed to coax the bigger man into a chair. "Take your time."

Jake took a few deep breaths as he fought to bring his anger under control. From the look of his swollen eyes it was clear he'd been crying. "Sarah's in Memorial hospital. We've been there all night. She was involved in an automobile accident. They say she's gonna be all right, given time. They had to remove her spleen, her right leg is busted up pretty badly and she's suffering from shock, but at least she's alive." The retelling brought on a bout of uncontrollable sobbing.

Marion enquired at the door if there was anything she could do.

"Yeah, just make sure we're not disturbed,"said Morgan as kindly as he could, realising how off hand he'd been to her earlier. Paitently he waited for the sobbing to subside.

Jake wiped at his eyes and, falteringly, he forced out what had happened. "They say that given time, she'll make a full recovery. Her friend Mary Lou, wasn't so lucky. In the emergency room I kept looking over at her parents and thanked God my daughter was still alive. You know, I almost felt guilty that Sarah had survived while their daughter was lying on a stone cold slab in the mortuary."

"What happened?" asked Morgan.

"They were driving home from the movies, when this car driven by a couple of pill heads sped around the corner and careered out of control, smashing into Mary Lou's car. They escaped with only minor injuries. Both of them were high on crack Morg! So fucking high they shouldn't have been able to open the fucking door to the car, let alone drive!"

"Best you go home, Blythe will need you."

"She's staying at the hospital. She told me to get the hell out. My temper wasn't helping anyone. You should have seen her Morg, my little Sarah, tubes sticking out of her from every which way. Her pretty little face a mass of lacerations, though the doctor says they'll heal in time. But what about her, Morg. Will she heal in time? Will the sight of her best friend bleeding to death at the side of the road, will that go away?"

"I don't know, I just don't know," said Morgan. An hour before he'd been thinking how lucky Jake was, how he still was, but for the grace of God. How quickly fortunes change, he mused.

"I wanted to go in that ER room and bust a cap on both of them creeps, then I thought, why them? Why them? Whenever you say the word Morg. I thought I could escape it. I thought we were safe in our cosy little world. Well last night taught me no one's safe. Complacency, that's what I'm guilty of. I thought it couldn't happen to me. Well I was wrong. It can happen to anyone. If you want to live in a decent world, you have to be prepared to pay the price. It's about time I repaid my debt. When do we go?"

"You're in no fit condition. Blythe needs you. Sarah needs you."

"Cut the crap Morg! I'm as useless as a fart in a cyclone. Blythe don't need me pissing and wailing about what I'm gonna do. John Junior's there with her. I'd only be in the way."

"You'll only get yourself killed."

"Right now I'm dying inside. I've thought it through, without me along, you ain't got a prayer. Say give me the word."

Jake was right, with him along there was just the smallest of chances they'd get out alive, thought Morgan.

"We go tonight!"

Chapter 27

Peace lasted longer than Zachariah expected. With the advent of martial law, a stability descended over the Plaza. It wasn't unusual to see as many as a dozen troopers inconspicuously patrolling the surrounding streets, while another dozen or so spent their free time in the saloons and gambling dens around the Plaza. Rumours began circulating about the mobilisation of troops at the local garrisons. Some said it was on account of the lawlessness in the Military Plaza area. Others, those that kept abreast of world events, said the United States was readying itself for war against Spain. Whatever the reason, the saloons and gambling dens in and around the plaza began to thrive. It wasn't long before half the clientele of the Military Plaza saloon were dressed in blue flannel. After a time their presence was hardly noticed, except by certain factions of Frenchie's and the Military Plaza saloons.

With gambling, whoring and drinking on the increase, everyone stood to make a great deal of money. A new building was quickly erected on the side of the Military Plaza saloon, allowing the proprietors, O D Clements and Jonathan Loudermilk to expand their gambling concession. Tom negotiating on Zachariah's behalf, managed a new deal that brought them in twenty five percent of the house takings. With the influx of hard drinking, hard fighting soldiers adding to the already explosive situation, both proprietors chose to take a back seat and left the running of the saloon to Tom and Zachariah. By Christmas they'd added Keno, Fan Tan and Chuck-a-Luck to their tables. Poker, Faro, Monte and Roulette were still as popular as ever, and with Billiards on the two new tables they'd shipped in from San Francisco, the Military Plaza saloon was coining it in.

Fanny Shelton brought in a couple of new girls all the way from Paris, France. Well that's what she told everyone. Chances were, they'd originated from the bayous of Louisiana. Culture wasn't high on the menu at the Plaza. Another couple of cribs were hastily erected out back, near the area where they staged the Friday night cock-fights. Any hopes of persuading Tom to pull up stakes ended with the new deal and his interest in a sporting gal who went by the name of Madeleine.

An inquest into the deaths of J W Barnes, Josh Randolph and Lucky Charlie, found that the Rangers Zachariah Trelawney and Ethan Book had acted in self defence. They'd expected opposition from Kendrickson but with the military flexing its muscle none came. Zachariah was grateful for the respite. It meant he could concentrate on courting Alicia. She'd told him they'd gone way past the courting stage, but he persisted in old fashioned Victorian values. It amused her, his stoic attitude to all things proper. She'd laugh out loud in public places, pull faces at the prudish old dears that looked down their noses at her. She was a free spirit and he loved her for it, despite the embarrassment she showered on him. They dined in the best restaurants, drank the finest of French Champagne. She introduced him to the theatre, the ballet and the opera, though he said it was his first and last time. She called him a Philistine.

He said, "You can call me what you want, I'll still love you."

He took her buggy riding though, unbeknown to her Ethan Book shadowed them from a distance. Everyone in town knew how deadly Book was with the Creedmour. They picnicked by a small lake, where he picked a small bunch of wild flowers and presented them to her. He knelt on one knee, she began to giggle, he looked annoyed, she tried stifling her silly laugh, he began to giggle himself, and then he asked her to marry him.

She looked away sadly, "If only," she cried. "Xavier wouldn't agree to a divorce, it's against all his beliefs."

"Then we'll go away, somewhere far, far enough so we can share our lives together."

"Live in sin, shame on you Zachariah," she said mockingly, the seriousness of the mood quickly dispelled. Yet as they drove back to town, with Alicia's tiny frame snuggled up close to him, Zachariah couldn't help thinking that the day of reckoning would soon be upon them. Xavier Morales wasn't a man to give up easily on a woman as beautiful and lovely as Alicia.

Ethan Book held back as Zachariah pulled the buggy to a halt outside the Menger Hotel. He watched from a distance as his captain jumped down from the buggy and extended a hand to his lady. He couldn't help but think how much his friend had changed since he'd faced down J W Barnes a little over a month ago. The hardness had gone from his face. He seemed different, happy, yeah that's what it was. The man had never been happier in his life, thought the tall blond Ranger.

Ethan wasn't one to socialise, preferring his bedroll and horse to the comfort of a soft bed and a sweet woman. He'd taken to riding wide loops as part of his rangering duties, returning to San Antonio once every couple of weeks or so. "I ain't far, if'n you need me. About a day's ride is all." The arrangement worked perfectly, being gone was when Ethan Book was at his most dangerous. No one had known he was there when Zachariah faced the range detective from Montana, by the time they did it was too late.

It was approaching noon, a week later, when Ethan spied a group of riders racing towards town. It didn't take him long to realise that the white haired man leading the bunch of vaqueros was Xavier Morales. Spurring his horse towards San Antonio he arrived fifteen minutes ahead of Morales. Jumping off his horse at the entrance to the Menger Hotel he threw his reins into the hands of a surprised doorman. Taking the stairs three at a time he was soon banging on Alicia's door.

Zachariah flung open the door, "What's up?"

"Best you get your ass down stairs pronto. You got company."

"Xavier?"

"I'd say, and about a dozen guns."

Zachariah turned towards Alicia, "Stay put, let me deal with it."

"The hell I will, your fight is my fight."

"You stay in your room!" There was no mistaking the command.

"He'll kill you."

"Maybe, maybe not."

"I'll get Tom," said Ethan. Without waiting for a reply he hurried along the corridor and disappeared down the stairs.

Alicia rushed into Zachariah's arms, "I'll go back with him. If I do he'll leave you alone."

"No! I love you and I ain't giving you back. I'd rather die than let that happen." He pushed her gently inside the room, kissing her softly upon the lips. Minutes later, he checked his Peacemaker before descending the stairs. He heard the clattering of hooves in Alamo Plaza as he pushed open the door to the Menger hotel. The doorman, quick to understand the situation ducked past Zachariah and raced into the lobby. The tall Ranger walked steadily out into the plaza. Xavier and a dozen riders fanned out in front of him.

"You don't need to die. Send Alicia out and we can forget this ever happened," bellowed Xavier.

"I told you I'd kill you if I have too," said the cold, calm Ranger. His eyes transfixed on the handsome face of his sworn enemy. "Alicia's staying with me."

"Then you're a fool, a dead fool," said Morales as his hand gripped the walnut butt of his holstered revolver.

"Gentlemen, gentlemen," came a cry from the shadows, "this is no way to behave. Back off sir before I blow you out of the saddle."

Zachariah and Xavier as one, looked towards a diminutive looking man with a sandy moustache and a pair of ridiculously small spectacles. Cradled in his arms was a large calibre hunting rifle and it was pointing very steadily at the chest of Xavier Morales.

"Now sir, now that I have your full attention, pray tell me what this commotion is in aid of."

Xavier glared at the stranger, then to Zachariah's astonishment he reined back, and turned his horse. "This isn't finished!" His eyes bore deeply into Zachariah, then with a vicious kick he sent his horse galloping away from the plaza. The tall Ranger stared after him in amazement.

Before he could turn and thank the stranger, Alicia was upon him. Her right hand slammed hard against his cheek. "How could you be such a fool! He could have killed you!" Then without another word she lifted up the sides of her dress and ran back inside the hotel.

"What! What did I do?" Bewildered Zachariah addressed the question to the man who undoubtedly had saved his life.

Small spectacles grinned at him. "You sir have a lot to learn. Any fool can see the woman's besotted by you. And furthermore the lady's right Morales would have cut you to pieces."

"You know him?"

"I do indeed, a fellow patriot, a believer in the cause."

"The cause?"

"Yes sir, the Cuban insurrection. Mark my words, the United States will be at war with Spain within a year."

"And that's good?"

"Freeing those poor devils from the tyrannical rule of Spain. At this very moment, atrocities, the like you've never seen, are being carried out in the name of that devilish country. Men, women and children, put to the sword. Rape and torture, just bywords to the Cuban people."

"You sound like a politician," said Zachariah.

"Heaven forbid," he said with a wry grin, "Allow me to introduce myself, Lieutenant Colonel Theodore Roosevelt, First United States Volunteer Cavalry."

"Zachariah Trelawney, Lieutenant, Frontier Battalion Texas Rangers. I think sir, I owe you my life."

"Maybe you do, maybe you don't. At the moment I think your mind is chasing petticoats. If you've a mind, perhaps we can meet later in the hotel bar, say around eight this evening."

"I'd be honoured."

Before Zachariah could break away, Ethan and Tom with three others came riding into the plaza at a hell of a gait. Tom reined his horse to a halt in front of the two men. "What happened?"

"Theodore happened," said Zachariah, by way of explanation. "Teddy Roosevelt, this here reprobate is Tom Tenpenny. The tall fellow on the dun horse that's Ethan Book, they're with me."

"Pleased to meet you gentlemen. I'm having drinks in the bar around eight, you're most welcome. Now if you gentlemen will excuse me, I have work to do." *With a quick doff of his hat he briskly walked back inside the hotel.*

"Who the hell is he? He don't look much like a fighter," said Tom.

"Don't let his size and demeanour fool you, the guy's got sand and then some," said Zachariah.

"I heard tell of him, he's some kinda politician or somethin, Did a bit of hunting and I heard he cowboyed for a time," added Book.

"Well don't that beat all," added Tom.

* * * *

Teddy was propped against the solid cherry wood bar when Zachariah walked in. He'd been staying with Alicia for almost six weeks but this was the first time he'd ventured into the hotel's bar. It was as he'd been told, an exact replica of the bar in the House of Lords in London. Apart from the cherry bar it featured a cherry panelled ceiling and walls, French bevelled mirrors and gold plated spittoons. More than a cut above the Military Plaza he thought as he walked up to his new found friend.

"So good of you to come," said Teddy as he extended his hand in greeting. "Shall we sit," he said and motioned to a quite table in the far corner. "Your friends, they couldn't make it?"

"Tom had to work and Ethan…well he ain't really the sociable type."

"And the good lady?"

"She's fine. It gave her quite a scare. Chewed me out good and proper for the fool I am. Everything's okay now."

"Good, I'm glad about that. What would you like to drink?"

"Just a beer, thanks."

"Zack, I can call you that?" The tall Ranger nodded. "I'll come straight to the point. I need men like you. Don't get me wrong, I've men falling over themselves to join my regiment, that's not the point. You're a Texas Ranger, you're used to taking charge. Making split second decisions, reckless, I've seen that with my own eyes, but sure of your own capabilities. I need men of your calibre."

"Teddy, I'm tired. I've done my share of killing. I can't say I have the taste for it, but I've done what was necessary. You've seen her Ted, she's everything a man could want, but I'm stuck in the middle of my own private war."

He proceeded to tell Roosevelt about his problem with Kendrickson, how he'd like to cut and run, how he can't on account of his two friends. Then he touched on the subject of Xavier Morales.

"What's with it with him. Why is he so godamn important. He aims to kill me or me him. He's a bad son of a bitch."

"He's a hard man, I'll grant you, but he's an honourable one. I've met him a time or two. He's witty, charming and a true patriot," said Theodore with some enthusiasm.

"He's all that, I can't disagree. But I watched as he shot dead two young rustlers who were in my charge. Then he hung them. If that weren't enough, the son of a bitch set them on fire! He ain't on my list of friends and I ain't on his either."

"You've stolen his woman. He'll kill you first chance he gets. If you decided to volunteer, I could guarantee you a commission. Morales wouldn't dare harm you whilst wearing the uniform. He knows I'd have him hanged from the nearest lamp post."

"I take your point Teddy, I thank you for your generous offer but the answer has to be no. After my wife died I never expected to meet another woman, let alone one so beautiful as my Alicia. She's what dreams are made of, she's every thing I could ever want. I can't explain how much I love her. Xavier might be out there waiting in some dark alley. Kendrickson might kill me before the new year. I might fall from my horse and break my neck, but while I can still breathe, I'll never give her up."

"A noble thought, I wish you well, dear friend."

* * * *

Lying awake, Alicia snuggled under his arm, he stared through the open window at the night sky. He should have been the happiest man alive. He'd cheated death by the finest of margins, he'd met an incredible man, and he'd just finished making love to the most beautiful woman in all San Antonio. Yet as he stared at the midnight blue sky he realised he was frightened, not of death but of living. He'd known her but a short time, time enough to fall helplessly in love. It was then he realised he couldn't face life without her.

* * * *

It was Christmas Eve when he next saw Teddy. He was just returning to the Menger Hotel when he heard the news that Roosevelt was in town and holding court in the bar of the hotel. Eager to see his new friend Zachariah made his way into the bar. It was crowded, far more than usual. At first he put it down to the festivities of the season, until he noticed most of the men were wearing slouch hats, blue shirts, brown trousers, leggings and boots and all were sporting spotted bandannas. Teddy was in the thick of them. The moment he saw Zachariah he broke off from his conversation and extended his hand in greeting.

"Compliments of the season Zack! Look at them! Look at my boys. Doesn't it make you feel proud. They might appear undisciplined, but don't let that fool you. Every man hand picked, every man dedicated to the cause. Remember them Zack, they are going to make history, they're my boys, the papers have even given them a name…they're the Rough Riders!" On hearing their name they let out a chorus of whoops and yells."

"They're a hearty bunch," said Zachariah.

Theodore motioned to a table. Both men grabbed chairs and sat down. Through the din of the crowd Teddy exchanged pleasantries, "I trust you are in good health. From the look in your eyes, I can see there's been no change in your circumstances. The Gods must be looking down on you."

"It's good to see you and yes fate has been kind."

"I'm glad to hear it. A man like you doesn't deserve to end his days face down in the dirt. Man was made for greater glory. I was hoping you'd changed your mind and decided to join me."

Zachariah shook his head. "No chance. We thought we'd winter here, then when the weather breaks we're thinking of heading for California. We've enough saved to buy a place near San Francisco. I've wired a friend there who's fixing me up with a job. If we can last out the winter without any interference from Morales, we've got a chance."

Teddy looked at his friend and smiled, "I've an early Christmas present. Xavier has accepted a commission and is at the present moment mobilising a division of soldiers at his ranch. We could get the call to arms at any hour, which means your old friend won't be bothering you for the foreseeable future. Merry Christmas."

* * * *

The events culminating in the climatic gunfight at Military Plaza on February 15th 1898, were overshadowed by the stunning news from Cuba. The battleship Maine, anchored in the Havana harbour, had been blown apart by several explosions and now rested at the bottom of the habour with the loss of 260 lives. Anti Spanish feeling, fanned by the jingoistic newspapers, brought Teddy's war ever closer.

Chapter 28

The old horse trailer bumped and rattled as it negotiated its way through the uneven streets of Nuevo Laredo. No one looked at the poor Mexican horse trader as he drew up at a stop light in the centre of town, just another peon going about his business. Tony sweated profusely beneath the battered straw hat. Even though all the windows of the old Chevy pickup were rolled down, the humidity, grime and pollution of the city streets stifled and choked him. "Fucking Mexico," he said for the seventh time that day. Bad tempered and thirsty from the long sweltering ride from Monterrey, he pulled up beside an old Coke machine and dug deep into his jeans.

Raising the bottle to his mouth he drank greedily. "Fuck, doesn't anything work in this God-forsaken town!" he cried as he spat out the sticky sweet warm cola. "Hey man! Where can I get a cold one?" he shouted at an old man who was selling cartons of cigarettes on the street corner.

"Try inside," the old man said disinterestedly, pointing toward a run down shop that displayed faded magazines and Hershey bar ads.

"Gracias."

Fortified by a cold Seven Up, Tony climbed back into the truck. Hanging a right he drove towards the river. At the border he took a left turn and drove for several miles. As the buildings faded away he slowed his speed and began looking for the rocky outcrop that Morgan had shown him a week after he arrived in Laredo. He didn't realise how much things looked different from his side of the river until he tried spotting the rocky promontory. If it hadn't been for a disturbed flock of birds at the river's edge he'd have missed the meeting point altogether. With relief he pulled onto a dirt road, and drove slowly towards the river and a small clump of cottonwoods. In the relative shade of the trees he switched off the engine. With an old bandanna he wiped the sweat from his brow, then he glanced at his watch. It was a little after four-thirty. He'd made it with hours to spare.

Settling himself for the long wait, he hunkered down in the seat and put his feet up on the dashboard. At once his thoughts returned to Lupe. He wished he hadn't left in such an all-fire hurry. He couldn't get enough of her, she was everything and more. It was as if he'd been struck by a thunderbolt. A little over a month ago, if anyone had said he'd fall in love with a foxy nineteen year old hooker, he'd have told them to screw themselves. But the fact was, he had, and he was loving every minute of it.

He knew Morgan would be mad, mad as all get out. The crazy gringo would have got it in his head that they were hitting Hacienda Morales early Friday morning, but Tony had other ideas. Without question he'd agreed to put his life on the line, to go back to the hellish life he'd led in Ciudad Acuna. He'd agreed readily because of the money he'd stashed in the sewer. What he hadn't reckoned for was Lupe. She'd entered his life like a cyclone, tearing him apart and rebuilding him every which way. If he and Lupe were to have half a chance, he needed to get his hands on the money. He'd do whatever Morgan asked, but not before they'd helped him retrieve his stash. Saturday was time enough for the Morales brothers.

He awoke in darkness, his back ached from the uncomfortable position he'd slept in. Panic brought him fully awake as he realised he'd closed his eyes for one moment, only to fall into a deep slumber. His blood ran cold as he searched the face of his watch. With relief he found it was only nine fifteen. Climbing out from the cab he stretched his legs and took a leak. When he was finished, he zipped up and walked slowly to the river's edge. Crouching down he scooped up handfuls of river and sluiced his face. The cold water ran through his hair, into his eyes, his nose and mouth, invigorating and revitalising his parched and dried out skin.

Back at the truck he checked his watch, it was almost ten o'clock. The sound of numbers being punched into his mobile phone echoed loudly as he dialled Morgan. He could feel his heart beating faster as the phone began to ring.

"Hello," came the cautious greeting.

"Morg, we're all set," whispered Tony.

"We're setting off right now. If the current's not too strong we should reach you within half hour."

Tony clicked off his phone and threw it inside the truck. Taking his nine millimetre from the small of his back he checked the clip. He'd been careful, but he wasn't prepared to leave anything to chance. He looked across the river at the varying lights of Laredo. The roar of traffic floated across the river, sirens blared into the night, the incessant sound of horns blown in anger and frustration, the all to familiar hubbub of a small city, and then he heard it. He thought he'd imagined it, but no, there it was again, the faint whinny of a horse. He stared into the blackness of the river for what seemed like an eternity, then the moon broke from behind its cloud cover and bathed the river in a surreal midnight blue. He recognised Morgan even without seeing his face, he was seated low in the saddle and was leading a pack horse. Behind that Tony made out the bulky frame of Jake Hamilton, and more importantly, trailing at the rear was a fourth horse.

Morgan emerged first from the river, his horse glistening wet in the moonlight. Within a couple of minutes all four mounts stood dripping and panting on the bank of the river. "Good to see you Tony," whispered Morgan. Jake climbed down from his mare and nodded his greeting. Without another word they lead their horses towards the open back of the trailer. Untying the pack from the second horse, they loaded it into the bed of the truck and covered it with an old tarp.

"What's wrong?" In the blue glow of moonlight Morgan had spotted the worried look in Tony's eyes.

"There's been a change of plan," said Tony abruptly.

The look on Morgan's face said it all, "Go on," he said sternly.

"There's no guarantee they'll both be at home on Friday morning. Our best chance is to hit them Saturday." Tony knew the odds of Morgan believing him were slim.

The sound of a round being jacked into the breech of a 50 calibre Desert Eagle was unmistakable. Instinctively Morgan pointed the gun at Tony's head. "You son of a bitch, what the fuck are you playing at. If this is a trap I'll blow your fucking brains all over Mexico!"

Tony threw his hands up in protest. "Jesus Morg, it ain't a trap. Now go easy with that trigger, man."

Jake worked the pump of his shotgun, "Start talking!"

"Okay Morg, I'll level with you. You ain't gonna like it, but believe me Saturday is the best time. When you called and asked if I'd help, I didn't hesitate, did I?"

"No, as a matter of fact, you almost jumped at the chance. I thought it was strange then, but I put it down to being your way of paying back that favour I did for you."

"Well, it was partly, but that's not the real reason. When I was working undercover, I had to make a few scores. Street cred, you know how it is, well I made more than a few. I stashed away over three quarters of a million dollars. I intended collecting it."

Jake stared in astonishment, "Three quarters of a million!"

"And that's because I ain't greedy," added Tony.

"But it's blood money! You were there to do a job, instead you're feathering your own nest. Fuck! Man, you're as bad as them. Doesn't the misery that filth causes bother you?" said Morgan as he violently shoved Tony hard against the side of the truck.

"Don't judge me!" Tony's dark eyes glared with murderous anger. "Who the fuck do you think you are? You ain't seen or endured a quarter of what I've seen. Sure I knew it was wrong, but it was my ass on the line."

Jake's clenched fist tore into the side of Tony's left cheek, "My fucking daughter's in intensive care because of that shit."

"Leave it Jake," shouted Morgan as he forced the big sergeant back.

"What was I supposed to do," continued Tony, "come clean, give it all back. Do you really think our government cares. I've been to hell and returned, not once but many times. It's mine, I earned it. That money belongs to me."

"It's morally wrong," said Morgan, realising the situation was almost out of hand.

"Taking the law into your own hands, that's right! What you're intent on doing is nothing less than murder," retorted Valdez.

"No, of course it ain't right, but it's gotta be done," said Morgan

"Don't preach morality to me Morg. Where was God when my mother needed him? Where was he when that policeman shot my father to pieces? Answer me that mister high and fucking mighty!"

"Cool it you two! This ain't getting us anywhere," said Jake. In the few seconds since Morgan had intervened he realised Tony had a valid point. The half-breed had seen at first hand. He'd risked his life on more than one occasion. Blood money or not, in his eyes Valdez had earned the right.

"I need twenty four hours," said Tony. "After that, I'll willingly help you send those bastards straight to hell!"

Morgan stared him straight in the eyes. "How do we know you'll come back?"

"Easy, come to Ciudad Acuna and watch my back."

"You're loco!"

"Why can't you collect your blood money after we've dealt with the Morales brothers," suggested Jake.

"Because of Lupe," his voice softened at the mention of her name.

"Who the fuck's Lupe?"

"She's the woman I intend spending the rest of my life with," said Tony by way of explanation.

Morgan looked at him incredulously, "You can't be serious!"

"More serious than anything in my entire life. I know with my track record that takes some believing but wait til you see her Morg, she's beautiful. She's everything I've ever wanted in a woman."

"What if I tell you to go to hell?" Morgan said acidly.

"Then I'd say you'll be signing your own death warrant. It's a lame plan at best, but without me you ain't got a chance."

"What's to stop you from taking off with your woman after we've helped you retrieve the money?" said Jake, his eyes narrowing in suspicion.

"You don't know Diego. He'd kill you two, then come hunting for me. Three quarters of a million ain't enough, if I've got to look over my shoulder for the rest of my life. Believe me, all I want is to get my money, kill them sons of bitches, then get the hell outta Dodge."

Jake exchanged a questioning glance at Morgan. "I guess we ain't got much of a choice," said Morgan reluctantly.

Chapter 29

Only one person was more pleased than Teddy Roosevelt when the United States declared war on Spain on the 25th April 1898. That man was Zachariah Trelawney. For the best part of ten weeks he'd been waiting for death to claim him. Not from the dreadful wounds he'd received in the plaza, but at the hands of a far deadlier foe, Xavier Morales.

After the gunfight in the Military Plaza, Zachariah's life had hung in the balance. For weeks he'd slipped between conscious and unconsciousness. Throughout the ordeal the doctor had feared for his life, expecting every morning to find a stiff grey corpse. Alicia, overcome with shock and grief arranged for a priest to read the last rites, and then against all odds Zachariah Trelawney slipped back into the real world.

The bullet that rendered him into unconsciousness had creased the side of his skull, and fractured it. An angry purplish bruising formed around the wound. But far more important was the severe concussion. The blow to the head had caused a swelling to build up inside his skull. The subsequent pressure resulted in a serious loss of oxygen and blood supply to certain parts of his brain. As the body began to heal itself the swelling became less and less. There was no way of knowing at that early stage whether serious damage had been done to the brain.

It was the wound to his left upper thigh that caused the most concern. The bullet had shattered the bone in several places. The surgeon from the nearby fort had wanted to amputate, in fact he was about to reach for the saw when Zachariah suddenly regained consciousness.

"Don't cut off my leg!" Somehow deep in his subconscious he'd managed to scream out.

"I have to, if I don't you'll die," said the surgeon slightly rattled by the unexpected command. He'd seen wounds like these at Chickamauga when he was a young surgeon operating out of a canvas tent; most times the soldier died. He looked sadly at the old Ranger and guessed his chances of lasting the night were pretty slim.

"The leg stays!" repeated Zachariah, just before he lapsed into unconsciousness.

"Hell sir, you might die anyway," said the surgeon to the unconscious man. But against all odds Zachariah began to improve. The doctor worked carefully at removing what splinters of bone he could from the gaping thigh wound, before he probed for the bullet. The lead projectile was lodged in an area halfway between the inner thigh and the groin. The old surgeon cut and probed for two hours before he finally managed to extract the bullet. Though tired from his labours, he carefully cleaned the wound and cauterised arteries before finally dressing the thigh. Turning towards the distraught Alicia, he said, "He's in the hands of his maker. I've done all I can do. Just pray that infection doesn't set in."

Alicia sat at his bedside and prayed. After five days without any improvement in his condition, she called in the local priest. He was reciting the last rites when Zachariah came round. "My leg, I can't feel my leg!" Alicia fought back the tears as she gripped his hand.

"Zack! My darling. You've come back to me."

"My leg?"

"Your leg's fine. The doctor managed to save it, but you won't be able to use it for a while." There would be plenty of time for her to tell him, he might never be able to walk unaided again. Doc Adams had said he wasn't an expert in rehabilitation but a positive mind always helped. Even if he'd had the strength, the splint on his leg made it impossible to move.

As the days became weeks, Zachariah drifted between two worlds. The wondrous world where Alicia saw to his every need, and the nightmarish dream world, where he relived over and over those fateful hours that led to the gunfight in the plaza.

He'd been dining with Alicia in the hotel when the sequence of events began to unfold. Relaxed and in good spirits since hearing Roosevelt's news, Zachariah had embraced his new life style, albeit some what clumsily; his embarrassment at his own loss of Victorian attitude long since gone. Just as in their lovemaking, Alicia had patiently coaxed him, nurtured and built on his confidence.

"Times were changing," so Alicia had said, "and we have to change with them." Zachariah sipped on his brandy and looked across the candle lit table at Alicia. Her sparkling brown eyes seemed more alive than usual. She was in good spirits and was talking excitedly about the forthcoming visit of Miss Lily Langtry, the famous actress.

"There's even talk she's going to be staying in the hotel," said Alicia excitedly. "I can't wait to meet her."

Zachariah laughed. He always did at her childlike enthusiasm, it was one of the things he loved about her. In her presence, it was so easy to forget the life he'd led before. For weeks they'd talked of the move to San Francisco. A new life beckoned. One free of the Xaviers and Jaspers of this world. They were running, not from, but to.

Against all odds, Zachariah had managed to persuade Tom to join them in their new venture. When the tall Ranger offered him a partnership in a gambling establishment on the Barbary Coast he jumped at the chance. His relationship with Madeline had blossomed into something far more serious. Both saw it as their last chance to escape their sordid pasts.

With the ever present army patrolling the streets, Kendrickson had had no choice other than to keep a low profile. Yet Zachariah knew that once the United States committed itself to the rumoured invasion of Cuba, the troops would disappear from the streets of San Antonio. The trick was to leave before Kendrickson unleashed his dogs. As for Ethan, they'd asked him to go along, but he'd insisted that he only knew rangering, and he'd continue going where the Rangers sent him. With Captain Platt not more than a day's ride away, Zachariah had to concede the tall willowy Ranger was capable of looking out for himself. Besides Kendrickson had no real grudge against him. With Zachariah and Tom Tenpenny gone, he'd soon lose interest in Book. And if he didn't he'd better make good and sure he'd finished the job, because not many men would bet against Ethan Book and the Creedmour.

Xavier was another matter. He'd come looking, of that Zachariah would stake his life. But with his new commission, it was looking more and more likely that the United States would get drawn into the conflict in Cuba. If that happened, there was no telling what could happen to Xavier. Whatever happened, Zachariah felt secure in the knowledge that he and Alicia would be long gone.

* * * *

Tom Tenpenny was dealing Monte while Madeline sat at the table next to him. "You bring me luck," he'd say and squeezed her bare shoulders. Since they'd been going together Tom had made her quit whoring. "If anyone's paying for the privilege, it's gonna be me!" It was an arrangement that Madeline found very agreeable, though Fanny Shelton found the loss of revenue more than a little disconcerting. But whatever else Fanny was, she wasn't a fool, and no way was she going to argue with the fiery Monte dealer. Not many people did, unless they were packing a concealed gun and were drunk enough to use it.

With the relaxing of tensions it wasn't unusual to see some Kendrickson men frequenting the Military Plaza saloon. That night was no exception. Nathan Kendrickson fired up with too much booze and carrying beneath his vest a short barrelled Colt 45, swaggered into the saloon with Billy Owens, Newt Padbury and Lee Blaisdell.

Ethan looked up from his table at the far corner of the room. He'd been back in town a little over an hour and was looking forward to a hearty meal and a bath. His Sharps Creedmour was propped against the chair next to him. Seeing the four men enter the saloon, he put down his fork and carefully lifted the rifle and laid it across the table, pointing it in the general direction of Nathan and Billy Owens.

Nathan and his boys bellied up to the bar and began drinking. Tom peered over but didn't react. Instead he looked across the room at Book. Ethan gave him a reassuring glance. There weren't too many men on the frontier who he'd trust with his life, but Ethan Book was one such man. Tom relaxed and returned his attentions to the card table. Everything was under control, but the tension in the room could be cut with a knife.

Ever since Newt Padbury's cousin Lee Blaisdell, rode into town he'd been desperate to show him off. Blaisdell came with the name of a man-killer. He'd rode a trail of terror across the Southwest for almost a decade. Texas was probably the only state in the South where there wasn't a warrant out for his arrest. Maybe it was the company he was keeping. Whatever it was, it wasn't long before the already liquored up Nathan began mouthing off about the Rangers, Zachariah in particular. "Who does Trelawney think he is, masquerading as a gentleman. Him and that Mexican whore. He thinks he's safe, he thinks he's got my old man treed. Well he's got it coming, and it's coming sooner than he thinks."

Tom exchanged a knowing look with Ethan and carried on dealing Monte. Zachariah had left instructions that trouble was to be avoided wherever possible. Deep down Tom wanted to have at it, but he'd given his word to Zachariah. 'Two weeks, then we're free of Kendrickson and his hot head of a son,' he thought angrily.

Getting no reaction, Nathan staggered across to the Monte table and Tom Tenpenny. Billy Owens and the two others followed not half a yard behind him. "Hey shorty, let's play some cards," cried Nathan. The remark was designed to inflame Tom's legendary temper.

"Your money's as good as the next man's but there'll be no loud talk around my table," said Tenpenny in a quiet threatening voice. Nathan seemed to sober, his vest was open and the short barrelled Colt was visible. If Tom noticed it he chose to ignore it.

"Well sir, if loud talk isn't permitted, deal the cards," said Nathan in an exaggerated whisper. "Second thoughts, don't deal the cards, what I want's a woman. And you pretty lady are about the finest money can buy." His voice had taken on a dangerous edge and his hand hovered close to the butt of his revolver.

Billy Owens and Blaisdell pushed forward as if to back Nathan's play. Newt Padbury moved to the right. The Monte dealer, seething with murderous rage, but realising Madeline was in the line of fire, sought to buy time. "If you gentlemen would leave, we'll forget this whole incident." The anger was evident in Tom's eyes. He wanted the hot head to cause something, yet he wasn't prepared to risk losing another woman to the guns of Nathan Kendrickson. Billy Owens and the others began to fan out. They'd caught Tenpenny in a vulnerable position and they weren't about to lose the advantage.

"Boom!"

A cloud of dust and plaster cascaded down over the heads of Kendrickson and his men. Spinning around they watched as Ethan jacked another round into the breech of his Creedmour. He aimed it at the chest of Billy Owens. "There'll be no killings in this here saloon tonight, unless it's of my making!"

In the commotion Tom, quick to see the advantage, instructed Madeline to get out through a side door. Without hesitating the frightened girl raced for the opening. Out of the corner of his eye Tom waited until she was safely through, then he addressed Nathan Kendrickson. The look in his eyes was unmistakable. "Now you got two choices, get down on your knees and beg for your life or have at it!"

"No Tom!" Bellowed Ethan.

Nathan, seizing his chance, pulled his Colt clear of his waistband and levelled it at Tenpenny. The little man grabbed at Nathan's gun hand, knocking his pistol from his grasp. At the same time his right hand reached for his nickel-plated pistol. In one easy motion, he pressed the barrel against Nathan's chest and squeezed the trigger. Immediately Nathan's shirt front caught fire. A look of surprise appeared briefly on Nathan's face, then still on his feet he staggered backwards for a couple of steps before his legs buckled from under. For the briefest of seconds Blaisdell looked as if he wanted action, until he looked down the still smoking barrel of Tom's revolver. Slowly he raised his hands.

"Oh Jesus," said Billy Owens as he crouched down and felt for Nathan's pulse, "He's still breathing, someone get a doctor!"

* * * *

Nathan Kendrickson lasted for almost an hour before he expired in an upstairs room above Frenchie's. Jasper, incensed by anger and grief, would have raced across the plaza with both guns blazing if it wasn't for the line of soldiers standing guard in front of the Military Plaza saloon. From an upstairs window he could just make out the tall imposing figure of Zachariah Trelawney as he strutted agitatedly back and forth on the sidewalk. His hatred of the man knew no bounds. He'd sent lesser men to do his dirty work and they'd all failed. His only son, in a desperate attempt to seek favour, had sacrificed his own life. For Jasper Kendrickson, the time had come.

* * * *

Newt Padbury was the first to notice the departure of the troops guarding the Military Plaza. He came charging into Jasper's room at around one fifteen on the afternoon of February 15th. Out of breath he pointed towards the window, "They're leaving."

Jasper watched as the soldiers formed an orderly line and marched from the plaza. "Newt, get the men together downstairs in fifteen minutes. This time I'm gonna handle things personally."

At the same time Zachariah stepped outside and asked a young corporal what was happening. "I'm sorry sir, it's orders from the fort. We're to return immediately."

Ten minutes later Zachariah heard the news. The US battleship *Maine*, anchored in Havana harbour on a peace mission, had exploded and sunk with the loss of 260 lives. The War Department had been caught on the hop. Orders were hurriedly sent out to mobilise all available troops. The battalion in San Antonio was put on immediate alert. More important to Zachariah, the shooting at the Military Plaza saloon was down graded and transferred to the Sheriff's department. However, Thadeus Youngerman and a number of his deputies were off in the brush country hunting an escaped prisoner.

"We got to sit tight until Youngerman gets back," said Zachariah.

"I'm for taking the fight to Kendrickson," snapped Tenpenny.

"God damn you Tom, ain't you done enough," shouted Zachariah in frustration.

"Hold it Zack! Tom didn't have himself an option. Nathan was on the prod from the moment he stepped inside the bar," shouted Ethan.

Tom looked surprised by Ethan's support, and upset by his friend's outburst. "You ain't got no call to be talkin to me like that, Zachariah," the man was clearly hurting. "In my place you'd have done the same."

'Done the same,' thought Zachariah as he lowered his head, Tom was right. They were both right. It had been Jasper and his fight from the start. There was no way anyone else should have been involved. His head was full of dreams for the future. He'd been such a fool, how could he expect to start afresh while Kendrickson lived? He so regretted hurrying out of the Menger Hotel as quickly as he had. There was no time to tell her he loved her. All he had was the memory of Alicia's sweet questioning face. It was etched in his memory. He'd told her he wouldn't be long. That had been more than sixteen hours ago. She'd have heard by now, she'd know the danger he was in. He wished he'd been able to kiss her one last time, but he'd been in such an all fired-hurry. Now in the dreary saloon he was faced with a dilemma. No spur of the moment shooting, no luxury of letting instincts take over. He was afraid, not of Jasper, but of the distinct possibility he wouldn't live to see Alicia again.

"I'm sorry Tom, I shouldn't have said that. It's my fight, it's always been my fight." To reinforce his words, he pulled his Peacemaker from its holster and began checking the shells.

"Hey Zack, Padbury's walking across from Frenchie's and he's holding a white flag," said Ollie Hammond, the new barman of the Military Plaza.

Zachariah watched from the doorway as Newt Padbury approached. Even though it was a mid February afternoon he could see Padbury was sweating. "Speak your piece," said the Ranger, keeping himself in the shadows.

"Jasper says his grievance is primarily with you. He says it's time."

"Tell Jasper I'll meet with him on the plaza in ten minutes."

Padbury wasted no time, he turned quickly and raced back to Frenchie's. The tall Ranger stared across the empty plaza. Only an old buckboard stood outside the dry goods store to Zachariah's left. To his right stood a solitary oak tree and in the centre of the plaza an old adobe well. 'Not much cover for a man to hide behind,' thought the Ranger.

"If I miss my guess I'd say old Jasper won't be gunning for me alone. If he gets me Ethan, you make sure he doesn't get off the plaza alive."

"You got it," said Book.

"If you're going out there, I'm coming with you," said Tom, his jaw set, ready for the argument.

"Obliged," grinned Zachariah. Somehow he just knew the little Monte dealer wouldn't take no for an answer. Knowing Tom was at his side seemed to quell the shakes he'd been feeling only moments ago.

"Ollie, throw me down that Winchester," said Ethan. "I reckon Jasper's intent on finishing it, so I figure he's coming loaded for bear. Sharps is a wonderful gun, but it ain't worth a damn in a fire-fight like the one we got coming."

Zachariah whirled around and gave Ethan a nod of gratitude. Whether Ethan noticed or not he continued to busy himself with checking the lever action and inspected the weapon. Ollie threw him a box of 44.40 shells. Catching the box, Ethan cried, "Thanks," and began feeding the cartridges into the Winchester's breech. Leaning the rifle against a chair, he drew his Remington from its holster and checked the cylinder.

Tom filled his jacket pocket with 45 calibre shells, his matching nickel-plated Colts clearly visible under his coat. Reaching behind the bar he brought out Bob Schaffer's old scattergun. "Well Bob, here's where we settle the score," he said cradling the Greener ten gauge.

"I figure Lee Blaisdell and Billy Owens, maybe Newt Padbury. There's no telling who else will have the stomach for it," said Zachariah as he pumped shells into a nickel-plated, scroll-engraved short barrelled Colt. Tucking it into his waistband he grabbed a handful of shells and put them in the left-hand pocket of his frock coat.

"Jasper's coming out of Frenchie's," said Ollie Hammond excitedly.

The three Rangers briefly exchanged glances then walked outside into the sun drenched street. Across the plaza they could make out Jasper, Billy Owens and closing in on the dry goods store Lee Blaisdell. Apart from Jasper they were all carrying rifles and belt guns. Newt Padbury was nowhere to be seen. Zachariah cast his eyes into the afternoon sun sweeping the upstairs windows and false fronts for the tell-tale glint of a rifle barrel. He figured Newt Padbury and one, maybe two, others.

"Let's do it," said Zachariah, as he walked onto the plaza. Tom, quickening his steps to stay in time with the taller man's strides, broke to his friend's right. As the adversaries advanced to the centre of the plaza Zachariah's mind wandered to the beautiful Alicia. He so desperately wanted to hold her face in his memory one last time.

Tom sported a maniacal grin as he drew closer to Billy Owens. Ever since he'd heard the alleged story of Owens backing down Short and Courtwright in Fort Worth he'd been waiting for this moment. He knew Billy Owens wouldn't let him get much closer with the Greener. Tom figured he'd raise his rifle just as he drew level with the oak tree. Any later and it would be pure suicide.

Ethan stalked gracefully close to the side walk. The buckboard was between him, the dry goods store and Lee Blaisdell. All the time he kept one eye on the windows opposite.

Jasper advanced, unafraid, grinning, his gun hanging at arm's length. Suddenly Zachariah picked up the pace and moved to within twenty feet. Jasper's gun hand came up and levelled on the tall Ranger's chest. Unnerved by the pace of the lawman he fired too quickly and the bullet missed its mark and tore through the fabric of Zachariah's frock coat. Unshaken the tall Ranger levelled his Peacemaker at Jasper's bulk.

"Crack, crack, crack!" A fusillade of rifle fire erupted from the second story window of Frenchie's. Zachariah was blown off his feet as a bullet tore an ugly gash in his left thigh, and another hit his right arm sending his Peacemaker flying from his grasp. Jasper quick to seize on his lucky escape, re-cocked his revolver and bore down on Zachariah.

Billy Owen reached the oak and raised his rifle quickly, only to stare in amazement as the little Monte dealer threw the scatter gun to the floor and pulled both his nickel-plated pistols from beneath his jacket. Stepping wide of the rifle Tom fired at the bewildered man. His deadly accuracy sent the man spinning to the ground as Tom's bullets found their mark, hitting Billy Owens in the chest and leg, before he could get off a single shot. Lying in the dust of the plaza, his life blood ebbing away through the faded store bought shirt, Owens somehow managed to muster the strength to draw his revolver.

"Crack, crack, crack, crack."

Unable to get a clear shot at Blaisdell, Ethan had switched his attention to a window on the second story of Frenchie's. Firing repeatedly, the window crashed inward. A cry of pain echoed through the sound of gunfire, confirming what Ethan already knew. Lee Blaisdell, firing from behind the rearing horses and buckboard, found it difficult to get off a killing shot and saw his bullets kick up dust harmlessly around the tall blond Ranger.

In the same span of time Jasper towered excitedly over Zachariah, his gun cocked, an evil smile of triumph spread across his face. Excruciating pain tore through Zachariah's groin as he desperately tugged with his left hand at the short barrelled Colt in his waistband. Thumbing back the hammer, he aimed it at the blur that was Kendrickson and pressed the trig-

ger. The evil smile froze in death as the 45 calibre slug tore his heart and part of his lungs from his body.

Billy Owens thumbed back the hammer and fired at Zachariah. The bullet tore into the side of the stricken Ranger's head.

"No!" screamed Tom as he saw his friend go down. Turning towards the slumped figure of Owens, he advanced on the dying man, firing, cocking, firing. When he was done, he battered the dead-man with his nickel plated pistol. As the rearing team of screaming horses fled in panic exposing Blaisdell, he fired across the plaza hitting Tom in the left shoulder. Seeing the fight was about over the lone gunman began to run from the plaza. Ethan Book took careful aim and fired. Lee Blaisdell felt a dull thud as the 44.40 slug tore into his back. He staggered a few steps, and haemorrhaged from his mouth before slumping to the ground. His dying breath was ragged and full of pain.

Gunfire from another building across the plaza died as the third Kendrickson man fell. An eerie silence filled the plaza of death. Only gun smoke and the smell of cordite lay testimony to the carnage that had befallen the Military Plaza. Ethan, rifle still hot in his hand, surveyed the scene. Jasper lay on his back, his sightless eyes staring up at the weak February sun. Close to him lay the large frame of Zachariah. He looked across to the oak and saw Tom was down but moving, He gave a cursory glance at the body of Billy Owens who appeared to have been shot to pieces.

Within five minutes of the final shot being fired, San Antonio's Citizen's Safety Committee arrived on the scene, all heavily armed and ready for business. "Where were you, when you were needed," enquired Ethan bitterly. The question was left unanswered as they discovered Zachariah was still alive. He was near death and looked to need a priest more than a surgeon. Quickly the committee carried him into the Military Plaza saloon. Doc Adams took one look at Zachariah and advised Ethan to send to the fort for their surgeon. In the meantime he did what he could for the tall Ranger. When he was done he began working on Tom's shoulder wound. It turned out the bullet had gone clean through. Madeline was there by his side, doing her best to nurse him. "What he needs is tender loving care," said Doc Adams.

"And that's what he'll get," said Madeline gratefully.

Ethan sent Ollie Hammond to the fort for their surgeon. He stared out of the window at the undertaker and his assistants as they carried the dead from the plaza. He prayed the surgeon would arrive in time. Then he remembered Alicia. Without another word he walked out of the saloon and mounted his buckskin. The Menger Hotel was but a few blocks away.

Over the next couple of days the Citizen's Safety Committee strutted around like peacocks. They found Padbury propped up against the far wall of a room in Frenchie's. Surrounded by shards of glass he sat motionless, three 44.40 slugs had all but blown his stomach to pieces. He died two days later. There was talk of arresting both Tom and Ethan and holding them for trial. The Committee saw it as a way of removing the unlawful element once and for all. Before any action could be taken, Sheriff Youngerman arrived and stepped between the Committee and the two Rangers.

"You ain't arresting anyone! We'll wait until the coroner's verdict before I decide if there's any action to be taken."

*   *   *   *

As the days turned to weeks, Zachariah's condition slowly improved. Since the battleship Maine had sunk, there had been talk of war, yet the United States was still reluctant to issue the orders. Unable to move, Zachariah grew fearful that Xavier would return and extract his vengeance. In his mind, the inactivity could only mean one thing. Xavier would grow tired of his commission and return to San Antonio and reclaim his wife and take his revenge. On that day, the 25th of April 1898, war was declared. No man slept more soundly than Zachariah Trelawney.

Chapter 30

They'd left Jake guarding the horses with the trailer while they drove the last three miles into the city. Dawn's early light was just breaking over the tallest of the buildings in Ciudad Acuna as they pulled up outside the back of Madero's. Reaching across, Tony took two hook-like tools from the glove box. Morgan's eyes surveyed the street; it was deserted. Climbing out of the Chevy, Tony indicated the manhole cover of the sewer, "That's the one."

"Just get the fuck down there and be quick about it," said Morgan, more agitated than he felt he had a right to be. It had been his idea to take the law into his own hands. He couldn't expect everyone to work from the same motivations. On the drive up to Ciudad Acuna Tony had told him of his meeting with Lupe Chavez. He'd left nothing out, so great was his love for her that he didn't care who knew what she'd done for a living. Jake had put his ten cents into the pot, but even that hadn't rankled with Valdez.

"I tell you Morg, she's like nothing you've ever seen before. Sure she's gonna lead me a dog's life, but who cares. I'm so crazy in love, it hurts. I can't wait to hold her in my arms when this is all over."

Morgan patted his friend on the shoulder, in way of saying, 'I know what you mean buddy'. Since before they'd crossed the river he'd been thinking about Laura. He hadn't been able to get in touch, but he'd made up his mind that once this business was over he was heading back to Austin.

"Give me a hand will ya," whispered Tony, as he handed Morgan one of the hook tools. Together they raised the cover from the sewer.

"You got five minutes," said Morgan, as he handed Tony a flashlight.

"That's all I'll need," said Tony as he began to climb down the metal ladder inside the sewer. He pulled a bandanna up over his nose as the toxic fumes began to make him gag. "Oh Jesus, this is worse than I remember," he said to himself. At the bottom, he caught his breath, and began to get his bearings. He counted out seventeen paces north along the sewage corridor, until he came to a left turn that ended in a dead end some eight foot from the main corridor. Tony swept the bricked-up passage with the flashlight, searching for the loose bricks near the ceiling. His heart was in his mouth as he feverishly felt the brickwork. 'Solid, solid, solid, something was wrong. It was here, it had to be.' Then as his heart was about to pop out of his mouth, he felt a brick move. Wiggling it free, he let it fall into the water, then another brick, and another, until he'd cleared a third of the wall. He probed with the flashlight along an old lintel, his eyes glinting feverishly as they sought the key to his future. His heart leapt as he glimpsed the black nylon of the old sport's duffel. Reaching in, he hurriedly pulled the bag out. Excitedly he unzipped it to reveal his ill gotten gains. Feasting his eyes on the cache of neat bundles of fifties and hundreds, he began to laugh excitedly. It was all just as the day they'd hidden it, wrapped carefully in plastic bags.

Within minutes Tony emerged from the sewer, his clothes stinking to high heaven. "Thank God, I'd almost given you up," exclaimed Morgan as they replaced the man hole cover. "Now let's get the fuck outta here."

As they drove out of the city the first of the day's commuters had begun to trickle in. Morgan sat with his head stuck firmly out of the window, while Tony giggled maniacally as he drove the short distance back to Jake and the horses. "Hell Morg, I reckon everything's gonna work out fine."

"Fine or not first thing you're gonna do is take a bath in the Rio Grande," said Morgan.

"Jesus H Christ, I ain't ever seen so much money," said Jake as he gazed at bundles of cash.

"It's probably close to eight hundred thousand," said Tony, "and fifty thousand of it's yours Jake, when we get safely back to Laredo. Same goes for you too Morg."

"Keep it! All I'm interested in is the job on hand. It's dirty money and I don't want no part of it," said Morgan.

"Don't be silly Morg. It's as Tony says, the money don't belong to anyone."

"You've changed your tune. Have you forgot Sarah, so quickly," said Morgan cruelly.

"The hell I ain't, this here money can help her. I don't want it for myself, but my little girl." The hurt look was unmistakable.

"Hell Jake, you know I don't mean it that way. It's just the waiting that's getting me down."

"I know," said Jake, "Let's get some breakfast, I'm starving."

They drove to Piedras Negras, found a suitable fast food chain and ate. Away from Ciudad Acuna the trio began to relax. On the journey down to Hidalgo both Jake and Morgan managed a few hours shut eye. Tony was so fired up with the recovery of the money that the chance of sleep was nigh on impossible. At a truck stop just outside of Hidalgo he pulled in. When neither man woke up he considered waking them, but thought better of it. Staring out of the windshield he noticed a call box in close proximity to the Chevy. He was on a roll; he had the money, in a few short hours the Morales brothers would be no more, and he and Lupe would be long gone. He needed to hear her voice just one more time. Mumbling something he climbed out of the pickup and dug into his jeans for some change for the phone. One quick phone call couldn't hurt, but as the coins dropped into the box he knew Morgan would be sore as all hell if he knew.

Miraculously he got through first time. The phone rang and rang and rang. 'She should have stayed at the apartment,' he thought angrily, though he hadn't told her not to go out. "Fuck," he said as he put down the receiver. Fishing in the top pocket of his shirt, he pulled out a piece of paper with her mobile number on it. Quickly he dialled the number, glancing furtively towards the truck. He was in luck, the boys were still sleeping. "Hurry up," he cried impatiently into the phone as the dialling tone rang loudly in his ear.

He was about to give up when a voice, not Lupe's, spoke up. He recognised it immediately. It was Emilio Ortiz.

"Ortiz! What the fuck are you doing with Lupe's phone? Where is she?" His voice took on a strangled cry as he began to realise what was happening.

"Ah Tony, I've been expecting your call," Ortiz said with a mocking edge to his voice. "My good friends Diego and Ignacio were a little concerned when they hadn't heard from you. They asked me to provide them with a little insurance. Lupe makes wonderful leverage don't you think." He began to laugh. It wasn't a nice laugh, it was one full of menace.

"I've got it in hand, all I need is another day," he stalled.

"Well then, we'll expect you with news that the job's done. In the meantime, Lupe makes a wonderful distraction, don't you think?"

"If you touch her I'll feed you your own intestines! You mother fucker, let her go! I've money, I'll give it to you, half a million in US dollars. It's yours if you'll let her go," he pleaded.

Fearful for Lupe's life, Tony failed to see Morgan and Jake until they crept up beside him. Morgan had woken when Tony got out the truck. Suspecting a double cross, he'd woken Jake and they'd crept out unseen by Tony. He was about to confront his friend with the large calibre Desert Eagle when he noted Tony's reaction. It didn't suggest a double cross, the drained look upon Tony's face implied far worse.

"Feed me my own intestines, now that I believe. You fool, do you think I don't know Esteban gave you orders to kill me. I'm not the stupid pig you take me for. Now half a million dollars that's something else, bring it with you to the Hacienda Morales tomorrow after you've eliminated De la Fuente. Then we'll see."

"Listen, you worthless piece of shit! Harm one hair of her head you're a dead man, you're fucking dead!" The phone line went dead. Tony stared into Morgan's face, unconcerned for his own safety. "They've got her, they've got my Lupe!"

"Easy Tony, calm down," said Morgan.

"You don't understand, they'll kill her!"

"Far as I see it, you go racing in there they'll kill you too," added Jake.

"Phone him back, no one says no to half a million. Convince him you've got the money. Tell him he can have it all on condition he brings the girl to you tonight." Morgan paused, his brain cranked into overdrive. "If I miss my guess, I'd say he ain't gonna share it with the Morales brothers if he can help it. Tell him you'll meet at any place of his choosing. Just convince him you've got the money."

Tony fed the callbox. After half a dozen rings Emilio Ortiz picked up the phone. "Don't hang up, listen to me," said Tony barely concealing the panic in his voice.

A minute later he put the phone back on the hook, "I think he bought it."

"Good. What time are you meeting him and where?"

"It's an old deserted truck stop, five miles east on the main road that leads out of Monterrey. He told me ten o'clock."

"He won't be on his own," chipped in Jake.

"No, but at least he won't have the Morales brothers with him," said Tony.

Three hours later Tony, Jake and Morgan pulled into the deserted truck stop. It was a desolate place, home to a few blades of grass that somehow managed to push their way through the cracked and crumbling asphalt. Wind driven sand swept across the lot making patterns in their wake. Slowly and surely mother nature was returning it to the barren landscape that surrounded it. Morgan checked his watch, it was a little after six. They had four hours left to formulate a plan.

Chapter 31

▼

For months the papers were full of the heroic feats of the American forces and their daring deeds in Cuba. Patriotism was at an all time high. The heroic charge up San Juan hill, albeit with the loss of many lives, was all everyone was talking about at the Menger Hotel. Teddy Roosevelt's name was heralded loud and clear. Together with his Rough Riders, you'd have thought they took the ridges of Santiago by themselves. One man scoured the papers more avidly than others. That man was Zachariah Trelawney, but instead of reading the blood and guts tales of bravery, he combed the obituary columns. His obsession with Xavier Morales was at fever pitch. He was not a well man, the fight in the Plaza had cost him more than just his mobility, it had robbed him of peace of mind. His moods were becoming as varied as the hours in a day. Irrationally he believed that Alicia's husband would descend on them like an avenging angel, destroying the only true happiness he had ever really known. He prayed the war would last for a very long time, or at least until he saw Xavier's name on the lists he scrutinised weekly.

Ever since Alicia had declared her love for him, he'd felt vulnerable. Before, he'd been able to face any adversity with the confidence of a man who had nothing to lose, but now things were different. Alicia was everything to him. The thought of losing her drove him to the brink of insanity. He thought of himself as a cripple though to be fair, he exercised the leg daily and was just beginning to hobble with the aid of a cane. Alicia was never far from his side. She was a tower of strength, someone who could bring the best out in him. But when he was away from her, his irrational mind fed on the snippets of conversations he heard. On one occasion he overheard a group of businessmen discussing the deeds of a captain under Roosevelt's command, who'd fought so savagely that he killed five Spanish soldiers single handedly at Las Guasimas. Zachariah's blood ran cold, when his eavesdropping caught the phrase "twice the age of his fellow countrymen." Alarmed and intrigued, he strained to hear the name of the captain in question. "I believe he's from your neck of the woods," said one man. "Morales, yeah that's his name Captain Xavier Morales." The words burned into Zachariah's brain. Alicia's husband was a hero of the Spanish American War. The news, accurate or otherwise was enough to send Zachariah on an all night drunk.

When he failed to come home, Alicia sent word to Tom Tenpenny. If he didn't know where to look, then no one did. Tom was up most of the night searching the bars and taverns that operated along the San Antonio river. It was a little before dawn that he found him slumped in a chair of an old cantina on the south side of the river, two miles from town

"Alicia's been worried sick about you. You can't go on like this. If you do, you'll lose her for sure!" They were hard words, and spoken from a man who had been there. Tom knew only too well, how self pity could destroy a man from the inside. "If you think this apparition is going to come back to haunt you, getting drunk won't solve the problem. Go home, show Alicia your determination to get better, show her how much you love her, forget about Xavier Morales until he becomes a problem. Work on your leg, and work on your relationship, it's the only thing worth a damn."

Zachariah took these words to heart, he'd been a fool. He'd fallen into the same trap that his old friend Dallas Stoudenmire had fallen into, the trap of self pity. He changed after that, spending more and more time with Alicia, working hard at rehabilitating himself. His mood swings became less and his calm demeanour returned. He slipped once very slightly during the following months, and that was caused when peace was declared. Some-

how he managed to pull himself together, partly no doubt to the obituary columns that he still read secretly whenever he got the chance. Fatalities from the war were as nothing compared to the reported deaths as a result of the tropical diseases found in Cuba. Malaria, typhoid and dysentery were rife and the scourge of them all, yellow fever, was killing men in there hundreds and spreading at an alarming rate.

The end of the war brought confusion and chaos to many. When sons never returned from the war the worst was feared. It was many months before their families realised they'd either perished in Cuba or had simply been drafted to the Philippines to help restore law and order there after the War. As each month passed without any news of Xavier, Zachariah's strength slowly returned. By Christmas he was able to walk almost unaided. The cane, now a fashion accessory, lent him a dignified air for the many festive functions that he and Alicia had become accustomed to attending.

For a time even the rough diamond Tom could be seen frequenting the theatre district and fashionable restaurants of uptown, in the company of his lady friend. Tom's affair with Madeline lasted five months, before fizzling out just as quickly as it had begun. The shootout in the Plaza had somehow softened the man. His hot and fiery temper had been exchanged for a man determined to get the most out of life. Since losing Loretta, he'd kept one eye on his emotions and the other eye on the ladies. His latest fling was with an up and coming actress called Sarah. He'd spotted her one night whilst watching a play. He thought she was the most wondrous woman he'd ever seen but then he thought that about most of the women he'd known. He neither sought nor offered a settled life. Tom Tenpenny had survived death by a whisker. In his own words: "Life's for the living, and brother am I about to live!"

In one of their quieter moments he told Zachariah that of late he'd been thinking more and more about his Sally, and the life they should have shared. It reminded Zachariah that Tom Tenpenny had once been a mild-mannered store keeper. He found it strange that fate could deal some of the most unlikely men such a hand.

Ethan, a man who chose his words carefully, had started out life as a teacher back East. There wasn't much known about why he travelled West, but Zachariah suspected a woman was at the heart of it. He was a solid enough guy. A man to depend on when the chips were down, but a man you never could get close to. After the coroner's verdict on the deaths in the Plaza he'd opted for duties far from the big cities. Throughout most of the year he'd been seen in town not more than a handful of times. Riding the border kept him busy most of the time. He was becoming known as the scourge of the border bandidos, a far more complex man than Tom ever was. A man content to play the cards that were dealt to him.

Zachariah's own cards took on a surprising new slant when he was dealt a royal flush on New Years Eve 1898. Alicia hadn't seemed her normal self and declined to dance. She even refused to see the year in with a glass of champagne.

"What's up? Are you unwell?" His concern was most touching, though naïve to the extreme.

"On the contrary, I'm better than most," smiled Alicia. Even then he hadn't got it. Sweetly she stared into his inquisitive sad eyes and smiled, "Oh you fool, can't you guess?" She watched as the cloud slowly lifted from his eyes and the uncertain knowledge began to sink in.

"You mean!"

"Of course I mean. We're going to have a baby."

* * * *

Alicia had always defied convention. Living with Zachariah was scandalous enough, giving birth to a bastard would be far too much for the Victorian clientele of the Menger Hotel. But Zachariah and Alicia didn't care. It was of no concern to him that to his face he was treated with respect but behind his back he was talked about as a callous killer. He was conditioned to the flaws in human nature, a keeper of the peace had to tread both sides of the divide. But a slight on Alicia's good name sent him into a rage. Rough talk and rude manners were something he couldn't abide.

Alicia laughed at his pomposity, "Zack darling, I've been called everything from a Mexican whore to a woman of easy virtue. It doesn't bother me. It's what's here," she said pointing to her chest. "I love life. I love everything about my life. I love you. That's all that matters."

"Just let me hear them once," he continued.

"Zachariah! You are impossible," she said mockingly.

For six weeks Zachariah was ecstatically happy, until he received a letter postmarked New York. On opening it, he found it was from the Governor of New York, Theodore Roosevelt no less. The tall Ranger read the letter with trepidation in his heart. He'd known Teddy very briefly, kindred spirit they might have been, but friends who send letters from afar? Zachariah didn't think so. The letter was pleasant enough, briefly dwelling on his time in Cuba and his surprise nomination and the ensuing election as Governor of New York state. The amazing thing was, Roosevelt knew about the gunfight in the Military Plaza. He even asked after his health; whether his leg was fully recovered. As Zachariah read on the tone of the letter was beginning to change. Even before he read it he knew what was coming. "Our mutual friend Xavier Morales fought gallantly alongside me and my Rough Riders and earned the highest decorations our great country has to offer. His bravery and extraordinary skill with a pistol, are quite remarkable. At Las Guasimas where he killed five Spaniards and later on Kettle Hill where he saved the lives of two of my closest friends, his courage was truly astounding. I might also add that his compassion for the wounded on both sides was equally astonishing. He's not someone I'd like to make an enemy of since he's held in high regard by both sides of the house, a true patriot."

Zachariah mused over the letter. Roosevelt was cryptically warning him, not just against the man's skills with a pistol, but that he had made many powerful friends.

He kept back the letter from Alicia, preferring to face the looming dangers on his own. What good would it do Alicia as the baby grew inside her? Instead he held it back, and watched as Alicia bloomed in the spring sunshine. He drew comfort from that fact. For the first time he could truly believe she was his, no wedding band could lay testimony to love more than the plumpness of Alicia's body.

Whatever happened, Zachariah vowed he would see the birth of his child. Nothing else mattered. He wanted to run but his injuries, though healed, meant travelling would be both arduous and painful. Besides, it wasn't advisable to travel while Alicia was pregnant. The only thing that worried him was Roosevelt's warning of Xavier's powerful friends. He was a man who had spent most of his adult years defending the rights of others. Not once had he stepped over the line. He remembered his oath, he remembered the constitution. Somewhere it was written, every man has a right to bear arms and defend himself. Safe in his interpretation of the constitution, Zachariah awaited the outcome.

*   *   *   *

Another problem worried Zachariah equally as much as the return of Xavier. The high life they'd been living, the luxury hotel, room service and expensive meals all had been paid for with Zachariah's percentage from the tables. That and the meagre savings Alicia had brought with her. Foolishly he'd squandered his life savings. Now there was hardly enough to pay his medical bills. With a new baby on the horizon Zachariah had to get back to work. Leaving town was no longer an option, it was a luxury he couldn't afford.

Alicia had two months to go when she happened to notice the worried frown on Zachariah's face. "Zack, my darling, what's wrong?" He tried brushing it off as nothing, but Alicia had known him long enough to know something was troubling him. "You can't fool me Zachariah Trelawney, I know something's up."

"It ain't that bad Alicia. We just got to tighten our belts is all."

"I don't understand?"

"The money's all gone. I need to get back to the tables, I need to earn a living. We won't starve, I'll look after you and the baby real well, you'll see."

Alicia sensed he had more to say, "Zachariah level with me, is that all that's bothering you?" The way she asked left him no choice, "What if Xavier comes looking for you? I ain't giving you up. I'll kill him before I'd allow that!"

"Easy Zack, if Xavier does come looking, when he sees me with child, he'll back off. He'll see I'm taken care of."

"He'll come gunning for me, there's nothing surer," he mumbled under his breath. At that precise moment Zachariah understood what cards he'd been dealt. He always thought it was a running flush but it turned out he was holding a pair of aces and eights, the dead man's hand.

As Alicia's time grew nearer, Zachariah's thoughts turned black. Officially he was still a Ranger, though he hadn't drawn pay for over a year. That fact alone hopefully would give him all the protection he'd need if he happened to kill Alicia's husband. By the laws of Mexico if Xavier had died in battle Alicia would inherit the ranch in San Antonio and the Hacienda near Monterrey. She stood to be a very rich widow if he died suddenly. It was widely known that he'd threatened to kill Zachariah on sight. If he came looking for a fight and Zachariah killed him, it wouldn't be murder, it would be self defence. He would have brought it on himself. With these dark murderous thoughts in mind, Zachariah began to make preparations. For weeks he practised in secret, getting the short barrel Colt that he'd used to kill Kendrickson, into action. He'd had a leather sleeve sewn into the left-hand pocket of his vest. Not for a second did the tall Ranger doubt the deadliness of Xavier Morales. If he came on Zachariah unexpectedly the shorter Colt would be the more accessible. Xavier would expect him to draw the long-barrelled Colt which he wore in plain sight under his coat, not the hideaway gun. It was an edge, an edge that could prove the difference between life and death. Coldly and with a calculated cunning, he prepared himself for the inevitable showdown.

Chapter 32

It was hotter than hell as the Blazer's headlights caught the old sign of the disused truck stop. Clicking on the indicator, Tony pulled off the road and entered the deserted parking lot. Even though the air conditioner was on full blast sweat trickled into his eyes. He wiped it away with the back of his hand. He was scared, more scared than he'd been all his life. It wasn't much of a plan, but it was all they'd got. As his main beam swept the empty lot he prayed Ortiz would show up. He prayed Lupe would be with him. He prayed that somehow they would both make it out alive. Tony glanced down at his watch, it was 9.55 p.m. Parking the Blazer, he switched off the engine. He pulled the Beretta from his waist band and checked the clip.

The bright green diodes of the dashboard clock registered ten o'clock. Absentmindedly Tony wiped his sweaty palms down the front of his jeans. Then he saw it, purring slowly to the entrance of the parking lot. The indicator lights of a ninety three Eldorado clicked into action. Tony braced himself. As the car slowly approached him, he strained his eyes desperately to make out the occupants of the Eldorado. He couldn't see clearly who was sitting in the car, only that there were four occupants. He flicked his main beam on to indicate that was far enough. The Eldorado came to a stop facing the Blazer. Tony judged that the distance between them was about thirty yards. He knew Ortiz for the greedy bastard that he was. He wouldn't try to kill Tony until he was sure the half million existed.

A door opened cautiously and Emilio Ortiz stepped out. Tony studied the older man carefully. On his face a smug look of triumph. A man who thought he had all bases covered. The driver's door opened and another man got out. Tony had never seen him before. He was around thirty, young and athletically built, weighing approximately two hundred and twenty pounds, and from the shape of him, all raw muscle. Tony pulled the nine millimetre from his waistband, then glacing once at the dash board clock, he stepped out, grabbing the sports duffel at the same time.

Dumping the duffel on the ground in front of him he shouted across the dark void. "Show me Lupe!"

"The money, show me the money," said Ortiz greedily.

"It's here, in the bag," answered Tony.

"The girl, she is quite well," said Ortiz, as he indicated for the interior lights of the Cadillac to be switched on.

Tony gasped and his heart leapt as he could just make out the small face of Lupe.

"The money," shouted Ortiz. He raised his hand and Tony could just make out the third man as he put a gun to Lupe's head.

"No," he cried out involuntarily.

"The money!" repeated Ortiz.

A blast of rock music punctured the still night air. "What the…!" cried Ortiz, as an old pickup and horse trailer clanked and groaned into the parking lot. The drug dealer stared mesmerised as the horse trailer drew level with him. A peon in a large straw hat unrolled the window of the pickup.

"Get the fuck outta here….!" Ortiz started to say, until he found himself staring down the barrel of a Winchester Pump action shotgun.

"No mother-fucker, do as I say or your head's mush," threatened Morgan.

Ortiz was a survivor. It took him a milli-second to control his surprise. "One word from me and the girl dies!"

"Tell him to send her out and I'll let you live," said Tony hesitantly.

"If I do that, you'll kill me anyway."

It was a Mexican standoff. The tall driver had his hand on the butt of his revolver. Ortiz was fingering something inside his jacket and the guy in the car had a cannon pressed against Lupe's head. Jake by now should have the man in the car in his sights from his vantage point at the rear of the trailer. 'If only he could get the man to put the gun down,' thought Tony. "Emilio, he's making me nervous, tell him to lower the gun."

The drug dealer at that moment was far from afraid. In his head he was calculating his chance of escape. He was short and fat, but he was quicker than most men half his age. The element of surprise had got him out of far worse scrapes than this, he needed a distraction. "Tell your friend to point that shotgun at someone else then maybe I'll tell him."

Sweat poured from Tony's brow, "Morg do as he says!"

"It's your call," said Morgan as he slowly redirected the shotgun. Ortiz watched as the barrel moved away.

"Kill her!"

"No....!" screamed Tony. It was hardly out of his mouth before he heard a sickening thud, followed a split second later by the sound of Jake's M15 opening up.

"Lupe!"

Caught off guard, Tony felt a searing pain as a switchblade sliced into his shoulder. "Ahhhh," he cried as Ortiz, quicker than a cat, brought the blade down for the kill. But Tony was even faster as he parried the knife thrust and brought the full force of his Beretta crashing hard against the side of Ortiz's head.

At the same instant the driver pulled his weapon and tried levelling it at Morgan.

"Boom!"

The shotgun in the Ranger's hands spat death as two hundred and twenty pounds of raw boned muscle crashed to the floor. The fight was over in seconds.

"Oh Jesus no....!" Tony rushed towards the Eldorado.

Before he could get there Jake grabbed him and pulled him away. "There's nothing you can do for her, she gone."

"No, she's alive, she's got to be!" Why had things gone so terribly wrong? One minute she's alive, the next....... He couldn't believe it. It was his worst nightmare. His mother dead in a car accident, his father shot by an over zealous patrolman, now this......God couldn't, no God wouldn't be so cruel.'

For that moment in time Tony hated Jake, and could've killed Morgan. Why had he listened to him. Why had he allowed himself to be brought back to this God forsaken land? Why had he fallen so desperately in love...? Why? Why? Why? And then his anger turned in on itself. Why hadn't he thought out the plan more carefully? "It's my fault, I shou......"

"It ain't your fault. It ain't anyone's fault," cried Morgan. Looking down at Lupe's body he realised the true horror of what he'd just witnessed. "She's been dead for at least twenty four hours. You couldn't save her. She was already dead, when you made that phone call."

"What......!" Tony slumped to the floor, "That's impossible!"

"I'm sorry Tony, it's true," said Morgan, "Tell him, you piece of shit." Then he kicked at the unconscious Ortiz. The drug dealer began to stir, "Wake up you murdering bastard, wake up and take what's coming to you." There was blood in Morgan's eye.

Emilio Ortiz rose to his knees, his hands clenched together in a vain attempt at mercy. "I didn't kill her, Ignacio ordered it done. The Albino killed her. There was nothing I could do." Morgan smashed him hard across the mouth with the barrel of the shotgun.

Tony pulled himself up with Jake's help and in a voice devoid of emotions said,. "Jake I want to see her. I want to see what those bastards did to her."

"No Tony, it's best you don't."

"I tried to stop them, I really did," spluttered Ortiz through his broken mouth, the front of his light coloured slacks stained with urine.

Tony pulled free of Jake and turned back to the cringing Ortiz. "You knew she was dead!" His pistol smashed into the side of Ortiz's face. "You weren't satisfied with violating her when she was alive, you had to violate her when she was dead. Look at me you fucking piece of dog crap, look at me! I want you to see it coming," he screamed maniacally. With his left hand he grabbed the drug dealer's greasy hair and yanked his head up so the crossbeams of the two vehicles almost blinded him.

"Please, don't kill me!"

Tony forced the barrel of the Beretta inside Ortiz's broken mouth and cocked the hammer. "I promised her I'd kill you. At least I can do that for her. Tell the Devil hello from me." Morgan and Jake watched sombrely as Tony squeezed the trigger.

An uneasy silence descended on the disused parking lot. It couldn't have lasted more than a few seconds but in the surreal atmosphere it seemed an eternity. Morgan was the first to speak."We'd better get the fuck outta here."

"I can't leave her, not with them," cried Tony. "I want to take her somewhere, somewhere she can rest in peace."

Morgan glanced across to his Sergeant, "I'll see to it," said Jake. "You go with Morgan, we'll follow in the Blazer after I've cleaned up here."

Dazed and in shock, Tony allowed Morgan to lead him to the old pickup. "See you at the rendezvous," said Morgan as he cast an eye back towards the big man.

Jake grunted, then effortlessly he picked up the body of the driver and dumped him into the front seat of the Eldorado. Then with even less effort he picked up the body of Ortiz and dumped him next to the driver.

As Morgan drove out of the parking lot he stole a glance back towards the scene of carnage. Jake lifted the tiny body of Lupe Chavez from the back seat and lay it gently in the back of the Blazer. Half a mile down the road Morgan heard the explosion. Looking in his rear view mirror he could see the telltale flames of the Cadillac. Jake had finished cleaning house.

Chapter 33

Folks young and old lined the streets of San Antonio for the annual 4th of July parade. Alicia, against Zachariah's wishes had insisted she attend.

"Jesus, Alicia! You're about ready to have the baby, the excitement might start you off," *he said fearfully.*

"Nonsense Zachariah, the fresh air and a little excitement will do me the power of good."

As usual Alicia got her way, but only after she promised that when the parade had passed Alamo Plaza she'd head back to the hotel and rest up. "Damn fine father I'm gonna turn out to be, if you have us a little girl. Guess I'll be run ragged every which way to Sunday." *Zachariah was happier than he'd been his whole life.*

The crowd cheered as the marching band led the parade through the streets. Kids in colourful costumes depicting colonial days followed closely behind, then the fire service with its brightly coloured tender being pulled along by a pair of dapple grey mares, brought in especially for the occasion. Captain Platt and his troopers followed at a safe distance riding two abreast in something that almost resembled a uniform. As Captain Platt drew alongside Zachariah and Alicia, he tipped his hat in recognition. A squad of foot soldiers from the nearby fort were close on the Rangers heels. Behind them, forming the middle part of the parade, were Texas's finest; a contingent of Roosevelt's volunteers. They were dressed as they were when

Teddy introduced Zachariah to his Rough Riders in the Menger Hotel more than eighteen months ago, riding four abreast, tall in the saddle, proud men.

Proud victorious men they might have been, but gone was the innocence and laughter that accompanied these men in the bars of San Antonio in the months before the war. Shell shocked, some racked with the aftermath of disease, men old before their time. And then Zachariah saw him. He hardly recognised the man. Gone was the flashy smile. The sunburned face was now yellow and gaunt, the once proud and impressive physique now feeble and stooped. But the eyes, Zachariah could never forget those eyes. They bore into him like the rays from the sun; burning, searing hot orbs of barbaric hate. And then he was gone, as the parade marched its way towards the cathedral.

Zachariah stole a glance at the heavily pregnant Alicia and realised she hadn't seen him. He was glad. He was ashamed and he was fearful. Supposing she felt pity and decided to go back to him? He cursed himself for such thoughts. Alicia loved him, not the poor pathetic wretch who had paraded past them today. From the look of him Xavier wasn't a threat anymore. The war had robbed him of his vitality and his strength, reducing him to an old man. Zachariah felt ashamed of what he'd planned to do. The wanton destruction of a fellow human being had never sat well with him.

After taking Alicia back to the Menger Hotel, Zachariah went downstairs for a drink and a chance to think about his future with Alicia. He took his drink outside and grabbed a table in the shade. Seeing Xavier had given him plenty to think on. He was relieved that the threat to his life was over, that he would never have to fire a gun in anger ever again. In the cool shade of an olive tree he reflected on the men he'd killed. Every one of them had, in his eyes, deserved the killing. Johnny-behind-the-Deuce, Jasper, Long Tom Carmichael, and the others. He'd been lucky. He'd survived. He'd come through his baptism of fire and lived. He had a beautiful lady and a new baby on the way. Suddenly he had an urge to visit his sister and his two kids, show off their baby brother or sister. It didn't matter what. It was funny looking back. When Carmichael killed Alicia's sister, he'd been preparing to visit his kids. How long had it been. He couldn't quite remember, more importantly he didn't really care. All he knew was that he was blissfully happy.

"Senor Zachariah," said the young Mexican kid that stood at his table. The tall Ranger looked up. "Senor, I was asked to give you this." The kid handed Zachariah a letter. Reaching in his pocket the Ranger fished out a quarter. "Thanks Senor," The kid snatched the money and ran off towards, Zachariah could only guess, the candy store.

He tore open the letter and unfolded the single white piece of paper.

Dear sir,

I would be grateful if you would meet with me tonight at nine o'clock outside the Alamo. This is a private affair and I urge you to meet with me alone. As you are aware honour is at stake.

Yours X

Zachariah read the letter over and over. Was it a trap? Was it a challenge? Was it to discuss a settlement on Alicia? After all Xavier must have seen she was with child. Why outside the Alamo? Why nine o'clock? Why not here, right now? That he had to meet with Xavier, was certain, but go alone? Trust a man who he'd seen kill two young boys in cold blood? There were too many questions. But at nine o'clock that night, outside the Alamo he would get all the answers.

*   *   *   *

A single gas lamp flickered into life outside the Alamo. Zachariah checked his watch in his right-hand vest pocket. Under the lamp he saw it was almost nine. The streets were still alive with people, the day's excitement still not quite spent. Zachariah welcomed the crowd, it helped put him at ease. And then precisely as Zachariah's watch struck nine, there in front of him stood Xavier. His jaundiced face laying testimony to the disease and deprivations he'd suffered fighting for a cause he so truly believed in. A cruel man, hard as iron, stubborn, savage and brutal, yet a man of honour.

Disarmed by the man's feeble bearing Zachariah nodded, "Xavier."

"Pardon my appearance. Yellow Jack, it took over half my company, decimated us worse than the Spaniards." As if to illustrate, he coughed up a black tarry substance into a silk handkerchief. "Damn cough, just won't quit."

At that moment Zachariah couldn't feel any hatred towards the man. He was, in Roosevelt's own words, a true patriot. And then Zachariah looked into his piercing dark eyes and knew. Xavier's hand was reaching inside his jacket. A surge of adrenaline coursed though Zachariah's veins. Instincts older than time, borne on a will to survive, sprang into action. The tall Ranger pulled the short-barrelled Colt and cocked and fired in one smooth motion. The look of surprise, the frenzied grabbing at the Ranger's coat, the falling to earth, all caught so vividly in the slow motion replay of Zachariah's mind. Then nothing.

He awoke to find himself lying on the floor of a cell. He couldn't quite make out where, but he figured it must be the city jail. Standing up he staggered towards the cell door to find that for some unknown reason the door to his cell was locked. Realising there must be a simple explanation, he shouted out for attention. Somehow in the ensuing fight he'd been knocked unconscious and been brought to the jail to recover.

He called again, "Hey sheriff!"

There was still no answer. The exertion of shouting had renewed his headache. His vision was blurred. He was becoming confused and had started to feel a little anxious. He couldn't remember a damn thing after he pulled his revolver, except the look of surprise on the face of Xavier. Angrily he shouted as loud as his head would allow. He could hear movement from inside the office. "Thad, Thadeus Youngerman!"

The door partitioning the cells from the main office opened and in walked the sheriff. "You done it this time Zack," *he said in a judgmental way.*

"What, what, do you mean? Who hit me?"

"You got hit from behind by one of this here town's constables." *Zachariah threw him a quizzical look.*

Absentmindedly the Sheriff rubbed at his jaw with his right hand. It was obvious to him the Ranger didn't understand what trouble he was in. "Jesus Zack, why'd you have to kill him. Damn town's gone and got itself civilised. It ain't something the town's people are prepared to tolerate anymore. The days of settling scores in the street are over."

"I had no choice, it was him or me. What was I supposed to do?"

"Zack, the man's a fucking war hero."

"What should I have done, let the son of a bitch kill me?"

"Face it Zack, those days are over. Sheriff Youngerman was no stranger to trouble himself. He'd crossed swords with the best of them, but even he'd seen it coming. "It's a New World order, our time has come and gone."

"That's what I'm trying to say, I had no choice, it was him or me."

"The man was old and frail. He wasn't a match for you."

Zachariah remembered the eyes, they weren't the eyes of a feeble old man. "He went for his gun, I had no choice," *he repeated.*

"You had every choice, the man was unarmed!"

"Unarmed! There must have been a mistake. He was reaching for his gun when I shot him!"

"A letter. The man was reaching for a letter."

Zachariah slumped down on the single cot. The sudden realisation of what he'd done came on him in a rush. He could have sworn, things happened so fast

"Thad, do me a favour please. Get word to Alicia, find Tom. Ask him to come see me."

"I'll see it gets done Zack. But I have to tell you you're in a tight spot and you ain't made too many friends over the last year or so."

"Thanks Thad."

✱   ✱   ✱ . ✱

Tom arrived just after Zachariah had finished breakfast.

"Thanks for coming Tom. You've got to help me. He was carrying a gun, he has to have been." *The desperation in his voice was unmistakeable.*

"Easy Zack, if he was wearing a gun I'll find it."

Zachariah's keen sense of instinct detected something was wrong. Tom couldn't or wouldn't look him in the eye. It was enough to cause him concern. "What's troubling you Tom?"

"Ah shit Zachariah, I guess you'd find out soon enough. Xavier Morales wasn't alone when he came. His nephew Rafael and a bunch of greasers came with him."

Zachariah remembered Rafael from the first time he arrived at the ranch. He'd been reluctant to point that rifle of his anywhere else but the centre of his belly.

"That son of a bitch hadn't liked me from the moment we first met! He figuring to lynch me?"

"Hell Zack, I wish there was another way to tell you." *Tom shook his head in frustration.* "Nope, he ain't even in town anymore. He's taken Xavier's body back to Mexico for burial." *He paused momentarily before adding,* "Alicia's gone with him!"

"What! She can't have, she's in no fit state to travel! You must be mistaken, she wouldn't leave."

"I don't know why she's gone. All I know is at seven thirty this morning Rafael stopped by the Menger Hotel with a carriage. By ten after eight, Alicia's bags were packed and she was heading back to Mexico."

"She wouldn't have gone without seeing me first," *said the shocked and bewildered Ranger.*

"She did come to see you. It was an hour after the shooting. According to Youngerman she looked in on you while you were unconscious."

"She must have said something, she wouldn't leave without an explanation. What did she say?"

"Well, I'm only repeating what Thadeus said, I can't vouch for its accuracy."

"Go on, spit it out will you," said the agitated lawman.

"She looked in on you. Her eyes were glassy like she'd been crying. She's supposed to have looked down at you and said, 'I'm sorry Zack, I'm so sorry.'"

"That's it!"

"The moment she said it, she turned around and walked away. I don't know why. Perhaps she's had to return to the Hacienda to arrange the burial. After all she was his wife." Tom could have bitten his tongue. He added quickly, "Maybe she's going to sort out the legal side of her estate. Maybe she's gone there to raise cash for your defence. I just don't know."

Zachariah slumped back on his cot, 'Yeah, that's why she went. She knows we haven't enough money to get a decent lawyer. Alicia was always smart. She'd be thinking on her feet. She wasn't the type to sob and wail. She was the type that got things done.'

For a month he languished in his jail cell, clinging to those very thoughts. As time passed without any news he began to fret. 'Perhaps she'd fallen ill on the journey. Maybe she's had the child prematurely.'

With long hours to kill, Zachariah dwelled on his predicament. It was an awful mistake. Months even years of expecting the worse had taken their toll. He'd believed the man was going for a gun, or had he? He was even beginning to doubt himself.

The trial began on the 16th of September 1899. A defence attorney was appointed by the state when it became clear no funds were coming from any other quarter. Zachariah's lawyer argued the case that a long standing feud had existed between the two men, that Morales, had on more than one occasion, threatened the life of the Ranger. But it was the gun that was crucial to the defence. Tom had spent long hours questioning witnesses. Unfortunately they all claimed Zachariah and Xavier Morales were arguing in the street when for no apparent reason the tall Ranger pulled a hideaway gun and shot dead the deceased. Not one witness came forward in Zachariah's defence. For an attorney paid for by the state he put up a credible *case for self-defence. But for every point in Zachariah's favour the prosecution made two. The alleged letter was produced in court. Its contents were deemed irrelevant to the case, but as the letter came from a mutual friend of the deceased and Zachariah, it could be presumed that Xavier was in the process of showing the letter to the Ranger. Both men's characters were put on public show. Xavier Morales elderly land owner, frail and ill after serving his adoptive country in the recent war with Spain. A war hero clearly wronged by his wife and the man in the dock. Zachariah Trelawney, legendary lawman, faro dealer and chief combatant in the infamous shoot out at the Military Plaza. A man living in sin with another man's wife. A man now so desperately broke, that there was no way he could support a child and continue living the lifestyle of a gentleman. With Morales dead, his undeserving widow would inherit all his worldly goods. With the motive now clearly in the hearts and minds of the jury, it didn't take the prosecution long before a verdict of guilty of murder was brought against Zachariah.*

"No!" Tom Tenpenny cried from the public gallery. "Morales gunned down two young rustlers in our custody. He took their bodies and strung them up to the gates of the ranch. Not content with that, he drenched them in coal tar and set them on fire!"

"Silence," shouted Judge Driscoll, "or I'll fine you in contempt of court." A God fearing man of impeccable morals, a stern believer in Victorian values, a man who showed no mercy to those that transgressed. "Zachariah Trelawney, you have been found guilty of the most heinous of crimes. Once this land, this violent land, had need of you and your kind. I thank God that time is now at an end. We are at the dawning of a new century, a new era, free of the violence and savagery that has marred the last hundred years." His sense of the dramatic sickened Zachariah's supporters. "I cannot see it in my heart to grant you clemency, therefore I have no choice but to pass the sentence of death. You are to be transported to the prison in Huntsville, where you will remain in custody until the 31st of December 1899. Then at 9 o'clock in the morning you will be hanged by the neck until you are dead."

Zachariah, head bowed, was led away in shackles to the town jail, where he was to be held until suitable transport could be arranged for his journey to Huntsville. Tom looked at his friend, a man he'd looked up to, a man who had stepped in when the chips were down, a man who had helped him overcome the ghosts of his past, a man who deserved a better fate.

Chapter 34

As Morgan drove past the gates of Hacienda Morales, he stole a glance at the Moorish towers silhouetted in the moonlight. He felt an involuntary shudder as a cloud slowly drifted across the moon, plummeting the hacienda into semi darkness. Never in his worst nightmares had he seen anything so menacing. He prayed that God would give them the strength to destroy the evil that dwelled within.

Stunned by the slaying of Emilio Ortiz and the grisly discovery of Lupe's body, Morgan's immediate concern was for Tony. He was slumped in the seat next to him, his face glazed in shock, his eyes staring blindly through the windshield. The man had had his dreams shattered in one cruel and devastating blow. From what Tony had told him of his feelings for the young girl, Morgan wasn't sure he'd ever get over the events of that night. In his opinion Tony was next to useless, his ability to function was gravely in doubt. Would he be able to shake himself out of his catatonic state before the dawn? It was the worst possible start.

Morgan drove for three miles following the fence line. At a junction in the road he turned right and continued until the landscape changed. Great chunks of ugly rock jutting up to the night sky, marked the beginnings of the foothills to the Sierra Madre. About then the road took on a series of twists and turns as it steadily climbed in altitude. In the distance he could see the pass, like a great black window, cut neatly in the side of the rock. The pickup laboured as the road grew steeper, causing Morgan to sweat profusely as he slammed his way down through the gears. He uttered a silent prayer to General Motors as he pushed the Chevy to its limits. At the top of the pass, Morgan gave a sigh of relief. Slowing to ten miles an hour he scoured the rocks looking for the clearing they'd agreed on earlier that day. At the large boulder he pulled off the road and bumped his way through rocks and brush until the road disappeared behind him. Switching off the engine he sat and waited. A shaft of moonlight cast a blue grey light across the impassive face of Tony Valdez. Morgan had hoped to bring their mission off without casualties. Looking at his friend he realised that was now impossible.

Ten minutes later he stood by the roadside and watched as the Blazers headlights lit up the road below. Waving the sedan down, Morgan climbed in beside Jake.

"How's he all doing?"

"I don't know Jake. He ain't said a single word since we left the truck stop."

"It's a bad break," added Jake.

The Chevy and horse trailer came into sight as the Blazer's headlamps illuminated the clearing. Jake switched off the ignition and doused the headlights. Morgan jumped down and walked towards the horse box. An inpatient whinnying greeted him from inside the trailer. "Easy boys, it'll soon be time to go to work," he said, his voice both soft and reassuring.

The door of the Chevy opened and Tony climbed out. Even in the glow from the moon, he looked to be still in shock. Suddenly he began to retch, turning away he vomited into the darkness. Morgan and Jake stood back helplessly and gave him time to recover.

Wiping his mouth Tony turned, "Jake, where is she?"

"She's in the back of the Blazer."

"Pop it," said Tony.

"No Tony, best you leave her be," said Jake, his voice faltering as he tried to save his friend further grief.

"No Jake, pop the tailgate. I need to see her, I need to see what they done to her."

"Do it," ordered Morgan.

Tony moved slowly towards the back of the Blazer. With a flashlight he peered down at the small childlike face of Lupe Chavez. It was mercifully untouched. "She looks as if she's sleeping," cried Tony. His heart gave a great surge, "Maybe she's still alive."

"She's dead Tony, the bastards killed her." Jake couldn't stand to look at his friend. He averted his eyes. He'd seen many sad sights in his lifetime but the look on Tony's face was the saddest.

"She's cold," sighed Tony. "I've got to make her warm."

"We need to lay her to rest," said Morgan. "You sit with her awhile, me and Jake will find a suitable spot."

With their knives, the two men stabbed at the hard ground, loosing rocks as they worked feverishly to dig out a shallow grave. Gathering as many small rocks as they could find, they finished an hour later and returned to the Blazer. Tony was sitting with his back to the rear wheel, Lupe cradled in his arms. He looked up as the two men approached him. "I don't want to say goodbye. I want to stay here and hold her forever."

"I know Tony, but it's best we give her a decent burial," said Morgan sympathetically.

Tony looked up at his Captain, "You'd have loved her Morg. She was so full of life. I knew from the moment I first laid eyes on her that she was the one for me. You wouldn't understand, no one understands. She was special, the most special person in the whole world, at least to me. I remember saying to her, the first time we met, 'Listen kid, I've spent my entire life chasing pussy. Searching for that one special piece of tail. You're it baby, you're my Holy Grail.' It don't sound much, but I know she'd have made me happy."

"We understand," said Morgan, though he doubted he ever would.

"Best you bring her over where she'll be more comfortable," said Jake.

Tony looked at him and nodded, "You're right Jake. Guess it's time." He stood up and effortlessly carried her lifeless body to the improvised grave. Gently he lowered her into the ground and looked up at his comrades, "Leave me do it, I want this moment alone." Morgan and Jake nodded and slowly turned away, leaving Tony with Lupe.

"I guess things ain't so bad," he said to her softly. "I reckon I'll be with you shortly." Leaning over her body he kissed her cold lips one last time. He lay there reluctant to move. In that moment he wished he could lay there forever. After a while he sat up, wiped his eyes, and slowly began covering her body with rocks. When he was done he removed the crucifix she'd given to him and draped it gently across the mound of stones. "I love you, my dark angel of Monterey, I'll love you forever."

Dawn's early light began filtering through the clearing as Tony walked back to the trailer. "It's done," he said.

Morgan looked at Tony, at the shell of a man he'd known for years. A man who had known much suffering, each time gaining a strength he'd never thought he'd possessed. This time it was different. His eyes though red and swollen told Morgan all he needed to know. Gone was the sparkle, where once a flame had burned brightly. He was looking at a walking dead man.

"Okay, here it is, decision time! We've come this far, we've struck the enemy a deadly blow. If any one of us decides to quit, I'll understand." He looked straight at his sergeant, "Jake your family is far more important than the vermin we've come to exterminate. Go home."

"I can't. I've come too far, seen too much, I can't quit."

"Jesus Jake, haven't you thought I might just want to quit. Life's better than death, even if you have to live it on your own," he said reflecting on the loss of Laura and Kathleen. "We can't change a damn thing!"

"Maybe not," said Jake as he untied the drawstrings of the oilskin, and unravelled their collection of weapons. He looked at Morgan, then glanced across at Tony. "I say we go!"

Tony knelt down beside him and studied their armoury.

"Shit," said Morgan as he pulled the Desert Eagle from his shoulder holster and checked the clip. "If I miss my guess, I'd say we're gonna give them sons of bitches a breakfast they'll never forget."

Chapter 35

▼

In the dim light of the livery stable Tom Tenpenny threw his saddle across his buckskin and cinched up. Working methodically he added his bedroll, saddle bags, canteen and fully loaded Winchester to his rig. When he was done he walked quietly across to Zachariah's mare and gently stroked her neck and withers. "Well ol' girl looks like it's time," he said soothingly, before placing the saddle blanket on the horse's back. He'd thought hard and long about his decision, yet in the end his heart left him no choice. Without his help Zachariah would spend his last couple of months incarcerated in the penitentiary, before ending his days at the end of a rope. To Tom, it wasn't a choice.

The streets were quiet and empty as Tom rode up Main towards the jail. Only the sound of his horses hooves and the gentle hiss from the gas mantles of the street lights broke the silence. It was nearing two in the morning as the old adobe jailhouse came into view. He had no clear plan, other than to bust Zachariah out and hi-tail it south towards the border. He didn't know how many would be guarding the jail, and frankly he didn't care. If he had the choice he'd do it as quietly as possible, but if push came to shove, he was ready to have at it.

Riding right up to the hitching rail outside the jail was risky, yet Tom couldn't think of a more natural play. Climbing down from his horse he checked his nickel-plated Colts, both were fully loaded. Pulling his hat down firmly over his eyes he stepped up onto the sidewalk. He peered through the window of the sheriff's office and found his luck was in. Only Jeb Taylor was on guard and he appeared to be fast asleep, his feet propped up on Youngerman's desk. With one hand Tom pulled his Colt from its holster and with the other he held up his Texas Ranger badge to the peep hole. He banged loudly on the door, loud enough to shock the deputy and throw him off guard.

"Hello the jail. Captain Platt, Frontier Battalion Texas Rangers! Open up!"

The ruse worked, Jeb Taylor was having the sleep of his life when he was jolted back to the real world. For one heart stopping moment he thought he'd slept the whole night and Sheriff Youngerman was hollering his ass off. He figured the Rangers were the ones to escort the prisoner to Huntsville. It was only as he slipped the bolt that he realised his mistake. Tom smashed him hard across the forehead with his nickel plated pistol, sending the deputy flying back into the room. Shocked and scared half to death, Jeb Taylor looked down the barrel of the Colt at the snarling face of Tenpenny.

"Oh Jesus! Tom don't kill me!"

"Stop your whimpering. Do as I say, you'll live to see morning. Where's the keys?"

Jeb began to stammer, "They'rrreee…innn the top drraweer."

"Get them!"

Zachariah hobbled to the front of his cell. "Tom! What in blue blazes are you doing?"

"What the hell do ya think I'm doing," *said the sandy haired Monte dealer. Within less than a minute Zachariah had freed himself of the shackles they'd kept him in since the trial, and was grabbing his pistols from the Sheriff's cabinet. Tom motioned Jeb into the cell. Bewildered at the speed of things, the deputy didn't see it coming when Tenpenny laid his pistol barrel across his head.*

"Thanks Tom, but I didn't want you involved," *said the ex lawman.*

"Guess I ain't got much choice now," *said Tom cheerily.*

Grabbing his dark frock coat and hat from a hook on the wall, Zachariah stepped swiftly outside into the cool night air. He stood and stared at the empty and deserted street. It was his first glimpse of freedom in three months. Zachariah's mare whinnied a greeting as the familiar figure of her master stepped over to pet her.

"How ya doing old girl?" he said affectionately, and patted her neck. Stiff from the months of inactivity, it took him three attempts before he got a foot in the stirrup. Tom watched the street while Zachariah brought his horse around, then both men walked their horses slowly down the main thoroughfare away from the jail. Ten minutes later they reached the city limits and kicked their horses into a gallop.

At daybreak they rested their horses at the edge of a stream. Zachariah took a swig from his canteen and poured the rest over his weary head. Then crouching down he refilled his canteen. Standing up he stretched his tired muscles and turned towards his friend. His hand outstretched.

"Thanks Tom. Thanks for giving me my life back."

"Don't mention it. You'd have done the same for me."

"Where you heading?"

"I kinda figured on riding with you awhile," said Tom.

"Well I'm heading for hell and damnation. Mexico. If I miss my guess, I'd say my Alicia's at the ranch-house near Monterrey. I've got to find her, I've got to see my child. I've got to find out why she ran."

"Mexico's fine. I kinda expected that's where we're heading.

"About now Youngerman's getting himself a posse together. I reckon he'll follow us until we make the Nueces river. Let's ride."

Zachariah was a little out in his deductions, Sheriff Youngerman followed them only as far as the Frio, then he headed back to San Antonio. He wasn't prepared to waste more time than was necessary. After all Captain Platt and his troop of Rangers had been informed, and had by now already set out after the two fugitives.

Captain Platt, a stickler for the rules, had taken it as a personal affront that two of his men should have turned bad. Before setting off on the manhunt, he'd wired Ethan Book in Laredo to be on the lookout for the law breakers Zachariah Trelawney and Tom Tenpenny.

Ethan Book read the telegram with incredulity. He'd been chasing bandits along the border for the last few months and hadn't any knowledge of what had been happening in San Antonio.

"Jesus H Christ!" The tall gangly lawman sat down and re-read the telegram. Zack and Tom were his friends, together they'd fought side by side against the Kendrickson faction. Now he was expected to hunt them down! If they resisted he was to turn his 50 calibre Sharps on them. It didn't make sense.

* * * *

The same mangy curs gave a cursory glance to the two horsemen as they rode into town. Zachariah looked across the street to the Jade Palace. It still looked as derelict and run down as the last time. Nothing much had changed in Dog Town. Tom guided his horse to the hitching rail outside the Last Chance saloon. As they dismounted Zachariah threw Tom a look.

"Yeah, well I kinda thought it appropriate somehow," grinned Tom.

A burly looking Irishman beamed a smile of welcome from the bartender's side of the bar, as Tom walked in. "As I live and breathe, Tommy Tenpenny, back to reek havoc or me name's not Patrick O'Dowd."

Tom took his gloves off and grabbed O'Dowd's hand forcefully. "Good to see you too Paddy. This here's Zachariah, him and me have rode some this past week. We're in need of a room, and a bath if that's possible."

"A room I've got, as for a bath the Rio Grande is out back aways."

"We're obliged," said Tom.

"You fellers look like you could do with a meal!"

"That'd be fine," said Tom, "but we ain't got a red cent."

"Most feller's that are on the dodge, seldom have," said Paddy.

Zachariah nodded his thanks.

"It's the least I kin do. Old Tom there, helped me out on many an occasion."

"Does that invitation stretch to a bottle?" Tom grinned.

"You have the cheek of the devil, and the luck of the Irish," roared O'Dowd as he reached behind the counter and produced a bottle.

Rot gut whiskey and a room infested with cockroaches filled their night. By morning Zachariah was ready to ride into Mexico. He didn't know why Alicia left when she did, he could only assume she'd been taken against her will. Powerless to find her whilst in his cell, Zachariah had been slowly going out of his mind. Since Tom had freed him from the jailhouse, he'd thought of nothing else but holding Alicia in his arms once more.

It was a bright Sunday morning when Tom and Zachariah thanked O'Dowd and walked out of the Last Chance. Shielding their eyes from the sun, they stepped off the boardwalk and began attending to their horses. They had a long ride ahead of them and a lame horse wasn't worth a damn. A careless man might neglect his horse's hooves but men like Zachariah and Tom knew a few minutes attention to detail could save a pile of grief. Zachariah had about cleaned the underneath of the mare's right rear hoof, when a cold voice from the shadows across the street bellowed out.

"Zachariah, you and Tom step away from them horses real slow!"

The hairs on the back of Zachariah's neck stood on end. He'd come this far, no way was he going back, unless it was in a pine box. Letting go of the horse's hoof he moved slowly towards the voice. At the same time he saw Tom doing the same. His hand inched towards the short barrelled Colt as his eyes located his target.

"That's far enough Zack! Move an inch forward and I'll drop you!" The voice was calm and somewhat familiar.

"Ethan! Ethan Book is that you?"

"I don't know what you done Zack, but I've orders to bring you back."

"Hell Ethan! Put up your weapon, we're old friends," shouted Tom.

"Don't move a muscle Tom. I can drop you in a second."

"You might get one of us. I'll grant you that, but it's my betting either one of us will drop you before you can bring that big old Remington into play."

"You might just have a point there. Guess if we all just ease off a spell, you might tell me why Captain Platt's after you two old boys."

"Sounds fair," said Zachariah, though his hand inched towards his Colt. "I up and killed that son of a bitch Xavier Morales. They claim I murdered him in cold blood, shot him down without so much as a half chance. Seems according to eye witnesses, he weren't packing. From the way it's told, I reckon that to be right, though I swear I believed he was pulling a gun on me."

"Zack weren't even given a fair trial. They took the deeds of a dead war hero against Zachariah's word. The town was baying for blood and that no good son of a bitch Judge Driscoll sentenced Zachariah to be hanged," added Tom, his eyes not leaving the hexagonal barrel of the Creedmour.

"Ethan, this here's a Mexican stand off. As things stand, none of us wins. Alicia was taken against her will, back to Mexico by Rafael Morales. She was carrying my child the last time I saw her. I have to know she's all right. What if I were to give you my word that once I've found out what happened to Alicia, I'll come back with you."

"Where's Tom figure in all this?"

"I busted Zachariah out of jail. And before you ask, I ain't going back."

Ethan looked at Tom and knew it. Returning his gaze to Zachariah, "I have your word!"

"You have it," said Zachariah.

Ethan lowered the Sharps. "You're heading for bandit country, an extra gun might come in handy," he grinned.

It was near dusk on the third day of hard riding that they reached the foothills of the Sierra Madre, another day's ride and they'd reach their destination. Tired and hungry they made camp in a clearing near a clump of cottonwoods. Ethan had spotted a couple of wild turkeys a mile or so back and went in search of supper. The sound of the Creedmour was unmistakable.

"I reckon Ethan bagged us supper," said Tom cheerily.

A second shot rang out, "Guess we're in for a feast," added Zachariah.

After a full and hearty meal, the three Rangers settled down for the night, each man lost in his own thoughts. Ethan knew that whatever the outcome of the next few days brought, taking Zachariah back to San Antonio would mean certain death for his friend. Book was a man who followed the law to the letter. He'd sworn an oath, yet Zachariah had been his compadre. It was an impossible choice.

Tom's mind was far clearer than Ethan's. Once Zachariah had found his Alicia and it was time to go back with Book, then Tom was going to blow the blond gangly Ranger out of the saddle. After all, he hadn't given his word.

Zachariah dreamed of Alicia and the child he'd never seen. In the dream, they all lived happily ever after. 'If only that were possible,' thought Zachariah before he too, drifted off into a peaceful sleep.

That was it, the trail ends.

Chapter 36

The early morning light shone on Morgan's improvised plan of Hacienda Morales. With Tony's input he'd somehow been able to draw a ground plan of the entire building area. Kathleen's nosiness had come in useful after all. With a policeman's eye he'd locked in his memory the tour Diego had given them. He still recalled the arrogant, cruel look in Morales's eyes. He'd played with the Ranger, toyed with his emotions. In a subtle way he'd let Morgan know that his life was for the taking. It still rankled how he'd appeared so smug and sure of his own security. He'd tried and succeeded in making the Ranger afraid. It wasn't something Morgan could forget in a hurry.

The small matter of an alarm system was worrying the three men. Getting inside the courtyard wouldn't be to much of a problem, but entering the house, that was something else. If the alarm went off, the entire police force of nearby Apodaca would be there within half an hour. "Seeing as it's Mexico, I reckon we'd have us around forty-five minutes to an hour," joked Morgan. "Our main problem will come from the house. If we can't get in, they'd be able to hold us off until the police arrive. Somehow we've got to get close enough to plant these," he said, holding up two small detonators and enough plastic explosives to turn the solid oak doors into kindling.

Each of the three Rangers was heavily armed. Apart from the 50 calibre Desert Eagle which he carried in a shoulder holster, Morgan favoured a Ruger Super Blackhawk .44 Magnum. It fitted snugly in a western style rig which he wore slung around his hips. Spare cartridges he carried in the deep pockets of an old oilskin duster. With his battered dark brown Stetson and faded Levi's he looked like a vaquero riding in from the night herd. At least that's what he hoped the guards would think. If they didn't he was ready to introduce them to his M16 assault rifle, which was slung in a saddle scabbard on his horse.

Jake was similarly attired, except he carried a Colt Anaconda .44 Magnum and the Winchester 12 gauge shotgun. In his belt he stuffed a Smith and Wesson 38 calibre revolver. He wore a greasy feed and grain baseball cap, a pair of Levi's and a ripped and torn red and black lumberjack coat, the left hand pocket bulging with shotgun shells.

Tony carried his favourite weapon, the 9mm Beretta and as extra insurance he was packing an Uzi Submachine gun, which he carried concealed under his duster. A bone handled Bowie knife he wore slung around his neck in an improvised sheath.

Morgan had chosen their weapons wisely. Not only were they capable of stopping a small army, they were the type mostly used by drug dealers. Working on the assumption that they'd all get out alive, Morgan wasn't taking any chances. He didn't want the Mexican police finding any weapon that could get traced back to the Texas Department of Public Safety.

"What are we waiting for?" Tony's face was set like stone. His only thoughts were of death and destruction. Ortiz had said the Albino did the killing, he also said Ignacio ordered it done. Both men's faces were etched into Tony's disturbed mind. Grabbing the pommel of his saddle he pulled himself up. "Good luck," he managed to say before twisting his horse around and advancing out of the clearing. Jake looked at Morgan, and gestured with his hand, "He's shaky man."

"He's also the only one of us that looks and speaks Mexican like a native. If he gets close enough to the guard at the house, he'll manage to plant the explosives."

"And if he don't," said Jake.

"If he don't, and they don't kill him right off, they'll raise the alarm and the Morales brothers will come down to see what's going on."

"Which means?"

"They'll think he's there to avenge Lupe's death. They won't suspect he's not alone. Either way the distraction should enable us to get close enough to inflict heavy casualties," said Morgan coldly.

Jake looked troubled, "What you're saying is Tony's our sacrificial goat." Morgan looked at his sergeant but said nothing. The time for talking was over.

They waited five minutes, allowing Tony a head start before mounting up. Morgan checked his watch, it was a little after six fifteen. He put spur to his horse and moved out of the clearing, Jake following a few seconds later. Together the two men rode silently towards their fate. A fate that had begun with a routine call to an old farmhouse. If Orville hadn't got himself so involved would they have embarked on such a mission. Jake doubted it.

As Morgan rode towards the great house he began wondering to himself just how many men were at the Hacienda. He had Tony's description of the guys at the party. Diego and Ignacio, the Albino for sure, the American with the Freedom Arms Capsull, whom he assumed fired the fatal shots that killed Juanita, and possibly the Mexican in the white shirt. Two guards on the front gate, another two in the Moorish towers, the servants and maybe another handful of guys in the living quarters near the stables. The more he thought about his plan, the more foolish it seemed.

* * * *

Hector Fernandez looked sleepily at his watch. It was six twenty five, 'another hour and five minutes, before my relief. Somehow that last hour always seemed to drag,' he thought, as he fought against his tiredness. It wouldn't have been so bad if he'd something better to do than just sit, watch and listen. From his vantage point in the left hand tower, he could see anything that moved within a five hundred yard radius. Any sign of movement or noise and the electronic sensors on his automatic searchlight switched on. Once to his cost he'd fallen asleep and the lights had come on automatically because of some damn coyote. Waking up with a start he'd sprayed the forecourt with a full clip from his Kalashnikov AK47. He'd woken up the entire household and for a breath taking five minutes he'd feared for his life. Instead Diego had taken the whole incident in good spirits. When Ignacio shouted out they'd found the bullet ridden coyote, Diego had turned to Hector and said, "It is a lucky thing for you that your marksmanship is so good," then he laughed. It was a laugh that Hector could only describe as the laughter of Diablo himself.

With the coming of dawn Hector usually relaxed and found himself drifting off. But this morning was different, he sensed something. His sensitive ears seemed to pick up a distinct sound, like a horse walking, very feint but increasing audibly. He strained his weary eyes, and in the distance he saw something moving slowly towards him. As the object drew closer, he could clearly pick out the shape of a horse and rider. They were coming towards the Hacienda slowly, and from the way the rider was slouched over, it looked like he was hurt. Hector trained the AK47 on the horseman, and waited.

While he watched the rider drawing nearer, he dialled the gate house on his mobile phone. "There's a horse and rider approaching from the Southwest pasture, looks like he's hurt."

"I thought the herd was grazing in the East section," said the gate-house guard. "I can't tell with them damn vaqueros. Check him out see if he's okay. I don't think you should disturb Diego if you can help it. Judging from the time the music stopped I'd say you wouldn't be too popular waking him up at this hour."

Hector laughed, "You're damn right. Let the patron sleep. I'll find out what's wrong, then I'll call you back."

As the rider drew closer, Hector Fernandez could clearly see the man was poorly dressed like most of the vaqueros who worked the ranch. His straw hat had seen better days, his boots were worn down at heel and the filthy ill fitting slicker almost dragging the ground as the rider clung desperately to the saddle horn.

"Quien es?"

The rider let out a weak cry, "I'm hurt, I need help…" Then slowly he slid out of the saddle.

"Holy mother," exclaimed Hector.

From a distance hidden behind a clump of trees Morgan and Jake watched the show. "I gotta hand it to him, he's got me fooled," said Jake as Tony hit the hard ground.

"We gotta hope his ruse works," said Morgan nervously. He brought the field glasses to his eyes and spied the guard coming to Tony's aid. Quickly he scanned the two towers, they were both empty. "If I miss my guess, I'd say drug dealers have cutbacks too."

They waited nervously as the guard knelt down to help Tony. With the speed of a cat, Valdez grabbed the guard around the neck. It was over in seconds, a glint of sunlight reflected off the eight inch Bowie that Tony wielded. Before Hector Fernandez had time to cry out, he'd already checked in for the one way journey. The two Rangers continued to watch as Valdez dragged the body into the nearby shrubbery. "Let's go," cried Jake.

"We wait a couple more minutes, just in case."

Jake glanced at his watch, it was six thirty. "Jesus Morg," he said impatiently. Morgan ignored his sergeant's outburst and waited the two minutes. Kicking their horses into a trot, both men rode towards the Hacienda. They trotted under the Moorish towers with the confidence of two weary vaqueros dreaming of a morning's sleep. Their horses' hooves clattered on the cobbles as they entered the front of the courtyard. Tony's horse was tied to the branches of an old cottonwood tree, close to an adobe outhouse. Both men dismounted and walked their horses over to the shade of the tree.

The plastic explosive was already in place when they hurried over to join Tony. "Good man," said Morgan in a whisper. "Right, the shopping list. Diego, Ignacio, the Albino, the short American with the Capsull, and anyone else that gets in our way. If we get all of them that's fine and dandy, but once the Morales brothers are down, we get the fuck outta there. Is that clear."

"The Albino's mine, I ain't leaving without finishing the job," said Tony. It wasn't the time or place to argue. They'd come to avenge a massacre, it was time to get the job done.

"Okay the Morales brothers and the Albino, after that the mission's over. We've accomplished our objectives."

"We need someone at the front to hold off any opposition," said Jake.

Valdez grinned and reached behind a stucco pillar and handed Jake, the coyote killing machine. "It's your birthday Jake. Me and Morg both been inside, we know the lay out. I'd be obliged if you'd watch our backs."

"It'll be a pleasure. You got it" said Jake, as he checked the working mechanism of the AK47.

"I reckon their men are quartered in those buildings across the forecourt," said Morgan pointing to a row of neat cream houses with red tile roofs. Immediately Jake rushed over to the large ornate fountain and took up his position. He rested the Kalashnikov across the arm of a golden cherub and propped the pump action shotgun up against the edge of the fountain. From his location he was able to get a clear view of the living quarters. For the first time since he'd agreed to go, he was having a good feeling about the mission. If they had outflanked the Morales brothers their chance of survival had gone up a notch or two.

Morgan and Tony set the detonators.

"Are you ready," said Morgan, his voice edged with tension.

"I reckon," replied Tony as he slipped the safety from the Uzi.

"Soon as the doors are open, we hit the centre stairs, with luck we should make the landing before anyone else......" The explosion ripped through the air, drowning out the remaining conversation. Great splinters of oak flew dangerously in every direction. A billowing cloud of black smoke filled the void. As one, both men charged through the opening. Chaos and confusion greeted them. Men and women, some in a state of undress, their faces bloodied and glazed with shock, ran terrified from the big house. Morgan checked himself, then swiftly cast his eye across the room and made for the stairs. A burst of machine gun fire echoed from outside as he reached the landing.

Jake had watched as the door to the living quarters of Morales' men burst open and six heavily armed Mexicans raced across the forecourt. He waited until they were in the open, then he let go with the Kalashnikov. Three men died instantly as the AK47 emptied its cargo of death. Another reeled in agony, his leg lying at an impossible angle. Miraculously the two remaining men had escaped without a scratch. Their small arms fire laying testimony to that fact.

Morgan's finger was on the trigger of the M16 as he kicked in the nearest door. On the bed a half naked couple froze in front of him. For a split second the sight of the naked female caused him to pause. The small man's eyes darted towards the large calibre revolver hanging in a shoulder holster on the bedpost. As he dived for the revolver, Morgan saw it was a Freedom Arms Capsull. Taking his eyes off the girl he began to depress the trigger.

"Look out Morg!" The staccato sound of Tony's Uzi filled the room. The woman jerked backwards in an obscene dance of death. A 25 calibre Browning Baby clutched in her right hand. Morgan swung around and fired instinctively at the short guy as he tried to bring the

Capsull into play. Fifteen rounds from his M16 sent the man hurtling through the closed window.

"Kill em all," cried Tony as he emptied the Uzi down the long landing. Ignacio, dressed in a sleeveless white tee shirt and jeans, burst from his room. His muscular body rippling with anger as he ran towards Tony, firing two semi-automatics simultaneously. Dropping the Uzi Tony reached for his eight inch Bowie, and screaming at the top of his lungs, threw himself at the charging bull of a man. Miraculously Ignacio's aim was erratic, missing Tony. Unfortunately a ricocheting bullet tore into Morgan's arm just above the right elbow. The M16 cluttered to the floor as the wounded Ranger cried out in pain and anger. Tony and Ignacio grappled the full length of the landing, one semi-automatic still held firmly in Ignacio's hand, the other discarded, allowing him to hold back the deadly blade of Tony's Bowie. Reaching the stairs, Ignacio smashed his head hard into the Ranger's face again and again. Blood poured from a cut above Tony's right eye and his nose was broken. He felt his grip on the big Mexican loosening. Ignacio gave a roar of triumph as he levelled the automatic at Tony's chest. Battered and bloodied the Ranger hurled himself forward. The momentum caused the Mexican to lose his footing on the stairs and together they tumbled to the bottom, losing the knife and the automatic in their fall. Struggling for survival both men used every ounce of strength to get to their feet. Ignacio didn't realise his left arm was broken until he tried to push himself up with it. A searing pain shot up his arm.

"Arrrrrhhh......," he cried.

Dazed and confused with blood stinging his eyes, Tony was momentarily blinded. As his vision cleared he saw the bigger man rising unsteadily to his feet. In desperation Tony looked for a weapon. His knife lay on the floor between him and the Mexican. With a speed he hadn't thought possible he grabbed for it, and dived at Ignacio, driving the eight inch blade deep into the man's thigh. He screamed in pain and toppled backwards, banging his head on the bottom stair.

Tony was on him in seconds. He pulled at the knife but his hand slipped off the bloody handle. Grabbing at the handle again, this time using both hands, he somehow managed to summon up all his strength and pulled the Bowie free. Ignacio's eyes opened wide with terror.

"Die you bastard!" Tony raised the blade above his head and plunged the knife into the centre of Ignacio's chest. In an orgy of bloody violence the Ranger plunged the knife again and again. "Die, you bastard, die, die!" In that moment Tony lost his grip on sanity, as he plunged his hand inside Ignacio's chest and tore out his heart. He held the organ and bloodstained knife high in the air and cried out in maniacal triumph.

Morgan screamed, "Tony!!!!!"

Valdez looked up the stairs towards the sound of Morgan's voice and stared in bewildered horror at the grinning face of the six foot eight Albino. In his hand a nine millimetre automatic. He started to descend the stairs when a burst of machine gun fire turned his body into a writhing mass of twisting tortured flesh. As the echoes of gunfire died, the room was cloaked in silence. Tony stared up at his saviour and saw the hulking frame of Jake and the smoking Kalashnikov.

"They ain't all accounted for," shouted Morgan as a warning.

Jake stepped past the mutilated corpse of Ignacio and ascended the stairs. At the top he barely gave the grotesque body of the Albino a second look. "Morg, you okay?"

"Yeah I'll live, but Diego's holed up in one of the other rooms."

Jake grimly loaded another magazine into the AK47. "How'd you want to play it Morg?"

Morgan looked at his watch. It was ten minutes to seven. At best they had three quarters of an hour, at worst fifteen minutes. They'd been lucky so far, only he had been really injured, and even that was something he could explain away. The longer they stayed the more hazardous it would become. Realising that Diego Morales wouldn't have any idea who or how many men had taken the Hacienda, he decided to try a bluff.

"Diego Morales, this is Morgan Trelawney, Captain of Texas Rangers. We met a few months ago. I'm here to bring you in for the murders of the De la Fuente family. I've been given my orders to bring you back alive. If you make us come in and get you, we'll shoot you down like the dog that you are. Your brother's dead, the rest of your men are dead, it's up to you. Either way, it's fine by me."

Morgan nodded to Jake, who walked to the nearest door and opened fire. Bullets slammed into the door tearing it from it's hinges. Jake strafed the open doorway.

"Diego, bringing you in without a motive ain't worth shit. If you want to live I need to build a case. Why did you have your sister killed? I ain't taking you back without evidence. I'd rather shoot you where you cower."

Jake moved to the next room and opened fire. Before the shots had died down a voice cried out from a door at the end of the corridor. "Okay, you win gringo!" An air of defiance still remained. "I'm coming out," he cried.

The door opened and Diego Morales stepped onto the landing. He had the same smug smile he'd worn when Morgan and Kathleen had paid him a visit. "I should have killed you when I had the chance. Your woman would have made wonderful sport."

"On your knees asshole!" The butt of Jake's Kalashnikov smashed into Diego's hip, dropping him to his knees.

Morgan stepped forward and pulled the Desert Eagle from his shoulder holster and held it to the top of Diego's head. "Okay asshole start talking."

"What do I get in return," sneered Diego.

"More of this you mother fucker!" The Desert Eagle slammed into the side of Diego's mouth, braking teeth and loosening others.

Shocked and surprised by Morgan's ferocity, he quickly answered. "Okay I'll tell you!" Gone was the cockiness, a prison cell was infinitely preferable to the other alternative. 'How foolish these Americans are, their sense of justice seemed so out of place,' he thought, as he began building a case to keep himself alive. "Juanita was a foolish girl, an inquisitive little fool. It was her curiosity that got her killed. If the bitch hadn't been making a bottle for her little one, she'd be alive today. It was around one o'clock in the morning, Salvador my father, was sleeping in his chair. Clemente his bodyguard had retired to bed earlier, it was the perfect opportunity. My brother Ignacio held him pinned to the chair, while I placed a plastic bag over his head. Even though he was weak from his illness, the old man put up quite a struggle. After it was done I heard a noise from the kitchen. When I went to investigate, there was no one there. On the drainer was a bottle of baby milk and it was still warm. We decided to wait until morning before taking action. It was an error of judgement on my part. In the morning Juanita was gone, the bitch and her entire family just disappeared."

"How did you find them in Laredo?"

"We have a massive organisation, we'd tracked her for five years and each time we got close she'd disappear. An agent in your Drugs Enforcement Agency located her for us, and was prepared to do the killing, but my stupid brother had been spurned by Juanita and wanted to handle things personally." Diego looked up at Morgan and grinned. "As you're no doubt aware, my passion is for the bizarre. When I asked my brother to record the killings it wasn't purely for my sole entertainment. Juanita hated my brother and I, her testimony would have put us both in the condemned cell. I had no choice, she had to die. Until she was dead I couldn't sleep safely in my bed at night. I had to see my sister dead."

"Why kill the Ranger?"

"He was getting too close. He was ambitious, he was like a dog with a bone. The fucker just wouldn't give up."

"Who killed him?" Morgan asked, but he already knew.

"Frank Jordan!" Diego allowed himself a half smile, he was home free. Quickly he added, "I'll testify to that very fact." He looked up at Morgan with a look of triumph and his courage returned. "Now are you gonna cuff me or not?"

"That Ranger's name was Tyson. Orville Tyson, and he was my friend!"

Diego froze to the spot, as realisation turned his blood to ice. He looked up fearfully into the merciless eyes of Morgan Trelawney and was dead before the echoes of the discharged Desert Eagle had died away.

Morgan stood over the body of Diego Morales and stared sightlessly at the man who had brought him to commit wholesale murder.

"Time to go," urged Jake as he placed a hand on his friend's shoulder and guided him towards the stairs. As they descended the stairs, they realised Tony was nowhere to be seen.

"Fuck," screamed Jake. They called his name but received no reply. Jake hoped he was outside with the horses.

The sunlight hurt their eyes as they walked out of the Hacienda and across the courtyard. Morgan's pony whinnied it's recognition. "We gotta find Tony," he cried as he awoke from his trance.

"There's no time," cried Jake.

As they untied their horses, Tony Valdez walked dreamlike from the hacienda, in his hands was what appeared to be a small bloodstained book. "I'll get him," said Jake.

When they were all mounted Morgan looked around the deserted courtyard and realised that God had been looking down on them that day. He paused momentarily before turning his horse in the direction of the Sierra Madre mountain range. They'd gone about five hundred yards when Morgan reined in his horse and looked back at Hacienda Morales. A cold shudder ran up his spine as he gazed at the hacienda of evil. "Ride on, I'll catch up!" He spurred his horse back towards the hacienda.

Tony and Jake looked at each other with indecision. They weren't prepared to leave without him. They waited five minutes, five agonising minutes until, to their relief, Morgan came riding towards them like a bat out of hell.

"Move it," he said as he drew level. Both Rangers heeded his command and spurred their horses into a gallop. An almighty explosion erupted behind them, sending debris high into the air. They rode swiftly without looking back until they came to the clearing at the gradual incline into the foothills. Morgan stopped his horse and looked back. A great plume of smoke billowed into the air, the hacienda was engulfed in flames.

"Burn you bastard burn, and may you never again rise from the ashes!"

Chapter 37

A year had passed since that terrible morning, yet listening to the voice at the other end of the line, it could have been yesterday. Morgan's blood froze as he realised who was on the other end.

"Morg, it's me Tony. I need to see you. I've something that belongs to you."

His first reaction was to hang up. It had taken an entire year to rebuild his life, and just when he'd thought he'd got it together, the past came flooding back. Yet there was something in Valdez's voice, that made him think again.

"Okay, I'll meet you at the Dead Mustang. It's an old biker's bar on the old highway just north of Laredo. It's between…."

"Don't worry, I'll find it. What time?"

"9 o'clock."

Morgan replaced the receiver and slumped into the soft leather chair in the corner of his study. A sudden stab of anxiety hit at his gut, his face took on a tortured look of inner torment, as he reluctantly began recalling the events of that day in late October of 98. A day that changed his life forever…….

While Jake and Tony herded their horses into the trailer, Morgan allowed himself one last look back at the funeral pyre of Hacienda Morales. To him the hacienda had taken on a life of it's own. It was as if an invisible force drove him to watch until every part of the building had been destroyed.

His quiet moment of solitude was broken by the urgent cry of Jake, to hurry it up. Spurring his horse towards the clearing he swiftly dismounted and led the mare into the back of the trailer.

Tony sat bloody faced and trance-like in the passenger seat of the old pickup, the front of his shirt stained the colour of dark burgundy. The sheer horror of what he'd done clearly etched upon his face. By his side driving the old Chevy was Jake, stone-faced and determined to get them all home safely. Morgan, though not really in any condition to drive, somehow managed to turn the Blazer around and headed unsteadily along the highway towards Laredo.

As Morgan began to relax, his arm stiffened up and he found himself in considerable pain. In the heat of battle he'd been too busy to notice but now as he drove the Blazer behind the slow moving pickup, he realised he would have to get medical attention. They were just outside Vallecillo when he was forced to abandon the vehicle.

Jake took the decision to drive it into a ravine and to continue on in the Chevy. Hopefully Morgan had driven far enough from Monterrey for the local police not to connect the burnt out Blazer with the killings at Hacienda Morales. Taking a cursory look at Morgan's wound he prayed it wouldn't turn poisonous before they could get to a hospital.

As they drew closer to the border Tony started to come out of his trance. At first it was a stutter of a sob, building gradually until he wailed with grief. Experience told his two friends that there was nothing they could do. No words of comfort could heal the rift in Tony's heart.

Dusk was falling as the lights of Laredo began flickering into life. A tantalising reminder that they were so near, yet so far. One slip and they could still face an uncertain future in a Mexican prison. Still cautious, they drove past the rocky outcrop and the clump of cottonwoods they'd come across on Thursday night. Jake continued driving the old Chevy and horse trailer for several miles before pulling off the road.

"Let's go home," cried Jake as he doused the lights of the pickup and jumped down. Within minutes they'd led the still saddled horses from the trailer and were heading back to the crossing.

Stealthily, under the shadow of darkness, they crossed back onto American soil. And it was there, bathed in moonlight that Tony Valdez said goodbye. Before going he offered Morgan and Jake a share from the sports duffel. Both men, sickened by what they'd had to do, politely declined his offer. With a weak smile on his face, he shook both their hands and disappeared into the darkness.

Within a month of their return, the body of Frank Jordan was found in his apartment. Someone had emptied a full clip from a nine millimetre into him. Judging from the autopsy report, he'd taken a long time to die. The Agency said it was the work of some drug crazed felon, but Morgan suspected differently.

Six months later Jake shocked everyone by taking early retirement, and had since moved to Sante Fe, where the most excitement he got was striking a ball off the seventh tee and landing himself a hole in one. "That's as much excitement as I need," he said once when he gave his old Captain a call.

As Morgan turned into the parking lot of the Dead Mustang, he began having misgivings about the meeting. Yet he owed the man inside a great debt. Without him, the Morales brothers would still be peddling their poison. They'd done what they'd set out to do, but at a cost that most men would balk at. It was impossible not to have been affected by what had taken place, each of them had paid a price, not the least Tony Valdez.

The place hadn't changed since he'd been there last. The same old hub caps, the tired Harley memorabilia, the grubby radiator grills. It was reassuring to Morgan, that some things don't change. As his eyes grew accustomed to the light he spied Tony sitting in a booth at the far end of the bar.

He was thinner than Morgan remembered, older than his years. His flashing smile and wicked sense of humour replaced by a more serious, harder exterior. He gave what Morgan took to be a semblance of a smile and stood up. "Hello Morg."

"Tony," acknowledged the Ranger Captain as he slid into the booth opposite Valdez.

"Let me buy you a beer," said Tony as he called the waitress over.

"What's this all about," said Morgan, his irritability showing.

"Relax. I'm not here to cause trouble. Just bare with me."

"I'm listening," said Morgan.

"The death of Lupe hit me hard, it tore me apart. I'd vowed on her grave that I'd return and see to it that she had a decent burial. You see, burying her on Morales land didn't seem fitting." Morgan nodded his understanding. Tony took a swig from the bottle the waitress had placed in front of him and continued, "A month after we returned to Texas, I found myself back in old Mexico. Funny though it sounds, Mexico was probably far safer for me than back in Texas," he said with a wry grin that contained no warmth. Frank Jordan sprang to Morgan's mind. "The Mexican authorities hadn't discovered Lupe's grave, so I was able to exhume her body and have her buried properly, in a decent Catholic cemetery." His eyes filled with tears, his voice faltered, as he recalled the event.

It was clear to Morgan that Tony was a long way from getting over the girl's death. Until now the Ranger Captain hadn't realised how much suffering the murder of Lupe had caused his old friend.

"They say there's someone out there for all of us, well Morg, she was that someone. She weren't perfect by any stretch of the imagination, come to think of it, who is? All I know is I loved her, and would have done anything she asked of me, regardless. Someone, I think it was an English guy, once said, it is better to have loved and lost, than to never have loved at all. That might be so, but it doesn't take into account the suffering that goes with it."

Morgan thought to tell him that given time he'd get over it, but changed his mind. He'd seen Tony deal with tragedy before, but this time it was different. There was only so much a man could take and come back from, and Tony had taken more than most.

"There's a reason why I'm telling you all this. I want you to think of what I've said when I'm gone." With that, Tony reached down and handed Morgan a package. "I meant to give it to you when we'd crossed the river, but Jake was so concerned about getting you to hospital that it slipped my mind."

Tony stood up and held his hand out to Morgan, "It's been a honour to serve under you."

Bemused by what Tony was saying, or not saying, Morgan gripped the outstretched hand and shook it firmly. Before he could react, before he could say anything, Tony was gone. For what seemed like an eternity, Morgan sat looking at the small package in front of him. 'What had been so important, that Tony needed to see me face to face? What was in the package, and why am I so hesitant at opening it?' Strangely nervous, he began to open the package.

Inside was a sealed letter, marked for his attention, and carrying an instruction to read the letter only after he'd read the bloodstained diary that accompanied it. In the briefest of flashbacks, Morgan remembered he'd seen Tony clutching hold of the same book when he'd emerged trance-like from Hacienda Morales.

Absentmindedly he put the letter into the top pocket of his shirt and stared down at the diary. Carefully he opened the book. On the inside page scrolled in long hand were the words,

Journal of
Lieutenant Zachariah Trelawney
Frontier Battalion, C Company
Texas Rangers.

Chapter 38

Morgan stared at the long hand script and gawked in disbelief. His hand trembled as he turned the first page of the Journal.

17th December 1899.

It is with a heavy heart that I record the events of the last few days. How I'm remembered matters little, but the memory of my good friends Ethan Book and Tom Tenpenny are worth more than a mention.

Tom broke me out of jail for the most valid of reasons known to man, he believed in me. Together we'd fought against insurmountable odds, not once in that time had he questioned my judgement, or me his. True, he could be a rough man, yet we lived in violent time and knew no better; except for what was right and what was wrong. His only transgression was cracking the head of my jailer. Ethan, a man honest as the day is long, allowed me the time to discover the truth. I wish to God he'd shot me down in the street when he had the chance. Let history judge these two men as the finest specimens of mankind it's been my privilege to have known.

14TH Dec 1899.

We'd made camp for the night in the foothills of the Sierra Madre. That night we dined like kings, Ethan having bagged us two sumptuous turkeys. It was a cold night, but with the food in our bellies and the tiredness of a *day's ride behind us we turned in for the night. We were blissfully unaware of the events that were about to unfold.*

15th Dec 1899.

I awoke to bird song ringing in my ears. It was a pleasing sound, the chirps and twittering of an American robin, a couple of warblers and if I miss my guess a wren or two. As I lay there listening, my thoughts wandered to Alicia and our baby. I knew we were but a day's ride from the hacienda. The thought of holding her in my arms grew ever stronger. I wanted to wake the others and hurry on our way. We'd ridden hard the past few days and I reckon the boys deserved to hug their bedrolls a little longer, so instead I brewed a pot of coffee and busied myself with saddling the horses. At least that way I could be guaranteed we wouldn't linger long over breakfast.

I'd no sooner put the coffee on to boil when my bowels started playing up. I gingerly hiked up into the under brush and dropped my pants. I'd just finished when I heard voices, Mexican voices. I quickly pulled my pants up and fastened by belt. From my cover I was able to make out five or six armed men. From the sound of them they didn't seem at all friendly. More importantly their rifles were pointed at Ethan and Tom, who were just rising from their bedrolls.

From the little Spanish Alicia had taught me, I was able to understand they weren't to happy at finding a pair of gringos so far into Mexico. The leader, I assumed he was their leader, a young Mexican, wearing a dusty black sombrero, a dirty white shirt and a black vest that matched his pants, was strutting back and forth, jabbering about hanging the gringos from the nearest tree, or shooting them where they stood.

I checked the Peacemaker, I had six rounds in the chambers and another eight in my cartridge belt. I knew that Tom kept one of his nickel plated pistols inside his bedroll when he slept. I could only assume Ethan would do likewise.

"Have at it boys, or get the hell out!" I shouted as I stepped from the undergrowth, my Colt pointing straight at their leader's belly. I was hoping

the sight of me would scare them off. Instead black sombrero, looked in my direction and I knew I had no choice as his hand reached for the gun he would never fire. His Latino good looks crumpled as a .45 projectile from my Peacemaker tore into his stomach. Out of the corner of my eye I saw Tom dive for his bedroll, then a blinding flash, then nothing.

I awoke a few minutes later to find my hands bound and my head bleeding just above the right ear. Either I'd been hit from behind or a bullet had creased my skull. Before I had time to discover what, a figure stepped in front of me. As my vision cleared I stared into the face of Rafael Morales.

"We meet again gringo," he snarled and then drove the butt of his Winchester into my stomach.

I grimaced with pain and would have cried out, if there had been air in my lungs. I gasped for breath, and looked around. Ethan had a cut above the left temple and was also bound. Tom was on his feet, his hands bound in front of him. From the look of him he was mad as all get out.

"I have your attention now, I think!" There was no compassion, no hint of mercy, just an evil glare. "We thought it was you. We heard shots early last evening. I hope you dined well," the hint of sarcasm his only concession to humour. "You are now a very famous badman, am I right! Even your own people turned against you. You are as nothing, you command no respect." It was obvious he was enjoying talking down to me. "Ever since you escaped from San Antonio I said you'd come. Well now you're here, you must be our guests at dinner." He laughed and the others around him began laughing too. Turning his back on me he mounted his horse.

Without warning I was pulled off balance and dragged forward for a few yards before regaining my feet. Tom and Ethan suffered the same fate, as the Mexicans began walking their horses. Within minutes we'd left our camp and our horses behind. I could understand why they made us walk, but why leave our horses behind? It made no sense then, but later, much later, I would reflect on it. It puzzled me for about twenty minutes, by then all of my attention was saved for keeping myself on my feet. Throughout the day we trudged behind the riders, sometimes walking, often at the run.

We'd fall and get dragged through the prickly pear that lined our route. Our escorts only laughed at our plight. I vowed if I ever got the chance I'd kill every last son of a bitch. But it was the sun doing it's best to fry our brains that caused us most concern. Midday, parched and dehydrated, exhausted beyond reason, we wanted to give up. Only the thought of Alicia kept me going.

My first sight of Hacienda Morales caused me to shudder. The last dying rays of the sun bathed the building in a reddish glow. I'd always known which way I was heading, but the sight of Hades filled me with dread.

As they dragged us like dogs into the courtyard, a reception committee began forming. These men, those and the others that rode with Rafael, they weren't vaqueros. I'd been around ranch hands all my life. Whether they came from north of the border or south, they had an easy going way about them. Hard men, but honest, men that rode for the brand. The men in front of me and the others that had dragged us across the vast foothills of the Sierra Madre were not those kind of men. The long march had taught us well. They were cruel, vicious, greedy and cunning. Soldiers of fortune, mercenaries, men that hired out to the highest bidder. What ever they called themselves I knew them by one name, bandidos! What were they doing at Hacienda Morales? And where was Alicia? I began to fear the worst.

We waited in the courtyard as Rafael dismounted and threw his reins to a servant. Without looking back, he entered the house. I looked at Tom, he was bloodied and battered, his face a mound of blisters from the effects of the sun. Ethan, so gaunt and thin, was holding up no better. I guess I looked much the same to them. As we awaited our fate, the first shadows of late afternoon began stretching across the courtyard, a cool inviting wind began to blow up, soothing us beyond imagination.

Two great oak doors opened and Rafael walked out into the subdued light. By his side was Alicia. My heart began beating wildly. Surely now our nightmare would be over. But to my surprise and horror she walked past without even a glance in my direction. I was battered and beat up but she must have recognised me. Instead she walked over to the ornate foun-

tain in the centre of the courtyard and gazed down at the young Mexican I'd killed earlier that day. Even in the poor light I could see her body racked with spasms of grief. The courtyard went deathly still as Alicia fought for control.

Then speaking in a voice as cold as death she asked, "Who did this? Who killed my brother?"

"God forgive me," I whispered to myself. I'd killed the brother of the woman I loved.

Rafael pointed in my direction. Without thinking I bowed my head. I don't know how many tortuous miles we'd walked, but in my heart I wanted to walk a thousand more, rather than face the woman I loved. Under my eyelids I saw her walk slowly towards me. I sensed her hand reach out and felt her cool tiny fingers raise my chin until I had no choice but to face her.

There was no warmth in her eyes, no hatred, no anything. "Oh Zachariah," she said, shaking her head. "You're a fool Zachariah! Why didn't you forget about me?"

"Alicia! What are you talking about? You knew I'd come for you. When you didn't come back, I thought something terrible had happened to you and the baby."

"There is no baby," she said coldly. "It was dead inside me, the baby was stillborn."

"No!" I cried, "It must have been the forced journey."

"There was no forced journey, I went of my own volition." She waited while it sank in, then she told me everything. "From the moment we met, when you told me of Teresa's death, I knew you had a liking for me. You were so full of yourself, how you were going to bring her killer to justice. I thought, what a brute of a man you were. I must say, you excited me, you were different. I had never known a man like you before. When you went away, I began wondering. Perhaps you could solve my problem, my dilemma. Xavier was kind to me, he'd given me everything I'd desired except one thing. Youth!"

I stared at her in disbelief, her face turned lovingly towards Rafael, and suddenly it became clear. She was right, I was a fool. It was so obvious, yet I was so blinded with love that I couldn't see. How could I expect a beautiful woman like Alicia to fall in love with a man like me?

"But why?" *I found myself asking.*

"I grew up poor. Do you know what that's like here in Mexico. The filth, the squalor, I wasn't going back. Xavier had shown me a life I couldn't have dreamt possible. Divorce was out of the question. He loved me with a passion only matched by his sense of justice and honour. His contributions to the Cuban cause were draining our resources. I had to do something before it was to late. I thought pitting you against him would solve my problem, but then he enlisted in that hideous little war. It wouldn't have been so bad, but he insisted Rafael accompany him. I thought by driving up to San Antonio and throwing myself at your feet, Xavier would come running. With your passion for me, and superior skill with a pistol, you'd kill him before he could go off to war. I hadn't counted on that dreadful little man Roosevelt. If he hadn't been with you outside the Menger hotel, Xavier and you would have killed each other for certain. After that, I had no choice but to wait out the war. It wasn't so bad, San Antonio is such a sophisticated city, and coupled with your generosity, how could I refuse. Only thing was, I hadn't counted on you having a little war of your own. When you got yourself shot up, I was left with no other choice but to stay with you until Rafael came for me."

"But you said you loved me!"

"I said a lot of things Zachariah!"

"We made a baby!"

"You don't understand. It was a mistake, it wasn't supposed to happen. I couldn't spend the rest of my life with you. You belong in the dark ages. You have only one skill, how could you support me. How many more people would you have to kill before someone killed you. Now Rafael is something different all together. He's young, handsome and ambitious. He knows how to keep a woman happy."

I felt sick to the pit of my stomach. My legs felt weak, not just from the forced march, but from Alicia's cruel tongue. I could feel the anger welling up inside. In front of me was the woman I loved, but at that moment I could have killed her. My heart was shattered into a thousand pieces. I tried turning away, but she pulled my face around. "You killed my husband, a fine and noble man, a nation's hero. That I can forgive, but you killed my brother, my beautiful handsome brother. You're nothing but a mad dog, all you know is killing. I should have listened to Rafael. He wanted to kill you when he heard you'd broken out of jail and were heading south. I told him not to, I said you were to be brought before me, I said you had a right to the truth. That letter, the one that Xavier was trying to show you before you killed him, it was from me to Rafael. Xavier discovered it and knew the truth. By giving it to you he hoped it would finish us. Instead it played right into our hands. You removed the obstacle that was my husband, and yourself at the same time. I was free to go back to Mexico, claim my estates and to marry Rafael. I was glad when you escaped, I wanted you to go free, I wanted you to know the truth, to forget me. My generosity caused the death of my only brother."

Her eyes burned into me, she'd taken my heart and torn it apart. She hated me, she hated everything I stood for. I felt limp, I wanted to die, I wanted her to end it. Instead she turned her back on me and began to walk back towards the house.

"You bitch!" cried Tom. I turned swiftly and saw him moving forward. He was bound and could barely walk, but he managed to advance several paces. "He's worth ten times as much as you!"

Alicia stopped in her tracks and nodded towards Rafael. Realisation came to me in seconds, I screamed, "No Alicia! No.........."

Rafael and three others pulled their revolvers and pointed them at Tom. I can still see the look of resignation on his face, just before the first bullet tore into him. His body bucked and writhed as if in a slow motion dance of death. His murderers continued firing until their guns were empty.

I raced to his side, but it was too late, all I could do was cradle Tom's head in my arms. He looked up at me, bewilderment and shock etched across his face. He tried saying something, but as the echoes of gunfire disappeared, his eyes glazed over and he died.

I looked up at Alicia with hatred in my heart. I wanted to cry out, but the words wouldn't come. She looked down at me and said, "I want him to suffer, I want him to dwell on what a fool he's become. I want him to beg for death. I want him hanged for the murder of Adriano. I want him hanged for the murder of Xavier. I want him dead an hour after the cock crows." Then she turned towards Ethan, who was still in shock at seeing a fellow Ranger gunned down in front of him. "And you lawman Ethan Book, I want you to go back to Texas and tell them Mexico has done their work for them. Tell them it was swift and merciful."

"Alicia, are you mad?" cried Rafael.

"No, my darling, I'm not mad. Give him back his guns, get him a horse, feed him and then send him on his way. Only an idiot would try something foolish, and from what I've seen of Mr Book, he appears a very sensible man. Besides I want him to carry the news, that Don Xavier's murderer has been brought to justice."

A Mexican grabbed me by the hair and led me towards an old hitching rail. I was knocked to the ground by a rifle butt and bound securely to the post and left there. Raising my head, I watched them cut Ethan's ropes and lead him into the servants quarters. He looked straight ahead and not once did he look at me. I wanted to cry out, I wanted him to say to hell with all this. Yet deep in my heart I wanted him to go free. He wasn't a part of this. Against his better judgement he'd allowed me to lead him into this mess.

I must have dozed. It was dark when the sound of a horse being led into the courtyard brought me to full consciousness. In the darkness I could just make out the gaunt figure of Ethan as he threw a saddlebag onto the back of an Appaloosa. I watched him mount and swing his horse in a wide loop. I wanted to tell him good luck and good bye, but a lump formed in my throat and all I could do was watch him leave.

16th Dec 1899.

Exhausted, and emotionally drained I laid my head on the hard ground and fell asleep. It was fitful and full of dreams. Alicia was there, dressed in white and looking as pretty as a picture. It was our wedding day and she kept telling me over and over how much she loved me. I didn't want the dream to end, I wanted it to go on forever. And then the spectre of death entered the dream, in the shape of Alicia's brother Adriano. His dead eyes staring sightlessly at me. I was a fool, I was an idiot..........

Coming out of my dream I felt a gentle shake of my shoulder and a voice speaking to me in hushed tones. "An idiot, that's what she called me. Well Zachariah, I guess here's as good a place as any for the fool and the idiot to make a stand." I looked up in surprise at the gaunt face of Ethan as his Bowie sliced through my bonds.

"Ethan, what the fuck are you doing here?"

"Said the fool to the idiot. What do you think I'm doing here!"

As I rubbed my wrists and ankles, he handed me my holstered Peacemaker and short barrelled Colt. "Had to trade that damn Sharps to get em," he said.

"We could ride out of here," I said. Although I had no intentions of doing so.

"We could," replied Ethan. The memory of Tom's death still clearly in his mind.

"How many guns you figure we're against?"

"I figure it's close to twenty six, thirty maybe," said Ethan.

"How much ammo we got?"

Ethan tapped his Winchester, "I got a full load." He pulled his Remington and spun the cylinder. "A full house, and I figure another ten in my cartridge belt."

I knew I had eight in my belt and another six in each of my guns, "Thirty you say. Well I reckon we're in good shape."

Ethan gave me a rare wry grin, just as the rooster began his wake up call.

* * * *

As I lay on the ground, pretending to be asleep, I realised Alicia was right about one thing, she said I had only one skill. I was about to see if that skill had deserted me. I could see them as they came across the yard. There were five in all. I guess it was their job to cause me enough suffering I'd beg for death. A couple of the men yawned, another was still dressing himself, while the other two seemed relaxed and were sharing a joke. To them torture and death were all in a day's work. Only two appeared to be armed, but all were unsuspecting. I waited until I could see the whites of their eyes and arose like a phoenix from the ashes and shot the nearest Mexican high in the guts at point blank range. The second I shot in the face as his mouth flew open in surprise. From the fountain I heard Ethan's Winchester as he opened fire, "crack, crack, crack!"

Three men all in a state of undress came rushing out of the house, one shouting, "I think Gregorio's killed the Texan!" It was a mistake he took with him on his journey to hell. My first shot missed but my second hit him squarely in the chest. The other two were similarly despatched as I heard the familiar sound of Ethan's Winchester, as it spat out its message of death.

Sporadic fire came from various parts of the house and grounds as I raced across the courtyard and found refuge behind an old adobe wall. Ethan, with bullets flying all around him stayed put behind the safety of the fountain. We'd been lucky, the element of surprise had been with us. Eight men were down and we hadn't suffered a single wound. From now on in we could expect things to start getting a little rough.

From the windows at the top of the house came a withering crescendo of rifle fire. None found their mark, but they succeeded in pinning me down. I watched helplessly as Rafael and six others took up positions behind the walls at the front of the hacienda. From his vantage point behind a stone pillar, Rafael barked his orders.

"Fabio, take three men and outflank the son of a bitch behind the fountain!" Gesturing with his gun in his hand he called to the upstairs window, "Santos, when I give the order you and your men lay covering fire."

Rafael hadn't served in Roosevelt's Rough Riders for nothing. His strategy was sound. Once Ethan was outflanked, the Mexican's in the upstairs window could pepper the wall I was hiding behind, while Rafael rushed me.

I watched as a group of men raced across the far side of the courtyard. One cried out with pain as he fell to the deadly aim of Ethan's Winchester, the others fell back. What Rafael hadn't banked on was Ethan's coolness under fire, not to mention his deadly accuracy. I shouted across, "Ethan, are you thinking what I'm thinking?"

"If I ain't, then you're dead," came the reply.

While we waited for the expected attack, I reloaded my Peacemaker. I figured Ethan had eleven maybe twelve rounds left in the Winchester. As yet his Remington had been unfired. I stole a brief glimpse towards the house, at a guess Rafael and his men were about thirty or so yards from my position. I began making mental notes as when to make my play, I could only hope Ethan was doing the same. It was all a matter of timing, and keeping of one's nerve.

We didn't have long to wait. The three surviving men at the far side of the courtyard had reached their allotted position. I have no doubt, given the ammunition Ethan could have taken them but selfless to the last, he'd restrained his trigger finger. Diving for cover behind the fountain, he came under fire from the stables to his right. A bullet nicked the heel of his boot, another tore a furrow across his cheek, yet the tall Texas lawman stood his ground and aimed his rifle at the upstairs windows of the house.

Rafael cried out, "Now Santos!"

A barrage of fire thudded into the adobe wall and ground, inches from my concealed position. As I braced myself for Rafael's charge, I knew a split second off timing and a bullet from the withering fire from the house would blast me out of the game. The familiar sound of Ethan's rifle joined in the melee of sound. "Crack, crack, crack." I knew Rafael would have left the stone pillar and would at that moment be racing towards me. I cocked both my guns in anticipation. In that split second of time, which only men in the heat of battle understand, I felt perfectly calm.

"Crack, crack, crack, crack," a window shattered, an agonising cry burst forth from the upstairs window. I launched myself to my feet. Rafael and a bearded man were less than a yard from my position. Their guns were pointing directly at me, they knew what they were supposed to do, but the message from their brains to kill, had been interrupted by my sudden appearance. In that millionth of a second, my Peacemaker barked death. Rafael's head burst open as my first bullet hit him between the eyes, tearing the back of his head clean off. My second, from the short barrelled Colt took the bearded man in the stomach. I moved swiftly to my left as a large Mexican charged straight at me. I fired and caught him in the side sending him sprawling into a heap at a far wall. Swiftly turning back I could see through the smoke and the dust, the others balk at the scene of carnage. A moments indecision, with guns drawn they had nowhere to run except towards me. Like a man possessed I charged at them screaming "Roll up boys, claim your ticket to hell! One went down immediately clutching his abdomen. I cocked and fired, I felt a bullet tug at my sleeve, another caught me in the side, sending me spinning into the dirt. The short-barrelled Colt flew from my hand. I braced myself for the end. Seeing my plight another six Mexican's plucked up the courage to attack.

"Crack, crack." Two spun backwards into the dirt as Ethan's Winchester barked it's last remaining shells. He was down and looked in pretty bad shape. From where I was lying I could see he'd been hit at least half a dozen times. His shirt sleeve was soaked in blood. He had a head wound and he appeared to have been shot in the upper right leg. Regaining their momentum the Mexicans charged. I cocked and fired, missing I fired again, but only heard the sound of a man scream in pain. My gun was empty, the short-barrelled Colt was a foot away. I dragged myself forward.

"Die gringo devil!" The first bullet missed, the second tore into my leg. Three men hovered above me, their faces in shadow as the sun began it's slow rise over the horizon.

"Come on you greaser sons of bitches," screamed Ethan, as he'd somehow managed to drag himself to his feet. The Remington spat fire, tearing one man from his feet, and blasting another in the gun hand. Seizing my chance I lunged for my Colt, and fired at the disorientated crowd. I emptied the gun, hitting nothing, but sent the few remaining Mexicans running for cover. Quickly I thumbed shells into my Peacemaker, ready for a further onslaught.

I lay there in the dust of the courtyard, the smell of cordite hanging in the air. I kept telling myself it was over, but somehow I couldn't bring myself to believe it. All around me were the bodies of Mexicans. To my left I could just make out the prone figure of Ethan lying a few yards from the fountain. Struggling unsteadily to my feet, I could feel blood trickling down my black pants. It was only a flesh wound, but I knew the hit I'd taken in my side was far more serious. I staggered over to Ethan, but I already knew he was dead. There were no more marks on his body other than when I'd seen him last. He'd been dying when he raised himself for one last hurrah. A man who'd watched my back in life, had watched it for the last time in death.

As the wind got up, and the dust and gunsmoke began to clear, I sensed a movement from the front steps of the house. I whirled around, my Peacemaker at arms length. Alicia stood before me, unruffled, unshaken by the death that was all around her. In her hand she held a nickel plated 38 calibre Colt Lightning. Never had a woman looked so deadly or lovely. She was wearing a long black dress, one that showed and complimented her figure. She was beautiful, her hair hug wantonly at one side, her lips painted a tantalising red, and her brown eyes sparkled and shone. We stood there for a moment, each of us pointing a finger of death at the other.

"You surprised me Zachariah. I knew you were capable, but this...."

"Put the gun down," I demanded.

"If only you hadn't killed him. He was my brother, he was so beautiful."

"I had no choice, he was about to kill Tom and Ethan."

"Of course you had a choice, he was my brother,"she shouted.

"Alicia, I didn't know."

"As kids we had nothing, yet we were happy, we had each other, Teresa, Adriano, and I. Now he's gone, I'm alone."

She'd hurt me more than she'd ever know, I wanted to hit back. "When I met Teresa, I asked her where she came from. The question seemed to frighten her. She said she would never go back. If I miss my guess I'd say something bad happened, bad enough to drive her into prostitution. She was more frightened of this place than of Long Tom Carmichael. She told me she had a sister in San Antonio, but she never mentioned a brother. Why was that Alicia?"

What came over me I'll never know, I'd deliberately tried to hurt her. I watched her reaction, as the implication I'd planted in her head took root. "It wasn't what you think," she screamed. The sparkle in her eyes went out, and she fired. I felt the breeze as the bullet whistled passed my ear. I was dying inside, I loved her, yet I hated her for all the lies and deceit, but my heart cried out desperately to hold her as I squeezed the trigger.

Alicia fell back with the force as it hit her high in the chest. Her beautiful face took on a dumb look of surprise, then turned white, then a ghostly grey. The shock of what I'd done left me stunned. I'd destroyed the only thing that made my life worth living. I dropped my gun and raced over to her. I knelt down and held her in my arms. I could see she was dying. "I'm sorry, I didn't mean for it to end like this," I cried. I wasn't a churchgoer, yet I'd always believed in the Lord. Not now, not now.

I rested her head on the steps and tried to make her as comfortable as possible. She tried to speak. I told her to save her strength, but she beckoned me to come closer. In a voice that was barely a whisper she said, "There isn't much time. Zachariah, I want you to know, I was attracted to you from that very first moment when you rode into our courtyard. Our time together, it...it wasn't just one sided. I really did love you. I know that now." She coughed and brought up a trickle of blood. She was frightened, I could see it in her eyes. There was an urgency in her voice, "Zachariah, hold me, hold me one last time."

I held her tight, "I'm here, don't worry, I'll protect you," I said, as I forced back the tears.

"Kiss me. Kiss me one last time," she cried weakly.

I lent over her and found her sweet and tender lips, and pressed my own against hers. In that moment her body grew limp and she died.

17th Dec 1899.

I spent yesterday burying the bodies of Tom and Ethan. I said a few words over their graves, and I told them my life had been made richer by having known them. They were men of this century, somehow it was a poignant end. I don't think the dawning of the 20th century would have treated them kindly.

After burying Tom and Ethan I returned to Alicia's body on the steps of the hacienda. I was feeling the effects of my wounds but managed to bend down and pick up Alicia. I carried her into the main house and found her bedroom. I laid her gently on the bed and arranged her so she looked like she was just sleeping. I stayed with her for as long as I could bear, then forcing myself to my feet, I said goodbye. With a heavy heart I closed her bedroom door.

Stepping outside into the sunlight, I saw the servants and peons, old and young, huddled together in bunches. They were in shock, bewildered by what they'd witnessed. I stared at them but none held my gaze. They stood back as I took an old kerosene lamp from the porch and lit it. Then I whirled it around a couple of times before hurling it into the great hall of the hacienda. The tinder dry furniture erupted into flame. I stood outside in the courtyard and waited until the fire had taken hold, then I walked across the yard and mounted Ethan's Appaloosa.

There was nothing for me here now, it was time to ride. I pointed the Appaloosa towards the mountains. From my vantage point in the foothills I watched as the smoke from Alicia's funeral pyre spiralled up into the heavens.

17th Dec 1899. Midday.

I hope that one day someone will find this testament, and see to it that Ethan and Tom are remembered for what they were really worth. As for

Alicia, I'd like to remember her as she was, the first time I saw her. And now I have only one chore left to do..........

Chapter 39

▼

Morgan slowly closed the bloodstained diary and sat there staring into the bar of the Dead Mustang. In Zachariah's own handwriting he'd finally discovered the mystery surrounding those empty saddles. 'If only Orville had been alive,' he thought sadly. Then he remembered the letter Tony had given him. Reaching into his shirt pocket, he stared at the letter. What was in it? What was so terribly important that he had to read it after he'd read the diary? Hesitantly he tore open the sealed envelope.

Dear Morgan,

I found the diary whilst in a catatonic state after I'd killed Ignacio. I don't know how or why I went in search of it. All I know is when I emerged from the hacienda I was clutching it in my hands. Something beyond my understanding, some force we'll never get to grips with, made it happen.

I read it, much like you've done now and felt intrigued enough to go back there and give my Lupe a decent burial. Whilst there I did some discreet enquiries into the Morales family. The baby wasn't stillborn as Alicia had told Zachariah. She had the baby a week after arriving at Hacienda Morales. It was a healthy baby girl.

Alicia, poor Alicia. She wasn't much more than a child when Xavier plucked her from poverty. He taught her social graces, a recognition of the arts and a grasp of the finer things in life. But what he couldn't give her was an appreciation of life itself. Loved by two older men, it wasn't suprising that she should fall for the charms of a much younger man. Rafael was dashing, reckless, and full of life. That he could manipulate her into doing anything he asked was an understatement. Away from his influence, I don't doubt she'd have made Zachariah the happiest man alive.

When she arrived back at Hacienda Morales she thought Rafael would marry her and bring her baby up as his. It was then that Alicia came face to face with the truth. He'd marry her, but bring up someone else's child, never. He even threatened to have the child killed if she didn't get rid. Frightened for her baby, Alicia gave the child to a servant couple who had no children of their own. Before she gave the child away she named her Angelina.

The baby grew into a beautiful woman, much like her mother before her. Her beauty was her ticket to climb out of poverty. She married a wealthy businessman and gave birth to a son when she was twenty two. A few years later they had another child, a little girl. She too had incredible good looks. As the years passed tragedy struck. The son, having immigrated to the States a year before the war, was killed in action somewhere over the Pacific just a few short months after Pearl Habour. Angelina was devastated, only the love of her daughter Pilar kept her sane.

Pilar married into one of the most wealthy families in Mexico and had several children. Angelina lived until she was eighty and died weeks after seeing the birth of her third great grandchild. A little girl, as pretty as all those who came before her. Her resemblance to a photo taken of her great grandmother at the same age was quite remarkable. She was a wild child, rebellious, spirited and full of life. She rebelled against the trappings of wealth bestowed upon her, so much so that she broke free of her family ties.

She'd been named for the wolf, and by changing her surname to the name of her great grandmother's adoptive parents, she became Lupe Chavez.

You see Morg, I think Lupe was put on this earth for one purpose. I believe it was Alicia's spirit through Lupe that kept us safe. When we

> *rode down to Hacienda Morales, the ghosts of Zachariah and Alicia rode at our sides.*
>
> **Vaya con Dios**
>
> **Your friend**
>
> **Tony.**

Morgan folded the letter and placed it between the pages of the diary. He paid his tab and walked out into the midnight blue sky. It was a starry night with no moon. A beautiful night, which was just as well, as he knew he'd be sitting up all night thinking. One question still remained unanswered, why were Zachariah's horses left at the campsite? It was a question he would ponder for many nights to come, but at least he wouldn't be alone, not anymore. Laura would be waiting. She'd been there at the hospital when he was treated for the gunshot wound. (Jake explained it off as a shooting accident) He'd told her everything. She listened sympathetically and was very patient with him. She stayed for a week until his arm felt better, then she drove back to Austin. A few days later Morgan rang her.

"When are you coming to visit again?"

"Why?"

"You know damn well why, cos I miss you…and I love you."

That had been eleven months ago. It was still early days, but somehow Morgan had a feeling he'd be waking up with Laura for a sight more years to come.

Epilogue

An extract from the **Laredo Epitaph,** dated 24th December 1999.

On the 17th of December of last week, a skeleton was discovered in the foot hills of the Sierra Madre. It is believed the remains are approximately one hundred years old. On closer examination the body appeared to be that of a male, six foot two in height, with what appears to be several wounds about the skeltal frame and a large wound to the skull. Close to the body the police found an old Colt Peacemaker. Historians have already begun speculating as to whether the remains are that of the Texas lawman Zachariah Trelawney, who disappeared under mysterious circumstances some one hundred years ago.

11 July 1999.
Michael Kennard ©
(*Revised 21 January 2003*)

Well, what's your theory of those………. Empty Saddles?

Extract torn from journal.

It was then that I realised the reason why our horses had been left behind. Rafael had not intended for any of us to live. By leaving our horses saddled and waiting, any patrol from across the border would assume we were within walking distance, and wouldn't think to search more than half a day's ride.

Zachariah Trelawney

Which is what happened. Captain William Platt rested his troop for a day, then searched the surrounding countryside for two days. The Rangers would have travelled no further than half a day's ride from the last known whereabouts of Zachariah before returning to camp. Hacienda Morales was a day's ride from the Empty Saddles.

I awoke to bird song ringing in my ears. It was a pleasing sound, the chirps and twittering of an American robin, a couple of warblers and if I miss my guess a wren or two……………

………………The last dying rays of the sun bathed the building in a reddish glow. I'd always known which way I was heading, but the sight of Hades filled me with dread.

Michael Kennard

mick-elaine@montanaskies.freeserve.co.uk

Notes

My spelling throughout this text has been in *English-English* rather than *English-American*. My apologies if this has distracted you in any way

Michael Kennard

0-595-27016-6